Ruthless REBEL

USA TODAY BESTSELLING AUTHOR
FAITH SUMMERS

Copyright © 2023 by Khardine Gray Please note : Faith Summers is the Dark Romance pen name of *USA Today* Bestselling Author Khardine Gray

All rights reserved.

Ruthless Rebel Copyright © 2023 by Khardine Gray
Cover design © 2023 by Book Cover Couture
Photographer—Wander Aguiar
Cover Model—Kaio

No part of this book may be reproduced in any form or by any electronic or mechanical means, including information storage and retrieval systems, without written permission from the author, except for the use of brief quotations in a book review.

This work is copyrighted. Apart from any use as permitted under the Copyright Act 1968, no part may be reproduced, copied, scanned, stored in a retrieval system, recorded or transmitted, in any form or by any means, without the prior written permission of the author, except for the use of brief quotations in a book review.

This is a work of fiction. Names, characters, businesses, places, events and incidents are either the products of the author's imagination or used in a fictitious manner. Any resemblance to actual persons, living or dead, or actual events is purely coincidental.

The author asserts that all characters and situations depicted in this work of fiction are entirely imaginary and bear no relation to any real person.

The following story contains mature themes, strong language and sexual situations.

It is intended for mature readers. All characters are 18+ years of age and all sexual acts are consensual.

Ruthless
REBEL

Chapter ONE

Jericho

I REST MY HEAD AGAINST THE CLUB'S SOFT LEATHER CHAIR and press my phone to my ear.

"It was you, wasn't it?" Knight's voice is boardroom-meeting stern. The tone brings out the slight hint of his French accent, making him sound more like me. "You put the paparazzi on Bastian, didn't you?"

With a triumphant smile, I glance at the newspaper on the glass-top table between me and my best friend Luc, who arrived moments before Knight called.

The damning words on the front-page headline flow into my mind with sinful delight:

Bastian Grayson exposed for his sexual relations with Governor Teddy Jamison's seventeen-year-old daughter...

Beneath the headline is a clear picture of Bastian, naked in bed, with Lana Jamison at his beach house.

As if to add dramatic effect, the club lights bounce off the words and the music below on the dance floor changes to the song "*Your dirt will come back to screw with you.*"

"I don't know what you're talking about." I feign innocence, but I know it won't work with Knight. In all the twenty-nine years of my life, it's never worked, so he already knows I'm guilty as fuck.

When the scandal hit the national news and the evening press earlier I expected this call from him. He's my superior in the Grayson empire. *And* my older brother.

In times like these, because of our one-year age difference, he always thinks he should take the moral high ground with me, like some patron saint. Despite the fact that I know he wishes he had the balls to do half the shit I do to men who cross me.

Even if the said man is dear old Bastian, our asshole half-brother and nemesis, second to our father—the head prick.

"Jericho, I *know* it was you." Knight's tone is reprimanding, but he should also be aware that I don't give a fuck.

Yes, *of course* it was me. The same way business is business, war is war, like any conqueror I simply removed an obstacle from my path.

My mission is to get my billion-dollar legacy, which includes the CFO position at the Park Avenue branch of Grayson Inc. and thirty percent ownership of the company.

I'm the senior investment analyst and infrastructure architect at Grayson Inc., but as Bastian works in the company's finance department my role crosses over with his.

Months ago, Bastian gave me the weapons to remove his ass as my competition when he threatened to ruin Knight's marriage to his wife, Aurora, and leak dark secrets that could have gotten her father killed. I retaliated by finding dirt on Bastian that fought fire with fire when I came across pictures and a sex tape of him and Lana Jamison.

The deal was we'd keep it quiet if Bastian ceased and desisted any actions he had planned to ruin Knight and his family. Or rather, that was what I wanted Bastian to believe.

Bastian played by the deal but he didn't realize I was the devil lying in wait for the right moment to expose him. I don't believe in swapping evil for evil.

It also didn't sit well with me that Bastian—a grown man of twenty-eight—was fucking around with a young girl of seventeen. I knew that couldn't have been okay with Knight either, so that worked well with my ulterior motive, which was to remove Bastian from my path when the time was right. That time is now.

I guessed that Bastian wasn't going to stop seeing Lana, and I was right. All I did was wait for the right time and place to tip off the press.

"I did nothing wrong." I widen my smile. "I wasn't the idiot who got involved with a minor. Let alone Teddy Jamison's daughter."

Luc laughs and I grin back at him. He continues listening with keen interest. He's heard and seen enough to get the gist of what's happening.

Knight sighs. "This might come back to bite us in the ass. Somehow, someway."

That comment there is the perfect illustration of the differences between us. People tend to think that because we look so similar with the black hair, muscular build, and six-foot-four stature, we have the same temperament, but we don't.

Knight is as ruthless as I am but he thinks too much. I, on the other hand, am the rebel. I don't waste time thinking about shit. I take action and dole out vengeance before any motherfucker can think of screwing with me.

"Dear Knight, I think you'll find that neither Bastian nor Father can do anything to us. They'll be more scared than ever because I have the sex tape."

"I know, but I'm sure you understand my worries. You can never tell what either of them will do, especially if they suspect you."

"Believe me, they won't do anything, even if they suspect I'm involved. The press caught Bastian live and in action in bed with Lana. On this occasion Bastian dug his own grave, lay in it, then buried himself alive."

Neither Bastian nor Father are stupid enough to come after me. If they're dumb enough to try they know I'll only come back stronger. And I would.

I'm willing to bet Bastian was with Lana before she turned seventeen. In New York seventeen is the age of consent, which means if I find one little thing that places him with her before her seventeenth birthday Bastian will go down for statutory rape.

I don't know what kind of legal punishment he'll get but I know Lana's father will raise hell. He won't allow Bastian to get away with screwing his precious daughter. Teddy will undoubtedly ruin him.

"I guess you're right." Knight sounds more at ease.

"I am. So how about you stop worrying and I see you at work in the morning?"

Knight sighs. "Alright. See you then."

We hang up and I focus on Luc. He straightens, moves a lock of his dark hair away from his eye, and lifts his chin toward the newspaper.

"I won't bother asking you to elaborate." He gives me a cunning grin.

"It's better if you don't." I sit forward and slide the newspaper to the side to give us room. "That's one more secret to shove under the rug."

He chuckles. "Well, let's leave it there. Knowing you, it's probably fucked-up shit that will get me in trouble."

"Indeed."

Luc has been Knight's and my best friend since we were kids. Knight and I lived in France until our early teens when we moved to New York to live with our grandparents. Before the move Luc was the friend we'd see first thing when we visited for summer breaks.

Luc is the same age as Knight so he did most of his schooling with him, including going to Princeton. However, Luc and I share a special villainous bond that I don't have with Knight.

Luc plays professional ice hockey now for the Hawks, one of New York's NHL teams. Although they're in the middle of the season, he made time to help me with my latest venture. He's the only person I can trust with the details of the plan to get my inheritance. I usually tell Knight everything but this is one time when I can't. And won't.

I trust Knight with my life, but sometimes he lives too far up my grandfather's ass. For the next part of my grand plan I need the kind of secrecy you take to your grave.

"Well, on to more important items to discuss." Luc pulls a document from the folder he's carrying. "I have some seriously hot women for you to interview."

On hearing that I smile and slide my phone back into my pocket. "Show me."

He chuckles. "I have a list of ten potential women I think will be a great match for you."

He sets the document on the table and opens the file to the first page, showing headshots of ten beautiful women who are most definitely my type.

I nod with satisfaction and flick through the pages, liking what I'm seeing from one page to the next.

Luc and I decided to meet here at Club Edge because it's more discreet than our usual hangout. It's a high-end gentlemen's club on the other side of town where the patrons who frequent the place are willing to spend a fortune just to get a lap dance.

Usually we come for the strippers but tonight Luc is here to help me with the hardest part of my plan—*finding a wife*.

Except what I need is a *fake* wife. A woman I'll hire to play out the rest of this game with me.

Ten months ago my grandfather announced his retirement from Grayson Inc. and decided to split the two New York branches into two separate companies.

My father would get control over the headquarters at Wall Street, while the three Grayson brothers would have to battle for the leadership positions of CEO and CFO of the Park Avenue branch. We would also get a share of ownership in the company too.

With the two positions available, there was only room for two winners.

Not three.

That's when the games began.

Knight fulfilled his task to become the CEO. Now I'm doing my part. To do so, my grandfather stipulated—*with no exceptions*—that I needed to get married.

Find a wife and fix what he thinks is a playboy image after my own little brush with the paparazzi, then I'd get the position I've come to crave.

It's ironic given the fact that at one time in my life I wanted nothing more than to create my own path and turn my back on the Grayson name.

Luc is here because I'm running out of time. I initially had three months but now I barely have eight weeks to find a wife. Then I have to be married to my said wife for six months before I'm handed the CFO position. The cherry on top of that shit is if I get divorced before one year of marriage, I forfeit the entire offer.

My grandfather is hell bent on me finding *real* love and settling down the way Knight did. That's the reason for all the rules and the timescale. I'm happy Knight found love, but I'm not about that life.

Grandfather believes I'm currently dating with a view to marriage, but in truth I'm doing things my way and just enough to tick all the boxes to make everything look legit.

The lucky woman I choose will enter a contractual relationship with me and receive a million dollars upfront for the job. At the end of our marriage she'll receive another million.

"Are they to your liking?" Luc asks, raising a hope-filled brow.

"Chef's kiss." I smirk, placing my fingers briefly to my lips. "You did good, Luc."

"Perfect. They've all signed NDAs and I've spoken to them at length, making them aware of what you need as well as the timescale."

"Thanks, man. I owe you one."

"No worries, bro."

Luc has done *way* better than I did. I think the gravity of the situation made me too anxious to get my head together. I kept finding fault with every potential bride. Then I realized none of them would be trustworthy enough to not try and screw me over.

Since the women Luc knows are slightly better than the company I keep, I knew he'd come through for me.

Mischief brightens his eyes and he flicks through the pages to a dark-haired beauty with striking blue eyes. Her name is Celeste.

"You might want to start with her. The gorgeous Megan Fox look-alike. She's twenty-five, a personal trainer with a great pair of tits and a perfect ass. You can't go wrong."

"Sure, I'll start with her."

"Cool. I'll set up a date with her first, then each of the other girls every day for the next week. I'm in Tampa all of next week for a few games, so maybe you'll make your choice by then and we can move on to the next stage."

"*The marriage.*" Every time I say that word I feel hollow inside.

"Yeah. The marriage."

I hate that I'm at the mercy of my grandfather but if there's one thing I know about him, the great Bradford Grayson, it's that you either play by his rules or lose by your own.

I have the greatest respect and love for my grandfather. For how he took care of Knight and me, and for how he built the Grayson empire to what it is today.

Grayson Inc. is a world-renowned multibillion-dollar international company that is second to none in the real estate and property development game.

It was built on the back of Grayson men but my grandfather started it all, and he wants his legacy to continue in the way he wants, so I'm either in or out.

Being out is not an option for me. A new path was paved for me the day Grandfather decided to split the company. From that day onward I saw no other way, so here I am—*planning to get married.*

"Have you thought about how this is going to really work?" Luc gives me a skeptical stare. "What if your grandfather finds out you're doing this?"

"He won't." Even I know I sound overly confident. No one should be like that because nothing is ever guaranteed, especially when you have to rely on other people to accomplish your goals. In my case I'll have to exercise some element of trust in the woman I choose to be my wife. That already rubs me the wrong way, but this has to work. "I can't let him find out, so that's not an option."

"Well, I'm rooting for you, and I'm here if you need me." Although he still looks skeptical, he nods and raises his glass of scotch to make a toast. "To success."

I lift mine too and clink my glass with his. "Success for both of us."

This is an important year for him, too. Last year he led his team to victory and they won the World Championship. This years' goal is to defend their title.

"Cheers to success for us both." He smiles with appreciation.

We drink, and the music changes again, growing a fraction louder to signal the start of the main show.

We're sitting in the VIP section, which is two floors above the main floor. Up here the music is usually low so you can carry a conversation without interruption, but when the main show begins the volume is cranked up for the first five minutes.

The lights dim and a spotlight illuminates the large stage between the two smaller ones by the bar where strippers undulate wearing nothing but barely-there thongs and feather boas.

I was told that the owners of the place used to be Cirque du Soleil stars who have an eccentric taste for mixing dark sexual fantasies with art. Months ago they had a Vegas-style burlesque show. Tonight it looks like they might be doing something different.

The curtains open, revealing streams of long, red, silky material flowing from the ceiling to the floor. Like a flower in bloom the center opens, revealing a fiery-red-haired aerial dancer who loops the material around her body, using it to somersault into some unreal split position.

Her long hair is tied up in a ponytail but it flows down her body, blending with the red material. The nude-color and the sleeveless leotard covering her toned body and perky tits leaves very little to the imagination. The only color on her is the red from the material and that hair, along with a dusting of glitter that sparkles as she moves.

The beauty and grace she exudes makes her look like she just drifted out of a dream.

I never watch anything like this anymore. It reminds me too much of a girl I once knew in a past life where my heart wasn't so cold, or dead.

However, this girl has managed to enchant and captivate me in the same way she has with the rest of the men here who can't take their eyes off her.

Maybe because her auburn hair and grace reminds me of the girl I used to call mine. *My ballerina.*

The same pang of guilt that always assails me when I think of the past stabs at my insides renewing the coldness in my heart and I shove the memories away.

"Wow, they really went all out tonight," Luc says, staring at the girl as if she's an exotic meal waiting for him to feast on.

"Yeah, they did."

I'm about to look away, but I get a better view of the girl when the spotlight hits her face and I realize she looks familiar.

My gut twists with that realization and I try to look at her properly, but I'm too far away.

Dark dread whisper to me as I continue staring that there's a reason she reminded me of my girl.

The crowd goes wild as she flips her lithe body through another round of somersaults, then makes it look like she's going to fall. They applaud louder when she lands into another aerial split just before she hits the floor.

A hoop floats down toward her and she steps onto it.

When she floats up and the hoop moves over toward us, I finally see her face and her emerald green eyes lock with mine.

At that moment all the blood in my body slams into the pit of my stomach, as if a brick wall has been shoved inside me. Then my lungs freeze, wrapping me in an Arctic storm of confusion, but realistically there's nothing to be confused about.

She looked familiar to me because she is.

I *know* her. The same way a person knows their name or the back of their hand.

At one point in my life I used to know every inch of her too.

The last time we were this close she was just a girl.

My girl.

The girl who was forbidden to me.

River...

River St. James.

She sees me, too, and the expression on her beautiful face that I haven't seen in eight years must mirror the shock paralyzing my soul.

"Oh my God," Luc mutters under his breath. I don't have to look at him to know he recognizes her too. Back in high school he was the only one who knew about us.

I never even told Knight about the girl I loved and lost on purpose.

Lost on purpose because of what I did...

The last time we were this close I broke her heart.

Now here she is.

Dancing in a strip club.

Chapter TWO

River

M**Y GOD. IT'S REALLY HIM...**
Jericho Grayson.
His face seems to loom before me, as dangerously handsome as he was eight years ago. Except his boyish looks have turned into the harder features of a man who looks like he was sculpted to perfection by the world's greatest artist.

The realization that Jericho Grayson isn't some figment of my imagination and he's actually here in front of me, slices through my body. Then the knowledge fills my mind with a weight as heavy as lead.

The heaviness spreads through my limbs, reaching every cell, and I almost feel like I might fall out of the air. Yet I can't will myself to look away from him. Shock has frozen me in time, and all I can do is stare back at those bright blue eyes that I haven't seen in forever.

It doesn't help that the mechanical aerial hoop is designed to stay dangling here for a full minute to give the VIP guests a good view of *me*.

Me, Club Edge's latest main attraction. Thank God my years of stage performance have equipped me with the concept of *'the show must go on'*.

I've managed to style out my shock by keeping my body still in a full split position on the hoop, but while the crowd below are cheering at what they think is part of the performance, I feel like I'm going to frizzle into the ether.

Jericho looks just as shocked to see me, and like he's trying to figure out if I'm really here or not. Although I've established that *he's here* and *he's real*, I'm doing the same thing.

The music rises and the hoop starts gliding again, severing our connection. It's only then that I notice Luc Le Blanche is sitting next to Jericho. In the same breath I note that he recognizes me too.

Instantly my awareness returns, along with a venomous dose of humiliation.

Embarrassment rushes over me like an army of fire ants, and I think of how cruel fate is to have done this to me tonight.

Fate has never been kind to me. Not once. This is just one more devastating *thing*.

It's bad enough that I work here, but seeing my ex and his best friend from *high school* has shoved what little remains of my pride deep into the earth where no one will ever see it again.

When you run into your ex you hope that you're in a better position than you were when they left you, but I'm still in trouble, just a different kind.

Before my mind can sink into a chasm of despair I will myself to focus and remember why I'm here.

This is for Aunt Gina, the only person in my life who's always been there for me.

By some miracle I find strength and am able to push Jericho and Luc to the back of my mind so I can continue with my performance, but I can still feel Jericho's eyes burning into me.

I always wondered how I'd feel if I ever saw him again. I hoped it would never happen because it was clear the day we broke up that he no longer cared for me.

I felt he'd wanted to find someone better. Someone more fitting to his social status. At the time, I wondered if he had. There was always some girl who was chasing after him.

I must have seemed so deluded when I went around thinking I was going to be with a guy like him who came from one of the richest families in America.

Now he's known for his net worth and position on the Forbes billionaire list.

Old pain stirs deep inside my soul and I'm annoyed at myself for feeling it.

Enough years have gone by for me not to feel anything for this guy.

Jericho Grayson shouldn't even be an afterthought, but his mere presence in my sphere of existence rattles me to the core.

I manage to complete the performance, which lasts another ten minutes—the longest ten minutes of my life.

The hoop floats back down to the stage and the crowd cheers for me.

I've been performing at Club Edge for close to a month. According to Penelope, the club owner, I've been a hit.

The sound of the applause takes me back to my glory days when I was the prima ballerina dancing with the Bolshoi Ballet. Those were the days I lived for, and I was so glad I'd gotten so far. The same thought saddens me now because I'm not that girl anymore.

I was lucky enough to get this job thanks to my dance and acrobatic skills, but in this skimpy leotard that exposes more than I'd like I'm hardly any different from the strippers. I'm not stripping *yet*, and I hope I never have to.

Pretending I'm still the River St. James I used to be I curtsey, receiving louder applause.

When I rise I chance stealing a glance at the VIP section where I saw Jericho.

He's not there anymore. Neither is Luc.

They must have left.

Good.

The curtains close and I release the sweltering breath I'm holding, but my body still feels like it's made of lead.

Placing my hand over my racing heart, I take a few deep breaths hoping my mind will climb down from the shock of seeing Jericho, but it doesn't work.

"Hey, River, are you okay?" Zara's lively voice cuts into my thoughts.

I turn to see her making her way over to me. She's the club's manager. Tonight she's dyed her mid-length hair a vibrant electric blue and is wearing a matching catsuit that makes her slender body appear leaner.

Quickly, I gather my composure and offer her my brightest smile. The one rule here is to always look like you're having fun, even when you're not.

"Hi, yes, I'm fine."

"You look like you froze up for a minute while you were in the air. I was worried." She looks genuinely concerned, a quality I like in her. She's shown it right from our first meeting when she could see how desperate I was for the job.

"Sorry, I just had a case of lightheadedness." I chuckle, hoping she can't see through the lie. "But honestly, I'm fine."

On hearing that she gives me a warm smile and seems relieved. "Great, because the crowd absolutely loved you. Penelope is having a field day." She clasps her bony hands and does a little hop.

"I'm glad to hear that."

"You should be. Everyone is obsessed with you. They're calling you the mermaid. I can see why." Zara laughs heartily, lifting the ends of my ponytail and making a show of staring at the red color.

I laugh, too. "I get that a lot."

"I'm sure you do. You also have private party bookings every night for the rest of the month, with the option of overtime if you want."

"Wow." That rejuvenates my mood.

"I know, right?" She grins, running coffin-shaped fingernails through her hair.

"That is amazing and will definitely help me out."

"I thought so." She nods and a spark of sympathy enters her eyes.

"Thank you."

"No worries."

My main job here is the aerial performances. I get a base pay of three hundred dollars a night to do that from eight p.m. to one in the morning. However, those party bookings are private functions that could add another three to five hundred per night, with tips if the men like me. Of course, they don't just want you there for your pretty face.

I've done five parties so far that have brought in an extra two thousand dollars. Half-heartedly, I also signed up for the auction on Friday night, where I hear you can bring in anything from ten thousand to fifty thousand dollars. Or more.

The parties and the auction are both way outside my comfort zone. I know I'll most likely have to do things I'll regret, but knowing I have a chance to make all that money and provide a better life for my aunt, *and myself*, gives me the strength I desperately need.

I'm still not anywhere close to my goal but at least I'm getting there.

"Anyway..." Zara sets her shoulders back, regaining her business-like poise. "I would love to stay and chat some more but you've got fifteen minutes before the Everton party begins."

"Okay, I'll go get ready."

"Great. Your dress is already waiting for you in the dressing room and Tony's on duty if you need him. Bailey Everton IV can get a little handsy when he's drunk." She grimaces and wrinkles her nose as if she's seen something disturbing.

Tony is the head of security but Zara's reaction doesn't exactly instill reassurance in me. In my frame of mind I don't think I could handle handsy tonight. My presence at these parties is just to mingle and basically flirt. I don't do lap dances like the other girls they book and sometimes the men don't like that.

"I'll be okay," I decide to say, because I have to be.

"Have fun."

"Thanks."

I leave her and make my way backstage. The instant I'm alone my mind goes straight back to Jericho.

Finding him in a place like this was no surprise. Club Edge is a playground for rich, powerful men like him who can own people like me. It was just a shock to actually see him.

I won't deny that I *have* thought about him over the years, especially when I first came back to New York. That was just over ten months ago.

It wasn't like I could escape the Grayson name either, with the press all over the family for one reason or another.

During the time I've been back they covered his brother Knight's wedding as if it were the royal wedding of the century, then they went after Jericho for hooking up with a *preacher man's wife*. Jericho's name was practically shoved in my face during that time.

And just today, Bastian Grayson was in the papers for his scandal with Governor Teddy Jamison's daughter.

No matter which Grayson I hear about it makes me think of him.

I just wish I never saw him tonight, when I've hit another low in my life.

I reach the dressing room, which is just as fancy and spacious as everywhere else in the club. It's been decorated to look like a French Provençal boudoir with ornate mirrors and period décor like something you'd find at the Moulin Rouge.

I make my way past a row of dressing tables and head to the section where mine is. I'm grateful to have the last one on the corner as it feels like I have the area to myself.

I turn the corner and my legs become stone when I see Jericho standing by the window.

Shivers erupt across my skin, as if I'm standing outside in the cold, and I slow to a stop then stare at him, wondering what he's doing here.

His back is turned to me but I can still see the hard outline of his jaw as he gazes at the bright city lights cascading across the scenic night-time view of the city.

If he's standing beside my vanity it's safe to assume he's here to see me.

But why?

My next breath stills in my lungs, captured by the tension in my nerves and my racing thoughts. My heart is pounding so hard it feels like it might hammer its way out of my chest.

I blink several times and try to calm myself so I can say something—*anything*—but I can't do either. I'm too stunned to even think of speaking to him because I don't know what to say.

What do you say to a guy who broke up with you after having a secret relationship with him for over three years?

What the hell do you say to him after he defied your father's warnings to stay away from you, then keeps the said secret relationship going for years, then suddenly tells you out of the blue that he doesn't think the two of you have a future? *Because his feelings have changed.*

My father hates the Graysons, so he went apeshit when he found out I was dating Jericho. Dad tried to stop me from seeing him *ever* again.

Tobias Grayson—Jericho's father—was my father's arch nemesis throughout high school and college. Dad said Tobias bullied him to no end, leaving the kind of trauma you'd need years of therapy to recover from.

Tobias even tried to mess with my father's job when he'd just started out as a software engineer.

Dad swears that's why he's never had the chance to climb up the ladder of real success. Given what I've heard and know about Tobias Grayson, that might be true, but my father is the type of person to hold on to a grudge for life. He also believes that the universe is continuously screwing him over.

So it was bad luck that drew Tobias into his life and good luck has never been on his side, even though he's been offered several notable accomplishments like getting a scholarship to attend the same prestigious academy every Grayson went to, along with Princeton.

I've always felt that Dad was so fixated on the Graysons and their insurmountable wealth that he never appreciated the good things he had in his life. Nevertheless, every time I was with Jericho I felt like I was betraying my father.

I feel like that again now.

Except *now* I also feel like I'm betraying myself.

"I don't remember you being able to stay quiet for so long." Jericho's voice swallows the silence around us.

Hearing his voice that I haven't heard in such a long time snaps my mind out of the stupor of thought. Slowly, he turns to face me and I prepare myself to speak to him.

He straightens and seems taller than I remember. I feel like a mouse in comparison to him.

In this light I can also see more of his uncut hard-meets-soft raw beauty. As if earlier was the sneak peek and this is the main attraction.

His onyx-colored hair cut in a sharp faux-hawk accentuates his piercing stormy blue eyes and the deep angles of his face.

The muscles beneath his suit and the tattoo peeking through the open top button of his shirt conjure the rebel I used to know. But the Rolex around his wrist and the black, tailored Armani suit display the wealth of the Wall Street man he became.

Jericho's gaze flicks over me, up and down and up again before he settles back on my eyes.

I keep my gaze trained on him and take in the raw intensity of his appearance, his expression, his entire presence.

The memory of how he broke my heart and severed the future I thought I was going to have with him comes alive in my mind as if it's happening now, then I see straight through to the asshole he is. The asshole he always was.

"I'm quiet when I come across unexpected surprises." Although there's a rasp in my voice, I'm grateful I sound confident. "What are you doing here, Jericho Grayson?"

"I was going to ask you the same thing." He raises sharp brows. "What are you doing working in a place like this, River?"

I guess I landed myself in that question sooner rather than later.

"I don't think that's really any of your business."

His jaw clenches and his eyes darken, showing he expected a better answer from me. He won't get any more of an answer than that, because whatever is happening to me *is* none of his business.

"What happened to you?" He ignores my answer, giving me a hard stare. Not the kind you'd see on a person when they're mad at you, but the sort you'd get when they care. I hate that look on him, because he doesn't *care*.

"I'm working." I lift my jaw higher.

"*Working?*" He makes a point of looking me over and lingering his stare on my virtually exposed breasts that I'm sure are visible through the flesh-colored fabric.

A flash of something sexual sparks in his eyes, igniting unwarranted heat in my core that surprises me. I don't want to feel anything for him. This man is just another smooth-talking beautiful devil with a cold heart covered in steel.

"Yes, I'm *working*."

"Something must have happened to you for you to want to work here."

"Nothing happened to me." If I add another dose of confidence to that lie even I might believe it. I'm not fooling Jericho in the slightest, though.

He knows I didn't work my ass off to get into Juilliard only to end up working somewhere like this. If he'd stuck with me a little longer and saw I got my dream to travel the world and dance with the Bolshoi Ballet, he'd know with certainty that I'm lying.

"You're dancing in a *strip club*." He places emphasis on the last two words as if I'm not aware of the true nature of the place I work in.

"As you saw earlier I do way more than *dance in a strip club*. Do you know the type of skills required to do what I can do?" I ball my hands into fists and hold them at my sides to keep my rage in. "How dare you come here and question my work?"

"Are you stripping here?" Again he ignores me. This time his eyes blaze with deep irritation.

"What?"

"You heard me."

I stare back at him, hold my breath, and count backwards from ten, hoping the therapy technique that's calmed me in many stressful situations will help now.

It works a little, allowing me to think on my feet and give an answer that will shut him down.

"Like I said, it's none of your business." There, that's the best answer to give him, and he looks as annoyed as I hoped he'd be.

I know I told him this wasn't his business before, but as I haven't confirmed or denied whether or not I'm stripping, hearing that answer again must feel worse.

"If you don't mind, I'm on a strict deadline I need to adhere to." I set my

shoulders back and keep my gaze leveled on his.

"You didn't answer my question." His tone takes on an abrasive edge. "Are you stripping here?"

My lips part in surprise and I give him a narrowed stare. "Listen, I think I've been polite enough to you. Now leave me alone. *My life* is none of your business. It hasn't been for the last eight years and it's not going to start now, so please leave."

I wish I could feel bad for talking to him like that, but I don't. Not even a little.

I'm more infuriated when he doesn't move. Then I realize he's staying put because men like him aren't used to not being in control. They always get what they want, and they don't like it when they no longer have the upper hand.

Since I have no time to argue and I'm done talking, I walk over to the clothes rail to get my dress, then I leave him.

That move would have surprised him but I walk away and don't look back. The same way *he* did all those years ago on the day I'll never forget.

Seeing Jericho tonight has been horrible, but in the grand scheme of shit happening in my life he is the least of my problems.

The dire financial situation Aunt Gina landed herself in came about because she saved me. Literally *saved me* from death.

I swear the stroke she had not even a month later was my fault too. Enough was enough at that point. My poor life choices affected her in ways she never imagined. Like with her health.

Now it falls on me to save her business and her home, because she can't do it herself. If I don't find a way I'll never forgive myself, so, no matter how bitter I feel for seeing my ex, or how many ghosts from my past haunt me, I have to focus on my family.

Perhaps if I'd done so years ago and heeded my father's advice to stay away from Jericho *and* anyone with the last name of Grayson, I'd be in a better position.

Jericho was my first heartbreak.

After him nothing was ever the same.

Chapter THREE

Jericho

MY DAMN MIND IS A MILLION LIGHT-YEARS AWAY. I'm lost in deep thought as I try to figure out what could have happened to River to send her into the arms of a strip club. This is the wrong time to lose my focus because I'm at Grayson Inc.

I'm on my way to the senior management meeting for today's battle among the Grayson men.

How ironic that I'd gone to Club Edge to discuss plans to find a fake wife, only to run into my ex.

My *ex*, who now looks like a fucking goddess with her vibrant red hair and a body that could bring a man to his knees.

Dressed in that seductress' leotard, River St. James was the perfect illustration of temptation.

Not even with the strict control I usually have over my dick did I have a chance of resisting the lust that riddled my mind.

I had a hard time speaking to her while I tried to push away memories of the last time I saw her perfect naked body.

She's filled out a lot more since, with curves in all the right places and a don't-mess-with-me attitude she wore as well as that leotard.

River looked like she was ready to hand me my ass. It pissed me off that the only answer I got out of her was to leave her alone and that her business wasn't mine.

She was right but that didn't make me feel any better or cleanse her from my mind.

Unknown to her, the last time I actually checked in on her was three years ago. She was living in Russia at the height of her career.

And she was engaged.

Clearly, none of that worked out. Unless her *husband* has a twisted mind and thinks it's okay for his wife to work in a strip club.

I didn't see a ring on her finger but that doesn't mean a thing. Many don't wear such things in places like Club Edge.

After I left the club I spent the night checking out River's records. My skills and expertise extend to digging up information on people and businesses that normally can't be found.

What I found on River left me more unsettled than I already was because while I didn't find much, from the intel I did gather the only sensible conclusion I could come to is that she needs money for something.

A lot of money.

River works at Kelly's Café on Crosby Street from six to eleven a.m. six days a week. On the weekdays when she's finished there, she works at the Riverside Academy as a dance teacher. After that she heads to Club Edge where she works until one in the morning. On weekends, she works with the Emerson Dance Company but that seems like it's for a production in the making.

In any event, it's all too much. She's working right around the clock with barely any time off to sleep.

She's been working at the club for the last month and at the café for the last three months. The job at the school seems to be her main one because she's been there for seven months.

It seems that something must have happened to her recently and makes me wonder how long she's been back in New York.

The type of schedule she has matches the behavior of a person who's desperate, or in trouble.

I know I shouldn't be thinking about her but I can't help it. She's the only person I've wronged in my life that I've regretted. At the same time, everything I did—including breaking up with her—was for the best.

And that wasn't because her father hated me for being a Grayson. That was the least, and the thing I would have continued to fight.

Our end was down to other important factors that I never discussed with her, and couldn't. Now she's back in New York making me crazy again.

I'd hate to think that she was stripping for money.

The idea bothered me so much that I spoke to her manager after I saw her and got a full listing of her job specs.

I got the confirmation that River isn't a stripper, but it didn't give me any reassurance to hear that she could be persuaded for the right price. I was more infuriated at being informed she's become a hit amongst the regulars who are booking her for their private parties.

Anything can happen at those parties. The men who book them pay for lap dances and attention from the most popular girls at the club. For the right price, they allow them to book girls for sex too.

Girls who are desperate enough take the money. Especially if they're being offered crazy money that might allow them to quit their job at the club after one night's work.

I don't want that to happen to River, but what am I supposed to do?

Surely her family can't be okay with what she's doing, but maybe they don't know.

I did a basic check on them, too—as in her father and Gina, the only other relative she's close to. It appears River is staying with her because I found a recent phone bill for her with Gina's address on it.

On the surface I didn't find anything to do with her father or Gina that seemed out of the ordinary, but I noted that River's ex-fiancé went by an alias.

Even though I was never going to like the guy, I found it suspicious that he'd have an alias. It's difficult but not impossible to find intel on people like that.

The question is do I keep looking? Should I dig deeper?

Do I reopen the deep wound between River and me that was created when we broke up?

I don't know.

I reach the management floor. The boardroom is at the end of the corridor.

Until my grandfather retires these meetings will continue to be held here at the Wall Street branch. I haven't been here in weeks as I've been working at the Park Avenue branch with Knight. After he assumed the role as the branch's CEO I went uptown with him because we work together.

After yesterday's scandal with Bastian I know this meeting is going to be one of those I wish I could miss. My grandfather is going to be pissed as fuck, and I'm sure heads will roll.

I also expect a confrontation from my father and Bastian, even though I know they have nothing to challenge me with. Any questions asked will be more to do with finding out if I'm planning to make Bastian's situation worse.

The two will also be riled up because they know that any chance of Bastian becoming CFO of Park Avenue is now out the window.

We originally thought he'd never want to work under Knight, until weeks ago when Bastian dropped the comment that he still had that option. That's when I knew I had to strike. There was no way in hell I was going to allow him to get my legacy when the motherfucker would also get control over the main branch too when our father retires, or dies.

It's a fucked up situation that Knight and I would be excluded from our father's inheritance, but that is how it is.

Father has three sons but has only ever acknowledged Bastian. He considers Knight and I to be his bastard children, which means—as he's *specifically* legally declared—that we get nothing from him after his retirement or death.

I'm a few minutes early but I decide to go in the meeting room anyway. When I walk through the already open door I come face to face with my rivals.

Father and Bastian are sitting on the left side of the long mahogany table, closer than two peas in a pod. The two of them glare at me with looks designed to kill.

I'm used to it, so I don't care.

My father told me on many occasions that he wished I'd never been born, so I'm sure if he could kill me he wouldn't hesitate.

Knight and I look like him. Bastian has the same resemblance, so you can tell we're brothers, but his hair is blond like Sloane, his mother.

Their seething eyes follow me as I make my way to the other side of the table and sit. The moment I do, tension fills the room like a cloud of smoke, then it grows so thick you could cut it with a knife.

Father leans forward onto the table and intensifies his glare. "The news yesterday…" His words pierce through the silence. "You didn't have anything to do with it, did you?"

I tilt my head and give him a wide-eyed stare. "In what way, *Father*?" I always call him Father with that disdain and mocking edge because he loathes Knight and me referring to him as our father. We only do it at our grandfather's request.

"You tell me, *son*." He borrows my tone.

I smile and look from him to Bastian. "Did I tell Bastian to keep seeing Lana Jamison? Or did I tell him to continue sleeping with her?" I raise my shoulders into a succinct shrug.

A sour look taints his face further. "You know that's not what I mean."

"Well, I don't *know* what you mean. The last time I heard anything about this we were making a deal to never speak of it again." I flick my gaze to Bastian, who looks more nervous. "From that moment I thought it was a given that Bastian should stop seeing Lana. Except he didn't. That was risky, don't you think, *brother*?"

"If I ever find out that you had—"

"I wouldn't be threatening me if I were you." I cut him off and keep my gaze sharp. "Especially knowing I have a sex tape. Or knowing that I might be able to get my hands on other things. Things that might confirm just how *long* Bastian has been seeing her."

Bastian already looked pale. Now his skin turns a deadly shade of alabaster, making me realize my suspicions about him being with Lana before she turned seventeen are right.

I hit him with a mirthless grin. "Was it *love*, brother? You really fell for a seventeen-year-old?" My tone is disdainful but as I say those words I think of myself and River.

I'm nearly three years older than her. When we met I was seventeen, mere months away from my eighteenth birthday, and she had just turned fifteen. It's funny how I thought I was too old for her back then but our age difference was *nothing*.

Father is about to say something but Bastian stops him by placing his hand over his.

"Just drop it, Father. *All* of it." Bastian's voice is as flat as the untuned keys of an old piano.

"I think so, too," I agree, giving them both a wicked grin. "Listen to your son, *Father,* and *drop it*. I'm not the one in trouble here. He is, and fuck knows what might happen next. Teddy Jamison is not a man to trifle with. But neither am I."

They look afraid now, because they know I'm right.

Light laughter falls from my lips at the sight of them—two untouchable men who made my life hell growing up.

Knight is always telling me how dangerous I am. Now my father and Bastian know it too. For once, I finally have the upper hand.

It's true what people say. Payback is one hell of a boss bitch, and revenge is a dish best served cold. I got both here.

Father and Bastian have treated Knight and me like filth all our lives. It was because he didn't want us. He even tried to deny that we were his after he broke things off with our mother *while* she was pregnant with me.

He made her believe they were going to be a family but upped and left when he got a better deal with Sloane. Sloane's family owns a diamond business. Marriage to her opened the door to more money and power, so my mother never stood a chance.

My grandfather stepped in and made sure we had the lives we were supposed to have, but that didn't stop the bad treatment that came from our father—or *the abuse.*

My abuse. Knight had it bad, but I had it worse because back then I wasn't as strong as him. Father used that to his advantage.

The saying *'Monsters are made, not born'* is true, and right now I'm looking at the man who turned me into the ruthless son of a bitch I am. This stunt of mine is hardcore retribution. My only regret is that I couldn't do much worse.

The sound of Grandfather's voice outside the room prevents the heated conversation from continuing.

Knowing my grandfather, he's already started to put damage control in place. A moment later, Grandfather walks in with Knight at his side and he looks just as angry as I knew he'd be.

The emotion becomes full bloom when he looks at Bastian. The redness in his face makes his hair appear whiter and the wrath in his steely eyes more pronounced.

Grandfather just turned seventy but he looks like he could give Bastian the fight of his life. I think he could. We got the Grayson height and build from him, and my grandfather is a man who never misses a day in the gym so he'd be equally matched with Bastian no matter his age.

I don't think I've ever seen him look so angry. That's saying a lot since my little scandal months ago with the preacher man's wife nearly lost us one of our top investors. Bastian's incident is different, though. We're talking about the governor's daughter here.

Knight walks over to sit next to me and we acknowledge each other with our habitual nod. Grandfather closes the door then takes his seat at the head of the table.

The room turns graveyard silent, a level of quiet below what it previously was. The nothingness is so potent I can almost hear the blood flowing through my veins.

"Good morning, men." Grandfather finally speaks but his tone is as harsh as his seething glare. I would feel worse about the situation if the ends didn't justify the means. "In light of yesterday's scandal we have a lot to discuss. I am so deeply embarrassed and enraged by what's happened." He presses his hands into the table's surface as if he's trying to force his rage into the wood.

"We tried to call you last night to explain," Father attempts but Grandfather holds up his hand, cutting him off.

"No. There is no *we* here. This is about Bastian." Grandfather's voice rises by several octaves and his nostrils flair like a bull ready to charge. "Bastian, what do *you* have to say for yourself?" I have to give my grandfather credit for the balls he always shows, no matter who he's dealing with.

Bastian sets his shoulders back and tries to compose his shame. "I can only apologize for my behavior. It wasn't my intention to make the company look bad."

"Our name always brings media attention. You should have known better than to get involved with that girl. We're only lucky that Teddy Jamison isn't one of our shareholders or investors, and the people we have who are affiliated with him have more loyalty to us."

That is exactly what made this plan so perfect. It's why I did what I did.

I would never put the company in jeopardy. Not like I did before. That was a genuine mistake.

When I hooked up with the preacher man's wife, I never knew she was married, or worse married to one of the most popular gospel leaders in New York.

Unfortunately for me, he also happened to be one of our biggest investors.

That was how I ended up with this marriage stipulation I'm still calling a punishment. I'm also certain it was Bastian who sent the paparazzi to follow me that night, but I have no proof.

"What is your decision on the matter?" Father asks, cutting to the chase.

"The board has voted to remove Bastian from the company. However, I overruled the decision." Grandfather keeps his eyes on Father. "The decision I've come to instead is to send Bastian to Hong Kong for the next three years."

Knight and I exchange surprised glances.

"Three years! Are you serious?" Bastian's face flushes red and he balls his hand into a fist.

"Of course I'm serious."

Father's eyes widen with a mixture of rage and annoyance. "Is there nothing better you can do?"

"That is my final decision and offer. This is still my company and I have the final word." Grandfather sits straighter and returns his focus to Bastian. "Take the offer or leave it, but if you decline it I'm afraid I'll be asking you to leave the company."

"I'm not leaving," Bastian speaks up.

"A wise choice. The remaining ten months of my stay here will be focused on making sure that the company is running smoothly." That means he's going to give them hell.

I get the feeling that if Grandfather weren't retiring he'd fire Bastian. This is him being compassionate.

"This new change means you will no longer be considered for the CFO position at Park Avenue. I'm sure that's understandable."

Bastian nods, but it's with defeat in his eyes. "I understand."

Good. Mission accomplished. Neither of them can get in my way anymore.

Grandfather continues talking about the plans he has for the company before his retirement. The meeting runs over two hours and ends on the same ominous note as it began; with a warning.

Bastian and Father are the first to leave. Once they're gone Grandfather focuses on me.

"It's all up to you now," he says with a slight dip of his head.

"Don't worry. I won't let you down," I assure him.

"I hope to meet the lucky lady soon."

"Me too," Knight cuts in, but he doesn't look like he believes there's a *lucky lady* to meet.

I have Knight believing the same thing I told my grandfather—that I'm dating.

Thank God I've Luc sworn to secrecy, or I'd have Knight on my ass for lying and scheming around with something so important to us.

"You'll both meet her soon." I feel like I'm walking on the edge of a plank by promising something like that, but at least I have a date with the Megan Fox look-alike in a few days. That should hopefully give me enough time to get River out of my head.

"That's really good to hear." Grandfather smiles, seeming more at ease.

"Thanks."

"Well, I guess I'll see you both later."

"See you later."

With that said, we leave and I know even before Knight opens his mouth that he's going to ask me more about my mystery woman.

"You've been super quiet about this girl," he states when we reach the hallway and are out of earshot of everyone else.

"Better to be quiet until you're certain."

"I guess so, but you'd normally tell me more by now."

"This is an abnormal situation."

"Yeah, I suppose you're right." He nods, looking as if he agrees with my reasoning but I know he doesn't. "I'm just concerned that the deadline is getting closer. With Bastian out of the way, don't think that Grandfather will automatically give you the position if you don't meet his demands."

"Believe me, I won't make that mistake. I saw how serious he was back there. He's shown more than once that he'll make you work for what you want."

"He certainly will. We've all had to work for what we want. And make sacrifices."

Knight wasn't exactly told to get married but he did it originally because Grandfather wanted him to own Sunset Cove, a resort in the Hamptons. It belonged to Aurora, which was how they got together, but Knight had to move heaven and earth to meet my grandfather's demands. In the process he almost lost his wife.

As I stare at Knight I think of how much he's changed since marrying Aurora and becoming a father.

He's been married to Aurora for eight months now. He already worshipped the ground his wife walked on, but the baby news transformed him into something else. Probably into the guy he wished our father could have been.

"Don't worry about me, Knight. I always come through." I smile back at him.

He smirks. "Funnily enough, you do."

"I do."

"Well, looks like you got everything under control. I've got back-to-back meetings until four, then I'm heading out. Aurora has a sonogram. I'm around until then, if you need me."

"Cool. Catch you later."

We part ways, and the moment I'm alone River resurfaces in my mind like a forbidden fantasy I know I should forget.

The sensible thing to do is to listen to her. I should leave her alone and worry about what the hell I'm going to do about picking this wife of mine.

I entertain the idea for all of one minute before I find myself planning to return to Club Edge later tonight. It's like I've lost my damn mind and I'm eighteen again, planning to hook up with the girl I was warned to stay away from.

I reach the club at the same time as I did last night and seat myself in the same seat in the VIP Area.

River comes on for her performance and we have that moment once more when she gets up to my balcony.

Tonight she's dressed in an emerald green spandex leotard with sequins and diamantes splashed over it.

The look on her face when she notices me is a deadly combo of surprise and fury, but like every other man here with eyes I allow myself the pleasure of looking at her. Looking and *fantasizing*.

Unlike every fucker in here who wants her, I'm the only one who had her first.

I took the cherry between her legs.

I claimed her virgin body, made her mine, and I'd be a goddamn liar if I said I didn't want her again.

Wanting her was never the problem. I always did.

Her cheeks flush crimson as if she can read my mind, then the aerial hoop floats away. Away from me.

Last night she didn't look back. Tonight she does. It's just for a few seconds, but her eyes lock with mine.

I don't know what I hoped to achieve by coming here again. Trying to talk to her like I did last night is probably fruitless. I could make it happen if I wanted to, but it's the wrong environment.

An idea crosses my mind for what could be the right place to talk, so I leave after her performance and catch up with her again the next morning at the café—the perfect place to speak.

But this is it. My one shot.

After today I'll leave her alone. I should.

It was my fault everything changed for her.

The one mistake I can't take back ruined her family and ruined us, too.

I took a job I shouldn't have, and her father paid the price heavily.

She doesn't know that was my fault.

I couldn't tell her and break her in such a way.

That was why I couldn't be with her.

Chapter FOUR

River

MY GOD, HE'S HERE AGAIN. Jericho is here at Kelly's Café and the fact that he knew where to find me suggests he checked out my details.

What else does he know?

Everything?

Or nothing?

Both could be reasons he's in my sphere of existence again.

I'm standing behind the counter with my hands frozen at my sides, gazing at him with the same shock I experienced last night. *And* the night before.

That first night I was in shock because it was our first meeting in eight years.

Last night I was surprised to see him again and that he seemed to be there just for me. The same way he is now.

There's no way this is a coincidence.

I was just about to replenish the napkins on the tables when he walked in.

He's wearing more casual clothes than last night. Today he's dressed in a T-shirt and Levi's. He looks more like the Jericho I knew from the past. The guy from school.

Seeing him this way, and again, only irritates me because I really do wish he'd leave me alone.

I'm tired. Tired mentally and physically. It's just past six thirty in the morning. I've only had about three hours of sleep. Less, if I'm being truly honest.

I don't have the strength for whatever this is.

Jericho walks toward the table at the back and sits. His eyes are riveted to me, and he has that same look of curiosity wrapped in desire I noticed from last night.

"Oh my God," Kelly mutters, coming up to me. "Is that seriously Jericho *Grayson*? In my café?"

I glance at her and take in the star-struck expression on her face. It shouldn't be surprising that she recognizes him. It would be more surprising if she didn't.

In a city like New York where he walks among the Wall Street titans, people like him are treated like celebs.

I gather myself and my scrambled, very tired brain to give her a curt smile.

"Yes. It seems so."

She gives me a wide-eyed stare and a matching smile. "He's looking right at *you*. Go, serve him before Talia does."

She lifts her chin toward Talia, the other waitress, who is serving the elderly couple who come in here every day. Talia is taking their order but her eyes are glued to Jericho. She's definitely Jericho's type. She's the same age as me with long raven hair and a Barbie-doll figure men love, and she knows it.

From the moment Kelly found out I was single she's been trying to set me up with every half decent guy who walks in here. She's in her late fifties so has that motherly presence about her that makes her treat us like daughters. On this occasion I wish she wouldn't try.

"I think we better let Talia serve him. She's closer to his table."

I nod, hoping my suggestion will help me avoid him, but judging from the deadpan stare Kelly gives me I already know she's not going to allow me to worm my way out of this.

"River. Don't let me march you over there." She slides a pencil into the messy brown bun sitting on top of her head that looks like a cute bird's nest. "This is exactly why you're single. You have to seize opportunities the way I did with my Ed."

Her eyes become dreamy, and I resist the urge to groan.

This situation here is nothing like her and Ed, her husband of thirty-five years.

Kelly has told me the story of how they met a million times over, so I'm well versed in it. The two met at a carnival kissing booth Kelly had arranged to work in just so she could kiss him.

It's a sweet story and Ed is amazing, but Jericho is not like Ed. *At all.*

Men like Jericho make me want to stay single for the rest of my days. So I won't tell Kelly that I've been there and done the relationship thing with this guy, and I have no desire to test those waters ever again.

"Don't keep the man waiting. He's our customer." She uses her I'm-your-boss voice.

"Okay, fine, I'll go serve him."

Ugh. This is just what I need to start an already hard day.

Feeling like I'd rather jump into a black hole and hide until the world ends, I grab my notepad and pen then proceed to make the arduous walk toward my ex.

I run through all the possible things I could say to him but my mind slows the closer I get, then I'm torn between wanting to scream at him and running away.

If I didn't need this job, I'd do both.

Jericho straightens, drawing attention to his football-player muscular shoulders.

He levels me a curious stare, then gives me that sexy half-smile that hooked me from the first night we met. That smile always got me in trouble. It did that night when my stupid heart decided it wanted one of the most popular boys in school. Someone who seemed unobtainable to me.

Our meeting wasn't sweet like Kelly and Ed's, but there were parts of it that were.

I met Jericho when I was fleeing from a party I shouldn't have gone to. I was the new girl, only a few weeks in at the Aster Academy, an uppity school I really didn't belong in.

Much to my evil stepmother's delight, Dad had just gotten a big job promotion at Jaeger Tech as one of their senior software engineers, so we made the big move from Colorado to the Big Apple.

Dad was thrilled too, because he always wanted to return to New York.

I got accepted at the Aster Academy because that was the school Dad went to, and as he worked for Jaeger Tech, my then step-sister and I qualified for a placement.

At school, I was a prime target who the bullies christened 'the dance geek' so the night of the party I had the misfortune of having my very own *Carrie* moment. I even got the pig's blood too. They said it was a close match to my hair.

I was in mid-flight when I crashed into Jericho, who then saved me from the bullies chasing me. It turned out he was the thing they feared. The alpha at the head of the food chain.

He, Knight, and Luc were the trio who owned the school. I never had any more problems with bullies after that night. Any problems I had came from being with a guy I knew my father would hate just for being a Grayson.

When I reach Jericho's table, my head feels heavy and light at the same time. The feeling infuriates me because it's his fault. The only thing I'm thankful for is that Kelly and Talia are out of earshot and won't be able to hear me. I have no shortage of words to say to Jericho for putting me in this awkward position.

"You know this borders on stalking, right?" I raise my brows and focus on his bright blue gaze, which brightens further at the mention of stalking.

"Yes, but when has such a thing ever stopped me?"

Old memories heat my cheeks as I recall him watching me from afar while I was with my family. Then he'd sneak into my room late at night to be with me when everyone had gone to bed.

"I suppose never." I try to keep my voice steady because he looks like he knows what I'm thinking.

"I'm glad you remember."

I roll my eyes and sigh. "What are you doing here, Jericho?"

"Can't a guy get a cup of coffee?" He flicks his palms over, a gesture meant to show that's all he's here for, but I know it's not.

I decide to play along and ready my pen and notepad to take his order. "Is that black or white, and would you like any sugar with it?"

He chuckles. "How about I get five minutes with you instead?"

My jaw tightens and I lower my pad. "No."

"Why not?"

"Why the hell are you doing this to me? I told you to leave me alone."

Most people would have taken my tone as a warning to quit while ahead, but not him.

Jericho presses his lips together and instead of the smile he gave me moments ago, his expression turns serious.

One of the deadliest things about this guy is that he never allows you to figure him out. One minute he's cocky and arrogant with a jovial, flirty personality you think you could work with. It's even charming at times. Until he switches and the next minute he becomes cold, calculative, and ominous. As if the malice that lives inside him can only be tamed and controlled for so long before it unleashes. That's how he looks now.

He sits forward, leaning closer, as if he's going to tell me a secret. "Five minutes."

He's doing that ignoring-my-comments thing again.

"No, but if you really do want coffee or anything else on the menu, I'll happily serve you. Anything else is a no."

Jericho gives me a narrowed gaze and considers me for a moment before speaking. "How about you give me five minutes, then I promise to leave you alone. You won't see me again."

I stare back at him, thinking about this new offer which isn't really an offer. It still suits him because I still don't want to talk.

"Why are you so hellbent on talking to me?"

"Because I want to know what happened to you." He gives me a clipped nod. "Regardless of our past, wouldn't you want to know what the fuck happened to me if you found me dancing in a strip club?"

His smile returns with mischief and I have to bite back mine. The thought of him dancing in a strip club isn't funny at all—in fact, I'm sure the place would be packed every night with women from all over the world. It's just funny because it's *him*.

"At least I can still make you smile." His smile widens.

"I'm smiling because it's crazy. That would never happen to you."

"But if it did, I'd hope you'd at least care enough to find out why." He searches my eyes and something softens inside me. "Would you care?"

I look away, glancing at the door, then at the people outside on the sidewalk walking past or getting ready to cross the road.

The question is do I still care if our situation were reversed?

Would I care enough to push past my hurt to find out why he'd hit rock bottom?

Knowing the answer, I look back at him and nod slowly, hesitantly. As if I'm afraid entertaining such feelings might crack the ironclad control I've held around my heart all these long years.

"Then give me five minutes, River. Five minutes, then I'm out of your hair for good."

I swallow past the tightness in my throat and release a measured breath. "Okay. But I'm not answering any questions I don't want to answer."

"That works."

I pull out the chair in front of him and sit, wondering what I'm about to get myself into. Did I really have a choice, though? No matter how much I pushed back he seemed to be determined to get an answer out of me.

Now that I'm in what feels like his lair my entire body is rigid with tension. I can also feel Kelly eyes on me. As Talia isn't across from us anymore, I'm sure she's joined her and they're talking about me.

"So," Jericho begins and steeples his fingers, "when did you get back to New York?"

I blink several times. The last time I saw him he would have had no reason to think I'd gone anywhere except Juilliard.

"I wasn't aware you knew I'd left."

"News travels."

"Right." I'm inclined to believe his answer over the possibility of him checking on me. He made it clear before we parted ways that his feelings had changed toward me, so why would he care what happened to me after? His recent checking/stalking is different. "I've been back in New York for over ten months now."

He seems surprised to hear that. "Oh. That's quite some time."

"It is. So, what else did the news tell you?" I want to know what he knows. That way I can prepare myself.

You have to be prepared when you talk to someone like him.

Jericho Grayson has a penchant for finding things others can't. I've never really known exactly how he does it, but he can. The same way he can solve any math equation within seconds and figure out the answer to...*anything*.

"The news told me that you stopped dancing with the Bolshoi

Ballet." His jaw tenses, a tell that he knows more details than he's giving me. It leads me to believe that he must have checked things out. "And you never married your fiancé."

Yes. He *did* check me out.

Jericho's gaze flicks down to my ring finger, bare of the ring that once lived there.

I wonder if he'd believe me if I told him I had to pawn it to buy food. I've never told anybody that story.

I still can't talk about Sasha either. I don't know when I'll be able to. My ex-fiancé left a hole in my soul as big as the galaxy. And it wasn't because of love lost. That would have been better. I could have handled it more easily than the truth of the lie he was.

That lie is part of the reason Sasha is behind bars in one of Russia's maximum-security prisons.

I hold my breath and push his deceitful face out of my mind. I don't want to think about him now, or ever again. Even if I fear the very real possibility that he'll get out of jail and find out that it was me who put him there.

Jericho's stare intensifies and I realize it's because I haven't said anything, so I think of the same lie I've been telling those who don't know the truth.

"It didn't work out." My voice holds a rasp of pain. "Neither of them. The Bolshoi Ballet and the engagement."

"I'm very sorry to hear that."

For some reason his answer irritates me, and I recall a movie I once saw with a similar scenario. I can't remember the name of the movie but in it a girl had run into her ex and got upset with him when he told her he was sorry to hear her engagement was off. At the time I thought she was overreacting, but now I get it.

She was upset because he was saying she didn't find happiness with this other guy, but deep down she wanted to be with her ex and have that said happiness with him.

While I don't wish to go back there with Jericho, I'm annoyed that he feels bad that I couldn't find happiness with someone else.

I know he meant my dancing career too, but my mind fixates on the broken engagement.

"Is that why you came back?" he asks, looking like he's trying to be careful with his words.

"Yes." That's the shortest version of what happened.

"Please tell me Club Edge isn't the end of your dancing career."

"No." At least I have some light at the end of this dark tunnel to look forward to, but it's not happening anytime soon. "I have the lead part in a production with the Emerson Dance Company. That's for the summer. Then I have an audition with the New York City Ballet in the fall."

He looks impressed to hear that. "Wow, well, that's fantastic."

"Thank you. I'm looking forward to it."

"I'm sure you are, and I'm sure you'll get in to the New York City Ballet."

"It would be great."

Those from the dance world will know how rare it is to get an audition with the New York City Ballet, but my previous credentials opened the door.

Teaching at the academy and the part I have with the Emersons Dance Company have also helped. Especially the latter. It's only a small production that will run from June to September but it's something active and shows I can still get dancing jobs. Too many gaps of not doing anything doesn't look good on a dancer's resumé. I've had almost two years of nothingness.

Only God knows how much I would have loved to go back to the Bolshoi and live the dream I'd had for as long as I could remember, but my position was filled long ago. In any event I know my heart can't handle the whole ordeal of returning to Russia.

"Until then, I'm teaching at a school, so at least I'm still dancing." I have a feeling he already knows that I teach at the school because he knew to find me here.

"That's good, too. What about everything else? You're working three jobs." He intensifies his stare and my breath stills.

I knew we were building up to that question, and for that answer I need to think.

"I have a few things I need to take care of," I say.

"A few things?" His brows knit.

"Just bills."

"Must be a lot of bills for you to be working at Club Edge."

Yeah, like a minimum of a hundred thousand. I'm not telling him that part, though.

"I can take care of them. It will all be fine, and I'm only working on the aerial hoop." I say that so he knows that I'm not stripping.

"Why don't you let me take care—"

"I think your five minutes are up." The words fall from my lips instinctively, cutting him off before he can finish his offer. His offer to help me with money.

Maybe most people would think I'm completely foolish to turn him down in such a way and not even consider an offer of help, but that would just shove me deeper into the hole of humiliation.

Jericho catches my meaning, and the understanding that I don't want his money forms in his eyes.

I wonder if he's shocked that this Cinderella turned him down when every woman he's probably been with since me has treated him like a king because of his wealth and status.

I might be the damsel in distress and, yes, I had the evil stepmother and stepsister who managed to rob my father blind of everything after his accident, but Jericho Grayson is not my Prince Charming.

With that reasoning I stand, pick up my notebook and pen. His gaze follows me then locks with mine.

"I should get back to work," I say.

He blinks, severing the tension filling the space between us. "Okay." He gives me a tight-lipped smile. "It was good seeing you again, River."

"You, too."

"Take care of yourself."

"And you."

I don't need to walk away this time. He pushes to his feet, dips his head, then makes his way to the door. Just before he walks through, he glances over his shoulder back at me.

At least he looked back this time, and I can replace our last goodbye with this one.

Goodbye, Jericho Grayson.

Chapter FIVE

River

"**K**EEP YOUR CHEST LIFTED AND EXTEND YOUR LEG AS high as you can," I instruct my students, watching the row of limbs rise into an arabesque, perfectly in time with the music from the piano Bernard is playing.

The floor-to-ceiling mirrors running across the left wall of the studio hold a beautiful image of them any dance teacher would be proud of.

This is my last ballet class for the day. It's also my favorite because I have ten eager-to-learn seventeen-year-old girls who have consistently reminded me of myself at their age. They have the same drive to learn and love for dancing that I've had all my life.

As they're all absolutely amazing I have no doubt that each of them has a fair shot at a career in ballet.

"Perfect," I praise them with an approving nod. "Now finish the sequence."

The girls continue dancing, flowing into each movement with the grace of swans while I watch them like a proud parent.

Bernard starts playing Bach's *Prelude in C major*, one of our favorites. The light atmosphere in the room changes with the sentiment, and I feel the beauty behind the talent from all of us. The dancers, Bernard, and me, the teacher.

Bernard's bushy gray brows lift and his smoky eyes brighten with the same satisfaction I feel for the work we've accomplished here. I take that as a small win for the day.

Bernard is a concert pianist who's been in the industry for over thirty years and has worked at the school for ten. It took some time for us to get used to each other because the teacher I replaced worked with him for longer than I've been dancing as a pro.

As the music plays and the dancers dance I allow myself a moment of reprieve.

Teaching these classes here at the school is my only joy in life. They keep me in touch with myself, my hopes, and my dreams. Teaching reminds me that I once knew the taste of success and I still want it.

The plan is to continue teaching until my auditions in the fall. If the New York City Ballet accepts me then I hope to be with them for many years to come. After that I want to open my own dance school. That's the dream I'm holding on to. After everything that's happened, I'm glad that's still part of me.

This job—courtesy of my best friend, Eden—feels like my anchor to the dreams I still want.

Eden is one of the music teachers here. We met at Juilliard and have remained friends all this time. Honestly, I don't know what the hell I would have done without her.

She's been my listening ear, my lifeline, and my support system throughout the duration of our friendship. We bonded on the first day of college because we both had mothers who died before we reached our teens, and we both had boyfriends who broke up with us weeks before college began.

When I got back to New York she put in a good word for me to get this job.

The vacancy had luckily just come about. Even though the school wanted someone with more years of experience under their belt, they picked me because Eden really sold me to them, and the head of dance had actually seen me perform several times across Europe.

The job comes with the perk of working for a prestigious school linked to many Ivy League colleges and professional dance companies.

I'm also, being able to use their beautiful dance studio whenever I want to practice.

The school itself is from the Victorian era so has that Gothic Revival architecture with curlicue trims and asymmetrical designs I've always loved about most of the buildings in Europe. The dance studio is no different.

I was here at four a.m. this morning, practicing for an hour before I went to the café. That was perhaps not the wisest choice given the fact that I got back from the club at two, but I couldn't sleep.

Seeing Jericho had me thinking about him and the past more than I wanted to.

It's been two days since he came to the café to see me. Although I knew that was goodbye, like an idiot I found myself checking the VIP section at the club for him when I went back that night. I checked last night, too, felt silly when I didn't see him, then realized I'd probably never see him again.

I should be okay with that. It's what I wanted, but I can't shake the weird feeling of loss from my soul.

Maybe it's because the part of me that still can't make sense of our breakup is struggling to figure it out.

I never saw it coming, and he left me when I needed him most. That hurt me more than anything.

It all started when my father lost his job after his team's designs for a new anti-virus software were stolen. Dad's business partner took matters into his own hands to issue payback. He blamed my father for the theft, so he broke in one night when Dad was working and tried to kill him. My father was shot in the back, and his business partner was killed when they fought. Dad barely made it out alive. Now he's in a wheelchair for the rest of his life.

Months before that happened, Jericho asked me to move to Boston to be with him after I graduated. Of course, I agreed.

The plan was for me to go in the summer so we could spend that time together, then I'd return to New York for Juilliard in the fall. He talked about traveling between Boston and New York until he graduated from MIT.

Those were all his plans. *His* ideas. All of which I agreed to. I was so in love with him that I would have said yes to anything, especially since it seemed as if Jericho wanted a future with me.

After many warnings to stay away from me, he'd even taken steps to confront Dad about our relationship, breaking free from the secret that we'd kept all those years.

Then my father's accident happened and Brielle, my evil stepmother, took control over everything.

When Dad started physio and it was clear he wanted Brielle's company more than mine, I thought it was the best time to resume my plans with Jericho.

But that's when he broke up with me.

I rest against the wall, keeping my focus on my girls as they dance, but in my mind's eye, I can still see that sickly look of dark dread and deep disappointment on Jericho's face from that night he broke up with me.

When he dropped the bomb on me it was like I was talking to someone I didn't recognize. Like the words were coming out of his mouth but someone else was speaking them.

Thinking back, I might have been able to deal with the breakup better if he hadn't told me *we'd* grown apart and it was time to move on. What he meant was *he* had grown apart, and *he* wanted to move on.

To take things back a bit further, I might have dealt with the breakup better if he hadn't continued our relationship after high school and if he hadn't asked me to move to Boston with him.

All of it screwed with my head. I was ready to defy my father and live my life with Jericho, but it wasn't meant to be.

I'm sure everything else that followed wasn't meant to be either because nothing worked out.

Like starting over with Sasha. That was a fucked-up epic fail of a mistake.

I met Sasha while I was touring in Moscow. After Jericho, Sasha was the first guy I let back into my heart, but I never saw him for who he truly was until I was miles too far on our journey.

He was the dangerous, controlling asshole who took over my life with his fists and his rage. He forced me to give up my career with the Bolshoi Ballet.

Ratting him out to the police was supposed to be my way out, but my trouble with him had only just begun. His debtors came after me for payment to settle his substantial debts. When they realized I couldn't pay, they kidnapped me, then contacted my aunt for a ransom of half a million dollars. Or they'd kill me. They nearly did when I tried to escape.

Aunt Gina is my mother's older sister. She already treated me like a daughter because she was told she couldn't have kids from an early age. When Mom died Gina became a mother to me, so knowing I was in deep, deep, deep shit she didn't hesitate to gather all her savings, all her earnings from her marketing consultancy, and worst of all, she got a loan not just from the bank but a loan shark too. All to save my life.

A month had hardly passed after she got me back when she suffered a stroke while driving. That's when everything really went to hell.

"River, are you okay?" Bernard's deep voice pulls me from the dark abyss of my memories, snapping me back to the present.

I straighten instantly when I realize everyone is watching me and the music has stopped. For how long, I have no idea.

Great. Nice one, River.

I hope I didn't look like I was bored or not paying attention.

Quickly, I plaster on a smile and shake my head at myself. "I'm so sorry. I was just thinking of some choreography I'd like to add to the routine."

"No worries." Bernard chuckles. "I'm sure the choreography will be as wondrous as what we did today."

"It will. We'll talk about that tomorrow." I look from him to the class.

They smile back at me—*believing me*—and I give myself a mental pat on the back for my quick thinking.

"Class dismissed. You all did amazing," I add in a chirpy voice.

"Thank you," the girls coo in unison, giving me that dreamy look of esteem and awe they always have on their faces when I compliment them. That's a remnant from my glory days. Everyone wants to be a prima ballerina. When you meet a person who is either doing what you aspire to or has done it, that person seems like a god to you. If only they knew how far I've fallen.

The girls and Bernard grab their things and leave.

My spirits lift when Eden approaches the door. We're going out to dinner and some much-needed catch-up time.

"Hey, girl." She leans against the door frame and her long black hair swishes over her shoulder.

"Hey, there. Great to see you." I go over to give her a quick hug.

I haven't seen or spoken to her in the last two days because she's been away on a four-day trip with her students. We have a lot to catch up on because she doesn't know I've seen Jericho yet. I wasn't going to tell anyone, but I think talking to someone about him will help relieve my mind of the added stress.

"How was your trip?" I ask.

"Amazing, and I met this guy." She brings her hands together in delight and laughs. "We're going out tomorrow night."

"Yay, that sounds great. I want to hear everything about him."

"Believe me, you will."

Of course, I will. She's been serial dating for the last five months and has been diligent enough to tell me about every single one of her many dates and conquests. It's enough action for me to live vicariously through her.

"Give me five minutes to change, and I'll be all yours."

"Cool, meet you downstairs."

"Alright."

I grab my things and head to the teacher's changing room. I have three hours before I need to be at the club. I've been dividing that time across the week so I can touch base with everyone, or catch up on lesson plans for class.

I try to see my father a few times a week and hang out with Eden, but I always go home to check on Gina before I head off to the club.

I get changed and meet Eden, then we set off for our favorite restaurant. A diner on Seventh that serves fattening comfort food like triple-sized burgers and house fries with giant chocolate shakes. We order exactly that before she starts telling me about her latest guy.

I'm thankful we're seated in one of the booths at the back because Eden has a flair for the dramatic and her sexy adventures are always of the X-rated variety.

I listen and laugh at her jokes, waiting for the right moment to tell her about Jericho.

I don't get an opening until we're nearly finished with our food. When I tell her, she has the precise reaction I expected. Her face becomes a sea of shock, amazement, wonder and mischief. The latter is always a worry with her because I never know what craziness she's going to tell me. Sometimes it's good and can get me out of a funk, but when it's bad, it's bad.

"I can't believe you ran into Jericho Grayson at the club." She blinks several times then bites the inside of her lip.

"I'm still in shock. Talk about coincidence and a twist of fate."

"No, girl, that's not how coincidence or fate works."

I roll my eyes. I totally forgot Eden is the girl who lives by her horoscopes and monthly psychic predictions. You can't mention concepts like fate and coincidence to her and not expect a deep dive into her truths.

"It seemed to work exactly like that with me," I say in a matter-of-fact tone.

She sighs with exasperation and tsks at me. "For God's sake, River. Think of what the universe could be trying to tell you."

"*Nothing.*" I cut her off before she can continue with her usual mumbo-jumbo crap. "The universe is telling me nothing except to stay far away from the man. This is just one of those unfortunate embarrassing-as-hell things you hope will never happen."

"I hear you, but he's Jericho Grayson." She sounds exactly the same as years ago when I first told her about him. Like most people, she knew who he was from the media attention the Grayson family has always garnered. "He's a freaking billionaire and one of the most eligible bachelors in the country."

"Yes, I'm aware of that."

"Don't you think it's noteworthy that he went to find you at the café?" She raises her perfectly-arched brows and the mischief in her eyes turns more visible.

"No. He was just curious. That's all."

"You think it's only curiosity?"

"Of course. There's nothing more to think. And I haven't seen him since."

"Did you want to see him again?" She intensifies her stare. "Sounds like you did."

"No. I didn't." Why the hell do I feel like I'm lying? I don't want to see Jericho again. There would be no point to it.

"It sounds like he was going to offer to help you." Eden gives me a heartfelt smile.

"I don't want his help." I inhale a deep breath, taking in the remaining aroma of our divine feast. I know I'm the last person who should be turning away money, but I couldn't allow Jericho to help me in such a way. My dignity already lives in the sewers. I want to hold on to whatever pride I have left.

"If all goes to plan, in six to eight months I'll be able to fix everything for Gina and get back on track." That will be just in time for my audition and hopefully acceptance to work with the New York City Ballet.

Worry pinches Eden's brows. "That's an awfully long time to wait and work at Club Edge." She drops her voice, mindfully aware of who might be listening to us.

Some of the teachers at the school who hate me would have a field day if they ever found out about my extracurricular activities at Club Edge.

Although I'm doing a great job and I'm loved by the students, there are haters who aren't overly fond of me because they think I'm too young to have a job that was previously filled by a teacher who'd worked in the industry for over fifty years.

They also don't think I fit because I don't come from old money, or any kind of money for that matter.

Eden is like me, but she doesn't catch the same flack because her great-great-great-grandfather was one of the founders of the school.

"You know I'm also not a huge fan of you working at that club." Her jaw tightens.

"I know." I'm not a huge fan of anything at the club either other than the money.

"*And* the auction." She swallows hard and I can see the worry filling her eyes.

"I know." I'd be a liar if I said that damn auction wasn't freaking me out, and it's an *anything-goes* auction. As in I've signed up to do anything with whoever buys me. I can't even believe I'm thinking those thoughts. Me, of all people. "I'm hoping a nice guy will just want a few dates."

"You *know* it won't be that." She blows out a ragged breath. "I'm probably the most liberal person you'll ever meet, and I've done some shit just to say I tried it, but this…"

"I'm just trying to think about the money. It's a lot to turn my back on when I really need it." I rest my hands on the table, suddenly feeling weak.

My stomach has been in knots since I signed up for the auction, but the money is the only thing that's been keeping my hopes up. I'm hoping to get a bid of twenty grand. That was the average bid at the auction last year.

The club takes twenty percent of the final offer, so if I got a bid of twenty thousand that would still leave me with a lump sum of sixteen thousand. Getting that money would mean I can pay some of the arrears on the loans.

The biggest one to worry about is the two hundred-thousand-dollar loan Gina got from an off-the-grid loan shark called Jones.

I don't even know how she came to know such a guy, but he's the kind of person you go to when you need serious money *quickly*, which was what she needed to save me. She only managed to get such a high-value loan from him by putting up her home and business as collateral.

That loan has eight months' worth of arrears. Jones has been what he classes as 'reasonable' because of Gina's stroke, but months ago he threatened to take the house and went as far as threatening to sell me. He was serious about both.

Gina doesn't know about the latter threat—*about selling me*—but that's what pushed me to get the job at Club Edge.

Poor Gina. She thought she was going to be able to pay everything off within a few months because she had a big job lined up. That fell through because of her stroke. The client who'd booked her wanted her specifically to work on their project, not her business partner.

The money I've been making has been taking care of the

mortgage and Gina's medical expenses that insurance won't cover. Sixteen thousand isn't a lot when I think of how much is still left to pay for everything, but it will help me a great deal.

Understanding enters Eden's eyes and she nods. "Hey, I get it." She clasps her hands. "I understand, so here's hoping everything will work out the way we hope. I guess I just wish I could help you more."

I reach across the table and tap her knuckles. "You've helped me more than enough. If not for you, I wouldn't have the job at the school. And remember, you gave me all that money after Gina's stroke."

Eden gave me ten thousand dollars, which helped immensely. "I still wish I could do more."

"I know, and I appreciate you for that." My shoulders slump with the weight of the disaster I've been living. "If anyone should have helped me, it's my father."

"Don't you think he wishes he could?" Her lips part, and she gazes back at me with surprise.

"I do, but he never says so because he knows he screwed up."

I can't help the resentment I feel toward my father for so many things. It started with his marriage to Brielle. I thought he got married way too soon after Mom died, as it was less than a year after she passed. Then, after his accident, he allowed Brielle and her bitch daughter, Michelle, to rob him of every cent he had.

He worried Brielle would leave him because he could no longer walk, so he gave her control over his finances and splurged on her to keep her. She left him anyway and took all his money. Money from the house she sold, money from Dad's other assets, money from his savings.

Dad ended up in a one-bed condo on the other side of the city. Because he can't work long hours, he does part-time at a software firm. It's a job that pays the bills and puts food on the table but it doesn't come close to the previous company he worked for. He's on an intern's salary, which is just enough to take care of his basic needs.

Apart from the finances, I hate that my father told me to stay with Sasha. He wanted me to stay even knowing how badly I was being treated. His argument was that he thought we could work things out. I only have myself to blame, but I know that if he'd told me to leave or found a way to get me out of that situation, many of the problems I now have wouldn't exist.

Neither of those options would have crossed my father's mind, though, because of Sasha's wealth. Dad would be more worried about looking like the bad guy than me.

The same goes for Club Edge. If Dad knew I was working there he'd be more embarrassed for himself. Not me.

That's why I haven't told him about it. Gina doesn't know either, but not for the same reasons. If she knew, she'd feel like she'd failed me, and I would never want her to feel that way.

Dad and Gina currently think I got a dancing job that's bringing in extra money to take care of the bills. I want to keep it that way.

"I'm so sorry." Eden sits forward and gives my hands a gentle squeeze. "Let's order dessert and talk about happier things, like your audition and all the amazing things you'll do when you get the job."

I give her a grateful smile. "Thanks for being so positive."

"It's the least I can do." Her face brightens. "Now, how does a hot fudge sundae sound?"

"Like heaven on earth."

"Then we should have it."

When the dessert arrives I try to enjoy it and stop thinking of the night I still have ahead of me.

At least it works to some degree, but as night falls so do my hopes.

I reach home at two in the morning, dragging my legs as if weights are attached to the soles of my feet.

Shit. Every cell in my body is screaming with exhaustion.

Every time I feel like this, I pray that my body doesn't give out and refuse to work. Especially when I'm on the aerial hoop.

Tonight, I almost fell.

Me.

That hasn't happened in so long I can't even remember the last time it did. It would have been long before Mom died. The same way she used to come to all my ballet classes, she'd attend my aerial classes, too. It was her who got me started on both from the tender age of five, because that was her dream. Her family couldn't afford lessons. When she saw that I was obsessed with both she made it her life's mission to make sure I did what I wanted to do.

She would have loved to see all that I can do now, but she'd want me to be sensible.

Being up on the aerial with no safety is dangerous enough as it is, but being up there when you're so tired you can't see clearly is downright foolish.

I have a break tomorrow for the auction and the two nights that follow for the time I'm supposed to spend with whoever wins me. Right now, I don't even have the energy to feel nervous.

When I get inside the house I see the light on in the kitchen, meaning Gina is awake. It's not often that she's up at this hour.

I hope she didn't wait up for me.

Earlier, when I checked in, Gina was worried about me because I'm working so much. She begged me to take the night off, and I was only able to get away because her support nurse came by for her physio appointment.

I make my way into the kitchen and find Gina sitting at the breakfast table with her laptop open and a stack of letters next to it.

She's in such deep thought that she doesn't notice me standing at the door.

Her eyes are glued to whatever is on her computer screen.

Her hair is a wild mess of long black and gray strands that hasn't been styled in months. She's only fifty, but the stroke has given her a gaunt appearance that's made her look several years older.

Taking care not to startle her, I walk in. When she looks up at me a weary smile slides across her lips.

"Hi, I couldn't sleep," she mutters.

Thankfully, her speech was one of the first things she regained after the stroke. It was slurred for well over a month before it improved.

The next thing to come back was the feeling in the left side of her body, but she still can't move around properly without the aid of a cane, or for too long.

"It's really late, though."

"Too late for you, too, and you're getting up in a few hours."

"Don't worry about me." I walk over to her.

She shakes her head. "You know I do. You're working way too hard, River. I know you feel guilty for our situation, but you mustn't."

"There's too much debt."

Sadness fills her eyes. "I know. I've been thinking of doing some online work. Anna helped me brainstorm the idea."

Anna is her business partner. I know she's trying to help, but Gina is in no position to do any kind of work, online or otherwise.

"I don't think that's a good idea."

"It wouldn't be stressful," she assures me with a determined nod.

"Aunt Gina, please, just allow me to take care of things. I really hope you aren't actually working." I scan the stack of letters, and now that I'm close I can read what's on her computer screen. It's an email with a list of things to do from Anna.

"This is all stuff Anna needed me to check for the company insurance renewal. And a potential contract." She says that last part with more caution.

"So, it's work?"

"River, I can't just—" Her words cut and she grabs her chest, then gasps for air.

I reach for her hand. "Gina, what's happening?"

She doubles over, panting and wincing in pain. Panic sends a jolt of adrenaline through me, eradicating my prior state of exhaustion.

I grab her shoulders and she leans into me.

"I'm going to call the hospital."

"No, I'll be okay," she says quickly, inching back so she can look at me. Her breathing slows, and then she almost seems normal but I can tell she's not. "This happened the other day, and I was fine. It's just… a sharp pain."

"Did you speak to the nurse about it?"

"Yes, it's nothing, sweetie. Probably gas." She tries to laugh, but it doesn't work. A raspy cough comes out instead. "I think I should go lie down and try to sleep."

"Yes, you should." I nod, still assessing her and contemplating calling the hospital. "Are you sure I shouldn't give the hospital a quick call to run it past a doctor."

"No. I'm okay. I just need some sleep."

"Okay. Let me help you to your room." I help her get up then take her to her room.

She lies down and is asleep within minutes.

Paralyzed with worry, I watch her, wondering what the hell just happened.

She said there was nothing to worry about, but it didn't look like *nothing* to me.

So, what could it be?

Something tells me there's more to worry about.

Like Gina could be more sick than I know.

Chapter SIX

Jericho

I REST MY HANDS ON THE TABLE AND FOCUS ON POTENTIAL wife number one—Celeste Wilder. *The Megan Fox look-alike.* Now that she's right in front of me I can see she's a dead ringer for the actress.

Tonight is our first date. We've been sitting in a private booth on the rooftop of The Mont Bleu for the last hour, getting to know each other over a gourmet meal and a bottle of wine.

I picked this restaurant because it's one of those places I go to when I need the ambiance of clarity to make important decisions.

Celeste is a former fashion model turned fitness enthusiast. She's definitely somebody my grandfather would love to see me with because of her career-driven mindset.

From the combo of her looks and personality, I know exactly why Luc placed her at number one on the list. It was because he thought she should get the job hands down. He's probably right.

Luc usually is. This occasion is no different, especially since there's nothing about the gorgeous Celeste I can find to hate *yet*.

She's been telling me about herself and I've been trying to listen without allowing my mind to slip back to a certain redhead I shouldn't be thinking about.

I should be psyched that my plan to find a wife is on the move and that it's quite likely, if I play my cards right, I could have a suitable candidate by next week.

However, my fucked-up mind has chosen to fixate on my ex.

At least I left River alone like I promised I would and haven't been back to Club Edge or the café. Against my better judgment, I even respected her privacy and didn't do any more research to find out what sort of money she needed to pay her bills.

Over the last two days, I've practically acted as if I never saw her at all. That doesn't mean she's left my mind, and although it gave me marginal assurance to know she was only doing her aerial performance, I don't know if that was true.

"I was a fashion model for five years before I decided to build my fitness empire, and I've been even more successful." A proud smile inches across Celeste's lips, highlighting flawless skin and high, exotic cheekbones. "I'm thinking of starting my own line of nutritional supplements next year."

"That's impressive. What made you go into fitness?" I try to sound like I'm genuinely interested to know more about her plans, but I'm not.

"I couldn't let this amazing body go to waste." She flicks her wrists and points at herself, pushing out her double Ds against her low-cut dress to show me more of her breasts.

"Of course not."

A lustful look enters her eyes, and she bites down on her glossy red lips. "So, we've been sitting here for a little over an hour. I'm interested to hear what Jericho Grayson thinks of me."

I think for a moment because I don't know what the hell to say. Clearly she wants to know if I picked her or not. As a rule of thumb

I know never to select the first option without looking at the rest and assessing them all together.

"You impress me." I school my thoughts, imbuing my expression with faux interest.

"Enough to make me your wife?" Her baby blues twinkle with anticipation, and I can see her go-getter attitude coming through.

"You'll find out in a week's time." That was the agreement.

She giggles. "A whole week. I'm often told that I'm one of those people you meet and want to get to know straight away."

"I don't doubt that."

"And as you can see, I'm definitely a great selection. You wouldn't be disappointed in the least." She winks at me, reminding me of myself. Maybe Luc picked her because she seems to be the female version of me.

"I'm sure I wouldn't be, but I'm sticking to a plan." This is me being nice. No matter the reason or scenario, I don't like anyone pressing or pushing information from me.

"Okay, I guess I'll have to understand. But just so you know, I'd be exactly what you want me to be and make sure our home and our kids are looked after at all times."

Kids?

No. Sorry, Celeste. There will be no kids.

Poor girl. She might have been in the running to become my wife until she said that.

Either she didn't read the terms and conditions I sent her, or she wants kids with me and thought to slip that in. I have a feeling it's the latter.

"I haven't seen any mention of how many kids you want." She gives me a challenging stare with a sassy smile, and I see that I'm right. *Again.*

A girl like her would have read everything in that document, maybe several times over. She's a businesswoman. A good one who's trying to be clever.

She wants more than a contract with me and obviously the security of being with a man who's worth billions.

"There was no mention of kids." My voice is flat and expressionless.

"Why not? Everyone loves kids." She giggles again. This time I find the sound irritating. "If we're getting married wouldn't kids just naturally enter the picture?"

"Not really."

"I'm sure I can change your mind." Her voice rises slightly higher, displaying her self-assured confidence.

"I highly doubt that." Very few people in my lifetime have managed to shift my mind once I've made a decision. I already know Celeste Wilder won't be the one.

"Just hear me out." She flicks her head from side to side so her dark locks cover her shoulder like a cape. Then she flashes more boobage, as if her tits are the winning ticket to unlocking my unyielding heart.

If I deposited a dollar for every woman who thought she could win me over with her tits, I could build my own empire and sustain it for a lifetime.

The speech Celeste delivers next is award-winning to say the least, and if I were some other guy, it might work. But I give her credit for trying. Trying to win me over to pick her to be my wife and trying to change my mind about having kids.

There's nothing wrong with wanting kids. *I* just won't be having them. That means I'll do this poor girl a favor and cross her off the list.

While Celeste continues talking about herself and all the plans she has for the family she wants with me, curiosity pushes my thoughts right back to River.

I'm not the kind of guy who gets hung up on a woman, or has the desire to chase, but River St. James was the exception to my rule. I think that's why she's still in my head.

Each time she floats into my mind—*like now*—I remember that she shouldn't be there.

River and I are in the past. Things are different now, and I'm not the same guy she knew. Honestly, a guy like me should have never been anywhere near her in the first place.

She's good. I'm bad.

She's kind. I'm selfish.

She loves to laugh, and I'm a malicious recluse without a humorous bone in my body, unless I'm being crude and sardonic.

She was too good for me. Too pure, too innocent, untainted. Until me.

That brings me to the crux of what happened. The selfish asshole I was back then wanted out of the Grayson empire because I didn't want anything to do with my father.

How ironic it was that River's father loathed me because I was Tobias Grayson's spawn. Her father never cared that mine wouldn't claim me as his son, and he never cared that I saw him as nothing but a sperm donor. It was simply enough that the Grayson blood flowed through my veins. Neil St. James told me exactly that when he warned me away from his daughter.

I got that warning five times and never listened. If I had listened even once, I might not feel as guilty as I have for the last eight years.

Then again, I know I would, because I wouldn't have wanted to do anything to hurt her. Yet I did.

Back then I would have done anything to get away from my father and his constant reminders of how his bastard children didn't belong to the Grayson family.

While Knight fought, I looked for a way out. That's where I went wrong.

I came across the wrong kind of people, who offered me a black-market job. They were hackers who I don't know the identity of to this day.

Being offered twenty-five thousand dollars for your computer hacking skills at the age of twenty-one when you were trying to create your own wealth sounded like a sweet deal.

The kind of deal you don't say no to when you don't have your own money, and your grandfather insists on keeping it that way so you can focus on your studies at college.

The job was to create a hacking device that could get past high-tech sophisticated firewalls similar to what you find in the military, or in government agencies like the CIA.

I was used to that shit as I was to the back of my hand. The deal was so irresistible I didn't even dig around to find out how the hackers knew about me and my skills.

There aren't many people like me who naturally understand how to hack, and I was no saint. I would hack a system just because I could, or wanted to create chaos and havoc for fun.

I did the job and later found out that the hackers wanted the device to hack into River's father's company, Jaeger Tech. They stole his designs and everything he and his business partner had created.

After that happened Neil and his team were fired, then his business partner took out his fury on Neil. That's why Neil is in a wheelchair and his business partner is dead.

Because of me. Because of my selfishness. Because I didn't think first before accepting the devil's deal.

I unknowingly opened the door to chaos and havoc and allowed both to screw with River's family.

There was nothing I could do to stop it—even though I tried—and there was nothing I could do to fix it. I tried that, too, hoping I could get Neil his job back, but I failed.

I wanted to buy back the designs but by then it was too late, the designs had been leaked and was already in production by competitors. Then the hackers threatened to kill me when they thought I was going to expose them.

It was grandfather who took care of them and stopped them in their tracks. I don't know what he did to get rid of them but I never heard from them again.

Grandfather never knew about Neil or River. I couldn't tell him about those parts because I was so ashamed of what I did and the repercussions.

That secret is one I've harbored for years and was my reason for breaking up with River.

There was no way I could be with her after that. Telling her wasn't an option. I know I never pulled the trigger on the gun and released the bullet that paralyzed her father, but I still saw it as my fault.

If I hadn't done what I did, none of it would have happened.

My father was the devil to Neil, but his son—*me*—became his destroyer.

The only people who know what happened are Luc and my grandfather.

Grandfather only knew about the hackers, but I told Luc the entire story.

I can't help but think that when this marriage thing came about that Grandfather was adding my past mishaps into the mix to come to his decision.

He values what I bring to the company, but he thinks I'm reckless.

Celeste's annoying giggle fills the space between us, telling me I'm done for the night. I showed up, gave this date a shot, and crossed her off my list, so there's no point sticking around.

Besides, even I know I'm being a prick for being on a date with one woman while thinking about another.

I'm about to tell her the night is over when my phone buzzes with a text.

"Sorry, I have to check this." I retrieve my phone and Celeste nods, giving me a little smile.

"No worries. I'll wait all night." She giggles again.

The look I return is stiff and as lifeless as a statue. I don't know what this text is about but I'm grateful for it. When I see it's from Luc, I open it.

It says:

FYI—just thought you should know what the mermaid is doing tonight.

The Mermaid is River. He hasn't dropped the name since he found out everyone is calling her that at the club.

Underneath his comment is a link.

When I click it, it takes me straight to Club Edge's event page.

The main event tonight is the VIP Auction.

Bid on the girl of your dreams and she'll do anything you want for two magical nights...

The moment my eyes land on River's face in the lineup of participants heated rage I haven't felt in years spreads across my skin like fire.

What the fuck is this? River has put herself up for a fucking auction!

As in auctioning herself to God knows who for fuck knows what.

Jesus. There's no way she's just taking care of a *few* bills. This goes right back to my theory about her being in trouble, so now I'm kicking myself for not digging deeper to find out what is really going on.

I hold back a growl and grip the phone so tightly it's a wonder it's not crumbling to dust in my palm.

"Is everything okay?" Celeste asks on noticing my reaction.

I flick my gaze up to her. "Yes." *But no, everything is not* okay. How am I supposed to sit back and allow River to do this because I promised I'd leave her alone?

And fucking Luc. He sent me this *FYI* to make me crazy.

Fuck him.

And fuck the promise too.

The auction starts in an hour. It will take about that time to get to Club Edge.

River St. James might not be mine anymore but I won't allow her to sell herself.

Chapter SEVEN

River

T HE AUCTION WILL BEGIN SOON...
My heart shrinks away at the sight of myself in the dressing room's full-length mirror.

I look like a cross between an exotic burlesque dancer and a confused prostitute.

I'm wearing an ocean-blue and green crisscross bra with diamantes splashed across the cups. The thing barely covers my breasts. In fact, it doesn't. It just covers my nipples.

The thong I have on—*if you can call it that*—just about covers the slit of my sex, so I'm practically naked. The only saving grace I have is that my hair is down in long waves and covers my ass to some extent. That's it, so hardly anything at all.

When I was given an idea of what I'd be wearing tonight I imagined something a little more tasteful, but this... This is degrading.

Tears sting the backs of my eyes and I have to fight hard to keep them from falling.

The last time I cried it took everything out of me to come back. I feel like that again, like I've truly fallen deep into the gutter.

How much further can I fall before I rise back up?

What if there's no option to rise?

What if tonight doesn't go well and all my plans fail?

You hear countless stories of women who choose the wrong path but end up finding the right one. I suppose the one thing they have in common is that they had to go through hell first.

This feels like my hell. I know I have to survive it, but I'm in way over my head.

What's worse is I'm starting to feel like I really did sell my soul to the devil by working here and agreeing to this auction.

Not even the prospect of the money I stand to gain from tonight will make me feel better about that. And I'm worried about Gina.

After last night I took the day off from working at the café and the school. I would have stayed away from the club, too, but of all the jobs I had today this is the one I couldn't miss.

Gina seemed fine throughout the day and I left her with one of the support workers from the hospital, but I'm still worried.

She's never complained about chest pains before. I know from losing my mother that chest pains are a serious thing that you shouldn't ignore.

Mom died of a heart attack. She had an undiagnosed heart condition that took her away from me way too soon. I was only twelve when it happened.

We were at Thanksgiving dinner with the whole family when she collapsed in the kitchen. That was the last time I saw her alive. It would kill me if the same thing were to happen to Gina.

Here's hoping that I get the money I'm praying for tonight and that I don't have to stay out too late. I'll head home as soon as I'm able to.

The door opens to my left and Zara pokes her head in with a big smile on her face.

"Wow. You look absolutely amazing."

I don't even know what to say to her. *Amazing* is not the word I'd use to describe me.

"Thank you." My voice reflects my inner thoughts but she doesn't seem to notice.

"We're ready for you now. The auction is about to start."

"Okay. I'll be out in two minutes."

"Sure, and please don't be nervous. It's gonna be a great night." She sounds like we've won some extravagant prize.

I guess *they* have. There are thirty-five girls taking part in tonight's auction. The club stands to bring in at least half a million dollars just from this event.

"I'll be fine," I assure Zara, hoping I sound believable.

"Okay, see you out there."

She leaves. When the door closes I drag in a deep, deep breath and try to focus.

Twenty thousand dollars, River, and that's a minimum. It could be much more but hopefully not less.

I *can* do this. I'm just tired. Physically and mentally.

But tiredness can't be my enemy tonight. Nothing can or will, not even the loss of my dignity.

Summoning courage, I take a final breath, shrug into my dressing robe, then leave.

I make my way to the backstage area of the main hall. It looks like the one I usually dance in but has an auditorium layout. And it's packed.

Packed with men of all different ages, shapes, sizes, and wealth.

I make my way to the section where the other girls are waiting in costumes as equally revealing as the one I'm wearing. As they're all veterans of auctions past and present, none of them seem to mind.

It's just me—the new girl—who's self-aware.

Zara arrives to give us some instructions, but my mind is so far away I hardly hear a thing she says. The only thing I got was that I'm to go on stage when my name is called, smile like I already have the money in my hands, and bring out my sexiest pose when I want the bids to increase.

It's all good advice, but I'm just thinking of putting one foot in front of the other.

The auction begins and Maribel, a platinum blonde, is the first to walk onstage.

The bid starts at a thousand dollars and slowly rises to twenty, where it closes and she's sold to a guy who looks like he just walked out of a Davidoff advert.

I might not know the ropes of how the event works, but seeing her get twenty thousand is a good indication of how the rest of the night might go.

The next girl, Laura, goes on and she gets twenty-five thousand. So do the other three girls after her.

I'm number ten, so I still have quite a wait. My nerves rise with each minute that passes and by the time my name is called I'm so anxious I can scarcely breathe.

Zara glances at my robe as I'm about to walk out on stage. I totally forgot I was wearing it.

When I shrug out of it that feeling of despair hits me again the moment I'm exposed.

With my legs shaking I walk out onto the stage. By the time I reach the center my heart is pounding so hard I feel like I should be holding it inside my chest to stop it from jumping out.

I manage a smile, but I'm not half as confident as the other girls. Given the fact that I'm the most desperate person here I should be skipping out naked and dropping to the ground with my legs open. Instead, I'm standing here like a terrified animal in a slaughterhouse.

The bid starts at five thousand, shocking me. Minutes later the voices rise with increasing bids, and soon I've reached twenty-five thousand.

Before I can blink someone casts a bid for thirty. It's the highest bid so far tonight. Hope sparks in my heart at the thought, but

I'm still too worked up to do anything more than breathe. And now I'm dreading all the things I'll have to do for that type of money.

The highest bidder, who seems dead set on winning me, looks old enough to be my grandfather and has a Hugh Hefner vibe.

He's sitting in the front row, so I can see the leery grin pasted on his wrinkly face.

No other bids come to outdo him, and my stomach turns when his smile radiates with sin.

"Well, it looks like we have a keeper for our beautiful mermaid," Zara speaks heartily into her microphone. "Going once, going twice—"

"Thirty-five thousand," comes a loud, booming voice from the back of the hall.

My blood stops in my veins as I follow the sound of the voice and find Jericho standing at the top of the steps leading down to the lower seats.

My God. The bid came from him!

He's here, and he just placed the bid on me.

What the hell is he doing here?

I was barely breathing before, but now I'm not at all. Shock has seized my brain, and the combination of humiliation and bewilderment has me rooted to the spot like a tree.

I'm too far away to read his face properly, but there's a hardness to him that reeks of power.

I can see the impact of Jericho's presence on the other men's faces, but the older guy who bid on me tries to look unfazed.

"Forty," he says.

"Forty-five," Jericho counters, but now he's looking at me and walking closer to the stage.

I can't take my eyes off him either.

Forty-five thousand dollars.

I'm numb just thinking about that amount of money.

"Fifty." The man cuts into our stare, and we both look at him. Silence settles over the room and the only thing that can be heard is the sound of Jericho's shoes on the floor as he makes his way toward the man. He stops in front of him and stares him down.

"Sixty thousand," Jericho announces, and a bolt of shock lances through me.

He just bid sixty thousand dollars.

Sixty. Thousand. Dollars.

Those words ripple through my mind like an echo in the mountains.

"We can keep going all night if you want, *grandpa*," he directs at the man, his accent sounding thicker with his annoyance. "A word of advice, though, if I were you, I wouldn't challenge me. You do know who I am, right?"

"Yes, Jericho Grayson." The man's voice is rigid with a hint of a challenge, but everyone can see from the sweat glistening on his brow that he looks like he's been backed into a corner.

"Well done." Jericho makes a show of brushing invisible lint from the man's jacket. "You know who I am, so you know you won't win. It would be best not to fuck with me."

My lips part. I can't believe what he just said any more than I can believe that he just bid sixty thousand dollars for me.

A deadly silence hangs in the air as the man seems to heed Jericho's warning and says nothing more. Neither does anyone else for what seems like an eternity.

"It seems we've come to an agreement," Zara announces in a cautious voice, glancing at me curiously. "Our beautiful mermaid is going once, twice, and sold for sixty thousand dollars to Jericho Grayson."

While whispers erupt all around me Jericho walks onto the stage like he owns the place. He's supposed to collect me from the office, where further arrangements will be made, but those rules obviously don't apply to him.

He moves toward me, takes off his jacket, and sets it over my shoulders to cover me.

Those bright blue eyes are riveted to mine as I stare back at him, speechless, and I hate, hate, hate that the shield of his jacket over my body comforts me.

I hate it even more that I feel like he just rescued me when he takes my hand and leads me away from what I had previously christened my latest descent into hell.

Chapter EIGHT

River

JERICHO MARCHES DOWN THE CORRIDOR WITH ME, STILL holding my hand.

All I can feel is the heat emanating from his palm as he tugs me along.

I'm moving, but I feel like a mindless automaton walking in a dream and I can't get my mind to focus past the raucousness of emotions writhing through me. Each of them wars with the pounding of my heart in my ears and the discordance created by the thud of his shoes and the click of my heels against the hard floor.

It doesn't help that his scent is laced into the soft fibers of his jacket. That scent of musk and the forest has never left me. It lingers beneath his expensive cologne, taunting me with the past and creating more chaos inside me.

I need to say something, but I can't think past the truth and the lie I've been trying to uphold that everything is okay.

Jericho has seen quite clearly that everything is *not* okay with me.

Everything is shit, and I've never been more embarrassed in my life.

Oh wait, actually, yes, I have.

There was one other time that I remember quite clearly. It was the night I first met Jericho, but this is so much worse. Saving me from high school bullies was tame in comparison to shelling out sixty thousand dollars to save me from selling myself.

The same guy saved me from both, but I'm not supposed to need saving from my ex.

My pride has fallen through the earth and the knots of tension living in my stomach have piled mountain high, rising into my throat.

Jericho takes me to the dressing room. It's only once we're inside that I realize where we are.

"Get your clothes on. You're going home now." His voice sounds as out of place in this room as it does in my life, but those commanding words spark the energy back into my awareness.

I yank my hand out of his, stopping just before we reach my locker.

He turns to face me, his face as stern as it was back in the auction hall.

"Why are you here?" I cry. I'm glad I've found my voice, even though the tremor rippling through my words shows how upset and embarrassed I am. "Why the hell did you bid on me?"

His brows snap together and he stares at me as if I've gone crazy. "Are you kidding me? What the hell kind of question is that?"

"Give me an answer. Why are you here, Jericho?"

"I'm saving your ass, so instead of asking me bullshit, you should be grateful you didn't end up with some old geezer who was one step away from putting you in his playboy mansion."

I'm so wound up I don't even bother to acknowledge that he caught the Hugh Hefner vibe from that guy, too.

"I don't want to be grateful to you. You promised me you'd leave me alone."

"I lied. But you obviously lied, too. This is not taking care of a few bills." He motions to the room with his hands. "What kind of trouble are you in, River? Clearly, you must be in some kind of shit. What is it?"

"I'm not in any trouble." *Not anymore.* This situation is the aftermath, but I won't tell him that.

He smirks, giving me an incredulous glare. "That's a bold-faced lie."

My temper flares and I don't care that I seem foolish again. I don't want to be grateful to him for saving me because I'm in a desperate situation. The traces of pride that I have left make me feel more ashamed of myself that he had to help me.

"Look, I don't have to tell you shit. You can't just waltz into my life and make demands. I'm not one of your lackeys or admiring fans who fall at your feet." The words fall from my lips without filter. "I didn't want *your* help."

"Well, that's too damn bad, because you got it." He squares his shoulders, looking enraged at my defiance.

"Don't you realize what you just did? It's an auction. Jericho, you just *bought* me." The gravity of this hits me and I feel worse, like my mind might implode on itself and the walls of strength I've built around my heart will collapse all around me into rubble and dust.

"Yes, that is what an auction is, so it looks like we're stuck together for the next two days."

That remark and the wild look dancing in his eyes cause my skin to heat and my lungs to tighten as if rope were wrapped around them.

"This is not a joke. You shouldn't have come here."

"And yet here I am, *Mermaid*." A spark of something I can't identify invades his eyes and he gives me a wicked smile.

"Don't you dare call me that. I don't have to put up with—"

He stops my next words, and my breath, by catching my face and crushing his lips to mine.

He moved so fast I didn't know what he was going to do until his mouth was sealed over my lips, robbing my mind of thought and reason.

Jericho pulls me closer and kisses the last shred of strength from my body. In his arms I feel light and vulnerable.

My knees turn to water and my insides liquify, melting against the burning kiss he brands on my lips.

The firmness of his kiss takes me back to the last time he kissed me. It's been so long I don't know how I haven't forgotten what it feels like. When his tongue sweeps over mine I taste him, and he takes advantage of the moment to taste me, too.

Then he draws back, breaking the kiss and snapping whatever spell he held over me.

My breathing comes hard, my heart beating faster and faster as I stare back at him with wide, wide eyes.

I'm surprised that he looks just as shocked as I am, but that unidentifiable look I previously saw returns to his eyes. I know what it is now. It's malice.

Malice mixed with the dark desire of a villain. The look a predator would issue to its prey before it strikes, before it consumes, before it devours.

I recognize it now from the past.

Jericho tilts his head, keeping his unwavering gaze trained on me. "I'll send you a message with my instructions in the morning. See you tomorrow night." There's no mistaking the promise in his words.

With that said he walks away without another word, leaving me stunned and speechless.

Feeling numbness spreading throughout my body, I watch him until he walks through the door and I can't see him anymore, but I still stare after him as if I can.

Jericho—my ex—just kissed me.

Jericho Grayson just bought me in an auction for sixty thousand dollars, then he kissed me the way passionate lovers kiss when they can't get enough of each other.

I don't think I could have made any of that up if I tried.

Earlier, I thought I was in hell. Now I feel like I've been pulled into a crazy episode of the *Twilight Zone*.

Sixty thousand dollars is deposited into my account before I even reach home.

The whole *sixty thousand*, meaning Jericho must have paid the club their cut on top to ensure I received the entire amount.

I was still in that numb frame of mind, so it took me several hours before I felt normal again.

Once I checked on Gina and saw she was okay and asleep, I went to my room. I got changed for bed, but I didn't sleep. The events of the night have run through my mind scene by scene, minute by minute, second by second.

It continued like that, stuck on a loop until birds began chirping outside my window and the first traces of sunlight brightened my room.

It's morning. I didn't sleep a wink all night, and I don't even feel tired.

It must be the shock. I participated in that auction hoping for someone to bid twenty thousand dollars on me, but I came home with sixty thousand dollars in my bank account. Courtesy of my ex I never wanted to see again, much less owe.

I know I don't have to pay Jericho back the money, but I do owe him.

As much as I hate to admit it, he was right. I could have ended up in the playboy mansion with the Hugh Hefner wannabe, or with someone else. I could have also ended up with less money.

I stopped Jericho in his tracks from helping me the other day, but he still found a way.

My pride is wounded, but truthfully…

I can't deny that there's a sense of relief in my soul at having that money. I can pay all the arrears on the loans and the house bills. If there's anything left, I can put it towards Gina's care. Having that money will almost put me on track where I can make the usual monthly repayments.

I'm not out of the woods, but the path is clearing. Now it looks like I should be able to leave Club Edge and the café in three months' time. That's moved up my departure date by several months. I could use the summer to practice, spend time with Gina, Eden, and my father. I might even be able to have some sort of a life.

My alarm goes off an hour later, and I get ready for the café.

Just before I leave, a message from an unrecognized number comes through on my phone. The instant I read the first few words I know it's from Jericho. It says:

I'll send a car to pick you up from your aunt's at seven. We're going to the Artisan. See you then.

J.

I note that he still refers to himself as J and that he must know I'm staying at Gina's. I'm still not sure exactly what he knows about me, but I don't doubt he'll be digging deeper for things he didn't know before.

I guess I'll find out more when I see him at the Artisan. It's not surprising he picked somewhere like that.

The Artisan is a trendy club that hosts nightly live art shows. It's somewhere I've always wanted to go but never expected to in my lifetime. It costs five hundred dollars just to get in, and there's a yearlong waiting list. I suppose that's for people like me.

For high-profile clientele like the Graysons, the doors will open the same way the Red Sea parted for Moses.

Quickly, I text back: *Okay.*

But I wonder what will happen when I see Jericho tonight.

What will he expect from me in return for this sixty thousand dollars?

Chapter NINE

Jericho

DAMN, I CERTAINLY HAVE A WAY OF LANDING MYSELF IN trouble.

If I had any hopes of forgetting my gorgeous ex then I shouldn't have kissed her.

Better yet, I shouldn't have claimed her as mine again by buying her in an auction.

If I were a better man I would have just let her keep the money and forget about the dates I'm supposed to get in return. The thought crossed my mind, but each time I contemplated leaving River alone I kept remembering the taste of her kiss. Then I saw her standing on that stage wearing next to nothing. Every man's eyes in that room were on the girl who used to be mine.

I don't know what the hell I plan to do, but the thought of having her for the next two days does something wicked to me.

Something wicked that sent me down another rabbit hole.

As River was determined not to tell me anything, when I got

home last night I picked up where I left off in my search the other day.

Had I done what I'm most skilled at I would have known well before now that River wasn't *just* taking care of a few bills. When she first told me that's what she was doing, of course I knew she was downplaying how much money she needed, but I respected her privacy. That idea went out the door the moment I found out she was taking part in the auction.

Now I'm sitting in the office of my tattoo shop reading through the last piece of intel I was waiting for about Gina's finances.

It's her who's in debt. *Gina*. River's aunt. From what I've found so far, she's in a ton of debt.

Although I know I've already crossed too many lines, I'm kicking myself for not digging deeper to find out what was going on with River days ago when I first had the thought to do so.

I did a background check on her father first. I felt if anybody needed money it would be him. I'm surprised to discover it's Gina, and now that I have all the information I feel like there is something more I can't see. Something else must have happened, and I'm looking at the repercussions.

From Gina's medical reports, I know she suffered a stroke what seemed like a month after River returned to New York. But prior to that she was receiving treatment for her heart and continues to.

I'm aware River's mother died of a heart attack, so I can imagine how worried she must be. Especially with the stroke on top, and the debt.

The details I found showed that Gina took out a loan from the bank and another from a known loan shark, then pulled all her savings and income from her business to pay half a million dollars to an offshore account in Kazakhstan. The date listed correlates with the time River returned to New York.

Piecing everything together has made me believe that something happened to River while she was in Russia.

I still have nothing on the fiancé, but I've seen enough darkness in my lifetime to connect the dots and conclude that he must have something to do with this. Something I want to find out.

There's a guy from the underground who I use when I get stuck—as in situations when I risk my name being exposed. Usually, I can conceal myself with standard firewalls not many people know how to get around, but as this situation looks a little riskier than I'd like, I emailed him and asked him to find out River's fiancé's real name.

My shoulders slump and I bring a weary hand to my head. I've asked myself the question of what I'm doing several times in the last twelve hours.

I'm doing it again now, and I'm coming up against that wall with no answers other than guilt over my past mistakes.

I have no heart, yet here I am, allowing this girl to be my exception again.

I usually keep Saturdays reserved to hang out at my shop, but I've used the time to cross another line in River's life.

Unknown to most, tattooing is what I do in my spare time. Knight sculpts like our mother does, but this is what I do. In our teens Knight and I used to own this shop, but we sold it just before college. I repurchased it five months ago, fixed it up, and decided to share the space with two other artists.

I was supposed to have a busy morning with clients who'd booked weeks in advance to see me, but I canceled at the last minute when the email came through showing details of the account Gina paid the money to in Kazakhstan.

Now that I have this information I don't know what to do with it, or if I should leave well enough alone.

Once again I have my own problems, and last night's date with Celeste did not go well. She's already messaged me twice asking about a second date, which won't be happening.

That's one down on the list with nine to go.

"You bid on her, didn't you?" Luc's voice pulls me from my haze of thought.

I turn and find him standing at the door with a huge smirk on his face. I wasn't expecting him, but I should have after the heads-up he gave me about the auction.

With the smirk morphing into a self-assured grin, he walks in and plants himself on the seat across from me.

"Well, did you?" he prods.

"Come to gloat?" I throw back, frowning. I can't even be mad at him. I'd be more enraged if he'd kept the auction from me.

"A little. Don't worry. I'm only here for a few minutes. I'm on my way to the airport, but I thought I'd check in with you because I heard back from the lovely Celeste."

I smirk. "She called you?"

"Of course, she did. Women like that don't get turned down. If they do, it's a shocker."

"Well, there's a first time for everything."

"She's concerned she fucked up. She said you looked freaked when she mentioned kids. She's willing to forgo the kids if you accept her."

I groan inwardly and wrinkle my nose. "No."

"Go on, tell me why."

"For one, she spoke too passionately about having kids to simply change her mind. I can't trust a woman like that not to trick me into fathering her child in some demented way."

"*Demented?*"

"Like Porter Coleman. Remember his wife drugged him into getting her pregnant when he threatened to divorce her for cheating?" It was big news last summer.

"Oh, yeah. That was whacked." He nods and chuckles lightly, tapping the side of his head.

"Also, if Celeste really does mean what she says, that doesn't paint her in a better light to me. Children are not assets you negotiate for money. They're people."

I will not become my father. Neither will I stand in someone's way who wants children. It's not like Celeste is poor. She'll manage.

She probably just wanted the endorsement of my name. I'm sure she'll find another rich bastard somewhere else. It just won't be me.

"Well said, Grayson. I agree with you."

"Good."

"So, now that's out of the way, what did you bid on River?" He leans in with a curious stare.

"Sixty thousand dollars." I bite the inside of my lip.

Luc wolf-whistles, then laughs. "Damn, man, she's definitely got you pussy-whipped."

"Fuck you. I'm not pussy-whipped."

"Says the guy who just bought his ex in an auction for sixty thousand dollars. And I know you. You would have kept going higher, wouldn't you?"

I roll my eyes at him, feeling annoyed that he knows me so well.

"The question is, what do you want for that sixty thousand dollars?" His expression becomes more devious. "I hear you get two nights with your chosen girl."

"I don't want anything."

He shakes his head at me. "I don't believe that for one minute. If you didn't want anything, you would have booked another date with Celeste, despite her talk about kids."

"That doesn't mean shit. There are nine other candidates on the list I intend to meet." Even though I've allowed myself to get side-tracked today, I need to stick to my plans. The clock is ticking. On Monday I'll officially have only seven weeks to find a wife and get married.

"It's good to hear you still plan to meet the girls on the list but seriously, what are you going to do about River? All you told me was that she was working at the club to take care of some bills. Clearly she needs serious money if she was in that auction."

"Her aunt's sick and in debt."

The humor recedes from his face. "I see. How sick is she?"

"Extremely. She had a stroke and has heart problems. I know she means a lot to River. She told me once that her aunt is like a mother to her. I think we all know someone who stepped up like that in our lives."

I have a fantastic mother, but she couldn't do it all because my father screwed us over for his new family. The person in my life who stepped up to help me to be where I am today is my grandfather. I can see Luc is thinking about his person, too—his uncle.

Luc was orphaned when his parents died in a boating accident. They left him their fortune in the sports world, so when he retires from hockey, he'll have part ownership of the New York Gladiators, the NHL team owned by his family, but his uncle took him in and raised him with the same love and care he showed his own kids.

The background of having a family member step up to take care of you when your parents either couldn't or wouldn't is one of the things Luc and I have in common. It was the bond that made us friends when we first met.

"Do you know if the money she got from the auction will pay off the debt?"

"It won't." By my count, Gina still owes the loan shark a lot of money.

Although he still looks concerned, the cunning smile returns to his face. "Are you going to help her?"

"She doesn't want my help."

"And you're going to leave it like that?" He raises skeptical brows.

"I can't force her to take my money, Luc." I remember how humiliated she looked when I tried to offer her the money at the café.

"Oh, please, you just bid on her in an auction. Men like us always find a way to get what we want. You just have to find the right price."

"I know, but there's a reason why you let sleeping dogs lie." Says the guy who did a deep dive into River's business.

"Sure, but you can't deny that River is the girl who got away." He sounds confident, as if that's the solid truth.

It is.

Not even I can deny it, and the memory of why she got away dulls my mood further. "You know what happened."

"I remember all too well, and you know what my thoughts are about it."

He understood my decision to break up with River, my decision to keep the secret about the part I played, and my guilt, but he thought I was too hard on myself.

Of course, I felt the opposite.

The only thing I accepted was that trick. That's as far as my compassion went toward myself. The shame of being in a position to be tricked made me see that I didn't deserve the girl.

"It's been eight years, *Grayson*, and your ex is fucking hot. And she's in *need*. That right there, my good man, is *a good excuse*. The past doesn't mean you're not allowed to help her or..." He pauses and gives me a sly grin.

"Or what?"

"Enjoy the next two nights. It's two nights, bro. Even if that's all you get. Food for thought." He stands. "In other news, I have ten more girls for you. I'm just waiting on them to return their NDAs before I give you the list. They're the back-up plan."

I'm relieved he's switched things back to business. "Alright, thanks."

"See you next week in Arizona?"

"For sure." Knight and I have business in Arizona next week, so we promised to attend Luc's game there.

He dips his head for a final nod, then leaves.

As soon as the door swings shut, I return my gaze to the computer screen and think about all I've found out about River.

The decent thing to do here is be *decent*. If only for tonight.

The only thing I should do is meet with River, enjoy the art show, and have dinner, then maybe I could offer to pay her debts again if she allows me to. If that doesn't work, maybe I could use tomorrow as back-up.

After that, I'll leave her alone. Honestly, that's as far as I can go with her anyway. The time to see her in line with the auction win will have run out, and I'll be crossing over into stalker territory again. So it's best to stick to the plan.

That's what I intend to do. Until I reach the Artisan and the sight of my gorgeous ex standing by the balcony on the terrace steals my senses.

A simple black mid-length dress with tiny straps over her delicate shoulders looks like it's been painted on her decadent body. The black of her dress combined with the shadows of the night makes her red hair look more striking.

She hasn't seemed to change much over the years. She still has that light of innocence about her, so I'll be willing to bet she has no idea how beautiful she looks in such simple clothes. Or that she's still the most beautiful girl I've ever seen in my life.

I was the devil who would have tainted that purity and corrupted her light.

I haven't changed in those ways.

I'm still the devil, and the wicked thing that made me kiss her last night has infiltrated my mind. It still wants me to own her in those ways too.

It reminds me that she's mine.

Mine for the next two nights.

Chapter TEN

River

As Jericho approaches me my heart stills and my lips tingle as if he's still kissing me.

The thought is not exactly the best to start the night with if I hope to concentrate and focus on staying sane.

I need to do both. Sanity is always a plus, but I don't know who would be able to concentrate around a man like him when he looks as if he just stepped off a billboard advertising Hollywood's latest movie.

Years ago, when he made my head spin, he was a boy. Now he's a man. One of the most highly sought-after men in this hemisphere.

Things are different now.

The soft glow from the moonlight shines down on him, illuminating his confident exterior, and the slight breeze ruffles his neatly trimmed hair.

Dressed in a silky black shirt, beige pants, and tan brogues, he looks every bit the man people talk about in magazines and on TV.

I always felt like a fish out of water back when I was around him. I feel no different tonight, yet he's looking at me as if I'm someone important.

He's certainly treated me as if I am. He sent a Maybach to pick me up from Gina's earlier.

Maybe I could believe that I'm important just for tonight, and tomorrow. Even if I'm a nervous wreck.

I paid the arrears on the loans and the bills earlier, but I've been walking on thin ice all day, dancing around the lies I had to tell Eden.

Of course, she wanted to know how the auction went and who I ended up with.

I told her about the money because I felt it was right she knew as she's worried about me, but I decided to tell her that an elderly man won me. To ease her worries further, I told her that he wanted my company to attend a friend's wedding. That's it. No funny business.

I couldn't tell her about Jericho because that would have opened the door to all manner of questions and assumptions I didn't want.

Now I'm here. I'm staring at the man who's plagued my mind for years, and we're standing on the terrace of one of the most beautiful buildings in New York with the starry sky above our heads and the skyline in the background. It's romantic and strange all at the same time because it feels like neither of us should be here.

Jericho stops a breath away, towering over me. Even though I'm wearing a pair of wedge heels, I'm still petite next to him.

The corner of his mouth slides into a sexy grin, and he looks me over when he notices my obvious nervousness.

"Hello." His deep voice is smooth, making his baritone tenor sound playful.

"Hi."

"Did you get here okay?"

"Yes, I did. Thank you." As awkward as this all feels for me, I know I also need to thank him for other things too. "And thank you for the extra money. You didn't have to do that."

"I know, but I did. Did it help?" His stare turns sharper, as if he's probing into my mind.

"Yes, it did."

"I hope that means there won't be any more auctions."

I shake my head. "There won't be." I preempted this discussion and came up with the perfect thing to tell him. Something to assure him I'd be okay going forward and restore a little of my tattered pride. "I plan to leave the club in three months. Everything will be okay by then."

"What about in the meantime? As in your job at the club. Will you have to do *other things*?"

Other things aka stripping or giving lap dances or prostituting myself for the right price. God, this is so embarrassing. The fact that he knows what happens at that club makes me feel more exposed.

"I promise I'll only be working on the aerial hoop."

"You said that before."

"The money helped, so it really is just going to be the hoop." I nod with surety. "The auction is the most outlandish thing I've done at the club. Even when I'm booked for a party, it's just to serve drinks."

He considers my answer as if trying to establish whether I'm telling the truth. That makes me feel worse, but there's nothing I can do about that. I practically work in a glorified brothel where he bought me in an auction. How can I expect him to believe I haven't done more than what I said?

"I suppose that sounds okay." He gives me a clipped nod, and a sense of unexpected relief loosens the tension coiling around my lungs. "Are you sure you don't need any more help?"

That sounds like a trick question because God knows I want to say yes. People say pride goes before a fall. They're right. I'm hanging on to what's left of my pride by the threads because I don't want to need anyone in such a way ever again.

That's nothing to do with Jericho. It's more a Sasha thing. Being with him taught me life lessons I don't want to rehash with anyone ever again. It taught me that no matter how great things appear to be, I need to *always* be able to take care of myself.

"I'm okay now." I nod.

Jericho straightens, and I'm grateful when he seems satisfied with my answers.

"Alright, sounds like you have a handle on things."

"Yes. I do. Thanks again for your help. Although I wish the circumstances were different."

"Me, too."

It's on the tip of my tongue to ask him why he kissed me but I hold back. As much as I would love an answer, I can't ask him that question.

"So… um, we're here." Nervously, I flick my hand, motioning around us, then I bring my hands together. "I've heard good things about this show."

"You'll love it." The curiosity recedes from his expression, lightening the tension between us. "We're having dinner first, then we'll see the show and have a chance to look at the artwork after."

"That sounds good."

"Perfect. Are you ready?"

No, I'm not ready for anything with you, Jericho Grayson. You mystify me in ways I can't describe.

He's not good for my present state of mind but what choice do I have?

"Yes," I lie, and shove my worries out of my mind.

"Let's go." His voice dips, along with his eyes to scan over my dress, then he stretches out his hand to me.

I step closer and he places his hand at the small of my back. His fingers flutter over the bare skin there, radiating heat through my body and something else—*desire.*

Desire stirs in my core like steam and pulses down to my groin, igniting something I haven't felt in years.

I glance up at Jericho to find he's already looking at me the same way he did last night. The look makes me nervous. *He* makes me nervous. Nervous of the feelings he's stirring inside me that have been dormant for the last eight years.

Focus and concentrate, River. Focus and concentrate.

No matter how hard being around him might be, this *date* is part of my job. If he'd been anyone else who'd won me in the auction, I'd still have to do this part.

Jericho Grayson may not be the guy you explain away as being like *everyone else*, but if I think of the next few hours I'm supposed spend with him as being nothing more than part of the job, I should be okay.

Should.

He breaks the stare and ushers me inside the building.

Ready to start the next part of our night together.

I just hope I make it out in one piece.

Chapter ELEVEN

River

THE FIVE-MICHELIN-STARRED RESTAURANT IN THE Artisan is exquisite. A blend of the delicious aromas from their European cuisine fills the air, and the exotic décor transports me back to my time spent in places like Rome, Monaco, and Sardinia.

We're seated in a private booth that offers a stunning view of the city.

When the waiter takes our order Jericho asks for an expensive bottle of wine with a name I can't pronounce, and that's where we start.

Because I don't really know what the hell to talk about with my ex, I fully expect the awkward tension living between us to metastasize into one of those dreaded silences people always fear, but it doesn't.

It doesn't because of him.

Jericho kicks off our conversation by asking me about my plans for ballet, a subject I could talk about in my sleep, and to anyone, no matter who they are.

While we eat a glorious dinner of Wagyu beef tarragon and roasted spring vegetables, I tell him about my work at the school and all the hopes I have for the future.

Given the circumstances, I'm surprised at how comfortable I am speaking with him. It shows I was probably eager to talk to someone other than Eden, Gina, and my father about my plans. Someone from the past who actually witnessed how hard I worked to become a dancer.

We enjoy the show after dinner. It's amazing. I've never seen anything like it.

It takes place over three floors of the building from the basement up and has a dark gothic feel to it.

The show is called *Metamorphosis* and goes through the stages of the life of bats and butterflies. The art comes to life in the way the artist has dressed the actors to represent the various stages.

The room that stands out to me the most is one that seems pitch black, but then I realize the darkness is created by the people attached to the walls. They move from side to side in a slow rise and fall, making the walls seem like they're breathing.

I haven't been to many living art shows, but I love artistic creations like this. You get to look into the mind of the artist. Art like this is so different from dancing, which is also an art.

The show lasts for two and a half hours, and we get the chance to look at the artistic props and paintings without the actors after. It's like getting backstage passes after a show. I didn't realize that this part was exclusive until the audience whittled down to just Jericho and me and two other couples.

We spend the last hour walking around again, seeing everything in a new light.

It's just us now. The other people left a while ago.

We're on the top floor, in a dimly lit room that has a Tim Burton dark fairytale vibe emanating from it. Giant silver butterflies are painted on the black walls, and winding trees the same color separate each section. It's also the last of the sets.

I look around the room with wild fascination, surprised at myself. I was so wound up before I got here that I can't believe I feel so… relaxed.

We stop by one of the steel pillars and gaze up at the ceiling, which is speckled with more silver butterflies that look like stars.

I walk over to the lowest one hanging by the wall to get a closer look.

"Eden would have a field day in a place like this," I say, scanning over the butterflies. Eden is the one who is always going to art shows and galleries. I wish I could tell her about this experience. Maybe I will one day when the dust settles.

Jericho grins back at me when I turn to face him. "Eden? You've mentioned her a lot tonight."

I just remembered he doesn't actually know her. Eden has been in my life for so long it's strange to think we only met after high school. Although that's still a long time, and like us, college is where most people find their lifelong friends.

"She's my best friend. We met at Juilliard. I probably talk about her a lot because she's the kind of friend who quickly becomes family."

"She sounds nice." He shifts his weight then straightens.

"She is. She plays the violin. While I was off in Russia she performed several concerts with a company here. Now she teaches music at the school I work at."

"It's great you two work together."

"Yeah. Eden's great." And so not like me. Eden followed her path and stuck to her plans. She did exactly what she set out to do and continues to do so with her teaching career. She still plays concerts from time to time. Whereas me… I'm stuck in the in-between.

"Do you still keep in touch with friends from high school?" He looks genuinely interested to know. He's going to be surprised by my answer.

"No."

"Really?" He looks as surprised as I knew he would.

I was very close to my two friends, Cindy and Vivian, but I haven't heard from them in years.

"The last time I spoke to them was probably freshman year of college. But I heard Cindy got married, and Vivian has two children." That's as much as I know. I sent cards and flowers to both of them. They did the same for me when they heard I got the job with the Bolshoi Ballet. That was actually the last time I heard from them.

"Wow, I'm surprised you lost track."

"Me, too. What about you? Apart from Luc are you still friends with the guys from high school?" There were three others who used to hang out with Jericho and Knight.

"Unfortunately, I am." He smirks. "We still see each other pretty much every week, but I'm still closer to Luc than anyone else. Then, of course, there's Knight."

"That's good."

It's strange talking about these people when most of them never knew we were together. My friends didn't know. Luc was perhaps the only person who knew on Jericho's side, and I'm not even sure when he became aware. I figured that Jericho told him but not Knight because of the feud between our fathers. His father was the worst back then, so I'm sure it wouldn't have gone down well if he'd found out we were dating, especially with the strained relationship they have.

"How is your family?" I add, hoping things might have gotten better with the passage of time.

He smiles, but there's no humor to it. "If you mean my mom, grandparents, and brother—as in Knight—then they're great. I have no other family outside of them."

And that says it all about his father and Bastian, his half-brother.

"I'm sorry."

"Don't be. There's nothing to be sorry for." He nods with conviction, but I wonder what it must be like to feel so disconnected from your father.

The years when Dad was married to Brielle were truly awful. The aftermath was even worse, and I've had my run-ins with him. Mainly because his mistakes were all down to his streak of greed and obsession with outdoing Tobias Grayson—something that would never happen.

Dad also supported Sasha, which made me stay in an abusive relationship for longer than I should have, but all things aside there was never a time when he treated me badly. Or made me feel unwanted. Not like Jericho's father did with him.

"How is *your* family?" Jericho lifts his chin and concern fills his eyes. It makes me wonder again how much he knows about what's going on with me.

I sense he's aware Gina is sick, so I decide to tell him about her but I won't tell him much about my father. It might not be the best subject since Dad and Jericho had no end of run-ins toward the end of our relationship.

"My father is doing okay, but Gina had a stroke. That's why I'm staying with her."

"I'm sorry to hear that."

"Thank you. The worst seems to be over so I'm hoping she'll be okay soon." Although I say that I'm still worried as hell about the chest pains she suffered the other night. She's been alright since, but it doesn't stop me from worrying about her.

"I wish her a speedy recovery. I'm sure it must be difficult on both of you."

"It is. We're just taking one day at a time."

"That's all you can do."

"Yes." Feeling my worries beginning to overpower my focus, I think of something lighter to talk about. Knight comes to mind. "So, um… in happier news, I heard you're going to be an uncle. Congratulations."

He chuckles. "Thanks, I think."

"Aren't you excited to be an uncle?"

"I'm happier for Knight to be the brother with the kids, not me."

That surprises me. He's never spoken like that before about kids. I just assumed he wanted them. "You don't want kids?"

"No. That's not me, but I'll happily be an uncle."

"Oh."

He pulls a cigarette pack and lighter from his pocket, then takes a cigarette out and lights up despite the no-smoking sign by the door.

I stare at him with my lips parted. This is just the type of guy he'd be back in high school. If he was ever caught smoking in the locker room or anywhere on the school grounds, there was never anything anyone could do or say to him because he was Jericho Grayson. The rebel who lived by his own rules. He'd just keep puffing away until he was finished.

"I'm pretty sure you're not supposed to be smoking in here." I glance at the sign again.

He answers with raised brows and looks at me as if I should know by now that those rules still don't apply to him.

"I can see you haven't really changed one bit," I add.

"I have. You're just seeing the parts of me you recognize."

"I guess so. I've changed, too." I try to sound assertive. The way I'd like to sound if my life were better. However, the sinful look he gives me when he looks me up and down throws me.

"I can see that." He continues looking at me, as if he can see through my clothes. It's unsettling to watch him look at me that way, and so effortlessly.

I swallow past the sudden thickness in my throat and take a quick breath. "I hope that's a compliment and you're not calling me fat." I know he's not but I'm trying to lighten the spark of undeniable arousal rippling between us. I can feel it again. It's the same entity that came alive between us last night when he kissed me.

From the flicker of awareness in his eyes I know he must feel it again, too. It's dangerous ground for us to tread on.

Keeping his gaze riveted to mine, he takes a drag on his cigarette and blows out a ring of smoke.

"You know I'm not fucking calling you fat." Jericho's eyes darken and he gives me a lopsided cocky grin. "I just like the way you filled out."

My entire body lights up with the heat I've been trying to stave off all night, and the nest of butterflies living in the pit of my stomach goes wild.

"I see," I mutter, because I have to say something.

"But you're still Miss Goody Two Shoes." He takes another drag and makes a show of blowing out the smoke in hazy rings.

Miss Goody Two Shoes?

I haven't been her in so long I can't remember ever being that girl. But he doesn't know that.

As I stare at him something crazy comes over me. Something completely and utterly crazy that pushes me to walk back toward him and take that cigarette.

He watches me with fascination, his eyes dropping to my lips as I put the cigarette between them and take a drag.

The last time I did this in front of him was on my sixteenth birthday. I coughed so hard I thought I was going to die. I'm pretty sure I even turned blue as I ended up on the floor in a coughing fit.

Now, to his absolute surprise, I'm handling the smoke with the ease of someone who's done this for a lifetime. I'm not a smoker. In fact I hate it, but I can smoke now.

"Very impressive indeed, *Mermaid*," Jericho states, watching the smoke float from my lips and rise into the air above us.

I was going to continue, but he takes the cigarette from me.

"Don't want to ruin your pretty little lungs." He puts the cigarette back in his mouth and slinks it to the side, so it sits in the corner of his lips.

"What about yours?"

"Baby, I'm already ruined." He flashes me a seductive grin and steps closer, too close. So close I have to look up at him.

He takes one last drag on the cigarette then puts it out on the edge of the pillar. All the while, keeping his eyes on me.

He tosses the cigarette butt into the metal bin across from us and moves even closer to lift a lock of my hair.

"Who taught you to smoke?" He smirks and searches my eyes.

"A guy in the show in Russia."

His eyes narrow with what looks like displeasure. "How did he get you to do it?"

"I lost a bet." It wasn't exactly the best experience, but since the alternative was forking up a month's wages, I learned to smoke.

"Interesting. This isn't some guy I have to worry about, is it? Someone who might not like that I won you in an auction."

"No. It wasn't anything like that, and I haven't seen him in years."

He smiles a little wider. "Is there anyone else I have to worry about?"

God help me, he's actually asking me if *I'm* seeing anyone. "No." I'd hope that if I were dating someone they'd be serious enough about me that I wouldn't need to be in an auction or be on a date with another guy when I should be with them.

"No?"

"No." Now I'm thinking about him and that kiss again. "What about you? I'm sure there's some socialite or fashion model who will hate that you won me in an auction. I'm sure they'll hate it even more that you kissed me." Saying those words sounds like I'm letting some secret out of a bag.

He reaches out and traces my mouth with the tip of his thumb. "No."

"No?" I borrow his previous question and tone.

Instead of answering he lowers his face to mine, almost in slow motion. By the time he's a breath away from my lips the desire to feel his mouth on mine again has me under its spell, and need is tugging at the walls of my aching core.

Against the reasoning in my mind whispering to me that I shouldn't want him, I don't move when Jericho presses his lips to mine for another forbidden kiss.

Unlike last night there is nothing fast or surprising. I saw him coming and wanted him. To deny that truth would be to lie to myself.

So many people have lied to me in the past, I promised myself I would never join them. I won't start now.

"No." He speaks against my lips between the kisses he plants on my mouth, his hot breath numbing my mind with raw desire.

Dangerous heat sizzles every nerve in my body, and suddenly it feels like it's too much. I realize it feels that way because it is. And I can't do this again with him.

The thought makes me pull away, but Jericho dominates my will once more by slipping one large hand behind my head to fuse my body to the steel wall of his chest.

There he inhales my hair and makes his way back to my lips.

"Jericho, we shouldn't," I whimper on the edge of a moan while he tastes me, flicking his tongue across the seam of my lips.

"I know, but fuck it. We're doing this." That's all he has to say for my body to obey and surrender to the desperate need clawing at my insides to give in to him.

We fall into a deeper kiss, one that feels different from any other we've ever shared. This one is full of fire and carnal desire. The sort of off-limits kisses people share when they shouldn't be together.

He moves with me until my back is pressed up against the wall, and there he devours my mouth.

Caught between the wall and the taut muscles of his body I feel all the ways he's filled out too, and I like it. His shoulders are broader, harder, and stronger, with solid ripples of muscle that I could sink my fingers into for miles.

And God… the hard bulge of his cock presses into my belly as he pushes into me. The hardness of it reminds me of how big he is and what he felt like inside me.

It's not something I'm likely to forget. Jericho was my first. The first man to have me. The first man to own me. The first man to break me.

If not for Sasha, Jericho would still be my only. It's almost a sad thought that it took so long before I could be with anyone else.

Here I am once more, with the same guy, and the pleasure pulsing through my body just from his kiss reminds me that I've always been helpless to resist him.

Jericho leaves my lips and kisses my cheek, my neck, my chest, then I melt against his mouth as he closes his lips over my aching nipple, sucking it through the fabric of my dress.

I moan from the pleasure claiming me from his hot mouth on my breast and the way he's sucking me.

He moves back up to my lips, but he cups my breasts and strokes my nipples while he kisses me.

I've lost control of my body in all the right ways, and I don't want him to stop touching me.

When he rolls the hem of my dress up to my hips so he can cup my sex and stroke my pussy through the lace of my panties I moan again, moving against his hand for more.

The sudden thought that he's touching me snaps my awareness back into focus and I remember where we are.

Although we're alone and Jericho has backed me into one of the darker corners where no one looking in can see us, we're practically in public. This is an art gallery. A public place. Someone somewhere will be watching.

"Jericho, someone could walk in or hear us," I rasp. With everything going on in my mind about us, it sounds strange to my ears that getting caught is what I'm worried about most.

"We have the place to ourselves," he answers in a husky voice, filled with sexual need. "No one will come in."

"But—"

He kisses my words away.

"River, you're wet for me." He licks my lips and sucks on my bottom lip, making me focus on how good he's making me feel again. "Let me take care of your pussy."

Before I can answer he slips his hand into my panties so he can slide his finger inside my pussy.

He pumps slowly into my entrance and it feels so good I have to grip his shirt.

"Your pussy feels so fucking good. I want to remember how you taste. Let me."

My cheeks burn at the sound of his dirty words, but I shove the shy girl away and nod, because nothing on earth sounds better than his request to taste me.

He gives me a grin filled with victory and sin, then pumps into my passage harder, finger-fucking me.

I moan with each thrust, trying not to be too loud and failing. Anyone outside the open door would be able to hear me as the sound carries across the room.

With his free hand he pulls down the top of my dress and my bra so that my breasts pop out. Exposed to the air my nipples harden to tight, painful peaks, but the ache becomes sweet pleasure as soon as his mouth closes over them, and he sucks. He sucks, alternating from one breast to the other while he continues pumping his finger into my needy passage.

Fuck, it feels too good and I can feel the start of a vicious orgasm building with every thrust.

Moments later I'm there at the precipice of pleasure.

That's when he crouches down, spreads my legs wider, and buries his face between my thighs.

He grasps my hips so he can push his face deeper into my pussy, then he thrusts his tongue inside me.

The impact is so potent and powerful I have to arch into the wall and grab his shoulders to keep myself from falling off the face of the earth.

Holy shit. I've lost my mind to this man again, and I keep disappearing into the deep abyss of madness as he eats me out.

Suddenly I'm coming on his face and my release is flowing into his mouth.

The release just flowed out of me like a river rushing through an angry storm.

My body comes alive with the wildfire flicking over my skin, scorching my brain and searing away all the reasons I know I shouldn't be with this man.

Jericho eats me out until he's drunk up all my arousal and I'm moaning out way too loud.

When he's done he stands and returns to my lips. I taste myself on his mouth and tongue. He kisses me harder than before, showing me how much he wants me.

The problem is I want him too.

I never stopped.

Not when he walked away from me years ago, and not days ago when I told him to leave me alone.

I want him now, more than I ever have.

Chapter TWELVE

Jericho

I DON'T KNOW WHAT THE FUCK I'VE BEEN TELLING MYSELF all these long years, but the only thing I know right now is that I want her.

Her—River St. James.

The girl who always felt like mine.

Right now she *is* mine, and the taste of her sweet pussy wraps around my tongue like a blanket, amplified by kissing her delicious, hot little mouth.

I don't hold back, and neither does she.

She must know by now that I want to fuck her. I've wanted to devour her right from the moment I saw her earlier standing by the balcony.

If I'm being honest, I'll admit the truth that I wanted to fuck every inch of her lush body from the moment she walked back into my life.

She grabs my shirt then touches my face, running her fingers over my beard with the same passion that I show her as I hold her against me.

Our kiss turns greedy and I can feel my already rock-hard cock aching to be inside her. Aching for the release from the years of pent-up need.

Her tongue tangles with mine, and as I lace my fingers through her hair I remember the last time we were together.

That last time, all the fears of losing her weighed down on my soul as I realized there was nothing I could do to fix the disaster I'd created.

She'd come to me after her stepmother threatened to pull her funding for Juilliard and send her to a community college. That wouldn't have happened because River's mother left money in a trust especially for her college funds, which was what she used in the end when her stepmother took control over her father's finances.

As I held her in my arms back then I knew I couldn't be with her and hold on to my secrets.

The same thought hits me now, and I feel that impending guilt over my selfishness and shame for what I did.

Sure, Luc will remind me that I was tricked into the situation. He'd also remind me that I was young and foolish, but neither of those things are excuses for what I did, nor what happened.

The hardest thing I've ever had to do in my life was break up with River, but I did it because I knew she deserved so much more than me.

In my heart I knew deep down that she deserved to be with someone better than a guy who could cause so much destruction to her life.

Her father didn't want her to be with me because of my father, but realistically he knew his daughter could do better too.

Better than the Grayson blood flowing through my veins that knows only darkness and deceit. That's how we built our empire and made our billions. It's how we continue to do so. It's not with love or compassion. It's with greed and all the deadly sins Pandora hid away in her box in hell.

Her father could have died as a result of my mistakes, then what would I have done? How would I have explained my part in such a mess?

I still can't, and I still won't because it's still a mess.

And River *still* deserves better than me.

Eight years later the answer is still the same, and I have to walk away again.

Summoning all the willpower in this world, I pull out of the ravenous kiss that would have taken me over another line with the red-haired beauty.

I release her and take a step back so she isn't pressed up against me anymore.

River stares back at me, at first not quite realizing that I'm ending our forbidden encounter, then I notice the moment realization enters her mind.

It's in her eyes. The spark fades, as if someone switched off a light.

"We… have to stop now." My voice sounds like someone else is speaking.

She looks worse for hearing the confirmation of what I'm doing.

"Why?" Confusion clouds her eyes the way it did the day I ended us, yet I still can't give her an answer.

"We just have to."

She seems to catch herself and remember that she hates me because she pulls back into the wall.

In the soft glow of the dim light I can see the pink stain of embarrassment racing across her cheeks.

Quickly she fixes her dress, covering her breasts and straightening the length back down her legs.

"River—"

"No, don't explain, please. I have to go anyway."

She turns, getting ready to flee. Instinct makes me grab her arm and pull her back to me.

"The car will take you home."

"No, I'll get a taxi." She tries to pull away from me but I hold her tighter, not quite wanting to let her go just yet and leave things like this.

"The car is outside."

"I'll be fine to get myself home."

"River, I..." My voice trails off, and I think of all I want to say. Like that I'll see her tomorrow at the ballet I booked tickets for, or at the very least that I'm sorry.

I don't apologize for anything, and doing so now doesn't feel like it would be enough for someone who means so much to me. So I say nothing more.

With a pained look in her eyes she stares back at me, waiting for an answer. I know how fucked-up this looks. After all, I was the one who broke up with her, but it's been clear all night that I still want her.

She waits until it's just as clear that there's nothing more to wait for and nothing to expect from me.

I release her and allow her to leave, the sound of her heels on the floor piercing my mind like double-edged daggers.

I watch her go, wishing I could turn back time, but I can't do that anymore than I can fix the past.

All I can do is what I think is right. It's just a shame that it will always be the wrong thing for me, and I will always be her villain.

♛

"It's been a while since the two of us sat down like this," Grandfather states with an easy grin.

"Long overdue, right?"

"Definitely."

He sits back into the wicker garden chair. I do the same while he lights a Cohiba cigar and looks me over, the way my mother would when she's trying to figure out what's wrong with me.

Neither of them would ever be able to guess the right thing, because something was always wrong with me.

We're sitting in my garden on the terrace overlooking the pool. This is more of a meeting than a visit, although it's at my new home. The new home I had to buy months ago in preparation for the wife I'm supposed to get.

Grandfather loathed my bachelor pad on Park Avenue and said it didn't suit a family. Months ago I accused Knight of living up Grandfather's ass. Now I've become the pot calling the kettle black.

"So, I have to say you look troubled," he notes. "More than usual, son."

I shake my head, trying to shift the memory of the beautiful girl I had in my arms last night.

"I'm just tired. It's been a long-ass week."

He laughs. Sometimes he likes the way I say things, but at other times it irritates the hell out of him.

"I have to agree with you. It has been a long-ass week."

Long-ass is putting it mildly. All I thought I'd have to do this week was gloat over Bastian's departure for his banishment to Hong Kong, then go on a few dates with potential wives.

I went on a total of one date, and I never even knew what day it was when Bastian left. It was Thursday but I was so wrapped up in River, Bastian was the furthest thing from my mind.

"I wanted to see you today, see how you're doing and give you another proposal you're welcome to turn down."

My interest piques. "I'm doing great, so how about you tell me this proposal of yours?"

"Well, things have kind of gone astray with this scandal of Bastian's. I thought I had everything under control, that everyone was working toward the end goal. He wasn't."

"Grandfather, is that really surprising to you?"

"Not so much. It's just disappointing. I don't want to have to extend the date for my departure. Your grandmother and I have been waiting for this time for years."

I nod, agreeing. "Then don't you dare do that."

"Well, that's reliant on you and Knight, and your father. I'd like you to take on Bastian's role at Wall Street until we find a replacement. I know you don't want to work with your father, but your extensive knowledge of investments makes you the best candidate."

"Then I'll do it."

"Are you sure? This would be an interactive role where you'd have to see him frequently again like you did before."

"I'm sure." It's taken me years to become the confident person I am around my abusive father, so my grandfather knows this is no mere feat for me.

"Thank you. I'm proud of you for doing this. I felt this would be a great opportunity for you to step up and show the board you can control the company."

"I agree, but I'm sure they know I can do it anyway." It was my father who influenced them into believing otherwise after my scandal. I wonder how he felt when he had to face them after what Bastian did. My asshole father wanted me gone before I even got the chance to explain myself, and made sure I didn't have a leg to stand on.

At the same time, I have to admit that I faced a buildup of things against me.

"You know what I mean. This doesn't affect the agreement we have for the CFO position at Park Avenue. It's more like a favor I'm asking that will be mutually beneficial."

"Then don't worry about it. God knows you've done more favors for me than I can count in this lifetime."

He smirks. "I'm your grandfather, son, it's what we do." He taps my hand. "That leads me to the other topic I wanted to talk to you about. I'm a little concerned that no one has met this girl of yours. Not even Knight."

My stomach actually twists with nerves, something I never feel. "You'll meet her soon."

"So you keep saying. I understand that my request for your marriage is unconventional and impromptu, but marriage changes a man. You need to change."

My temper flares the same way it did when he first dropped the bomb on me about finding a wife.

"That's not fair."

"Life is not fair boy, and neither is business. I'll say the same thing to you that I have to the others. I won't do anyone any favors, and I won't show favoritism or hand you your legacy on a silver platter. To do so would be insulting to me and the work I've put into this company."

"I understand that."

"Good."

"So, I do hope you're keeping to your end of the contract." He gives me a death grip stare, one that's sharp and searching, probing for the truth.

To make everything official, he made me sign a contract. It might as well have been in blood. I needed to find a wife within the time frame he set, and in return I'd get the CFO position and my share of the company.

Those were the terms and conditions, but my grandfather knows me the same way a father would. That look in his eyes tells me he suspects there is *no* potential wife I've been dating all these months.

I love and respect him to no end. I also want my share of the Grayson empire more than anything because that's all I have in my life to look forward to, but my grandfather is not the boss of my life. No one but me will wield that sword.

Just like a game of chess I will be the king of my court, so I will continue to do things my way. However, I know that still means I have to meet him halfway.

"Of course, I'm sticking to my end of the contract." I give him a clipped nod.

"I hope so. I could have arranged your marriage myself, but I opted against that because I feel you should have the freedom to choose who you marry."

At least he gave me that much. "I'm grateful you gave me the choice."

"I thought that was only fair, but time is passing fast. We're already in the middle of March."

"I know. I've just been busy. I'll organize a dinner where we can all meet as soon as I can."

"Actually, I think it would be a better idea for us all to meet this girl of yours at the fundraiser next Wednesday."

Shit.

No. Fuck no. That is not good. Not good at all.

This is what happens when two titans bump heads and try to overpower each other. Both fight with everything they have in order to outdo the other.

"The fundraiser?"

"Yes. That shouldn't be a problem, should it?" He raises his gray bushy brows questioningly.

"No." I do my best to appear nonchalant when really I'm shitting myself.

"Great. I think the fundraiser would also be a great opportunity to announce your engagement and get publicity under control. You know what the media are like. I also think news of your engagement would take the heat off Bastian's scandal."

Just fucking great. This is all I need now to make me go fucking crazy. "I suppose you're right."

"Believe me, I am. Your grandmother is also eager to meet your wife-to-be and start planning your wedding." He nods, and I feel guilty for the spark of pride in his eyes.

If he looks like that, I can just imagine what my grandmother will be like. She adores me. For some reason, although she loves us all without playing favorites, I'm the grandchild who garners all her attention. I get extra everything. Cookies, hugs, and grandma's special birthday treats. *Jesus.*

"Well, Grandma won't have to wait too long." I can't think of anything worse, but I look at him as if everything is happy, shiny, and wonderful.

"Then next Wednesday works perfectly."

No, it's not perfect at all. God. Next Wednesday cuts my time down significantly. I'll have ten days. No longer seven weeks. What the hell am I going to do?

So far, I've only met one woman from Luc's list. I have dates lined up this week and next between my trip to Arizona, but that's not enough time.

Ten fucking days is *not* enough time to find a wife.

But… it has to be.

I have to make it be enough if I want my share of the empire.

In all honesty, I'm not going to meet anyone on that list or the new back-up one Luc created who's going to blow my mind, so I might as well just pick the girl who's the closest fit, whether I like her or not.

A contract is a contract, and all I need from her is a year of our lives. That is all. There are no more expectations from me other than to give her the two million she'll receive for becoming my wife.

I think I've been making things harder than they really are because of River. Because I can't get her out of my head. Because… touching and tasting her felt great, and it's been like some forbidden fantasy having my ex-girlfriend in my life again.

Now I need to stop messing around and get serious.

That means I definitely can't meet River tonight. I already considered not seeing her, but I hadn't officially decided until just now.

"That will be fine." I nod ignoring that sinking feeling in my soul.

"Great. I look forward to meeting your wife-to-be." Grandfather smiles and points his cigar at me.

I guess last night was my official goodbye.

Goodbye, River. I really am sorry.

For everything.

Chapter THIRTEEN

River

DAD TAKES A SIP OF HIS BEER AND WRINKLES HIS NOSE as he watches Bastian and Tobias Grayson on TV.

The crow's feet at the corners of his eyes deepen and he shakes his head with disgust, allowing the ends of his gray hair to brush against his shoulders.

"I wish the whole lot of them would burn in hell." His tone is more venomous than the poison from a snake bite. "Every last man by the surname of Grayson," he sneers, not caring if the men he's cursing are related to the Graysons in New York or not. He loathes anyone with the Grayson surname that much.

He mutters something more I can't hear, and I watch him wondering how enraged he'd be if he knew I not only saw Jericho again but he bought me in an auction, then rejected me quicker than you would a two-dollar whore.

Every time I think of last night I feel sick to my stomach.

Dad and I are in the living room of his ground-floor condo. We just had dinner and settled in here to watch some TV before I leave.

I was hoping to watch a movie with him but he switched the TV to the news channel before I could even suggest the idea.

He's been watching the news special showing Bastian Grayson with Tobias in the background. Bastian is issuing a public apology for his behavior with Lana Jamison. The footage is from last week, before Bastian went to Hong Kong.

I haven't been following the story but I know there was very little Teddy Jamison could do to Bastian because his daughter was seventeen, the age of consent in this state. The other day, though, Teddy got on national TV to condemn Bastian and let the world know that people like him are poor excuses for human beings. He also promised that he wasn't going to let anything slide because his daughter is seventeen.

No one knows what that means yet but I'm sure that's one reason why one of New York's most eligible bachelors now lives and works in Hong Kong.

I, of course, have my own Grayson problem to deal with, and I'm not sure if I still have said problem as I haven't heard from Jericho today yet.

After last night I'm not sure I will, and if I see him tonight for date number two I don't know what the hell kind of atmosphere I'll be walking into.

What do we say to each other or do after such a wild and reckless encounter?

I, for one, have no idea how I'm supposed to face him.

Embarrassment and hurt feel like meager words to describe how I felt when he rejected me. Then I realized I'm not mad at him. I'm mad at myself.

I was practically naked in his arms. I allowed him to eat me out, and I came on his face, then I wanted more.

I wanted him. How stupid can one person be?

I'm like the moth to the flame who keeps getting burned and

going right back moments later. I want to chastise myself because I should know better.

Jericho Grayson is my ex. He's also a known asshole and playboy.

I truly should have known better, but before he rejected me we felt the way we did in the past. But like older versions of ourselves who still wanted each other.

But I was wrong. So very wrong.

"Dad, don't you want your dessert?" I offer, looking at the bowl of lemon meringue pie sitting on the table next to his wheelchair.

He likes to sit in the armchair when he's in here and keep the wheelchair to the side. I'm sitting on the two-seater opposite him, again, where he likes me to be, because it reminds him of how we used to sit together as a family when Mom was alive.

"The sight of those people turns my stomach every time." He's still looking at the TV but his hatred is directed at Tobias. "What a pity it's the son and not his asshole father. There must be so much dirt on the man. Why the hell can't someone, somewhere find something to destroy his ass?"

I have no doubt that if Dad could be that special someone, he would spill that dirt quicker than a heart can beat. I'm even more sure that if such dirt existed on Tobias Grayson he'd have every grain under lock and key. Men like him always have their darkest secrets guarded by the devil himself.

Bastian isn't so careful. It's always been clear that he believes he can do anything because he's a Grayson. He thinks his name or his father are get-out-of-jail-free cards. That's how he was in high school, and he's no different now.

"Dad, this isn't good for your blood pressure. Why don't we watch something more entertaining?"

He gives me an incredulous glare. "My girl, this for me is classic entertainment. I simply wish the situation were worse."

I stare back at him wishing he would just let go of this thing between him and Tobias. The worst thing about it is that the animosity between them—or rather in Dad's head—was the main cause of our downfall.

All my life I've had to hear about Tobias Grayson, but I'd be willing to bet the man doesn't even remember my father.

Why would he? The two might have gone to the same schools but they come from different walks of life and would never travel in the same circles.

I'm not discrediting my father or his past achievements but it's like thinking that someone like Elon Musk or Bill Gates would remember you just because you might have shared the same air space in an elevator.

It's not going to happen. Those men are so rich and powerful, people like us are specks on their radar.

"It never ceases to amaze me how assholes like the Graysons keep getting more and more wealth and recognition while men like me suffer and are destined to never climb the fucking ladder," Dad continues.

This is what he's like when he gets into his the-world-loves-the-Graysons-and-hates-me mode.

I'm not exactly a huge fan of the family, and I hate the stories Dad told me about the various run-ins he had with Tobias, but I think there comes a time in life when you have to disconnect mentally and emotionally from people who wronged you in the past. Especially when they haven't been in your life for over twenty years.

My father, however, is not like that.

His obsession with outdoing Tobias Grayson fuel him.

That cocktail was the deadly poison that made him marry Brielle after Mom died. He never even considered that Brielle was only after his money. Because Tobias' wife, Sloane, was a former Victoria's Secret model, it was an automatic tick in the box for Brielle because she was a model, too.

Then, because Tobias lived upstate, Dad had to live there, too. Because all the Grayson kids went to Aster Academy, his daughters had to go there too.

We lived well beyond our means for years, but anything to keep up appearances and keep his wife happy. Dad worked overtime pretty much every day to make sure he could afford to keep Brielle and her daughter happy, and when he couldn't afford it, he'd take out loans.

I was in the background watching it all unfold. When I couldn't stand being around either of them I'd head to Gina's, and she happily accepted me.

Dad almost, *almost* got to that rung of the ladder of success that would have lifted him higher to where he needed to be, but then his designs got stolen, and further destruction struck when he lost the use of his legs.

Although he doesn't talk about it much, I know it must have messed him up even more to kill a man he'd worked with for over ten years out of self-defense. Then he lost the wife he worked so hard to keep and she took all his money.

When last I checked, Brielle had married an oil tycoon mere months after she divorced Dad. And spoiler alert but no shocker—they were dating while Dad was still in the hospital recovering. Now she and Michelle live in Dubai, while we're here barely surviving on the breadline.

The news special ends and an infomercial for car wax comes on. I take the remote control from Dad and switch the channel to a documentary about the rainforest.

"Sorry." Dad's chest caves. "I don't mean to get so worked up or cuss like a sailor around you."

"It's okay. I understand your frustration."

"I'm just glad you didn't end up with that Grayson boy."

If only he knew.

Sorry, Dad, I didn't mean to fall for the one boy you told me never to see, and I certainly never meant to run into him eight years later and lose my dignity all over again.

"Yes, let's be happy that never happened." I pray he can't see through me. It would be hell on earth if I told him I might be seeing the Grayson boy he's talking about tonight.

Dad seems to relax on hearing my anti-Grayson comment.

"What are your plans this week, sweetie?" He smiles, and the angst he previously exuded fades away. "I was thinking we could go to the outdoor cinema. They're playing *The Sound of Music* all week."

I return his smile. "Sure, we can do that."

"Great. You're working too hard, kiddo. I can see it in your face. Your mother would never forgive me if I let something happen to you, and I would never forgive myself either. I can't do much, but these small things help."

I nod with appreciation that he's acknowledged how hard I work. "It will be great to go to the cinema with you and maybe we can have dinner, too."

"Sure thing." Concern dims his expression once more. "Are you okay? You've been quiet all day. I know you're worried about Gina."

He knows about the chest pains and has been as worried as I have.

"I am, but she's been okay."

"Good. That woman is a fighter. You are, too. I know it must be hard to go from living the dream with your career and the man you were supposed to marry to this."

"Yeah. It's hard." I really hope this isn't going to be one of those talks where he glosses over the fact that Sasha was a monster.

"I was really hoping Sasha would have taken care of you and given you a good life. I'm sure he still would if he could. He loved you."

Here we go. My entire body goes rigid. I hate when he says things like that.

Dad knows the story. He knows what Sasha did to me and how he ruined my career. He knows the abuse I suffered, yet instead of being happy I got away he chooses to see things in a way I don't know who else would.

I understand Dad regrets the loss of opportunity we would have gained from Sasha's wealth, and that they got on like fire and gasoline, but it's beyond me that he can forget all the horrible things that happened.

"Dad, Sasha was an abusive asshole. I'm happy he's not in my life anymore. You keep forgetting the bad parts."

"I haven't, sweetheart." He shakes his head. "There's nothing wrong with me expressing remorse for something that could have been perfect. I know you. You loved him too. If you hadn't, you wouldn't have given him the time of day when he first approached you, and you would have never accepted his marriage proposal."

I also hate when he raises valid points I can't deny. I did love Sasha. I loved him a lot, but that love turned to hate when he used his fists on me.

It was hard to love him after that and harder to wrap my head around how he could tell me he loved me then hurt me in the same breath.

What my father doesn't realize or understand is that Sasha changed. When things didn't go the way he wanted, he changed and took out his frustration on me.

"Sweetheart—"

"I don't want to talk about him anymore." My voice rises, and I hold my hand up to stop him from continuing. If I don't put a stop to this conversation he'll go on for hours, and everything he says will hurt me even more. Dad doesn't get that I don't even want to hear Sasha's name. Every time I think of him or hear his name, I think of how awful he was to me. Then, of course, there was what happened to me after he went to prison. I was kidnapped, held at gunpoint, and taken to Kazakhstan, where I was locked away in a dungeon until Gina came to get me. All because of one guy.

I still have nightmares, and when I remember what I went through it cripples me.

Dad doesn't think about any of those things.

"I'm sorry, Dad." I swallow the rising panic. "I don't mean to be so harsh. It's just hard talking about him."

"That's okay, sweetie." Dad nods, understanding, but I know his understanding only extends to me not wanting to talk about Sasha, not about my abhorrent feelings toward him.

Or why I knew my only escape from our relationship was to sell my ex-fiancé out to the police.

The only people who know that secret are Dad, Gina, and Eden.

The *only* person I wouldn't have told out of the three is my father. Gina ended up telling him because she felt she had to give him the full story. Dad was always in touch with Sasha, and Gina wanted to highlight the gravity of what happened to me so Dad would cut contact.

It was Gina who gave me the strength I needed to work with the police.

I never told her about his abuse and dangerous ways until I had a way out because I knew she'd try to get me away from him and I worried he'd hurt her for trying.

To my knowledge, Sasha doesn't know I left Russia and he doesn't know I'm back in New York. I want to keep it that way. He's in prison for the next eight years, but people like him can do things from prison when they find out you wronged them.

I also have the worry that he might get released early because of the people he knows and his importance to them as one of the best drug traffickers. Those words in my head sound so wrong, and I remember how he lied to me, telling me he was into doing up cars.

By the time I found out the truth I was in too deep. Sometimes it feels like I've lived several lifetimes. I don't feel like I'm only twenty-six. I would believe it more if someone told me I was actually sixty-two.

"I didn't mean to upset you." Dad places his hands on his lap.

"It's okay. I just need you to remember that things between Sasha and me didn't end well for several reasons."

"I know. I just wanted to see you happy. That's all." He nods. "I'm working on something that might change things soon."

I smile and try to look enthusiastic. It's not the first time I've heard this. Every year, he does something new. He has a genius mind but nothing he's come up with has ever been quite as good as the designs that were stolen.

"What are you working on?"

"A piece of software open-world computer gamers will find useful. Maybe this idea of mine could be my gamechanger."

"That would be great." At least I sound like the dutiful, supportive daughter I've always strived to be.

"Here's hoping it could be better than what I did in the past. I'd just need the funding, though."

Sadness fills his face. The same sadness I witness when he talks about the designs he and his team created that were stolen. Those ideas went into making an antivirus software now used by major companies and governments worldwide. It was developed by the competing company, who eventually bought out Dad's old company Jaeger Tech.

"I'm sure you'll get the funding."

"I hope so." He grins with pride. "Come on, let's eat this pie and watch one of our classic films. I think that will make you smile."

"It will," I agree and smile just to humor him.

The rest of the time we spend together I try to keep my nerves from overriding my mind. Not hearing from Jericho doesn't help.

I get home at three to find a big box of bright yellow roses sitting on my bed.

As no one I know would send me these types of flowers, my mind goes straight to him.

I open the little envelope tucked into the side and take out the note.

It is from Jericho and says:

I'm sorry about last night and for tonight, too.

I'm not able to make it, but I think it's for the best.

It was good to see you. I hope everything works out for you, but if you need me, you know where to find me.

You deserve the best, River,

Always,

J

I gaze at the note, my hands shaking. After last night I had a feeling he would cancel, but getting the confirmation makes me feel worse.

Gina approaches the door and smiles at me.

"Please tell me those are from someone special," she beams.

I stare back at her wishing I could tell her the truth. She knew about Jericho way back when, but telling her about him now will lead to my other secrets that she doesn't know about, like me working at Club Edge.

"No," I decide to say. "They're just from work."

Her smile falters. "Oh, darn. Well, I suppose it's still good. The flowers are beautiful, just like my little niece."

She walks toward me and gives me a hug. "Are you staying in tonight?"

"Yes."

Trying to get my mind off Jericho by getting to the dance studio at one this morning was not my wisest idea.

Gina and I watched films and binged on junk food until she went to bed after midnight. I unfortunately couldn't do the same.

Since dancing is like food for my soul, I went to the studio and practiced my audition piece until it was time to head to the café.

That plan would have been fine if I wasn't already exhausted. Now I'm at school and so drained I feel like I'm going to pass out.

I don't know how I'm going to get through the day. Thankfully, I have the night off from the club, so after school I can go straight home and sleep.

Until then I have to make it through the rest of the day.

It's only lunchtime now and I've already had quite the day. I ran into Mrs. Aspen talking about me to her group of bitches who are all married to billionaires and notable men. Those women are in their late thirties and forties, but they could give the Plastics in *Mean Girls* a run for their money.

I can usually handle them but today they got to me. Now I'm on my way to meet Eden in the park for lunch, but I'm not in the mood to talk or even to see my best friend. That's saying a lot because I'm always able to talk to her.

Jericho put me in a foul mood I can't shake. I couldn't even keep the flowers he sent in my room because the sight of them kept reminding me of what happened between us.

I placed them in the living room so Gina could enjoy them since she liked them so much.

I spot Eden sitting on a picnic blanket by the duck pond. As she had a free period she grabbed us sandwiches and pastries from the deli and bakery we love uptown.

When she sees me she waves. I wave back and quicken my pace.

I reach her and my mouth waters at the sight of the delicious spread of food she's laid out for us.

"Behold our feast." She waves her hand over the food. "Isn't this the best way to start Monday?"

I smile at her, liking the lightness in her mood. "I agree. Thanks for getting this for us."

"No worries. I thought we could do with something different."

I set my bag down and sit cross-legged opposite her. "It was a good call."

"I also thought that some good food might make you more open to telling me about your weekend. You do realize you've hardly told me anything, right?" She leans forward and beams at me with inquisitive eyes.

I bite back a groan. This is the conversation I was trying to avoid.

"There's nothing more to talk about. I told you everything." *Everything that made my story legit.*

"There's seriously nothing more to tell? You never even told me how the wedding went, or if he wanted to see you again."

"He understood it was just an arrangement for the two days, and the wedding was fine." Now I feel bad for lying. "I'm more excited about the money I got. I paid the arrears."

Her face brightens, and I hope she'll go with the subtle subject change.

"Praise God. You have *noooo* idea how happy that's made me. And you really think you'll be out of Club Edge in three months?"

I nod and smile with hope. "Yes, maybe before. I have some vacation I can take in the last month to cut my time down by maybe a week or two." That's providing I don't take any unscheduled days off.

She claps her hands with delight. "That makes me even happier. I was thinking that maybe we could go on a girls' trip after. Somewhere like Palm Springs or an island where we can get some sea and sun."

I'm already nodding before she can finish talking. "Yes. I wouldn't say no to that."

She giggles and grabs one of the sandwiches from the platter. "Great. I'll come up with something amazing. You deserve it."

"So do you. You've been working nonstop, too."

"River, my work is normal. You've been going at superhuman speed. And running into people from the past." She quirks a brow. "Like ex-boyfriends who tried to reconnect with you."

I also preempted this discussion. "Yes, I've been through quite the storm."

"Have you seen Jericho again?"

"No." She doesn't know all the things that happened between Jericho and me since the last time we spoke about him, but I don't feel I'm lying by telling her I haven't seen him.

"Are you okay to just leave things the way they are?" Her expression softens. "It feels a little… unfinished."

Jericho and I have been *unfinished* for the last eight years, but Eden makes a valid point.

It's perhaps that unfinished element about us that's making me feel so rotten.

"I don't think there's anything I can do about that, and maybe it's better this way."

"Is it?" She presses her lips together and looks me over. "I know things have been crazy busy and you must be so damn tired, but you haven't been yourself since you ran into him."

"Can you blame me?"

"Not at all. But that dullness about you from college is back. I don't mean the anger from your breakup. It was more about the loss. That was the biggest difference between you and me back then. My breakup was a long time coming, so I expected it. Yours wasn't. I just don't want you to keep thinking about this guy. Sometimes we need closure to end things properly."

I'm listening, and I feel like she could be right. "Maybe."

"Yeah, maybe. Anyway, let's enjoy this delicious feast and talk about this upcoming trip of ours before our time runs out." She perks up and grabs another sandwich.

We eat and talk, and I think.

The more I think about this possibility of closure, the better the idea sounds.

Jericho got to say goodbye to me, whereas I feel like I've been left hanging in the wind.

Regardless of how Saturday night went, Jericho is the reason I was able to pay off sixty thousand dollars on my debts.

I feel like I need a proper goodbye. Something more than what we had and enough to move on.

Instead of going home when school ends I find myself pulling up at the Park Avenue branch of Graysons Inc.

In my little beat-up Miata I already look out of place in the parking lot amongst the host of luxury cars like Porsches, Ferraris, Bugattis, and Maybachs. I almost wish I'd parked the car around the corner by the park and made my way on foot.

It's okay. I don't plan to stay long. I might not even see him.

When I get inside the building I head to the receptionist who gives me a haughty glare and looks me up and down as if I've lost my way.

I don't know what her problem is because my hair and clothes look fine. I guess it must just be me, my presence. Maybe she can smell that I don't fit in with the type of high society people who normally frequent the building.

I half expect her to send me away and I'm thankful when she tells me to go to the twelfth floor and wait to speak with Jericho's secretary because he's in a meeting.

He's a busy man, so him being in a meeting is perfectly natural. I'm also here uninvited and unexpected.

I make my way up to the twelfth floor but I already decided that if I don't see him today I won't be making an appointment.

This is it, and it's for me.

There's no one up here walking around like downstairs, only what looks like offices and meeting rooms. The place is impressive, though, and perhaps the most exquisite building I've ever been in apart from the opera houses and theaters in Russia and other parts of Europe.

I sit in the little reception area and wait in the silence.

Half an hour passes before I hear footsteps, but they're not anywhere near me. Moments later, I think I hear Jericho's voice. I listen closer and realize I'm right. It is him, but I don't know where he is.

I stand and follow the voice, which I now realize is coming from outside on the balcony. He must have come from the other side of the building.

I make my way around the corner and find him through the floor-to-ceiling glass wall. He's on the phone, standing on the balcony.

Seeing Jericho again warms my body in an unwarranted way and I can't resist the memory of how he touched and tasted me.

I decide to get closer so he notices me. What I have to say to him won't take long. Maybe not even a minute. He should be able to fit me in after his call.

I can hear him better now, and I realize it's because the glass door to my left is open. It leads out to where he's standing.

"Luc, I just need to pick one of those women to be my wife before next Wednesday."

On hearing those words I stop short in my tracks, my ears burning as if someone placed hot coals in them.

Did I seriously hear him say the word *wife*?

Wife as in *wife*?

And *picking a wife*?

What the hell?

Quickly, I hide behind the column and continue listening.

"Just narrow the list down to the best five. I won't have time to go through all the others. I'm already way out of time." He sighs with frustration. "Cross off anyone you don't think I can trust and leave the girls who will appreciate the money. I'm sure you can agree with that. A million dollars before the wedding and another at the end of the marriage in a years' time is more than sufficient."

My mouth drops when I process what I'm seriously hearing, and I think of all that money.

Two million dollars to marry Jericho Grayson. *Why?*

Why would *he* need to pay someone to marry him?

A man like him wouldn't need to make that kind of payment to anyone.

Unless it benefited him in some way.

That must be it, and whatever it is must be worth more than two million.

What could that be?

"Alright, I'll speak to you later." He hangs up and walks down the length of the balcony to where he must have come from.

Feeling dazed, I stay where I am and process the plan I just heard.

It doesn't make sense, yet it does. I can bet that list of Luc's holds nothing but the finest women. Pedigree women cut from the best cloth with fathers who will worship him. They'll be daughters of moguls, socialites and heiresses.

Not a girl like me.

Listen to me. As if *I* want to marry Jericho Grayson.

I don't, but the younger version of myself did at one point.

Perhaps this was the closure I needed. The reminder that Jericho and I come from two different worlds and he was always out of my reach.

Sometimes, Cinderella is destined to be Cinderella. The floor-scrubbing, home-cleaning girl who works her fingers to the bone. *That's me.*

On that thought I leave, and as I drive away I promise myself I'll never look back.

I get home an hour later feeling worse than I did when I left in the early hours of the morning.

The TV is on in the living room so I assume Gina is in there.

When I walk in my heart falls through my stomach when I find her lying on the ground. Next to her is a broken cup with tea spilled all over the white rug.

"Gina!" I cry, rushing to her side.

I check to see if she's breathing.

But she's not.

Chapter FOURTEEN

River

I HAD TO DO CPR ON GINA TO BRING HER BACK TO LIFE.
Me.
I had to do that to save my dear aunt's life, and if I'd done anything wrong or been any later than I was, I might have come home and found her dead.

She would have died, just like Mom.

I called the paramedics before I started CPR and they picked up where I left off when they arrived.

I've been at the hospital for the last hour, sitting in the waiting room, waiting for the doctors to update me with what's happening. Dad and Eden are on the way, so I've just been here by myself going crazy with worry.

The doctors have been running various tests and scans. The last time we were here like this, Gina had had the accident and was in surgery for hours.

It was horrible, but at least we had more of a sense of what was happening and a bit more hope. I feel this is to do with those chest pains. The moment I told the doctors about them, they looked worried.

Dr. French, the consultant who has been taking care of Gina, approaches the door, and I jump out of my seat, rushing toward him.

I've seen him a few times when I've brought Gina to her appointments. He's an elderly doctor in his seventies who has worked in the field for years, so I know Gina has been in good hands.

"How is she?" I talk so fast I'm tripping over my words.

"She's stable at the moment."

"Can I see her?"

"In a little while. I'd like to talk to you in private first." He gives me a kind smile but it's the sort you give a person when you pity them, not the kind you give because there's nothing to worry about.

"Okay."

"Let's go into my office." His pale gray eyes take me in with more pity.

We head to his office on the next floor. My trepidation increases with every second that passes. By the time we sit I just want to scream.

"It's her heart, isn't it?" I cut to the chase.

"Yes."

"What's wrong with her? There was nothing wrong before."

He blows out a ragged breath. "Actually, there was. Gina has been a patient of mine for over fifteen years."

All the air in my lungs stills, then it drains into the ether. "*What?* That can't be right. I didn't know."

Why didn't I know? That length of time means Gina has been seeing him since before Mom died.

"She's only just given me permission to speak with you, so I'm able to tell you more about her condition. She's always had a congenital heart defect that we were able to manage for quite some time with treatment, but things have gotten worse within the last year or so, and now her heart is failing. That was actually the cause of the stroke."

I suck in a sharp breath. "Her heart was the cause of the stroke?" I've never even heard of that.

"Yes. This looks like the same sort of defect your mother suffered, but in Gina's case we were able to treat it. However, the condition has gotten to the stage where she needs surgery."

I swallow hard. "What kind of surgery?"

"My recommendation is valve replacement surgery. That should fix a lot of the problems she's having and, of course, if successful, extend her life but the treatment plan would be quite extensive and we'd have to factor in the recovery from the stroke. Gina and I have talked about this before."

"How long ago did you talk about this?"

"Since she had the stroke." He opens his palms. "That was the moment things got worse. She didn't proceed with the treatment plan for financial reasons. Her insurance won't cover it and she didn't have the finances."

Oh God. She didn't have the money because of me. Because she saved me.

"How much will it all cost?"

"In excess of a hundred thousand dollars because of the level of care she'll need."

My entire body squeezes as if clamps are attached to my joints, tightening with every breath I take.

I drop my head. I don't have that kind of money.

Over a hundred thousand dollars.

Fuck, this is absolute shit, and I just paid all those loans the other day. Had I known about this, I would have used the money for Gina's health.

Slowly, I lift my head and meet Dr. French's gaze with tears in my eyes.

"I'm sorry to be the bearer of bad news. We've done a lot within the remit of her insurance coverage, and we will continue to do so, along with anything else we can offer but that won't be enough. She needs the surgery now. If we don't do it soon she'll get to a stage where there will be nothing we can do because her body won't be able to handle surgery."

My soul trembles on hearing that. "I understand."

"Take some time to think about everything and get back to me. Here is my business card with my number." He hands me his card.

"Thank you. I appreciate all you've done for her."

He nods respectfully. "Go, spend some time with her. I'll take you to her room."

"Thanks."

I feel like a shell of the person I was hours ago as I get up and follow him to Gina's room. The feeling worsens when I find Gina in her hospital bed looking so frail I fear she might dissolve into the air.

She looks at me, then at Dr. French and in her eyes I read the realization that he's spoken to me.

He leaves us and I move toward her. She has tubes attached to her wrist but manages to lift her hand out to me.

When I take it the tears just come.

"Oh, Gina," I whimper.

"Please don't cry my sweet, sweet girl." Her voice is a muted tone, and as she breathes in her chest rattles, sounding like a broken engine.

I wipe away my tears and shake my head. "Why didn't you tell me?"

"I hoped it wouldn't come to this. I really tried to take care of myself, especially after your mother died. Things were okay for some time, until they weren't."

"I will find that money for the surgery." I don't know where to start but I know I have to find it. "If not for me you would have had it."

She gives my hand a gentle squeeze. "River. No. I won't lie here and listen to you blame yourself."

"It's my fault, though, all that money you had to find to save me because of my stupid mistakes and Sasha." I'm trying to hold my tears back but I can't.

"I don't want you to blame yourself. I never want you to do that. All I want is for you to live and be happy. Do you remember the story about how you got your name?" She tries to smile but it doesn't quite reach her lips.

"Yes." I stifle a sob.

She gave me my name. Mom allowed her to because Gina delivered me when I arrived two months early while she and Mom were camping in the woods by Yellowstone River. Gina's favorite place on earth. That's how I got my name.

"Good. Now is the time to be as strong as that river, because you have to be. I don't want you to worry about this surgery. It's not an option. It can't be. I'm going to continue with my treatment but I know it will only keep me going for so long until it stops helping. That's when I need you to let me go."

My shoulders wrack with a sob. "I can't."

"You must. You have to." She closes her eyes, then opens them again. "You have to, River."

I won't.

I can't.

I hold on to her hand as if for dear life, and I know deep in my soul that as long as I draw breath I'll never be able to let her go.

If our situations were reversed she would move heaven and earth to save me. I will do the same for her no matter what it takes.

And I already have one solution stabbing at the insides of my mind.

It's something I shouldn't know about and *wouldn't* if I hadn't been eavesdropping on Jericho earlier.

That feels like it happened days ago but it was only today. Only mere hours ago.

I'm sure if I asked him for a loan he'd help me, or give it to me, but I don't want that for the same reasons I turned him down when he tried to help me at the café.

I don't want to owe him in that way. Besides, two million dollars is more attractive than anything I could possibly conjure up in my mind.

I could do everything and more with that kind of money. I could take care of Gina, pay her back for everything, take care of Dad.

Take care of myself.

Jericho's help is my only viable solution right now.

But what if he doesn't pick me?

I'll have to swallow my pride once more and find out.

If he doesn't help me I might end up in a worse position by going back to Jones to get a loan.

Either way, I have to try. In this instance not trying means failing.

I can't fail.

Chapter FIFTEEN

Jericho

R IVER WALKS INTO MY OFFICE AND CLOSES THE DOOR. With her hair pulled into a tight bun and a business dress perfectly fitted to the curves of her body, this is the most formal I've ever seen her.

It's a good look on her. She looks like she's ready to close a deal on a billion-dollar contract but as I stare at her, I can't shove the memory of her half-naked body in my arms away.

Half-naked with her perfect tits on show while I had her pressed up against the wall with my face buried between her legs, eating out her pussy.

I'm having a hard time keeping myself seated and calm when all I want to do is lay her out on my desk and bury myself deep inside her.

Shit. What is she doing here?

Saturday was supposed to be goodbye. Imagine my surprise

when I got a message from her last night asking if she could meet with me today.

At first I wondered if she was going to ask me about canceling on her on Sunday, but I quickly shoved that thought away. That's not her style. She would have accepted the goodbye after the way she left me at the gallery.

So my next thought was that she must need me for something, and she must be desperate enough to contact me. That's why I suggested we meet first thing.

"Morning," I greet her first.

"Hi."

"Do you want to sit?" I point to the chair in front of me. "Or we can go grab some coffee or something?"

"No, that's okay. I don't plan to take up too much of your time."

I narrow my eyes, curiosity eating up my insides as I watch her lower herself into the seat.

"What's going on, River?" I lean forward, resting my hands on the desk.

Her lips part, and she looks paler than the soft cream of her complexion. "I heard you were looking for a wife. I'd like to be considered for the job."

As the words fall from her lips, I wonder if I heard her right. When I realize I heard her perfectly, my back snaps straight as if someone shoved a steel rod up my spine.

What the actual fuck?

How the hell does she know that?

"What are you talking about?" My voice has a chilling edge to it I would never normally use with her.

She swallows and seems to regain some of the confidence she exuded when she first walked in. "Jericho, please don't bullshit me or beat around the bush. I heard you on the phone yesterday talking to Luc. I was… here."

Jesus Christ. How the hell did I let that happen?

How could I have been so fucking careless? No one was

supposed to be around because they were all in the lounge for the meeting. I slipped away during the break to take Luc's call.

River heard me. She could have been anyone. Not that they come here much but she could have been my father, or even one of Bastian's minions.

The information she has is the sort that could destroy me, but if she wants the job—of being my wife—then she's not looking to destroy me.

"What were you doing here?"

The color returns to her cheeks but she schools herself again. "That doesn't matter now. Did you hear what I asked you? I want to be considered for the job. You might not want to be with me but you know you can trust me, and two million would be more than I could ever hope to make in this lifetime."

The money.

She needs money again. Coming to me in this desperate state can only mean one thing.

"What happened to Gina?"

The deep worry in her eyes tells me I'm right but she seems surprised that I would guess the answer.

Her eyes turn glassy and her bottom lip trembles. "She needs life-saving surgery." A tear slides down her cheek, marring her flawless skin. "I went home to find her on the floor. She had a heart attack. I... had to do CPR."

"Jesus, I'm so sorry." Cold shock grips me. I knew things were bad with Gina but I didn't expect this. She could have died.

"Thank you." River wipes the tear away and blinks rapidly, attempting to stop the rest from falling but she fails.

I pass her a box of tissues and she gratefully takes out a couple to wipe her face.

I hate seeing her cry. I've only witnessed her tears a few times during the time I've known her because crying is not something most are privy to with this girl, so I know this must cut her deeply.

"What's happening with Gina now?"

"She'll be in the hospital for quite some time. They're continuing with her treatment but it won't be enough. The doctor said that eventually there'll be nothing they can do. The crazy thing is I didn't know Gina had heart problems. She never told me," she stutters and my heart goes out to her, making me feel worse for knowing before she did. "She has the same defect that took my mom. I didn't know she would need this type of surgery. I spent all the money from the auction to pay her debts and the arrears on a loan she got for me."

That must be the loan from the shark.

"What was that loan for? It seems you had a lot of money left to pay." It's best I act like I don't know anything.

"Yes. My ex-fiancé got me in some trouble I couldn't get out of myself."

My jaw tightens, clenching. "What kind of trouble did he get you in?"

Her hands tremble, the tell-tale sign of deep psychological stress. "There was a lot of stuff and I… he…" Her voice fades into nothing, making me think that she must have gone through a lot worse than I imagined.

"What did he do to you, River?"

She shakes her head and the tremor ripples through her body. "I… um, can't talk about him now." Her voice chokes and she pulls in a deep breath.

I want to press her for more information but decide against it because I've seen this type of reaction in women before when they've been abused.

That word in my head in relation to my girl makes me see red. *My girl…*

I keep needing to check myself when I think of her as mine. She's not and hasn't been in a long time, but there are parts of her that will always belong to me and I hate that I wasn't there for her when she needed me.

That hatred makes me want to find her motherfucking ex and

skin him alive, then kill him for hurting her, but I'll deal with his ass later. Getting worked up right now won't help her.

I wonder what her father thought of this ex. Neil hated me, but I would never have hurt his daughter.

"Okay." I try to keep my voice calm for her sake. "You don't have to talk about him."

"Thanks." She presses her hand to her mouth and wipes away more tears. "I came to you because I don't want to go back to the man who gave Gina the loan. He's not a good person. But I'll go to him if I have to."

As in, if I say no—which I'm not. There's no fucking way I'm allowing her to go back to some loan shark, and there's no way I'm not helping.

"I don't know why you suddenly need a wife but it's the only thing I know that you need. It would help both of us." She pauses for a moment and I realize she's suggesting it from this angle because she doesn't want to owe me.

She doesn't want a handout from me. Maybe she also knows I would never allow Gina to die and am a breath away from depositing the money she needs for the surgery, even without getting anything in return.

"If you pick me I'll do what you need me to do for as long as you want." She stares me dead in the eye as if she's about to fight.

Her words stick to my mind like tar, and I consider this new possibility.

Her—River St. James being my wife.

Of everyone *anyone* could possibly come up with as a good candidate, she'd make the perfect temporary wife.

River might be wrong about me not wanting to be with her but she's right about the other stuff. I know her, and I do trust her. My trust doesn't come easy, and I trust very few people in this world.

She's one of them, whether I want her to be or not. I trust her enough to take my secret plot to the grave, but this idea...

It's bad for all sorts of reasons.

Number one being that I shouldn't be with her.

However, my selfish mind is already running wild, wanting to hold on to the idea that I could be with the girl who got away. Especially when she's offering herself to me—offering to be my fake wife.

God knows I do need the kind of help she could give me.

"You're just staring at me." River presses her lips together. "I need some kind of an answer, even if it's a no."

"I have to think about it." I can't believe I just said that, but if I don't think I'll listen to my dick and agree in a heartbeat, shoving away all the elements of this request I need to consider.

That numb look I've seen twice before invades her expression and posture. The first time I saw her look like this was when I broke up with her. The next time was Saturday, when I had to stop myself from fucking her against that wall.

I can tell she thinks I don't want her. Or worse, that I have someone else lined up for the job. I don't, and I do want her.

"For how long?" Her voice is small and as careful as someone trying to preserve their last breath.

"Thursday. I'm in Arizona until tomorrow night." I leave later today for the business trip. I fly back tomorrow night. That will give me time to process how this could work.

"Okay." She dips her head briefly, the weight of her worries showing. It grieves me to see her look so pitiful and even I, with all the darkness that lives inside me, wish I could fix everything for her. The bad hand time has dealt her, her aunt's illness, the death of her mother, and her father's paralysis then eventual downfall. Money can only alleviate the burden of those things. It can't fix it.

"Thank you. I guess I should leave now." She stands and without another look, she leaves. She walks out of my office as if she's nothing more to me than one of my clients.

I watch her go and contemplate my answer.

I know what I want it to be, but nothing is easy when it comes to River St. James.

That ex of hers was no good for her, but neither am I.

Yes.

No.

Yes.

I don't fucking know…

I'm trying this thing out, to be a better man. That's why making this decision is so damn hard.

On one hand, I'm so fucking rich I could give River the two million dollars I'm putting up for this new position of mine. It would be like pocket change to me. She'd have money to take care of herself for the rest of her life and everyone in it.

I could give it to her and still pick a girl from Luc's list, but that's just the thing.

I don't want to.

Now that I know River wants the job, she's so perfect for the job no one else seems to suffice.

The fucking problem is me.

I struggled with the decision all morning. My brain cells are fried by the time I get to Arizona. Knight notices but doesn't say anything.

Fried brain cells are not what you want when dealing with a multi-million-dollar project that could give us more public endorsements. The job is to turn an old rundown parking lot into luxury apartments.

Knight and I are used to managing projects of all sizes with big and small budgets, but this one is significant because it's the first job this year under the new company structure.

Until Grandfather leaves we're still under the Grayson Inc.

umbrella, but we're officially in charge of the contracts that come into Park Avenue.

My mind settles a little after work and we're at the bar after the hockey game. Luc's team won, as predicted, and we join his teammates to celebrate.

Carl, the team's coach, is prouder than anyone. He buys us all a round of drinks, then we listen to him praise the team—which sounds more like a pastor giving a sermon.

We're in the VIP section of the sports bar. Knight and I are sitting across from each other at a table while Luc is with Carl and his team members.

Knight taps my hand and I realize I've zoned out again.

"What's going on with you, Jericho?" He's eyeing me seriously. "You've been like a fucking zombie all day."

"I'm fine, just thinking about work."

He doesn't believe me. I'm starting to get used to the look now. That's the problem with being around people who know you so damn well. Luc can do that with me, too, but my brother seems to have telepathic abilities that enable him to figure me out before I can process a thought in my mind.

"Are you sure that's all you're thinking about? *Work*? You've been more off-center than usual since Grandfather mentioned meeting your girl next week."

He gives me that uncanny look again that I've been noticing more recently. I'm starting to see through him, too, because I know he knows there is no girl. *Yet*.

He knows it's a yet because he's more than aware that I would never fuck with my chances to get my legacy.

"I'm fine."

"I hope so. You've been quiet about this girl, especially with me."

There's a reason for that, and I have to admit it's not because I think he lives in Grandfather's ass.

It's because, as devious as he is, I know he wouldn't agree with what I'm doing because I'm deceiving our grandfather.

Knight wouldn't understand it either because he's the kind of guy who planned for marriage even before he knew he wanted it.

We've had different experiences and I don't want him to dictate what I do with my life either.

"Don't worry about me, brother. Shit just got real and it's a little daunting. You know as soon as the world knows I'm engaged the press will be all over my ass *again*. That's not exactly something I'm looking forward to." I might be glossing over the facts but I'm being entirely truthful. I hate the media attention I'll garner when my engagement is announced. All eyes will turn to me and I'll have to make sure there are no loose ends that need tying up.

"I guess that's understandable." He drinks a sip of his beer but continues staring at me over the rim of the glass. "I just hope there's nothing more you're worrying about. You're definitely not yourself."

"Everything's cool."

"Alright. If you say so."

I give him a curt nod then look back at Luc and Carl. Anything to avert Knight's ever-increasing suspicious gaze.

The night wears on but I don't stop thinking about River, of how worried she must be, and how eager she would be to hear back from me.

It's wise, though, that I take the time I need to think.

It's not like I'm picking out a new car. This is marriage. Marriage for a year where we'll be together all the time, under scrutiny from the public and from my grandfather.

Luc comes to my hotel room the next morning with his new improved list. We haven't had the chance to speak since the other day, so he doesn't know about River. I purposely didn't tell him because I need this decision to be mine.

"I've got five of the best girls for you." Luc beams, sitting in the armchair. He crosses one ankle over the other and looks real proud of himself. "You will definitely be able to pick someone from this list and I've arranged for you to meet each of them over the next two days."

Everyone should have a friend like Luc. I know I'm a lucky bastard. I just don't feel like one.

I throw myself down in the chair next to him and wince.

"What? What's going on now?"

I bring a hand to my head and shake it. "River."

He gives me a cunning smile. "What about her? Ready to tell me how your date went?"

I've been avoiding the subject and any discussion about her, but now I don't know if I can keep it up because I'm too torn.

"What's happening, Grayson?" His stare intensifies with impatience.

I sigh and tell him about River's discovery of our plans and her offer to be my wife.

"What did you say to her?" He sits forward, his stare intensifying as if he's just been handed the biggest news of the year.

"I told her I'd think about it."

"What the fuck? Why the hell did you say that?" He throws his hands up.

"Luc, don't do that to me. You know exactly why I told her *that*."

He grits his teeth, then blows out a ragged breath. "Okay, I won't act like I don't know, but, Jericho, think about this, bro. It's perfect and maybe, just maybe, if you do it you'll feel some redemption from the past. If you help her in a way where she feels she doesn't have to owe you and gives her aunt a chance to live, that has to count for something. You could both move on at the end."

Redemption.

That sounds like a bittersweet notion I don't deserve but I want it so badly my soul yearns for it.

Could it be so simple? It still feels selfish.

"That's what you need to think about. How about I hold fire with my list and you get back to me when you're home? We can take things from there."

I run a hand over my beard and nod. "Alright, and thanks."

"No worries. FYI, Knight looks like he's starting to question things." Luc quirks a hard brow and clasps his fingers together.

"I know. Has he said anything to you?"

"He just thinks it's strange he hasn't met your *girl*. It's going to get real hard for me very soon if you don't pick someone, and I'm starting to feel like I'm coming between you guys. You're brothers, and I'm your best friend. Apart from when the shit hit the fan way back when with River's dad, this is the only time I've had to keep a secret between you two. Please don't make things harder for me."

"I hear you, and I won't."

"Cool, so take my damn advice and pick River."

I give him a stiff smile.

My phone buzzes with a message and I look away. I retrieve the phone from my pocket and look at the home screen, my interest piques when I realize the message is from Zeke, my contact from the underground who I asked to get more information on River's ex-fiancé.

I open the message and the pit of my stomach fills with rocks when I read what he's sent me.

Her ex is Sasha Konstantin. He's in prison in Russia on an eight-year sentence for drug trafficking but he'll likely get out a LOT sooner. His godfather is Dmitriyev Pertrinkov, who has ties to the Russian mafia.

I found details which suggest that Sasha's debtors came after River when he went to prison. They took her captive. They demanded half a million from her aunt.

That's all I got. Let me know if you need any more intel.

Each word in the message stabs into my mind, but reading that River was taken captive—as in kidnapped—sends undiluted rage rippling through me.

Fuck.

River went through shit. She went through actual fucking shit and God knows what else her ex-fiancé did to her. That motherfucking bastard.

She could have been killed.

Sasha Konstantin is lucky he's in fucking prison but I still want to hurt him, and I don't give a shit who he is or whose godson he is.

Everything I previously discovered about River and Gina adds up now.

It all culminated in the disaster they're in today where the two of them need my help.

"Everything okay?" Luc asks, looking me over.

"Yeah. It's okay." It will be. I know what I have to do.

I'm taking River up on her offer or rather, I'll make her *my* offer, with the workaround that I won't be selfish about it, even if her being my wife helps me.

My plans still stand the same as they would if she were any other woman.

Look but don't touch.

This is business, not a real relationship.

We just need to look real to those who need to believe we're legit. Like my grandfather and the rest of my family. And the world.

It's a win-win situation for us both and as Luc said, maybe this could be how I redeem myself from the past in some small way.

I just can't touch her.

Chapter SIXTEEN

River

EDEN STARES BACK AT ME WITH A VACANT EXPRESSION tainting the soft hazel color of her eyes. I don't know if I would have preferred for her to be mad at me. I've never really lied to her before.

We're in the living room at Gina's house.

Eden arrived about half an hour ago to check on me and make dinner. That's when I told her the truth.

The truth about everything and my offer to be Jericho's wife.

The latter is not information I probably should have shared, but Eden isn't any old person who will go bragging to the first tabloid or gossip magazine. My friendship with her means more.

I just wish I knew what she was thinking.

Telling her the truth might not have been the best idea with all that's going on, but I was going crazy keeping it to myself.

I felt she had to know the truth so she could understand my hopes to help Gina if things work out with Jericho.

I can't believe I've put my trust in the same ex who I vowed never to trust again, or that I broke down the way I did in his office.

The mere talk of Sasha did that to me. The people in my circle know how he treated me, but speaking to Jericho—for what little I said—really got to me.

In the same breath I was basically begging for an opportunity to be his wife.

God knows what Dad would do if he found out what his daughter did. Going to a Grayson for help, much less *that Grayson boy* he forbade her to see.

I've been a mess for the last few days, but knowing my father will lose his shit if all goes to plan actually made me feel sick.

We spent most of today at the hospital with Gina. I know it's unfair to say this, but I didn't hear Dad coming up with any grand plans to save her.

And poor Gina…she isn't doing well at all. She seems to be getting worse.

She's been able to talk to us since she's been in the hospital but today wasn't like that. She barely spoke and had a glassy, fragile look about her, as if looking at her too hard would shatter her body into a million pieces.

I don't know if that's the effect of the extra medication or if she's just getting worse. Then again, if she weren't getting worse she wouldn't need *extra* medication.

I'm so worried and shit scared. I also haven't been at work since Monday, so I'm losing more money but there's no way I can work in this frame of mind.

I'm deeply distressed and so anxious the tension in my body could dissolve my organs.

Eden makes her way over to me on the sofa, sits, and blows out a ragged breath.

"I'm sorry I didn't tell you the truth," I say quietly, pushing my palms down on the sofa. "Please don't hate me."

She shakes her head. "I could never hate you, River." She sighs, bringing her hand to her cheek. "I suppose I also couldn't be mad at you even if I wanted to be. I feel like I would have done the same if it were me."

"Would you?"

She nods slowly. "It's complicated, right?"

"Yeah, and strange to talk about."

"I guess I was right. You and Jericho seem unfinished." She bites the inside of her lip.

"Something seems to keep one of us hooked in, one way or another." I raise my shoulders into a short shrug. "Maybe I should have stayed in Russia."

"What would that have achieved? The situation would still have been the same."

"I guess so. I'm just tired of feeling like this is all my fault."

"It's not."

"But Sasha…" My voice cuts. I can't even mention that man's name without getting choked up.

"Don't even go there. You weren't to know he was going to turn out the way he did. No one did. I was so happy for you when you two got together. I thought he loved you, but he was a fucking psycho."

"I'm glad you acknowledge that. Dad still can't seem to wrap his head around that part."

"That's because your father only sees what he wants to see. Forgive me, I don't mean to be offensive." She wrinkles her nose.

"No offense taken, believe me. I completely agree."

She sighs again and brings her hands in to her chest. We stay in silence for a few seconds, processing and wondering.

"What are you going to do if Jericho agrees?"

"Rejoice, then hate myself even more than I already do for crawling to him for help." I give her a weary smile and my face feels like it might crack. "I can't believe I had to go to him. I've been stubborn and Miss I-Can-Take-Care-of-Myself all this time, but I've hit a stumbling block that I can't work my way around."

I feel like I've been teetering on the brink of insanity since I saw Jericho. The problem with him that worries me is that he's as unpredictable as a tornado.

"All things aside, my heart goes out to you for being that girl who'll do anything to save someone she loves. Here's hoping it works out."

"I hope so, too."

"Keep strong, River." She smirks. "At least if this works out you'll be two million dollars richer and married to a seriously hot billionaire."

I attempt to laugh because I know she's trying to cheer me up but I can't even do that.

"A seriously hot billionaire who might have wanted to marry someone like Paris Hilton or Kim Kardashian."

"Or he could want you. He did before. And just for the record, Paris Hilton and Kim Kardashian have nothing on you, my friend."

Now I laugh but without humor. "If only, but thank you for saying that, even though I'm the perfect illustration of the girl from the wrong side of the tracks. I wasn't even thinking about that part when I presented my offer to him."

"Because it's not relevant. I don't think it is."

"Maybe not."

My gut tells me Jericho would help me in any event with Gina's surgery, but he knows I want to earn that help. That doesn't stop me from worrying he'll say no to the whole thing. If that is the case I don't want to think of the alternatives.

After Eden leaves I have another rough time getting to sleep. I doze off in the early hours of the morning, then stir as the first traces of sunlight slither into my room. That's when I feel a heavy presence near me.

At first I think I'm imagining it, but the shuffling sound makes me realize it's real.

My awareness awakens with me and I turn to find a shadowy figure standing by the window.

On seeing I'm awake, it moves closer into the light. It's Jericho. The room is just bright enough for me to see his Adonis face with that brooding expression trimmed with malice.

He's dressed in a mid-length black coat and full black everything right down to the Tom Ford boots covering his feet. No wonder he blended so well with the darkness.

With my heart triple-beating and my breath lodged in my throat, I sit up and yank the sheets close to cover my breasts. Except for my panties I'm naked. I'm not sure how much he saw, but he was looking.

And damn it, he saw me naked again.

I always sleep like this when I'm anxious. No matter how loose-fitting my bed clothes might be, they always feel tight against my skin.

Leisurely, he allows his gaze to slide over my body and I feel exposed even though I'm covered up.

"How did you get in here?" I glance at the door, which is open. I didn't leave it like that. I never left the window open either.

When I look back at him he arches a quizzical brow, and I remember he's the same boy from high school who broke into the science building and the principal's office when his stash of pot was confiscated.

He's the same boy who pulled a Houdini on a police officer after being arrested at a beach party when a fight broke out between rival football teams and, more importantly, he's the same boy who used to sneak into my room to see me at night.

That was how I lost my virginity, right there in my little room in my family home with my dad downstairs in his office. I swear Jericho did it like that to prove the point that he could.

He's the same boy.

Boy.

No. *Man.* I keep forgetting he's a man now and I shouldn't, because he hasn't looked like a boy in a very long time. At seventeen he hardly looked like one when I first met him.

Breaking our stare, Jericho pulls a small envelope from inside his coat pocket. He holds it up then sets it on the nightstand.

"Your contract should you wish to accept my offer," he states in a flat tone, keeping his eyes fixed on me.

"Your offer?"

"*My* offer." He places emphasis on that word as if to remind me that he's the one with the control even though I asked about the *job*. "The contract of marriage is for one year."

"A year?" My breath tightens even more. I knew the time wouldn't be short, but I wasn't expecting it to be that long either.

"Is that a problem, *Mermaid*?"

I hate that mermaid name, and he always sounds like he's taunting me with it, but now isn't the time to get annoyed.

"No. It's not a problem at all."

"Wonderful. You get a million after the wedding, which will take place in one month, then another million at the end of our marriage in one years' time."

It's so weird to hear him talk about ending before we've even begun, but the prospect of all that money fills me with new energy.

"That sounds fine." I nod.

"I've taken the liberty of paying for your aunt's full medical care. Her surgery is tomorrow."

My mouth drops open and a rush of warmth fills my soul, relieving the heaviness of my worries. "*What*?"

His face softens. "I didn't want Gina to wait any longer than necessary."

"Oh my God." Tears of joy swell my heart but I hold them back. He's seen me cry enough. "Thank you so much."

"No worries."

If I weren't naked in bed I'd jump up and hug him. This is more than I expected but suddenly the matter of the money occurs to me. He paid for Gina's surgery but I haven't done anything yet.

"That money was supposed to come from our agreement."

"You and I are a separate matter. I don't want this to be about your aunt."

"But then I still owe you."

A salacious smile slithers across his face. "I'm sure there will be plenty of opportunities for you to make it up to me. We have time." He winks at me and, damn me, desire stirs low in my belly at remembering that those hands of his have the power to make me feel unimaginable pleasure. I push the thought away and focus on the fact that he paid for all of Gina's care.

"That's not what I wanted."

"It's part of the deal. Take it or leave it."

"I'll take it," I say quickly. I won't be a fool and argue. He just solved my problems and placed me on a new path. A clear path.

"Perfect. I've also taken the liberty of handing in your resignation at Club Edge. You will not be going back there."

"I'm not going back to the club?" I suck in a breath and grip the edge of the sheet.

"No."

I didn't know that the night of the auction would be my last. A sense of relief washes over me that I never knew I would feel.

"I don't want you working at the café either," he adds. "But you can resign from there yourself. You seem to have more of a special relationship with them."

"I do." Kelly will be sad to see me go but she'll understand. She knew I'd be leaving as soon as I could get back on my feet.

"Of course, your work at the school and the dance company can continue as you see fit. We'll talk about all the other details when I next see you."

"When will that be?"

"Saturday morning. You have until then to move your stuff to my place."

My God. I didn't think of that side of the deal at all—moving in with him and living together.

"Okay." I swallow past the constriction in my throat and try to breathe around the sudden adrenaline pumping through my veins.

"You will also need to speak to your father and Gina. Tell them whatever story you like, except the truth. Tell them we got back together."

That's going to be hard. Not for Gina, but Dad is going to hate me. "Okay."

"I can't risk anyone knowing the truth. I hope you understand that."

Instantly, I think of Eden. "I understand completely, but please can I tell my best friend? It's easier to make something up to tell my father and Gina but I can't keep something like this from Eden."

"River, this is serious shit, and my legacy is on the line."

That makes me question his reasons for needing a wife even more.

"You have Luc. He knows about this plan of yours." I talk fast before he can cut me off. "I promise you on my life that Eden is just as trustworthy as Luc. She would never say anything to ruin either of us." I pray he doesn't say no given the fact that I've already spoken to her.

"Alright." He nods, but I can still see his reluctance. "She'll need to sign an NDA but please make her aware that if she breaks her silence there'll be hell to pay."

"I understand."

"Well, we shouldn't have a problem then. I'll need you to read the contract and sign it today. I'll have my assistant pick it up along with Eden's NDA at midday."

"That's okay. I'll have everything ready."

"Great. Looks like we're in business. See you on Saturday."

"See you then."

He tears his gaze away from me then heads out the open door.

I watch him until I can't see him anymore before I allow everything to sink in.

We're getting married.

I'm marrying Jericho Grayson, my ex-boyfriend.

In one month's time I'll be his wife.

This is going to be one hell of a business deal but I'm not sure which will make me crazy first. Jericho or my father.

Chapter SEVENTEEN

River

"No." Dad holds up his hand to stop me from saying anything else. "Absolutely not." The wrath in his grimace could incinerate me if such a thing were possible.

I've just dropped the bomb on him that Jericho and I got back together, and we're getting married next month.

At first Dad looked at me as if I'd lost my mind. Now he looks like he wants to strangle me.

The angle I've gone with is that Jericho and I ran into each other months ago and realized we should never have broken up.

I mixed truths with lies and deserve an award for my acting skills because I served up a story so believable, I could believe it myself.

It took me several hours to gather the courage to speak to Dad. I would have left it until tomorrow or even another time, but as Gina's surgery is scheduled for later today I wanted to get it off my chest as early as possible so I can keep my focus on her.

I wish I could have told Gina first, but when I got to the hospital she was asleep and looked so much worse than she did yesterday. The fearful thought hit me that we might just be in time to save her with this surgery.

"Dad—"

"I said no," he clips. "How dare you do this? There's no way in hell you'd think I'd be okay with you marrying that boy. No way."

"Dad, this isn't about you."

"Jesus, girl, how can it not be about me? You're my daughter, and you're about to marry Tobias Grayson's son. *Tobias Grayson.* The same fucking guy who made my life hell for so many years. High school, college, and after. How do you think I'm going to feel on your wedding day while he's standing there with his wife, and I'll be there in my wheelchair? *Me*—divorced, paralyzed, and on minimum wage."

God knows I understand where he's coming from, but there's a bigger picture to think about.

"Dad, I completely understand how you feel but this is my life we're talking about." I feel absolutely terrible for lying to him and for the same lies I plan to tell Gina, but this is what you call survival. Everyone will thank me in the end, including my father.

"I can't believe this. You've been lying to me this whole time."

"I didn't mean to."

"But you did. On Sunday when I saw you, you had every opportunity to tell me you were seeing him but you kept it from me."

That was when he was ranting about Tobias on TV.

"Jericho proposed this morning. I didn't know things were going to get so serious."

Dad gives me an incredulous glare. "That's not good enough. At least Sasha had the balls to ask me for your hand in marriage and propose to you in front of people who mattered to him. And he had a fucking ring." He glares at my bare finger. "That's love and decency."

My blood heats and I can't restrain the hot flash of anger that flows through me. "I keep telling you Sasha didn't love me, so for the love of God, please stop talking about him." My voice is way too loud but I can't help it.

"You think this Jericho is a saint? He's not. He's the same kind of asshole as his father. Just look on the Internet. It's all there for you to see. You know I'm not lying to you or trying to poison your mind against him. It's there in plain sight. Him with one woman or another. That guy is not good for you."

"He can take care of me," I snap back. "He didn't even hesitate to pay for Gina's surgery when he found out she needed it." I told him that already but he just glossed over it.

He winces and grits his teeth. "I'm not against saving Gina but we could have fought harder to find another way. Seriously, River, don't you think there was another way to get that money?"

His crude words cover me like droplets of fire. They sear into my mind, burning straight through to my heart, and I realize there's more I have to tell him to set him straight.

"Dad, I've been working at Club Edge for nearly two months," I blurt, staring back at him with sharp eyes.

His face pales at my declaration. I always thought I was going to have to explain to him what Club Edge was, but he knows.

"What the hell are you saying to me?"

I swallow hard and try not to cry. "You heard me, so please don't ask me if there was nothing more I could do. I did *everything*. But what about you? What did you do? You have the audacity to bring up Sasha, but all those times when he hit me, you told me to stay. That's what you did, and you didn't come for me when I was seconds away from death. Gina did. She was so sick, yet she still came through for me." I don't realize I'm shaking until I look at my hands and see the tremor in my fingers. "I hope you never know what it's like to have a gun pointed at your head while you pray your next breath won't be your last."

Anguish fills his face and he reaches out to me, but I step back. "River—"

"No. Don't. There's nothing to say."

"These people think they're gods because they have money."

"I'd rather be with a guy who can take care of me and my family than one who could get me killed." I dry my tears. "We're getting married, whether you like it or not, Dad."

"Well, I guess there's nothing I can do, is there?" He stares back at me and I watch the stubbornness leave his face, but the tension remains.

"I would really appreciate it if you didn't make this difficult. It doesn't have to be. I'm getting married, and I'm asking you to try to accept Jericho. He's never done anything bad to me."

My words sound lifeless and I'm so drained out from everything that I can't muster the emotional conviction I need to convince him to support me.

Despite my exhaustion, I'll admit that it's partly because the girl inside me is still hurt by what Jericho did all those years ago, but it's time to get over it.

My entire body sighs with relief when Dad nods.

"I'll do it for you, but I'll never be happy about this."

"Okay." I suppose that's the best I'll get out of him, and I'll have to accept it.

By midday I'd handed over my contract along with Eden's NDA to a well-dressed posh elderly man called Brady, who introduced himself as Jericho's assistant and custodian.

Three hours later Gina had her surgery, which was a success and a relief off my shoulders. Just seeing Dr. French looking optimistic gave me hope and encouragement that Gina would be okay now.

More than anything, I felt like I'd given Gina the chance my mother never had. I also imagined Mom smiling at me with the deepest gratitude for saving her sister, a woman who is a literal angel walking on earth.

While Gina has spent the last few days recovering, I've been preparing for my new life by moving.

On Friday night Eden and I moved all my things—which technically wasn't that much—to Jericho's luxury oceanfront home in the Hamptons.

Eden and I were completely stunned to silence when we found out where he lived, but when we actually saw the house, the two of us had the kind of star-struck experience you have when you see how the other half lives.

Jericho's home has six bedrooms and the same number of bathrooms, two living rooms with ornate fireplaces and artwork on the walls. He has an outdoor pool and private access to the beach, a gym, two garages filled with all sorts of luxury cars and motorcycles. The grounds are also extensive enough to fit the same size house on it twice over.

I have my own room, which is breathtakingly beautiful with a terrace balcony offering a scenic view of the sea. I am also told one of the storage rooms will be turned into a dance studio so I can practice.

The extravagance of everything is impressive and, for once, as daunting as this all is, I have that Cinderella feeling in a good way. Like I'm in an actual fairytale and not some twisted version where villains like my evil stepmother and sister win the happily ever after.

It might be a temporary fix but it hits the spot and at the very least soothes the angst I felt after arguing with my father.

But… I haven't seen Jericho yet. I'm eager to learn the extra details of our arrangement and to have some idea of what will happen next.

I heard he was working, but I expected to catch a glimpse of him at some point. It seems, though, that he hasn't been here at all. At least his staff have been nice and really accommodating toward me.

Saturday morning comes and I wake with the sun. It dawns on

me that I don't know what time I'll be seeing Jericho, so I decide to get dressed and stick to my loose plan of heading to the studio to practice.

Jericho knows I have rehearsal with the dance company in the evening, so unless I'm told otherwise, I figure he'll probably see me later in the day.

It's barely seven now and the house is so quiet my footsteps on the floorboards sound out of place.

When I reach the garage and make my way past his row of Ferraris, Porsches, and the Aston Martin, to where I parked my car last night, I get the shock of my life because it's not there. As in, it's gone.

"What the hell?" I mutter to myself as I look around. "Where the hell is my car?"

"I got rid of it," the silence answers in Jericho's voice and I nearly jump out of my skin.

Across from me Jericho slides out from under the black Mustang on one of those roller trolley things mechanics use when they're fixing cars. I suddenly realize that's what he was doing.

And he's shirtless.

With a smirk on his face, he pushes to his feet, showing off the masterpiece of muscles and tattoos on his abs.

My unrestrained eyes, which have no shame, move straight to those abs and explore the peaks and valleys chiseled in the expanse of each muscle group.

The boy I used to know had a six pack, a dragon tattoo on the right side of his torso, and more dragons on his arms. Knight did those for him when they owned a tattoo shop way back when.

Jericho was what the girls at school—*to my misfortune*—called lickable.

Now his chest looks like it was sculpted from rock and has more inky designs. There's a wolf and an eagle, Japanese characters mixed with Celtic swirls and Egyptian hieroglyphics. Black roses on his arms add to that hard-meets-soft look that's darn right sexy.

If I were to explain it to anyone they'd think it sounded like too much, but it's not, and each design is so intricately done to perfection, the temptation is to stare and stare and stare.

"Gonna stare at me all day, Mermaid?" he asks with a cocky grin and an equally arrogant wink.

My eyes snap up to meet his. "Um…"

"I never said I minded, especially if I get to look at you too." He scans my body the way he's done every time he's seen me.

I shake off the rising arousal clogging my throat and remember what he said about my car.

"Did… you just say you got rid of my car?" I narrow my eyes at him and fold my arms under my breasts.

"Yeah." He raises a brow. "It's a miracle that thing could even drive."

I glare at him. "You got rid of my car?" My voice is firmer, with emphasis on each word. "I had stuff I wanted inside it."

"The stuff is in the living room in a box and, no, that piece of shit is no longer *your car*. Your *new* car has been ordered from the dealer. It will be delivered sometime next week. Until then, George will drive you wherever you want."

George is his driver. I didn't see the need for him when I had my own wheels to get me around from A to B, particularly on early mornings like these when I want to go to the studio.

"There was nothing wrong with my car."

"The wheels were shit, the bodywork shit, the steering shit and just begging for an accident, the car was fucking shit. Also, no wife of mine is going to be driving around in junk like that." He intensifies his stare and nods with conviction, but I focus on that weird word in reference to me that sounded so strange on his lips.

Wife.

He said wife, and it's the first time this is really sinking in.

I'm going to be *his* wife.

I can't wrap my head around it, not even a little bit, but I must.

"In any event, where were you off to at this hour? I certainly hope it wasn't work."

"No. I practice sometimes at the dance studio."

He walks to the table opposite me, giving me a good view of the dragon tattoo inked into the muscles of his hard back. He grabs his t-shirt and pulls it on, covering the view I'm sure most women would pay for with their last cent.

"George can take you there in two hours, if that works for you." He searches my eyes.

"That works."

"Great, in the meantime we could have a quick chat about the rest of my plans."

I'm dying to find out more details about this very strange situation of ours, so I won't say no.

"I'd like that."

"Then follow me." He points to the door across from us. It's wedged open with a large wrought-iron doorstop that looks like an anvil. It looks out of place in comparison to everything else but still carries that cool edge you can't help but associate with Jericho Grayson.

I follow him as he leads the way and gear myself up to hear more about this plan of his, which I'm sure will lead me deeper down the rabbit hole.

Chapter EIGHTEEN

River

Using the side entrance, we re-enter the house. I haven't come in this way before because I've been using the main section.

This route leads into one of the narrow hallways that have paintings of landscapes and ships on the walls.

We reach his office. I've only seen the closed door and the windows from outside. It will be interesting to go inside. I've never been in a home office or known anyone who had one. Dad came close, but his was more of a workshop. At least that's what he called it.

Jericho opens the door and we walk inside. The scent of musk and leather greets me, along with mahogany furniture. There are rows of bookshelves on the wall, a drinks cabinet with an espresso machine next to it, and a wooden chessboard I recognize over by the long casement window.

He had that when he was in high school. He told me his mother made one for him and another for Knight. She sculpted all the pieces. The gift was a reminder that life can be like a game of chess.

I've always agreed. People like the Graysons are the rulers, while people like me and mine are pawns.

Jericho catches me looking at the chessboard.

"You still have that," I state.

"I've tried to take care of it over the years."

"Still the king?" I'm sure he wouldn't have it any other way.

"Yes. I'm still the king." He walks over to the board and lifts the king piece. "What about you?"

I'm not the queen. We used to have a running joke that I was. He's looking at me like he expects me to pick up the queen piece.

I don't. I stand where I am and shrug.

"Just a girl." I'm sure he can hear from the dead-weight tone in my voice that I'm a shadow of my former self. In fact, in the past, I was already a shadow but trying not to be. Life has made me so tired I can't even try anymore. I just have the energy to live and hopefully survive the next minute, the next second, and hopefully the next year of marriage to my ex.

As strange as things go for me, this is right there with them.

Jericho steps away from the chessboard, a sign that conversation is over. It's better this way. There's no point walking down memory lane if there are places you don't want to visit.

"How is Gina? Did the surgery go okay?" He studies my face and rests against the wall.

"It was a success. She's been out of it for the last few days and will probably be like that for a while yet, but she's extremely grateful. I am too. Thank you again for your help."

My skin heats with a mixture of gratitude for his effortless help and awkwardness that I needed him.

When I think back on the last few weeks—or months, if I'm being honest—I was on a one-way trip to burnout. I was never going to be able to fix everything and, yes, my pride got in the way several times, making me stubborn.

It's okay to work hard and achieve things on your own but not when the length of time to do so ends up affecting others—the people you love. The people you're working hard for. This thing with Gina would have been my downfall, and I would have hit a wall that I couldn't see my way over.

"I'm glad Gina is okay. And you can stop thanking me now." He gives me a boyish grin.

"I actually don't think I'll ever stop thanking you." I clasp my hands and touch them to my heart. "Gina means the world to me."

He nods, understanding. "I know she does, and I'm glad you don't have to worry about her like that anymore."

"You've taken a massive weight off my shoulders."

"Good." The warmth leaves his face and his gaze becomes sharper. "How about your father? Should I expect him to spit on me when I next see him?"

He raises his brows, his expression so skeptical there's no way I can bullshit him with a lie.

I sigh and drop my shoulders. "I can't promise he won't."

To my surprise Jericho smiles wide, but realistically, this reaction is typical of him.

"Your old man still hates my ass. This is going to be fun."

"I've spoken to him, and I will make sure there won't be any problems going forward."

"I'll schedule some time to meet him during the week."

My eyes widen. That's the worst idea ever. "I don't think you should do that."

"Too bad, Mermaid. I'm going to. Regardless of the past I'm marrying his daughter. It's going to look strange if I don't make the effort to speak to him before the wedding."

I remember what Dad said about Sasha asking him for my hand in marriage. Those traditions matter to my father, so maybe Jericho speaking to him will help ease the tension.

"Okay. It's not like things can get any worse."

"Oh, they can."

"What do you mean by that?" I narrow my eyes.

"Sit." He points to the leather sofa next to us.

We sit across from each other and he picks up the envelope sitting on the little table next to him.

"This is yours." He hands it to me. "Read it later. It contains all the things I need you to do and memorize by Wednesday. Think of it as an extension of our contract."

"Oh, okay." I glance at the envelope, trying to determine from its weight what could be inside. It's not heavy, but not light either.

"The person you need to focus on is my grandfather," he says, and I sense from the seriousness in his tone that he's about to tell me why he needs a wife.

"Bradford Grayson."

"The one and only." He rests back against the sofa and sighs. "He's retiring at the beginning of next year. He decided to split the company so the Park Avenue branch would be its own corporation with a new leadership structure. He's given Knight and me the chance to own it and run it, but we had to earn our stripes. Knight's done his part. Now I have to do mine."

I see exactly where this is going.

"Your grandfather wants you to get married," I fill in. Jericho nods with a strained look on his face, showing his disdain for the subject. "He just demanded that of you?"

I've heard about things like this happening all the time in the circles Jericho travels in, but there's something about this request of his grandfather's that sounds odd. Like it didn't come out of the blue.

"He thought it would fix my image after a story came out that made our investors crazy."

I was right, and I'll bet I know which one it was. "The preacher man's wife," I supply again like a human search engine.

Jericho doesn't appear surprised that I know about that story—I'd call it more of a scandal, though.

An uneasy look invades his expression. "Yes. It was that."

I should feel nothing for being right again, but instead my stomach squeezes with the twist and tightness of envy—*my old friend*.

God, I used to get so jealous when any girl would simply look at him in high school. Because we were a secret I couldn't let the world know he was with me.

I was always watching from the outside. Like I am now.

It's stupid to feel anything. That woman—*the preacher man's wife*—was a hundred percent Jericho's type and extremely beautiful.

His PR people tried to do damage control to let the world know that he wasn't aware of who she was, and if he'd known she was married he wouldn't have gone there, but she was his type. I know him. He would have done everything under the sun with her.

"I'm not a playboy, River." Jericho's voice is knife-sharp, slicing through my thoughts.

"That's none of my business."

"Maybe so, but I don't like that title. Just because someone appears to be one way, it doesn't mean they are."

I want to tell him he has a funny way of seeing things. From all the articles living on the World Wide Web about him, I would definitely conclude that he's the billionaire playboy the tabloids have labeled him. It's strange that he's trying to tell me he's not.

It's been long accepted that if something walks like a duck, acts like a duck, and flies like it, too, chances are it totally is a duck. But far be it from me to question him.

Jericho Grayson is the exception to society's rules.

"So, your grandfather thinks getting married will improve your image for the company." I decide to switch the subject back to what matters. "And you decided to do it your way."

This marriage arrangement sounds exactly like the sort of thing Jericho would do because he hates being controlled by anyone.

"Yes. And that's why you're here."

"I'm guessing the one-year stipulation means something, too." *Everything* we agree to will have some significance. His grandfather is no fool. What Jericho is trying to do here is outsmart the leader of the pack.

"We need to be married for six months before I get awarded the CFO position and my shares in the company, but if we get divorced before a year, everything will be voided."

As I stare back at him, all I can think is his grandfather must know him incredibly well.

I'd even go as far as to guess that he could have suspected Jericho might cheat the rules to do exactly what he's doing now but beneath it all, his grandfather might secretly hope things work out. *Poor man. It won't. Not with us.*

"Obviously, it goes without saying that you're not to speak about this to anyone. Not even your friend, Eden. She doesn't need to know those details." There's a tick in his jaw. A tell that he might be uncomfortable with what he's doing.

"My lips are sealed." He saved Gina, so having my silence goes without question.

"Okay, well, now that's out of the way we can get straight on to the events we need to worry about. The first is the fundraiser this Wednesday. Our engagement will be announced then. That's when the real game begins, and the press will be on you like dogs. Will you be okay with that?"

"I have to be." I don't really like having that sort of attention but it's part of the job. I had to suck it up, too, when I did interviews back in Russia and various other countries. This is way different but I'll try to think of it as the same thing.

"Good. The wedding will be next. I'll be away a lot over the next month on several business trips, so you won't see me too much until the wedding day. During that time you'll most likely have to do interviews on your own. It's important that you only give the press information in bite sizes. Don't say too much and don't say too little. In my absence Brady will talk you through what you need to do. I'll try to touch base as much as I can, but I might not always be with you."

"I'll be fine." I smile with confidence.

"Alright, then. I guess there's only one more thing left to do."

He stands and walks over to the table to pull out one of the top drawers. When he takes out a small pink velvet box, I guess what's inside.

The ring.

My ring.

My stomach squeezes for different reasons this time. Reasons that shove the envy I previously felt to the side, because I have bigger fish to fry.

Jericho returns to me and flicks the box open. Inside sits a gorgeous white diamond and platinum engagement ring that you know came from some specialist upmarket jeweler normal people would never be able to buy anything from.

The ring looks like something royalty would wear. Certainly not anybody like me, especially because I'm only playing a temporary part.

Sasha didn't give me anything that came close to this. He could have afforded something a lot nicer, but I guess back then he wanted me to believe he wasn't buying everything we owned with drug money. Although it was clear from the start that he was quite wealthy, I suppose getting a reasonable ring the average Joe could afford appeared more legit to those like the police he knew could be watching him.

Jericho reaches out his hand to take mine. My gaze flicks between his outstretched hand and the ring.

I set the envelope down and stand although I don't need to. He would be able to slip that ring onto my finger just fine with me sitting. It just feels awkward.

I give him my hand and he slips the ring onto my finger. It fits. Another surprise.

I didn't think about this part, although of course there would be a ring.

Jericho says nothing. I don't know what I expected him to say, but saying nothing hurts in an unexpected way. To counteract the hidden emotion, I act like I wasn't the girl who used to spend hours on end daydreaming about this moment.

At eighteen years old I'd already dreamed up when and where we'd get married, where we'd live, all the names for the four kids we were going to have, and what we'd do for the rest of our lives.

Little did I know I'd find myself in a juxtaposition of shit years later when Jericho would be giving me a beautiful engagement ring to be his fake wife.

Attempting to school my thoughts, I take a measured breath hoping it will clear the fog from my mind, then I think of something to say because he looks like he's expecting me to comment.

"It's beautiful." Best to talk about the ring.

"Glad you like it."

"I don't know who wouldn't." I take another breath and realize I need to do more than just breathe. I need to go outside and get some actual air. "I suppose we're done here. I'll get on to this paperwork right away."

I grab the envelope and turn to leave, wanting to get away from this situation as quickly as possible, but Jericho catches my arm.

He turns me back to face him and holds on to my hand with the ring on it.

I look at him, not knowing what to expect but the hardened look on his face throws me.

"This ring on your finger means we're officially engaged now, River." His face is a stony mask, but something dark I've never seen before lingers in his eyes.

"I know. I get it." And I wish he would let me go.

"Good, it means you will act like my fiancée at all times. This marriage might be arranged but we need to act like we're *real* in front of everyone else. That should be simple, yes?"

"It's very simple." I try to imbue my voice with poise and stare back at him with faux aloofness, as if he hasn't fazed me.

"Glad we're on the same page." He runs his eyes over me and releases my hand, but only to press his fingers to the side of my jaw.

The gesture would almost be endearing but it feels too possessive. "To clarify, we kiss for the cameras, we touch for the cameras, we look legit for the *cameras*."

His eyes hold a sheen of desire that grazes against the wall he's trying to build up between us. For a moment there's a shift in his expression, and the desire filters down to the seriousness he's trying to portray. It's confusing, and I hate it because of the warmth stirring low in my belly.

"That means away from the cameras we're friends." His finger glides down my neck, lingering by my collarbone.

"Friends?" It's almost laughable. Jericho and I have never been friends, and he doesn't feel like a friend now.

"Friends." His eyes drop to my breasts and there's no mistaking the lust creeping into his gaze. It's powerful and dark. Possessive and dominating. But then his business face returns, chasing away the desire and unwarranted lust. "Friends who will mutually benefit from a marriage, so there won't be any unnecessary kissing, no unnecessary touching, and no fucking me. Or anyone else."

Translation—*except for the part about fucking*—we won't be having a repeat of last Saturday.

My cheeks warm, but not with arousal from the memory of the wild encounter we shared. It's more like rage that he's trying to lay out the boundaries between us and I mustn't get the wrong idea. As if I'm not aware of those damn boundaries. *Newsflash, Jericho: I got that memo already. More than once.*

I guess he thinks I need the reminder because I might have behaved as if I was pining over the past when I tried to leave. I'm also not some slut who's going to sleep around and create additional scandals for him.

I want to set his silver-spooned ass straight, but I don't.

I *won't*. It wouldn't be wise to give him a piece of my mind when he's done so much to help me. But seriously, what an asshole.

"Do you understand me, River?" His stare is as sharp as the end of a needle.

"Perfectly." His words are clearer than the diamond sparkling on my finger and I know exactly what to tell his high-handed egotistical ass. "Don't worry, *friend*, I'm sure I can go a year without fucking. I'll be sure to make up for it the moment I'm released from our *fake marriage*."

I step out of his touch and Jericho's lips part but he holds back whatever he was going to say. It must be hard to keep his inner control freak at bay.

Jericho Grayson might still be the king but I have him checkmated because he has no say in what I do when this arrangement is over between us.

I already assumed we'd create some ugly story that will lead to an acrimonious divorce—he'll probably say I cheated to make himself look better with his grandfather. So my guess is we won't even see each other again after this.

"Are we done here?" I tilt my head up and level him a hard stare.

He stares at me for a second too long before he gives me a clipped nod and a ghost of a smile cracks his face. "Yeah. We're done."

"Great. Thanks." My tone is cold, callous, and aloof.

I turn away from him once more, and this time he allows me to leave. For a moment I feel a sense of triumph for what I said. It lasts until I reach outside then the gloom envelops me because I know as ballsy as I sounded, I'm not.

It doesn't matter. Nothing matters now, only that I do what I agreed to do.

I glance at the gorgeous ring on my finger. My new brand of ownership and a reminder that my new job has just begun.

Fake fiancée today.

Fake wife in one months' time.

Think of the money, River, and all the things you'll be able to do with it.

If this is the price of my freedom, I'll take it and shove the memories of the past out of my mind.

Forever.

Chapter NINETEEN

Jericho

I DON'T LIKE THE WAY SHE SAID *FAKE MARRIAGE*.
Or the way she called me *friend*.
I hated the nonchalance on River's face, too, as she basically confirmed she'd be having a fuck fest the moment the ink is dry on our divorce papers.

It serves me right that she grew a pair of balls and handed me my ass with that comment. I had it coming. Even I know I was an asshole to her. Human one minute, cold-hearted villain the next.

My gaze is fixed on the swans swimming together in the river across from me.

I'm in the park across from Royal Enterprises, Neil's workplace.

I thought meeting somewhere neutral would be best so I chose the park. It's somewhere he can get to in five minutes, and it won't feel like an intrusion like if I'd gone to his home.

Neil agreed to meet with me here at noon. That's in ten minutes.

I got here early to establish the comfort and control I'll need for this meeting I really don't want to have.

It would help immensely if I could get my head together and stop thinking about River being with other men.

I can't blame her for what she said to me. Not for any of it.

It's just that thinking about River being with some other guy has riled me up in all the wrong ways I shouldn't feel.

Our marriage *will* be fake, so she'd be entitled to be with whomever she wants when it's over. In fact, she wouldn't even need to wait. Being fake means not real, so it wouldn't be cheating.

And what about me? The same could be said for me.

Since the preacher man's wife scandal I've been more careful. So careful I haven't been with a woman in months. A first for me.

But then there's also the matter of being so fixated on my ex I could hardly think straight when it came to choosing a wife.

Now the possessive bastard inside me can't leave well enough alone.

It's Monday, I've been going crazy all weekend, and I'm still torturing myself at the worst possible time.

I haven't seen Neil in years so I need to be on my game. The last time we spoke was on the doorstep of the house he used to live in.

I'd decided I wasn't sneaking in anymore. It was just before shit went down and he lost the use of his legs. I'd wanted to make River and me official, so I showed up at the door.

Neil told me to get off his property, then he followed that up with telling me that if he had a gun he'd shoot me. I believed him. There wasn't anything in his threat to not believe.

Had Neil not been my girlfriend's father, I would have responded by telling him he should try it, and I'd fuck him up all six ways to Sunday. I'm glad I held my tongue because it was the following week that I found out that my device was the instrument used to steal his designs.

The next time I saw him he was in his wheelchair, but he didn't see me. Neither did anyone else. I wasn't there to be seen.

God knows what kind of meeting we'll have today.

I'll have to lie through my teeth about my *fake arranged marriage* to his daughter.

It's strange I haven't thought of the end yet, but I know it's something I need to start thinking about. That will need to look more legit than us being together for both our sakes. Mine more so, because of my grandfather.

The sound of wheels against the pavement makes me turn.

It's Neil.

He's already looking at me, staring me down as he draws closer.

On seeing him in his wheelchair, shame and guilt rush over me with the kind of deep, raw emotion that I couldn't begin to explain to anyone.

I wish the accident never happened. I accept that he hates me, but I'd give anything in this world for him to get up and walk out of that chair.

Even if it was to come over and punch me.

Guilt is already riding my shoulders like the devil, but then the nerves in my stomach knot so tightly I expect them to combust. It's an odd feeling for me. I'm not a nervous person, but this man… he gives me all kinds of nerves.

Back when his designs were stolen my initial instincts told me it had something to do with me. I knew the moment I saw the story on the news that something like that couldn't just happen by accident.

You'd need someone like me to get into the system. I found out I was right when I tracked the activity of the hackers to establish how it all happened. Everything leaves a digital signature. No matter how well you clean it, people like me can find it.

The device they used took me straight back to its creation in my room at MIT.

That's how I knew it was me.

Neil's face hardens to stone when he reaches me. His expression is so tense he could pass for one of the statues around us, but I don't let his I-don't-want-to-be-here attitude bother me.

"Neil St. James. Thank you for coming out to meet with me." I hold out my hand to shake his.

He looks at my hand as if it's diseased, then waits for a few awkward seconds before extending his for a brief handshake.

I'm surprised he touched me. I suppose stranger things have happened.

"I've heard the news," he puffs, and his skin reddens. "I assume you want to talk about my daughter."

"Yes. I thought it was right that I speak with you. Out of respect." Although I'd rather be pulling out my damn teeth. The man has the emotional range and personality of a rock.

"Wow, at least we can agree on that. Although I will tell you that you are a poor choice for my daughter. You Grayson people only care about yourselves and your power over others. I never wanted my daughter mixed up with any of you."

Well, damn, not even a minute into the conversation and he's already spoken his mind. Typical Neil. At least you know where you stand with him.

"I can assure you that your daughter will be well taken care of."

"The internet is littered with articles about you. How am I supposed to believe someone like you can take care of my daughter?"

"Because I'm telling you." I use the firm tone I normally reserve for my staff. "I'm also a changed man."

"I'll believe that when I see it." He squints and tilts his head. "Jericho Grayson, one of the things I've always wanted for my daughter is marriage for love."

I grit my teeth and straighten. I wanted River to have that too. With the sordid views I have on marriage, I always ask myself what I would have wanted for us eventually had she and I stayed together.

At twenty-one marriage was the furthest thing from my mind. All I knew when I left for college was that I wanted my girl with me.

"I had real love with her mother. River will remember that," Neil continues.

I never knew River's mother but from what I've been told she was like Gina, so I'm not surprised Neil didn't mention his second wife. It was obvious Brielle didn't marry him for love. The real kind or otherwise.

"I'm sure she will."

"Exactly. We were good examples for her, which is why I don't believe there's any way you could have waltzed back into her life after so long and she thinks you're in love."

He's not wrong. "Well that's exactly what happened. She loves me and I love her." As I say those words it doesn't feel weird, or like a lie. Maybe because I'm talking about River, and I've said those words to her father before. Saying them now feels like an echo from the ghost of the guy I used to be.

Neil silently assesses me with his hawk eyes then he gives me an arrogant glare, lifting his chin so he can stare at me over the bridge of his nose.

"I hope so." His jaw tenses and he rests his hands on the arms of his wheelchair. "I hope so for your sake. I'm only going along with this marriage because there isn't anything I won't do for my daughter when it's in my power to give."

"I suppose that's the best I can hope for."

"It's the best you're gonna get from me, and God help you if you hurt her."

Neil doesn't wait for my answer. He spins his chair around and wheels away, leaving me standing there with the buildup of words I wish I could have said gnawing away at my insides.

That man is a threat to me. A threat I can't ignore. I need to ensure I don't give him anything to use against me.

Anything more than his hatred for me being Tobias Grayson's son.

Thanks, Father.

This is one more thing to add to the very long list of ill-fated shit that comes with being your son.

Wednesday night descends on me way too fast.

Tonight is the big night, when River meets everyone and the world will know she's my fiancée.

I just want to get everything over with. Whatever happens tonight will guide the decisions of tomorrow.

Tonight will also be the first since Saturday that I'll see River.

I spoke to her on the phone earlier so we could go over everything in preparation for later. She definitely didn't disappoint. She remembered everything I gave her to study in the file. Now we just have to put ourselves on show.

I just got home from a long, long day at work, and we're supposed to be leaving in a few minutes. *Oh, the joy.*

I'm already dressed and ready to go, but I need a glass of scotch and a Cohiba to get my head in check.

I head to my office to grab both and savor them while I read over the business plans for the rest of the week.

Knight and I are working on a new project alongside the Arizona one so we're going to be living on a plane for the rest of the month.

Our goal is to increase existing revenue by four million by the end of the year and double it by the end of next. Knight and I have worked together like one brain since we were in our late teens interning at the company.

He has the knack for property development, whereas I turn everything I touch into serious money. Like King Midas, I have the golden touch to create fortunes.

The best thing about what we're doing now is that it will be all about us, the first leaders of what will be Graysons LP when Grandfather retires. That's history in the making. History I want to be a part of.

A knock on the door disturbs my ambiance.

I had one more minute left to myself.

"Who is it?" I gruff.

"It's me, Jericho." That's Lauren, my head maid.

She pushes the door open and pokes her blonde head in with a proud smile brightening her face. The staff like her who've worked with me since I was an infant are loving the fact that I'm engaged. They were the first to know, and of course they're celebrating as though it's real.

"Everything okay?" I take a drag on my cigar.

"Perfect. Just letting you know River is ready and she looks absolutely breathtaking. You will be a hundred percent satisfied with your bride-to-be."

I return her smile and set down my drink. I have no doubts that River looks breathtaking or that I'll be satisfied. The problem is being overly satisfied.

"Thank you. I'll be out in a minute."

"No worries. Have fun at the fundraiser." She places a hand on her necklace and grins back at me. "I'm sure everyone will be so excited to hear the news of your engagement. Congratulations again, Jericho."

That would be the millionth time she's congratulated me. I didn't know so many were eager to see me married off. I suppose most of the people around me are like parents and grandparents who wish you well no matter how ruthless you can be at times.

"I appreciate that."

"See you later," she pipes, clasping her hands together in glee.

Lauren leaves on that note. I down my drink and take one last drag on my cigar before I put it down and leave, too.

When I reach the hallway with the grand sweeping staircase that won me over to buying this place, I'm just in time to watch River making her descent.

As I stare at her in the silver-slash-nude strapless gown hugging her body my mind goes numb, and all my thoughts evaporate.

Literally every ounce of thought I've carried in my mind all day, it's gone, and my only focus is her.

The gown's bodice and long flowing skirt are covered in gemstones from head to toe. The thigh-high split gives a great view of her sun-kissed legs and, fuck me, that glorious red hair pulled back in a high ponytail completes the look of temptation.

To say River looks breathtaking doesn't come close. This woman has a body made for sin, and poor souls like me are fucking hopeless in her presence.

She gives me a tight-lipped smile when she sees me, which grows into something more polite when she reaches me, reminding me that she's still mad about the way I spoke to her on Saturday.

"Hi." She sounds mad, too. She was a little perkier on the phone earlier, so I thought she'd be less tense by the time I got home.

"Hey, you look great." I'm trying for subtle.

"Thank you." Her tone is simple and I can tell that, once again, she has no idea whatsoever of the effect she has on people or how stunning she is. "Ready when you are."

"That would be now."

I put my hand out to take hers. She gives me her dainty hand with the engagement ring on it—*my* engagement ring.

Something primal flashes through me at the sight of it on her finger, knowing it makes her mine. That's real. I'm looking at it on her body. A symbol that she belongs to me regardless of the arrangements we've made.

God help me tonight. I think this is going to be so much harder than I thought.

River St. James is the chink in my armor.

But then she always was.

Chapter TWENTY

Jericho

WE GO OUTSIDE, WHERE GEORGE IS WAITING IN THE Maybach.

We get in, then we're off, but I'm fucked because I can't stop looking at River.

The drive to the Astoria is an hour and a half in the evening traffic. I've spent forty-five minutes of that time stealing glances at my wife-to-be while we drive in silence.

She's been looking out the window, and I've been shamelessly staring at her breasts, the curves of her waist and hips, then down to the smooth skin of her thighs where the dress splits.

Every time she almost catches me staring I look away, but I know she can see me watching. I haven't been completely covert.

"You should have added unnecessary looking to your list, too," she says when my gaze returns to the rounded swells of her breasts.

"What?" I heard her. I just want her to clarify.

"I said you should have added *unnecessary looking* to your list."

I grin back at her for taking that ballsy attitude with me again. It's even sexier tonight.

She gives me a sharp stare with those green eyes of hers that I could swim in and raises perfectly arched brows.

"A man can look, can't he?"

"Not when he's not supposed to be looking." She smirks, batting long thick lashes at me.

"You look beautiful."

"Thank you," she says after a few beats, but there's that polite tone again.

I don't like it but I realize she's setting boundaries, too, so I think of something safer to talk about.

"Are you nervous?"

"A little. I've never been to the Astoria before so I don't know what to expect. Eden played there once for a function. She says it's beautiful."

"It is. You'll like it."

The Astoria is an invite-only association for the world's elite which hosts a number of fundraisers and other gatherings. It's also the only social club I can tolerate where I can coexist with my father's side of the family.

"Sounds like I will." She nods but then looks more nervous. "This will also be the first time I meet your family, even though I know of them."

That's right. Tonight will be the first introduction of us as a couple.

It's strange when I think back to the reasons for our secret romance.

We're a different kind of secret.

"It'll be fine," I assure her, but it's for my benefit, too.

"Yeah. I'm sure we will." She knows that I'm the sort of ruthless that will make it okay because failure is not an option.

"Yeah."

We stare at each other for a moment before she goes back to looking out the window. I do the same, but on my side.

Not long after that we reach the Astoria and I can see the press already waiting outside.

River spots them, too, and looks back at me.

"Seems like it's showtime." Her voice rises a little.

"You ready?"

"Yes."

The moment the car pulls up the press are on us and my, oh, my, do they go crazy when River steps out and I slip my arm around her, making it overtly obvious that we're a couple and she is my leading lady tonight.

Flashes from the cameras go wild, looking like a lightning storm, but with her pressed up against me all I can focus on is the feel of her soft body and the sweet magnolia scent of her.

River is a natural, smiling for the cameras, showing off her decadent beauty. She gives the pack just the right amount of attention as if she's done this all her life.

"Jericho Grayson, who is the gorgeous beauty with you tonight?" the nearest reporter asks. He's an artsy-looking guy with a Van Gogh mustache.

"Why don't you let her tell you?" I lift my chin toward River, giving her the go-ahead to speak.

"I'm River St. James." She smiles wider, and I can tell the press love her just from that smile. It's the kind of endearing and winning smile that I need to redeem myself from my past scandals.

Translation—she will paint me in all the right colors I need to look like one of the future leaders of Grayson Inc.

One of the female reporters spots River's engagement ring and alerts the others like a vulture who's just spotted a fresh carcass.

"Oh my gosh, is that an engagement ring?" she shrieks, looking from River to me.

"You'll find out later." Of course, that's as good as confirmation, so more questions are thrown our way but I hit them with my trademark cocky smirk and usher River away from them.

We look at each other before we step inside, silently acknowledging that was round one and we both know we did well.

Once we walk inside the Astoria River's eyes grow wide with amazement as she takes in the marble floors and the Renaissance paintings on the walls and ceiling.

I've been here so often that I forgot what it's like when you first see the place.

This part of the building looks Vatican-inspired with décor common to that in European opera houses. There are other rooms and halls in the Astoria with a similar style, so this is just the beginning. I'm glad River looks so taken with the place.

We move toward the hall where the fundraiser is being held and walk right into round two when my grandparents, Knight, and Aurora notice us.

This is it. The moment we've been building up to. Time to survive it.

As we make our way over to them, I study each member of my family in turn. Grandfather, Grandma, Knight—who looks so relieved to see me with my mystery girl that a weight appears to have lifted off his shoulders—and then there is Aurora, his wife.

Holding hands, they look like the model couple the magazines have deemed them to be. Aurora's platinum blonde hair looks lighter against the room lights. Next to Knight her dainty features make him appear sharper and stronger.

Everyone is also loving that her baby bump has just started to show.

That was the news today, which I'm sure Grandfather was pleased with.

People gobble up those types of stories, and now they think Knight looks like a family man. The kind of person who wins over a crowd and multi-million-dollar clients.

Grandma is the first to greet us when we walk up to them.

Dressed in an elegant sapphire gown with her silver hair rolled into a perfect chignon, she looks amazing as usual.

She does her ritual hug and squeeze of my cheeks. They were chubby for most of my childhood and she took every opportunity she could to squeeze them.

My face is more chiseled now and the only resemblance I bear to my childhood self is my eyes, but that hasn't stopped my grandmother.

With the ritual over, all eyes switch to River.

"Hi, everyone," she says sweetly with a little wave of her hand. The hand with her engagement ring—which they notice, too, and smile back at her.

"Hello," Grandfather answers, as if speaking for the entire Grayson clan.

"Everyone, this is my fiancée, River St. James." The words outside my head sound strange now that they're out in the open. "River, these are my grandparents, my brother Knight, and Aurora, my sister-in-law."

"Great to meet you all," River says, placing a hand over her heart. That's not an act. That's really her.

"Oh my gosh, my heart is full," Grandma gushes with tears in her eyes. She's always and ever the overdramatic one. "Welcome to the family, dear. You are absolutely breathtaking."

"Thank you so much."

Of course, Grandma has to hug River and me once more.

"It's an absolute pleasure to meet you," Grandfather says, extending his hand to shake River's.

"You, too." River smiles.

The two shake hands, then he looks at me and nods with approval.

The simple gesture and the proud look in his eyes slide the weight off my shoulders, and I give myself credit. I'm more than halfway there.

Knight and Aurora pull us into an engaging conversation, which eases River into telling them all how we met.

For this I had to mix the truth with amplified lies, so I kept the truth that we met in high school. That was just in case anyone checks River out and realizes we went to the same school. I also thought the length of time we'd known each other would sound more acceptable and not like we're arranged. *Or fake.*

The story switches up to when we ran into each other months ago. I didn't want to bring our high school relationship into it. That was for Knight's benefit. He's aware I went through dark shit around that time but I've never given him any details.

Everyone looks impressed with our story, and I feel more relaxed that I won them over.

As the night wears on we catch the attention of many others, including my father and his bitch wife, Sloane, who looks down her nose at me.

They never speak to Knight and me unless they have to, so I don't worry about them.

The time comes when Grandfather announces our engagement and the press swarm us again for more pictures and more questions. We're stuck with them for at least half an hour. It's more time than I've ever given them but this is part and parcel of the show, which makes Grandfather look even more pleased with me.

The press gobble up our romance story, oohing and awwing at all the sentimental parts River and I serve them on a platter.

I know without a doubt we'll be all over the news tomorrow on every newspaper and channel. Our story will be selling for weeks because I was the least likely of my three brothers to get married.

"Can we get a kiss?" asks a petite brunette, readying her camera.

"Of course," I reply, pulling River closer to me.

Our eyes lock for a flash of a second, and I take in the beautiful emerald with specks of hazel color of her eyes. This would be the first time we've kissed since that date night. I prepared for this and tried to school my mind but, when my lips touch hers, the alluring taste of her mouth becomes the gateway to my destruction.

It's the pathway to every sinful need I've ever felt for her. Raw, carnal desire rips through my body, tearing at my soul and all the walls I erected to keep me from wanting her.

I don't want to stop, and as soon as we pull apart I want more, so much damn more.

River thinks the boundaries I put up between us are for her. To set her straight about what we are and what we can't be.

They're not.

They're for me.

"Well done, brother," Knight says, resting his arm on the glossy counter. "You two make a good couple."

"Thank you."

We're at the bar. This is the first chance we've had to ourselves.

Grandma dragged River and Aurora off to gossip with her friends, and Grandfather is with his, probably playing poker. Any opportunity for a game.

We've been here for close to four hours. It's been a successful night and a good one too, if I do say so myself.

Knight and I each have a glass of whiskey. He raises his to toast, and I do the same for tonight's success.

"To your upcoming wedding and your new life." Knight sounds proud. It's not often that I get that from him in regard to me. Nowadays, he looks like that with anything to do with Aurora or their baby.

"To your new life too, father-to-be."

He chuckles and we clink our glasses. "I still can't believe it. We find out next week what we're having."

"What do you want?" I'm genuinely interested to know.

Knight's smile widens and I can't get over how content he looks.

"I just want a healthy baby and for my Aurora to get through it all. I've been reading way too much about pregnancy and labor."

I stare back at my brother, feeling like I'm trapped in an alternate reality. The one with this new version of Knight. In the one where I belong he used to talk about fast cars, hot women, anything to do with business, and art.

This Knight has a real thirst for life and seems to become more obsessed with his wife and child with every passing day. That said, even though I don't have a paternal bone in my body and I hate that I was forced to find a wife, I can accept it's good to hear him talk like this. He truly seems to be complete.

"She'll be okay, and you'll get that healthy baby," I assure him.

"Thank you." He rests a hand on my shoulder. "I think this girl is good for you, Jericho. You actually said the word *baby* without looking like you're going to barf."

I smirk. "I guess some things change."

"They certainly do but, yeah, River is definitely good for you." He nods with approval. "And she's certainly getting on well with Aurora. You'd think they've known each other for years."

"I know." I thought the same thing.

"That's a good thing. Everything seems to be good. I was starting to worry about you for a minute there."

"Nothing to worry about, as you can see."

"I can, and I guess this means you're definitely enroute to getting the CFO position." He raises his glass again, and I follow.

"Enroute."

"You pretty much have it in the bag. Grandfather was talking about going ahead with the company separation when he awards you the role instead of when he retires."

My spirits lift on hearing that. "That would be great. We'd be in complete control over Park Avenue sooner rather than later." More importantly, we'd be free from our father. That part would be even better.

I've worked with him a few times since Grandfather asked me to take over Bastian's duties. It's a good thing I have the backbone and tolerance to deal with my father's shit now because every time I've seen him has been horrendous.

He was pissed as fuck that his precious Bastian was sent to Hong Kong and even more pissed that he had to work with me. I truly, truly can't wait for the day when I don't have to see him anymore.

"I'm working on Grandfather. I think he just needs that final assurance but I'm sure he can see that we're ready to take the lead."

"We always were," I say with reflection, thinking about how hard we've worked since we were in our teens.

Knight bows his head. "It sure has been one hell of a road. Tonight gets us one step closer. Your wedding will be another." He looks over my shoulder and grins. "Duty calls, brother. Our girls are back."

I follow his gaze and see that River and Aurora have returned. River is looking right at me as she glides across the hall.

All the kisses we shared tonight flow right back into my mind and lust shoots straight to my dick, making me rock-hard for her again.

This is where I'm supposed to control myself, but those reins have slipped right out of my grasp.

"I guess this is goodnight, then," Knight chuckles, but I barely register he's spoken.

I'm already on my feet moving toward the beautiful mermaid, loving how the light bounces off her silky hair. It makes her look like she just stepped out of a dream. *My dream.*

We meet in the middle and desire compels me to kiss her again, but I stop myself. The cameras are gone now. There's no need to continue the act.

Except I was never acting.

I indulge myself by leaning close to the shell of her ear and inhaling her scent. I want to lick her skin, and other things that will get me in trouble.

"Ready to go?" I ask, brushing my cheek against hers.

"Yeah. I guess it's late." She smiles.

"Did you have a good time?" I straighten, facing her.

"I did. Your family were all nice."

"*All*?" She knows I'm referring to my father and Sloane because hell hasn't frozen over yet, so there's no way they'd be nice to anybody.

"The family that counts." She grins.

"That's better. Also, you did good."

A soft smile spreads across her beautiful doll face. "Thank you."

I nod and take her hand. A delicate blush colors her cheeks and flushes down her elegant neck, but she looks away and waves to Aurora, who is back in Knight's arms with his hand resting on her belly.

Hand in hand we make our exit and slip into the car, which is already waiting for us when we get outside.

The moment we sit River's dress rides up her thighs, and I'm screwed with the same kind of curse that got me on the way here.

My eyes are glued to her smooth, silky skin as George sets off, and I'm so fixated I don't even look away when River catches me checking her out.

"You're doing the unnecessary looking thing again," she states, glancing at me.

I tear my gaze away from her thighs and meet the amused expression on her face.

I stare back at her and decide to be myself. That way I can rebel *against* myself.

"Yeah, I guess I am."

"Just for the record," she leans close, "that's not how *friends* look at each other."

I touch her face and trace the outline of her neck. "No, it's not, but you know me and rules."

"I do." She purses her glossy lips, directing my attention to her mouth. "No pun intended, *friend*."

I'm about to kiss that smart, sassy mouth of hers, but the mermaid moves out of my grasp and makes a point of staring out the window.

Fuck me.

This is what you call beating me at my own game. And she's good at it. Along with being too beautiful and sexy for her own good.

River keeps up the show of ignoring me for the entire journey home. Not once does she look at me while my eyes are all over her.

I get a moment of reprieve from my lust-stricken haze when we walk inside the house but the moment we're in the hallway and she advances ahead of me, my eyes go straight to her ass, screwing with me all over again.

"Goodnight." River tosses the word over her shoulder like an old jacket she doesn't want.

I stop in my tracks and watch her getting away from me. I should allow her to leave, to run from me if she needs to.

It would be best for both of us if we parted ways here and said goodnight or goodbye for now. That is exactly what I'd need from the business relationship I expect from our marriage.

After tonight she'll hardly see me until our wedding day.

No contact with each other for close to a month is perfect but as I watch her go I realize I can't say goodnight or goodbye for now just yet.

Because I want what I never got from her the other week.

I want what I haven't had from her in eight years.

I want to explore all the ways her body has changed from the shy eighteen-year-old girl I left behind.

And… I need her.

I actually need her as badly as my next breath. Fuck reasoning and rules, exceptions, and all my sins from the past. I need her *now*.

The thought pushes me forward and I rush toward her, catching her arm just as she's about to turn the corner.

"Jericho—"

I don't give her a chance to stop me. I yank her to my chest and crush my lips to hers.

The kiss I give her is the kind that says 'you make me horny as fuck and I want to fuck the hell out of you'.

It's the kind of kiss you keep to yourself, not because it's secret but it's too scandalous. Although I've never cared about that. I'd kiss her just like this wherever and whenever I want.

She only encourages my reckless behavior by kissing me back.

I shove her up against the wall but the moment gives her the chance to turn her face away from me.

"What are you doing?" River asks breathlessly.

"I want you." I nibble the side of her neck.

Her eyes meet mine again. "Friends aren't supposed to want each other."

"You and I are not friends, River St. James." I plant more kisses along the side of her neck and lick the shell of her ear like I wanted to earlier. "Friends don't want to ride the fuck out of each other."

A little moan escapes her lips and I lap up the sound. "I…"

I guide her face back to me and like a crazed lunatic I get off on the war waging in the depths of her eyes. Desire and reason clash against the logic of what we should and shouldn't do.

"Tell me I'm wrong," I challenge, stroking the hollow of her throat. She whimpers and catches her breath, trying to regain some of that bravado she had previously, but she can't.

"Remember I know you." My voice drops low at the same time my hands do, and I roll her dress up, feeling my way through the slit so I can touch her pussy. She's wet. Wet again for me. "I know what your body wants. What your body needs. You need *me*. Me to fuck you properly. The way I used to."

Her breath hitches and her cheeks are so red they almost match her hair. "You said no unnecessary touching or kissing. Or fucking."

"This is necessary." I kiss her again, and she kisses me back, unyielding and without restraint. *Good.* This is how I want her. This is what I want.

River melts against me, pushing her breasts into my chest.

I want to lose control for one damn night. Just one night, then I'll reconvene.

"Tell me, Mermaid. Are you on the pill?" I whisper along her lips.

"Yes."

"Good, because I want to fuck you raw."

Chapter TWENTY-ONE

River

As soon as I give Jericho my answer, his lips move right back to mine for a ravaging kiss that makes the blood dance in my veins and sizzle as if I've been thrown into the fire.

Jericho's touch was already intense, but I'm unprepared for the fierceness of his need when he pauses our kissing to pull me into the closest room—*the piano room.*

A dim light snaps on the moment we enter and crash back against the wall. There he continues devouring my lips like a man starved of sustenance for

centuries. Whatever was holding him back before has unleashed and infiltrated my mind and body too.

I can't think, and I don't have the control to stop myself from wanting this, or wanting everything he promised, or wanting him.

Damn me and to hell with everything. I don't want to care

about the million and one things I have weighing on my mind like unwanted guests.

I don't want to think about how well we did tonight at playing the couple, or that the wedding is only a few weeks away.

I don't want to think about the past or my father's disapproval of us.

I *don't* want to think about *anything* that's not Jericho Grayson for however long I have him.

I know I'm a fool. I know where this road leads, yet I'm still a willing participant ready to travel the dangerous path of crossing the line with this man again.

Pressing his hard body into me, Jericho tears the bodice of my dress open. The dress is one of the most beautiful things I've ever worn in my life, but I don't care if it's been ruined.

With one flick of his menacing fingers, he undoes the clasp of my bra, causing my breasts to fall out. Each one is heavy with arousal and nipples so tight they hurt.

"I've wanted to suck these all night," he groans.

I gasp when he latches onto my right nipple and hungrily sucks it into his mouth. I moan into the sweet pleasure as his tongue flicks across the taught peak and swirls around and around my nipple.

On seeing my delight, he alternates from one breast to the next, giving each one the same amount of attention.

Streaks of liquid heat flow into my body, straight down into my core. Then he sinks his teeth into the tender flesh of the swells of my breast and sucks more into his mouth.

Fuck, it feels so, so unbelievably good, and this is so hot.

I was wet from before he kissed me, but now the moisture has started leaking down my inner thigh.

Moans of pleasure fall from my lips as I lose myself in his wild suckle and I writhe against him, riding the shockwaves of delight surging throughout every atom in my body.

I don't even care that I'm so loud someone could hear me. The staff who live in stay on the other side of the house and would have probably retired to bed already. Still, the kitchen isn't that far from us, so there's nothing to stop someone from roaming by and hearing me.

Hearing *us*.

I still don't care, and neither does Jericho.

He pulls back with a wicked smirk, then rolls my dress down my body in one fluid motion, taking it off and throwing it to the side.

"Time to feast on you, Mermaid." He tweaks my nipples playfully then rips my panties off in the same pirate bodice-ripping manner he used with my dress.

He stares at my naked body with wild eyes, his chest heaving and his jaw clenched.

That wildness sends thrills racing through me. It's like my heart didn't start beating until this very moment. The way he wants me makes me feel like…

Like I'm everything and not Little Miss Shy Girl from the wrong side of the tracks.

Jericho drags his shirt off over his head, and I admire the view of his beautifully sculpted body.

Lord, he's utterly exquisite, and the huge bulge of his cock pressing against his pants is making my mouth water.

Men like Michele Morrone, or whoever everyone is fantasizing about these days, have nothing on Jericho Grayson.

He is the essence of every fantasy. The man they were all built on.

And right now, he's with *me*.

When he picks me up I wrap my legs around his waist, securing my body to his.

He doesn't take his eyes off me as he carries me to the piano and sets me on top of it.

With a devastating smile, he leans in to nibble on my neck. "Spread your legs for me, River. Let me feast on your pretty pussy."

"*Yess*, do it," I moan.

"With pleasure, baby."

His dirty words send a shiver of heat coiling down my spine, then he pushes my thighs wide and lowers his mouth to my pussy, thrusting his tongue inside.

"Jericho," I moan his name out loud, and I don't stop moaning as he eats me out, pumping streaks of hot pleasure into my body.

Oh. My. God. This is everything and I don't want him to ever stop.

He licks my clit and sucks on it until I'm squirming against his face and moaning like a cat in heat. Watching him is so wild I can barely contain myself.

Just when I think he's pushed me to the brink, Jericho lifts my leg so he can bite a greedy mouthful of my ass.

I wince, but not in pain. It's a weird sensation that feels twisted and delightful in all the right ways.

"Bad girl, you like me too much."

"You just bit my ass." I giggle.

"And I'm about to do it again and again."

He does, but this time he takes slow, leisurely nibbles across my skin, trailing fire in the wake of his touch toward my inner thigh.

Laid out on the surface of the piano, I'm moaning and writhing, rocking against his face. One more lick over the slick wet opening of my passage and I come.

My orgasm is rapid and furious. An eruption of potent pleasure.

I scream his name and grab his shoulders, digging my fingers into the thick cords of hard muscle.

Jericho straightens then rips open the fly of his pants, releasing his massive cock.

I take the moment to look at it.

It's huge, longer and thicker than I remember, and so erect precum has beaded at the tip of the fat round head.

Seeing me looking at him, he grabs my ankle to pull me closer, then he shoves his rock-hard cock deep, deep, deep inside me. My breath goes short and his next thrust sends me reeling with pleasure. More pleasure than I ever thought possible. It feels so good we both groan at the same time, and I grip on to him tight again to keep myself from drifting away.

"Fuck, you feel so fucking good, River. So fucking good."

I'm only able to answer with a desperate moan that grows louder as he starts moving inside me.

My pussy contracts around him and my body stretches with the combination of sweet pleasure and arousal as it remembers how he feels.

The memory starts flowing back, but he fractures it with his possessive touch, showing me that he's not the same guy from the past, and this is not the same thing we used to do eight years ago.

The raw difference is in his eyes as he holds me and I get the message loud and clear, then he fucks me hard, deep, and ruthlessly.

My heart pounds with the same ruthlessness, my lungs throb, then my soul shatters.

Jericho drives into me relentlessly, incinerating me from the inside out.

The mixture of my helpless cries and the sound of our flesh slapping against flesh makes me come again.

He continues hammering into me, and I don't stop coming. Jericho pushes harder in response, moving faster and faster showing me he's not finished with me yet.

After what seems like forever where he has me in this lock of perpetual pleasure a wicked smile spreads across his lips and he picks me up off the piano so we're closer. I wrap my legs around him and he drives into me so much deeper.

"Oh God!" I cry out from the intensity.

"You're mine, River. All fucking mine."

We go back to the wall, crashing against it once more. There he fucks me against the wall, and into it, like he never stopped owning my body and this is just a reminder of who I will always belong to. Every thrust feels like a new brand of possession to ensure I never forget this mark of ownership inside me.

I'm utterly lost in the wild, thrilling sensation of this man and everything about him I know I mustn't want, crave, or desire. I take it all like an addict getting their next fix.

When Jericho speeds up and his cock tenses inside my passage, I know he's reached his own climax in our wild, passionate lovemaking.

Through the haze of lust we stare at each other. Me holding onto him for dear life and him gripping my hair.

He comes inside me with a series of succinct, jolting thrusts, and the hot cum flooding my passage pushes me to orgasm one more time.

As his pumps slow to a stop and he touches my face I wonder what we'll do now.

We just had wild, raw sex on top of his grand piano, then up against the wall.

Us.

Me and him, who have been broken up for almost a decade.

Not days ago, I signed up to a fake relationship where we agreed to be married but strictly without the physical. Now look at us.

He's still buried balls deep inside me, and I want him again.

I want him again. The realization scares me. I don't want to be one of those women who are so hung up on their exes that they have no control over themselves.

But it's him—*Jericho Grayson.*

This is what he does to me. What's more scary is that I know I'd be like this whether I could control myself or not.

We stare at each other and, with sadness, I watch the confusion play out in his eyes. It's the same way he looked the other week but I'm not going to wait for him to send me away.

I pull away to move but he stops me, cups my face and kisses me.

"Stay... I'm not done with you yet." He kisses my lips, then the bridge of my nose, and moves on to my cheeks. "I'm never done with you, River."

I stare back at him, allowing those words to sink into the layers of my mind. They feel like they hold a deeper meaning than just for tonight.

"Aren't you?"

"No. Never. Spend the night with me." He holds my gaze, locking me into his allure all over again. The kind that's so spellbinding there will only ever be one answer.

"Yes," I say on the edge of a whisper.

Jericho lifts me up again and I wrap my arms around him.

"Where are we going?"

"My room. You haven't been in my bed yet." He winks at me as he carries me out of the room.

We go to his bedroom, then moments later he's inside me again.

Claiming me again.

I give myself to him.

Again, and *again*.

Chapter
TWENTY-TWO

River

I WAKE TO THE SOUND OF STILL SILENCE.

It fills the room.

Jericho's room.

I quickly remember that's where I am. Where I spent the night with him buried deep inside me, and me not wanting him to stop touching me.

We had sex all night, and it was nothing like the past.

Our adult selves took whatever we did before to a whole other level, then it was as though we were stuck on repeat, destined to repeat the same thing over and over again as soon as we'd regained our strength.

I've never felt so consumed and every inch of me feels claimed.

I can't even remember falling asleep. Now my core aches in the most delicious way, and my greedy body still wants more.

As my awareness returns fully, I open my eyes and meet the

long casement windows. The curtains are drawn but slices of sunlight are peaking through, bright enough to let me know it's not that early.

I find the clock on the wall and see it's seven. I need to be at the academy in a few hours. Not even a week ago, I would have been at Kelly's Café serving customers at this time. Now I'm lying in my ex's bed.

My ex, my fiancé, my soon-to-be husband. The man I spent the night with last night.

Is it bad that my first thought hasn't been something along the lines of: *what the hell did I do?* Or, *I can't believe I just slept with my ex*!

Honestly, my thoughts feel like they're stagnant in my mind, and I can't really pick them apart. The only thing I know for sure is that I don't regret last night, and I don't know if that's good or bad.

Yes, Universe. My life is definitely one big bundle of confusion.

I scan the masculine tones dominating the room. Midnight blue mixes with shadowy shades of gray on the walls and the wooden furniture. It reminds me of the colors you'd see before a storm. Dark and unpredictable. Just like Jericho.

Most would consider the decor gloomy, but its opulence carries that touch of elegance that speaks of Grayson wealth.

This is the first time I've been inside this room since I moved in. I like it. Everything about it feels like Jericho, and the scent of his power and presence clings to the air.

I wonder if I'll ever see the inside of this room again.

Maybe.

Maybe not...

The silence suggests I'm alone. To my knowledge, Jericho is supposed to be flying out to Arizona later for his business trip. I don't know when I'll see him again before we say *I do*.

Is he here now?

Maybe downstairs. It's early enough that he wouldn't have left for work yet, but what should I say or do when I see him?

Maybe I'm not supposed to say anything, or do anything.

Jericho asked me to spend the night with him, so maybe that just means last night was last night.

A one off.

Did I want it to be more?

Did he?

His words float back into my mind like a blissful lullaby—*I'm never done with you.*

So many things about Jericho don't make sense. Since we came crashing back into each other's lives, the one thing that's been *clear* is that he acts like he still wants me.

The auction. The date. Last night. All those events weren't part of the contract. But maybe it means nothing and I'm reading too much into a night that was only supposed to be fun.

The shuffle of footsteps outside the room catches my attention.

I sit up quickly, wondering if he's outside.

Against my better judgment I languish in the thought of seeing him again, and my body heats from the ghost of his touch moving from the top of my head to the tips of my toes.

The wild sensation stops me from thinking with my brain, and I find myself slipping off the bed and grabbing one of his worn shirts from the clothes basket by the ensuite.

I pull it on and it swamps my tiny frame, but I like the woodland forest smell of him against my skin.

I pad across the room, open the door, and make my way out.

The shuffle of footsteps sounds again, and I realize it's coming from the storage room at the end of the landing.

I move closer, gearing myself up to find him and hoping I don't have terrible bed hair.

Damn it, I didn't even check, or rinse my mouth.

No matter. I'll just pray to whoever is listening that I look and smell good enough.

"Jericho?" I call him, but Lauren steps out of the room with a set of neatly folded peach towels in her arms.

"Nope, it's only me." She greets me with a warm smile that

I return while I try to hide my obvious disappointment. "Good morning, dear."

"Good morning."

Her gaze switches from my face to the oversized shirt hanging from my body, which she knows belongs to Jericho. When her eyes sparkle, it doesn't take a genius to figure out that she knows I've just come from his room and am wearing his clothes because I've got nothing else on underneath.

"Do you know where Jericho is?" I ask, changing the focus back to him.

"Sorry, my love, he left earlier for Arizona." Lauren nods.

My brow furrows. "Oh, I thought he was supposed to be leaving later tonight."

Lauren shakes her head. "No, he said he was heading out early."

Is that strange? It's barely seven. Why would he leave so early?

Maybe it's not strange at all and I'm overthinking again, or not thinking properly at all.

Maybe his schedule changed.

Or maybe he didn't want to hang around to see me.

Why do I feel like that's the answer?

"Do you know when he'll be back?" I try to hide my disappointment again, but I'm sure I must fail because a look of sympathy crosses her face.

"No, dear, you never can tell the days apart with those Grayson boys. They're always busy. It's gotten to the point where being at home is a rarity, and this is one of those months when Jericho will be all over the place."

"I see. Did he maybe leave any message for me?" I sound desperate to my own ears, but I can't believe he'd just leave like this after the night we had.

"He didn't. But don't worry, we will take care of you." She nods with enthusiasm. "You are in the best hands. The wedding planner will be around later today when you're back from school, and we have all sorts of fun things to do in the run up to the wedding."

Lauren's face brightens with delight. Like everyone else she believes our engagement is real and I can see how happy she is for Jericho and me.

This is just the first time the whole arrangement feels weird to me because I know I foolishly crossed a line.

"Thank you." I gather myself and find the confidence I'm used to summoning to calm my mind.

"We're all so excited. The next few weeks are going to be fun. I'm so glad we don't have to wait longer than necessary for your wedding."

Necessary.

There's that word again. The word that got me in trouble last night when Jericho practically said being with me was *necessary*.

I think now that he meant for the moment, for last night.

"Breakfast will be ready in an hour, but go grab some coffee and pastries."

"Sure, I will." I give her a curt nod before I walk back the way I came.

The tightness in my gut tells me I need to snap out of this funk.

If nothing else, I shouldn't read any more into last night than what it was because wanting a man I can't have is a mistake my heart can't afford ever again.

"Hello, sweet girl." Gina pulls me in for a big hug. I've just arrived for my daily visit.

"Oh, Gina, it's so, so good to see you sitting up." I smile and hold her a little closer to my heart, appreciating the moment and the fact that she seems stronger.

When we pull apart I look her over, noting how she looks as if someone poured new life back into her body. This is the absolute best I've seen her look in months. Maybe years.

"I felt like I could get up this morning, so I did. I even walked around for a little while." Her eyes glitter with restored hope.

"That's amazing. And you look great."

"Thank you."

All the other days I've been here she's been completely out of it because of the strong medication she's been on. Last night Dr. French told me he'd adjusted the dosage. So she should be more like herself over the next few days. I never expected it to happen so soon.

"I feel tons better." She rests her hands in her lap while I pull up the chair next to the bed and sit. "How about you?"

While she stares back at me eagerly, I mull over what to tell her.

She knows about Jericho, what he did for her, and my upcoming wedding, but up until now she's been too weak to talk to me about any of it.

Today marks twelve days since her surgery and an entire week since Jericho and I had our reckless rendezvous.

I haven't heard from him.

Not one word.

Not even a message about the wedding, or any relayed messages from the staff. Nothing. *Nada*.

In the same breath the unwritten message I received is clearer than clear that what we had was a one-nighter between exes and we're back to being business partners.

Back to this fake arrangement where I'm simply a contract and little more than the business transactions he makes on a day-to-day basis.

I got the car, which is an absolutely beautiful white Porsche, but it felt more like a perk for being with him. Like a benefit from a job.

So, *how am I?*

The truth is I feel like absolute shit.

"I'm okay." My tone is plain dull. Gina can usually see through my lies, but I pray she's not well enough to do so today.

"Just *okay*? Girl. I have been fighting to come back to you so we could have a good old chat about your Jericho." She beams. "Getting married is big, exciting news."

I smile back to keep up appearances, but what I really want to do is throw myself into her arms and tell her the truth. Tell her about the newest hole I've dug for myself.

"I know. I'm just a little tired. I did some extra practice this morning at the studio."

"River, you need to slow down. Especially now that you don't have to work so hard to take care of me." She brings her hands up to her cheeks. "I still can't even believe this is possible. That I'm here after receiving life-saving surgery, and you're getting married in a handful of weeks."

"I know. It's crazy, right?"

"Yes, it's completely crazy. I am eternally grateful to Jericho and for all he's done for us." She nods, showing that gratitude. "But is everything okay with you guys? You never told me you were even dating him again."

"After what happened in the past I didn't want to say anything. I wasn't sure how serious we were."

"Well, he must be *seriously* serious about you if you're getting married in a few weeks." She reaches forward and takes my hand.

"Yeah." I chuckle. "He's serious alright."

"How has your father been?" She bites the inside of her lip. "He's been colder than fish when he's come by to see me. I might have been out of it but in my lucid moments I remember him looking like he was ready to kill someone."

"Things have been hard with Dad and he's worried about me becoming a Grayson, but this isn't about him."

"It's not about him at all and I'm glad you're being so firm because I know how devastated you were when you and Jericho broke up, but, sweetie, I have to confess that I'm worried about you becoming a Grayson too."

"There's nothing to worry about." I spread my smile wider.

"I'm sure there isn't, and no one is more ecstatic than me, or as grateful, but this wedding is just so… *sudden*. This time last year you were still engaged to Sasha. How are you feeling about that?"

It's best I don't think about that part.

"I understand your concerns. After the whole ordeal with Sasha I never expected to get involved with anyone ever again, let alone be engaged, then Jericho came along like some knight in shining armor." *God,* it's so hard to lie to her, especially when Jericho isn't exactly one of my favorite people at the moment. "He wanted to get married right away. He felt that the years lost between us were long enough to wait."

"Eight years is a long time, but it hasn't escaped me that Jericho helped me just in time too." She tightens her grip on my hand. "You know I would never want you to marry someone with money just to save me, right?"

It wouldn't be like her to not be suspicious. I was waiting for her to say something like that. It makes me wonder if she's been talking to Dad. He's been saying stuff like that, too, only harsher, as he drops snarky comments he doesn't expect me to reply to. I might if I felt stronger, but the arguments aren't worth the stress. Especially when I'm already dancing way too close to the edge of sanity.

"No, Gina, it's nothing like that." I try to say that with as much assurance as possible.

She taps my hands, looking relieved. "Oh, good, then I'm glad. I know you'll do anything for me." She holds my gaze. "I love you for that, but I don't want you to do anything that will cost your happiness."

I nod, understanding, but my happiness is a small price to pay.

Everything good I have in this world came from Gina. All my achievements are because of her.

When Mom died and Dad wanted me to stop dancing, it was Gina who fought for me to keep going. She took me to my classes and paid for my lessons. She made sure I had everything I needed.

And it was her who gave me hope when she saved me from my captors.

I will never forget being seconds away from death, then hearing her voice on that phone confirming she'd gotten the money they demanded.

So, yes, I will do anything to save you, Gina, including marrying my ex.

"When Jericho heard how sick you were, he helped without question." Telling her these elements of truth helps me feel better. "He knows how much you mean to me, so he jumped to getting everything organized for the surgery straight away. He didn't want you to wait for that either."

Her eyes swell with a mixture of tears and gratitude. "My God, I'm in awe of his kindness. Things have been so hard for so long, and I accepted that death was knocking at my door. To be given new hope is something I can never repay."

"There's nothing to repay. All you have to do is focus on getting better."

"Thank you, my sweet, strong River. You are my something good."

"And you are mine, Aunt Gina."

"I hope I'm well enough to come to the wedding. This is the best news we've had in a long time. I'm so glad you found true love." She sounds as hopeful as a Disney character making a wish.

"Me, too." Back to telling lies.

I've come to accept that things like true love are myths.

Such things don't exist. Or maybe they do for some people, just not me.

I'm proven right and put further in my place when the days roll by and the non-communication between Jericho and me grows and grows.

Days turn into weeks, then suddenly it's our wedding day, and I'm walking down the aisle to get married.

I'm on the beautiful grounds of the world-renowned Oheka castle, surrounded by three hundred guests and the press, who started taking pictures of me the moment I stepped out of the limo and they saw my wedding dress.

Today is the day everyone who is anyone has been talking about, and the day I've been dreading.

The only good things around me are that Gina is here, Eden is my maid of honor, I have guests like Kelly from the café, who was ecstatic to get an invite to the wedding, and Dad is beside me.

He's walking me down the aisle.

Despite what he said the other week about his wheelchair, he insisted that this was his job and he wouldn't pass it up for anyone.

I love him for that. Having him next to me is keeping me from withering away as I stare at Jericho at the head of the altar, standing between the priest and Knight.

His eyes are on me.

Those same eyes stared at me as he claimed my body weeks ago.

I want to hate him. Hate is an easier emotion for me to deal with.

Anything else with Jericho is too much and so complicated it could enter the *Guinness Book of World Records*.

As I draw closer I realize I might not have a choice in how I feel about him for good or bad. Better or worse.

That doesn't mean I should play love's fool again.

Even if the man I shouldn't want is seconds away from becoming my husband.

Chapter TWENTY-THREE

Jericho

"YOU MAY NOW KISS THE BRIDE," THE PRIEST announces, sealing our union of marriage.

His words flow into my mind, bringing reality home, and I stare back at my beautiful bride, the realization hitting home that River and I are now husband and wife.

I just got married, and River is now my wife.

My wife.

It's strange to think of her as such but those words in my mind feel like something wicked and sinful, luring me back into what I tried to escape for the last few weeks.

My eyes lock with hers for another heartbeat before I lean in and kiss her, but the kiss…

It's nothing like I expected.

It's not like the kisses we've previously shared that were filled with passion, need, longing, and desire.

This kiss is empty.

Sure, she's kissing me back, and we must look as real to everyone as I want us to, but something's off, and it feels fake.

There's no emotion, no feeling, and no River.

A pang of desperation surges through me and I try once more to feel her as I deepen the kiss, but I'm only met with emptiness.

The same type of hollowness I've experienced over the last eight years of being without her.

She's gone and just like before, I can't blame her.

The lack of emotion and coldness toward me suggest she understood my message.

She quite rightly understood my complete absence and lack of communication to mean that we couldn't have more than that one night.

I became the asshole again the moment I woke up the morning after the wild night we shared.

I took one look at her and wanted her again, then I remembered my solid reasons for staying within the boundaries I placed between us.

I'm no saint, so I won't think of myself as the kind of man who sacrificed what he wanted for her sake, but at that moment I had to remember she didn't deserve that trip down memory lane with me.

That's why I left and stayed away.

We pull apart, and our guests applaud loudly and cheerfully. There are people here who I see all the time and those I haven't seen in years.

To all of them, that kiss of mine must have made me look like the eager, doting husband, but I was just searching for my girl.

The priest says something more but I can't hear him over the battle of thoughts in my mind, each one warring with the other over what I should have done and what I shouldn't.

Gathering my composure, I link River's arm with mine and resume the show, smiling for the crowd as we make our procession down the aisle as Mr. and Mrs. Grayson.

Among our esteemed guests are my mother and stepfather,

Maurice. They are sitting in the front row opposite my father, Sloane, and Bastian. They aren't here out of the goodness of their hearts or to support me as family members. They're here at my grandfather's demand.

Neither of them attended Knight's wedding last year, and it didn't go unnoticed with the press. My grandfather didn't want that to happen again.

I find Grandfather next, standing tall and proud with his arm around Grandma. When I meet his proud stare something that feels like shame fills me.

I've stood by my end of our agreement and got married like he wanted me to, but like the ruthless conqueror I am, I did it my way. Time will give me my share of the empire.

This should be my moment of triumph because I did it. I outsmarted my grandfather's rules. I found a woman who is able to adhere to our contract of silence, but I don't feel the euphoria I imagined I would.

The sour thought pushes me into a trance where the next few moments go by in a daze that sees me on autopilot doing what I previously rehearsed. River and I speak when we're spoken to, smile when we're supposed to, and move around when we need to.

There's an hour of nothing but pictures and congratulations from our guests.

The only lucid moments I have are when I speak to River's father and when I'm talking to Gina as she thanks me from the bottom of her heart for my help in saving her, then proceeds to congratulate River and me on our union.

As we speak to Gina I get glimpses of the River I know. The warmth returns for those precious minutes but she's gone again the moment we finish, and I go right back to the block in my mind.

I don't get her to myself again until the reception starts and we walk out to the center of the hall for our first dance as husband and wife.

I hate the song that's playing. I don't even remember the name of it but I recognize it as a classic forties jazz song that most people love. It's just been used too much.

"Who the hell chose this song?" I mutter under my breath, low enough for her ears only.

"I did," River responds with a seething glare. "What the *hell* is wrong with this song?" She borrows my tone and continues giving me her death glare.

"It's overused."

"Well, maybe if you'd been around and didn't leave me to plan the whole wedding by myself, you could have chosen the song." Her words are sharp and direct, like a bullet to the heart. And I know I landed myself in that.

I stare back at her, my jaw set. This little woman is the only person in my world who would talk to me like that and live to tell the tale.

"I was working." She's also the only person who could elicit an answer from me when I don't feel the need to explain myself. "I was too busy."

"Of course, you were." The sarcasm that drips from each of her words is enough to poison a snake. "That's okay. I was busy, too, *friend*."

I hate the way she says that word. She might as well tell me to fuck the hell off.

I'm *not* her friend.

A friend wouldn't be remembering how fucking sexy she is when she's naked and I'm pounding into her from behind.

My calm slips and I pull her closer, pressing my mouth to her ear.

"You are my *wife* now, River." I kiss the shell of her ear to make my grip on her look less threatening.

"On paper only, Jericho. On paper only." She moves her face away from me so she can look at me again. "That's the only place in this world where I will be *your* wife."

I want to correct her, but there's nothing to correct.

She's talking about the contract we signed.

Before I can answer with the non-existent answer in my mind, the song changes and people applaud for us, then they join us for the next dance.

We're supposed to break apart now and dance with our guests, but I feel as if the moment I let her go she'll be gone forever again and only exist to me on paper.

"Mind if I steal your groom, sweetheart?" Great-Aunt Bernice's hearty tone cuts into the thick fog of tension between us.

"Not at all," River replies, sounding as if Bernice just offered to rid her of the plague.

River slips out of my arms, and Bernice takes her place.

I start dancing with my aunt, who starts gushing about how lovely the wedding was and that it was good to see my father there with his family, but I'm not paying attention.

I'm too busy looking at my wife, who just started dancing with Corey, one of my assistants.

I could kill that little fucker just for touching her. River smiles at him, and the two laugh at something he's joking about. While I was traveling around I left him back here to help with the wedding. It seems he did a little more than that.

It irritates me more that River would like him. He's the same age as me, and he's normal.

As Bernice proceeds to tell me how proud she is that I found such a beautiful bride, I try to tamp down my murderous thoughts, but my temper flares again when Corey gets a second dance out of River.

His eyes are all over her. Of course, they would be. She's stunning, and her wedding dress isn't that different from the one she wore to the fundraiser.

The two of them are either oblivious to my stares or ignoring me. I suspect River is doing the latter because she avoids me for the rest of the day.

Night falls and I find myself behind the bar. We're supposed to be leaving for Italy in an hour but I just want to go to bed. Today was absolute shit and I'm only going to Italy because I have business there. I thought I'd kill two birds with one stone and have our honeymoon there too. Or rather, take my wife there so she could check out the place while I work—so not really a honeymoon.

River and Eden are sitting at a table across from me with my mother, Maurice, Knight and Aurora.

I retreated over here for a much-needed drink. Since I wanted to mix my own cocktail I got behind the bar to do it myself. The bartender is at the other end of the bar serving my guests.

I mix a shot of vodka and whiskey because I need a strong hit.

"Don't tell me you're already drowning your sorrows," Luc taunts, joining me behind the bar. He grabs a shot glass and I pour him a whiskey.

"I'm not drowning anything," I reply, but I look back at River.

Luc follows my gaze and grins. "You sure about that? You look like a cross between a psycho and a man about to take his last breath."

"I look just fine," I snap, gritting my teeth. "If you don't have anything sensible to say, fuck off."

He laughs. "Jesus, Grayson. Cool off, man. How about we take a moment to acknowledge the fact that you did what you planned to do? You did it."

"Yeah, I did."

"She's River Grayson now."

"River Grayson." That name in my head and on my lips stokes my primal instincts again, but I hold them back and remember what she said. *Wife only on paper.*

"Now what, bro? You haven't talked about the next part."

He means the in-between. The pocket of time before River and I are supposed to end. I haven't spoken about it because I haven't been thinking about it.

"We just live," I reply. "We both have work to do and we'll be busy with that. It's not like we need to be glued together."

"But what if you weren't working? Would it be such a bad thing to be stuck together?" Luc sips his drink.

"Yes." I knock back my cocktail in one gulp. When I set my glass down I look at my wife again.

Luc leans in. "Looks like that's going to be quite the challenge. You don't seem to be doing so well."

"I told you I'm fine."

"I'd beg to differ. And just a friendly word of advice you might want to take…" His voice trails off, and I glare at him.

"What? What advice?"

"Have you considered that just maybe you could be happy with her?"

I smirk without humor. Of course I have. I've thought about it a million times over and then some, but that confession won't leave the confines of my mind.

"I'm being serious, Jericho."

"I know you are."

"Then listen to me. The past is the past. Why not leave it there?" He holds my gaze.

I drop my voice to a whisper and say, "You're assuming I want this."

He gives me a wide toothy grin. "Because you do, *my friend*. Take it from a guy who's known you all your life." Luc nods then pours himself another drink. "The only thing I've ever known you to want in life is her. Now she's your wife. Go figure."

He grabs the glass then marches away, leaving me with that thought.

I look back at River again. She must feel my eyes on her because she looks back this time.

From all the way over here I note a shift in her expression, like a peek of emotion poking its head through, but then she looks away and continues ignoring me.

Everybody seems to be right except for me. Even when I choose the right thing that will benefit everyone.

The only sure thing I seem to know at this moment is that if I fuck my wife again I'll be nothing more than a doomed fool, destined to dig the pit for his own downfall and ruin.

Luc's words stay with me long after he leaves, and I'm still thinking about what he said as I board my jet for Italy.

River has already boarded but I had to hang back to discuss some last-minute stuff with Knight because he'll be in Arizona while I'm away.

Traveling with me are Lauren to keep River company at the villa we'll be staying in, Brady, and Corey. Even though Corey annoyed the fuck out of me earlier, he's here in Knight's absence to help me with the admin work and contracts.

River must be in one of the cabins in the back. The jet is a Bombardier Global 6000, so there's plenty of room for us to continue ignoring each other. There are three bathrooms, bedrooms, and three full-service lounges. So if she doesn't want to see me, she doesn't have to.

When I get seated I decide to distract myself by checking my emails, so I grab my laptop and jump into it. We take off ten minutes later, and I think of how this will be the first time that River and I will be away from everyone.

I'm on the third email when I hear the distinct laughter of my wife. When Corey's voice follows suit, telling her some joke about college, my blood boils.

I couldn't hear either of them before so I assume they must have moved up to the cabin next to me.

I'm also assuming that whatever intelligence is in Corey's pea-sized brain told him not to come in here because he knows I'd skin his ass for slacking around when he's supposed to be working. That's on a minor scale. Not even I know what I'd do to him for messing around with my wife on my wedding day.

My hands still on the keyboard, I listen out, trying to hear what else they're saying.

River laughs again, much to my irritation. She used to laugh like that with me.

Only with me.

What the fuck could be so funny that she's laughing like that now? If she's trying to drive me crazier, it's working.

"You should have seen it. I called it a mushroom cocktail in the end," Corey gushes on, the sound of his voice grating on my nerves.

I've worked with him for as long as I've worked for my grandfather and *always* found his voice infuriating because it has that boys' choir high pitch that could shatter glass. I only tolerate him because he's good at his job and alleviates my stress levels.

Except today.

"That sounds disgusting," River chuckles.

"Believe me, it was totally gross. I learned to never mix mushrooms with vodka. At the same time, that was the start of my side hustle as a masseur."

The fuck?

When in hell did Corey become a masseur? And *side hustle*? He makes himself sound like a man struggling to make ends meet who needs to moonlight as a masseur when he's done working for me. He's nothing of the sort.

I hate when rich people talk like that, but maybe Corey is doing it because it would make him seem more endearing to my wife.

"Well, thank you so much for offering the foot massage. My feet are burning after wearing those heels all day."

On hearing that my back goes ramrod straight. Under no circumstances is that asshole giving my wife a foot massage.

"You are most welcome," Corey says.

I was already getting up, but I was trying to exit my email. However, the moan-like sound that hits me next, followed by a whimper and the words *that feels so damn good*, has me shoving the laptop to the ground and storming forward with my hands folded into tight fists.

By the time I reach the door and shove it open I fully expect to Hulk out and turn green, then breathe radioactive fire or some fucking thing. I just know this won't end well.

River's gaze snaps toward me. She's practically lying on her seat, which she has tilted backward. She's changed out of her wedding dress into a green summer dress that will be perfect for the weather in Italy.

Corey is on his knees in front of her, holding her foot at the ankle, which has made her dress ride right up her thighs.

At least the fool has the good sense to look terrified when he sees me. With his tight curly black hair, lanky stature, and freckled face that looks like it never developed from his pubescent years, he already looks weak. Terror on him looks pathetic and for some reason infuriates me more.

"Jericho—"

"No," I cut him off. I don't want to hear any form of bullshit. "What the fuck do you think you're doing?"

River straightens and glares at me with the same daggers she used earlier when we were dancing.

"I was just giving River a foot massage. She said her feet were hurting. I didn't think it would be a problem."

"Really? And *River*?" I stare him down. "That's *Mrs. Grayson* to you and, *yes*, it is a problem that you thought it was okay to touch my wife."

"Jericho, stop it." River stands, setting her hands on her hips.

I flash her a seething glare, warning her to not interrupt me again. I look back at Corey, who is now standing and looking like he might wither away.

"I'm sorry."

"Yes, you should be." I nod, baring my teeth. "If my wife wants a foot massage, I'll give her a fucking foot massage. Now, get out before I throw you off the fucking plane. Go and do the fucking work I hired you to do." I point to the door behind him.

"Sure thing, Jericho." He scampers away the way a rat would and closes the door.

In all my years of working at Graysons Inc. I've never spoken to any of my employees in that way but, fuck, Corey had it coming. Who the hell would think it's okay to give someone else's wife—*his boss' wife*—a foot massage on their wedding day?

I look back at River. From the appalled look on her face I can tell she thought he did nothing wrong.

"You are such an asshole," she snaps, raising her fists as if she's going to fight me. The thing is, I wouldn't put it past this new version of River to fight.

She's certainly looking at me as if she just might claw out my eyes or cut off my balls and make a purse out of them.

"*Yes*, I am an asshole." There's no point in denying my personality as it's a widely accepted concept that I am indeed an asshole. It's the same as knowing the sun is warm and the sky is blue. "I also happen to be the kind of asshole who doesn't want his wife messing around with his employees."

"Absolutely unbelievable." She grabs the magazine on the table and throws it at me. "Did I look like I was messing around to you? It was a freaking foot massage."

"It sounded like a little more than that." I know I'm crossing the line now and acting way outside my usual level of reckless, but this woman makes me crazy in a way that I want to shout at her and fuck her at the same time.

Of course, she doesn't like my comment, so she looks more enraged than before.

"How dare you? I haven't seen you for close to a month. God knows what you have been doing. With your track record, you could have been with that preacher man's wife again."

My temper heightens even more. "I wasn't with anyone and that shit was a mistake."

"Of course it was. I'm sure she just mistakenly fell on your dick."

"Jesus Christ, stop it," I seethe, knowing she's thinking of me as the playboy again, when I'm not. "I wasn't doing anything besides working." Working, trying not to think about her, then stopping myself from catching the next flight back to be with her.

"I don't know that." She folds her arms and pouts.

"Right, so you thought you'd make me jealous on our wedding day?"

She shakes her head at me and gives me a cruel laugh. "To be jealous you'd have to care about me. You don't."

I'm aware people can hear us and she's saying things that will fracture the image of the fairytale couple we created for the media, but I don't care about that.

I actually don't care that she could ruin me with two words—*contract marriage*.

The realization of this surprises me nearly as much as the fact that I care more about her than anything else. And I care that she thinks I don't.

Again, Luc's words come back to me, but this time they feel like a sledgehammer landing in my gut.

When I don't respond quickly enough her eyes become glassy and she turns to walk through the door Corey used.

Instinct shoves me forward and I grab her arm. My reaction is fueled by that fear again that if she walks out that door, I'll lose her for good.

I'm already losing her. I don't think I'll ever forget the kiss she gave me after we said *I do*. It was like kissing a statue. Or a corpse. Something with no life.

"It's not true. I do care." I sound like I'm taking my vows again.

"Leave me alone," River huffs.

She's about to shake my hand off her arm but I pull her closer and crush my lips to hers. This is maybe the third time I've done this.

Grab her and kiss her. Grab her and fuck her. Grab her and

make her my wife. Grab her and show her the only way I know how that I more than care about her.

This reaction has come to be a default for me because I know no other way than to be the rough, reckless, ruthless rebel.

She struggles against me, trying to get out of the kiss, but I keep her there with my lips sealed to hers, trying to find the missing emotions in her.

There's still nothing there.

"You've been screwing with my head since high school," she stutters against my lips, still trying to get away from me. "This stops today."

I kiss her harder. "No. You're my wife, not just on fucking paper, or a damn contract." I risk saying that word—*contract*—as a desperate attempt to reach her.

It works. There's a shift in her kiss that's not so cold. The warmth appears to return to her lips and I feel her—my River.

"My wife," I repeat, and those words, like magic, soften the tension in her body.

I move with her to the wall and deepen our kiss. She slips her arms around me and relinquishes that resistance.

"*My wife*," I mutter, pausing to look at her while she holds me.

A tear slides down her cheek and I realize just how much I must have hurt her by staying away.

Not just this last month. She's right. Since high school.

"My... wife." I speak the words as if I'm taking my last breath.

It's her who moves toward me next, and we fall back into our kiss. Except this time we explode together in a wild, hungry, devouring kiss as if we've become ravenous beasts, starved for centuries.

I press her up against the wall, feeling my cock shoving into her belly, and she rubs against it, tightening her grip around my neck.

There's only one direction this can lead to, and I choose it.

I choose it because I need her and I will do everything that will keep me with her, including signing the ink on my downfall.

It's better than nothing.

I'm tired of feeling *nothing*.

I push the zipper of my pants down, freeing my cock, which is aching so badly to be inside her I don't know how the fuck I'm going to control myself once I'm in.

In the clash of teeth and tongues I push up her clothes and move her panties to the side so I can cup her sex.

Just like always she's wet and ready for me, so I guide my cock to her slick entrance and push in all at once.

My cock impales her tight passage that feels so fucking good I know now I was a complete idiot for thinking I could deny myself of her body, or of her.

I unleash, pounding hard into her body, and fuck, fuck, fuck, nothing has ever felt this good in my life. I had the same thought last time I was with her. Maybe the difference is that now she's my wife.

The same girl who has driven me crazy with wanting her for the last twelve years.

Luc is right. River is the one thing I've ever wanted in my life and the only woman I've ever craved.

I stop kissing her so I can fuck her properly, allowing her the freedom to moan however much she wants.

"Jericho," she cries out my name on the edge of a strangled moan.

That's better. I want to own every sound that comes from those lips and all her pleasure. Whoever is listening—*Corey*—can hear that she's mine, and they better hope they never fuck with me again.

"Hold on tight, Mermaid. I'm going to fuck you harder."

I grip her waist and barely give her a second to catch her breath before I slam into her pussy harder and pound into her body with wild ferocious lust and need.

I fuck her until she's coming and her slick juices cover my cock, arousing me even more and fueling my stamina.

Her body weakens against me and her grip loosens around my neck, but still I keep going, fucking her hard, and she takes what I give her.

I cup her face and kiss her again, sucking her lower lip as our bodies continue slapping together in filthy carnal pleasure.

Then I feel it. My climax is rising and building. My balls draw up, and I come.

I explode into her, the release taking over my body as if I've been possessed.

River trembles against me, the walls of her passage wrapping around my cock as she comes again.

The feeling of our shared release is glorious, and I'm lost in her in all the right ways.

When I slow I notice the thick white of my cum sliding down the inside of her thigh, and I have the perfect idea.

"Jericho."

"Shhh, Mermaid." I touch my fingers to her lips. "You and I… we're just getting started." I finish the rest of that sentence in French because I don't want the ears on the wall to hear me telling my wife that I plan to fuck her pussy so raw she won't be able to walk when we get back to New York.

I pick her up and carry her to the shower, then I stay inside her for the rest of the flight.

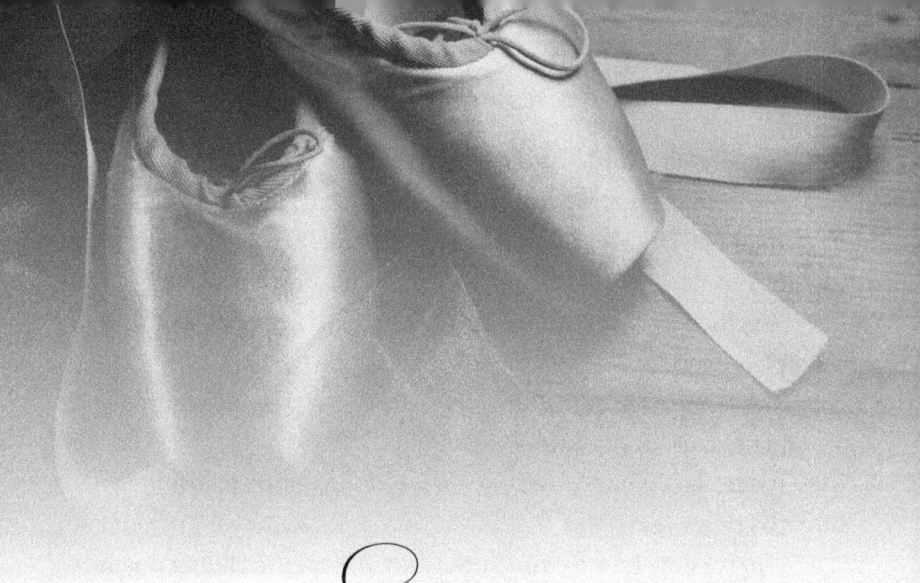

Chapter TWENTY-FOUR

River

THE DULCET MELODY OF *CLAIR DE LUNE* FILLS MY HEAD, lulling me from a blissful sleep.

He knows this is my favorite song.

Not many people are aware that Jericho Grayson plays the piano like a pro.

It's not unless they visit his home and see his piano, or he tells them that he plays, would they even associate a musical instrument with him.

I found out that he played the second time I saw him after he saved me from my bullies in high school.

I was practicing late at night in the school's auditorium, unaware that I had an audience.

When said audience started playing the music I was going to use for my audition at Juilliard it shocked me to hear it, then it shocked me to find him, the boy people called the rebel, playing the music as if he owned every note ever played.

After that night we'd meet there. He'd play while I danced.

It became a thing for us. Whenever I heard it when I wasn't dancing I knew he was trying to get my attention.

He's doing it again now.

Now that we're husband and wife.

Day three of being Mr. and Mrs. Grayson.

With a smile on my face I open my eyes and sit up in the king-size bed taking up most of the attention of our room in the villa.

I keep being thrust into the most beautiful places.

When Lauren told me Jericho was taking me to Naples for our honeymoon I tried my best not to get too excited because I wanted to stay mad at him.

However, I'm a complete sucker for the picturesque beauty.

Even if we hadn't, uhm… *made up* on the plane, I would have melted just at the sight of the villa.

The villa which we have to ourselves while the staff stay in the guesthouse adjacent to us.

The villa has that European exotic architectural design I love. There are two bedrooms, two living rooms, an Olympic-size pool with a jacuzzi built on the side, and then there's the view of the Marina Piccola Beach. The one and only that was made famous by Homer's *The Odyssey*.

The place is like our own little getaway and absolute heaven.

And dare I say it… Heaven seems to be including my husband, too.

My husband.

It feels so weird to think of myself as married, much less married to Jericho Grayson.

I'm River Grayson now.

God knows what time it was when we eventually got off that plane. We arrived sometime yesterday but stayed on board for a few hours after it landed.

At least we knew we were the only ones on board as we continued reacquainting ourselves with each other.

It was almost night time by the time we got here. We spent a little while checking out the place and the scenery, and just managed to get something to eat before we were in bed again.

Now a new day has dawned and it seems that Jericho wishes to start it the same way we ended last night.

The night of the fundraiser when we were together, I shoved logic into the back of hell. I did it again over the last few days but now I'm thinking of good old logic again, which has been screaming at me to be careful.

'Don't fall for this guy again,' it keeps saying, but can logic ever make sense when nothing else does?

When your heart seems to beat for one man and *you know* it's only ever going to beat for him, what do you do then? Or now?

I'm not weak.

The strongest trait that people often discover in me is that I'm not weak. I've been through too much to call myself anything of the sort, but Jericho Grayson makes me feel like it's okay to be weak with him. Like he might wrap all my vulnerabilities in the chasm of his heart and guard it with his life.

It sounds so stupid for me to even think like that when I'd hardened my heart moments before we took our vows. More so because there is nothing solid about a relationship like ours except the contract we signed. But it's how I feel.

How I choose to react to those feelings is my problem. All he has to do is touch me for my resolve to fade away. That's not good. And hearing him call me his wife…

God, it did something more to me that I can't describe to anyone, along with the added bonus of telling me that I wasn't just his wife on paper or in the contract.

It means more to me, and something has changed between us. I just don't know what, or if I should entertain it.

I don't want to get hurt again. Neither do I want to let Jericho hold all the cards, but the part of me that wants him knows that all this thinking is a waste of time because I'm already in trouble when it comes to having any sort of feelings toward him.

This is Jericho Grayson. The guy I classed as the love of my life.

Maybe it's true what people say about first love. That you never forget it and that it gets all of you. A part of your heart, mind, body and soul remains with it always.

I never believed it until him.

I never knew I could love anyone the way I loved him, so I already know I can't say no to him.

But… I can promise myself that I will be careful.

I must.

The alluring piano music continues calling to me and like an enchanted spell I allow it to take control over my mind.

I get dressed quickly in a little summer dress and pull my hair into a ponytail before I make my way downstairs to the piano room where I find Jericho sitting on the stool shirtless, playing.

He glances over his shoulder at me and gives me a cocky smile.

"Finally, she's awake," he says, his hands flying across the piano keys in perfect harmony.

I smile back at him. "You got my attention."

"I thought I might."

I walk around to him and lean against the piano. He looks me over while he continues to play and I make myself believe that the ghost of the couple we used to be is trapped in the music. Us together right now is the ghost having one last play out of their whirlwind romance.

"It's been a while since I've seen you play the piano."

"It's been a while since I played, Mermaid."

"Why's that?" While he looks me up and down I allow myself to do the same, taking in the mass of hard muscle on show.

"I lost my dancer."

My stomach squeezes and I stare back at him, wondering if he realizes that whenever he talks about the past he makes it seem as if something happened to break us up. As if he doesn't realize it was him.

So many questions come to me that I'm compelled to ask during these moments: Like, what really happened?

Why did he break up with me if he thinks he lost me?

What happened to us?

He glances away for a moment then back at me.

"We're going out today," he declares.

I give him a narrowed stare. "Aren't you supposed to be working?"

"Not today, baby." He fixates on my breasts and allows his gaze to climb back up to meet mine.

"I see." I'm actually happy to hear that I'll have him to myself for the whole day, but I decide to make him crazy to test the waters. "I was hoping to check on Corey while you're working. He was going to take me to see the waterfall."

The music stops abruptly and Jericho swivels around to face me with a stern expression.

"Come again?" The sharpness in his tone reminds me of nails scraping across a gritty surface.

"We were just going sightseeing." I nod with nonchalance, secretly loving the possessive reaction I'm getting from him. "I didn't want to be bored so when he offered I gladly accepted."

Corey was actually super nice to me over the last few weeks, so I genuinely felt bad for the way Jericho treated him. However, I definitely saw where Jericho was coming from in being enraged. I'm only not more upset because I'll admit that now that I think of it, I feel Corey might have a thing for me.

"No." His tone is flat.

"No?"

He stands, towering over me, then he leans in close to brush his nose over mine. "No. And if you want that little asshole Corey to keep his job, and his *life*, you will end whatever the hell this fascination is with him."

I laugh because it's hilarious to see Jericho Grayson getting worked up over someone like Corey. A man who would never begin to compare to him.

"What is so funny, wife?" He tweaks my nose.

"You, *husband*," I try out the word and like it *way, way* too much. It feels like getting high on adrenaline. From the cunning smirk that lights his face I can tell he likes me calling him my husband too.

"Why am I funny, wife?"

"Because jealousy looks odd on you." I giggle.

"Then don't make me jealous. Never can tell what I might do if you make me that crazy." He reaches out and slides the band out of my hair, allowing it to tumble down my shoulders.

"What are you doing now, Jericho?" I shake my head at him.

"Getting you ready for the first activity of the day."

"And what would that be?"

He gives me a look so scandalous my insides blush. "First, this comes off." He turns me around and pulls the zipper down on the back of my dress. We watch the dress float down my body and pool at my feet.

"This next." He undoes the clasp on my bra and takes that off, too, then he turns me back to face him and takes in my bare breasts.

That look of wild adoration that always weakens my resolve fills his eyes from corner to corner, turning them darker and filling them with sin. When he looks at me like that it's difficult to breathe, much less think about anything else besides him touching me.

"You want me naked?" I try to sound composed although my blood is rushing through my veins like hot lava waiting to erupt.

"I want you naked and on your knees, sucking my cock, then…" He flutters his thick fingers down to my breasts, then lowers his head to taste my already tight nipples, aroused from his request.

"Then what?" My voice comes out with a tremble.

He flicks his tongue over my nipples, sucking one then the next, and I feel him deep inside my core. He stops stroking my breasts then crouches down to roll my panties down my legs.

I step out of them, trying to bite back the smile of pleasure spreading across my face. Of course, I fail miserably. By now we both know that one of my favorite things is the attention he gives my body.

He lifts my leg and licks the skin on my calf then kisses his way up to my thigh, leaving tingles on my skin. He stops at my pussy, where moisture has gathered and licks over my clit. When he pushes his tongue into my passage he inches back to smile at me, and licks up the wetness that has gathered there.

"You're leaving me in suspense," I moan, tipping my head back.

"I know, but I needed to taste you." Jericho chuckles then straightens and stares at me with wanton, lust-filled eyes.

"What comes next?"

"I'm going to bend you over the piano and fuck you. I think that's a good start to the day. Don't you?"

My gaze drops to the big bulge of his cock pressing against his sweatpants and my mouth waters, hungry for everything he just laid out.

"Yes," I rasp, meeting his gaze again. I can't think of a better way to spend my time than us devouring each other the way we have for the last few days.

"Great, baby, so how about you get on your knees for me?" He raises a brow and his face hardens with desire as he gives me that I-can-have-you-anytime-I-want look that has made many women line up to lose their dignity.

When I sink to my knees his smile broadens, making him look like the bad boy badass I remember from high school.

He pushes his pants down and takes out his cock.

Seeing him so hard for me brings out the sexy in me, so I grip him at the base and run my hands up and down the length of his shaft, savoring the thickness and hardness of his arousal.

Jericho runs his hands over my hair, lacing his fingers through the strands.

"Suck me, Mermaid. Suck me hard." His jaw clenches. I love that I can bring out this reaction in him just with my touch.

"With pleasure," I reply, summoning the confident woman I wish I were and shocking him in equal parts.

His lips part with a sexy half grin and his cock grows harder in my hands.

I keep my gaze trained on his as I move my mouth toward his cock and lick the tip, tasting him. He closes his eyes and groans, deep and guttural. Triumph surges through me at the sight of this pleasure I'm giving him, and I take the greatest pride in making a man like Jericho Grayson go weak for me.

It's like I own him and he's mine. Mine in a different way from all the ways we used to belong to each other.

Using my tongue, I circle the head of his cock, then take him as far as I can into my mouth.

He's too big and thick for me to fit all of him but I take as much as I can, allowing him to hit the back of my throat. Then I suck him.

I suck his cock hard and fast and with possession. He thrusts his hips against my mouth, fucking my face and looking like he's barely controlling himself.

"Fucking hell, River, you're too good at this." He groans again and takes a handful of my hair, gripping it tight to control my movements.

I keep going, but arousal grips me as my breasts bounce and he tweaks my nipples.

Suddenly wetter than I was before, I feel like I'm going to come. I can tell he's close, too, so I run my tongue along the underside of his shaft, licking him in quick, fluttering strokes.

His breath becomes choppy and his hands shake against my head. I take him deeper and just when he groans, I taste pre-cum on the tip of my tongue.

His cock jerks so I move faster but he pulls out, then he grabs my arms to pull me to stand and straight up to his lips.

"I want to finish inside you." He kisses me so hard my lips feel bruised.

I can't answer. I'm too consumed with his lips on mine and his promise of bending me over the piano to think of anything sexy or intelligent to say.

I melt into his kiss and enjoy the surge of longing that spreads throughout my body. It's so fierce and powerful I feel it in my soul.

Everything is amplified when he flips me around and bends me over the piano. We're on the side where I can get a good grip on the lid. I do so as he fits himself against me and I revel in the sensation of his cock entering my body, then me welcoming him as if he always belonged inside of me.

I like the way I feel when we're joined like this and we're so close it's difficult to remember not being with him. The feeling is like nothing else.

Jericho starts pumping into me, then pounding, creating the perfect storm of pleasure as he fucks me into delirium.

Sparks of white light flash behind my lids, turning into fireworks with every thrust.

My orgasm sneaks up on me like a thief in the night, then swallows my senses whole.

I grip the piano lid tighter, moaning out loud as my body takes the deep pounding of his cock.

Then he blows my mind further by reaching between us to cup my sex and massage my clit with his fingers.

The demand in his touch makes me explode and I scream as my orgasm detonates inside me.

The fierce pleasure makes me shake as my walls squeeze his cock. He groans, coming too. The sensation of us sizzles through my veins, short-circuiting my brain, then I'm falling into bliss and light where nothing exists but this moment where we own each other.

I'm still catching my breath when he pulls out of me and turns me slowly to face him.

Breathing hard, Jericho cups my face. I expect him to kiss me but he touches his forehead to mine.

"You're going to ruin me all over again, wife." His warm breath tickles my skin.

"Am I, husband?"

"Fuck, yeah. How about we head to the pool next? We haven't christened that yet."

"I'm all yours."

He scoops me up and I wrap my arms around him, deciding to savor this—whatever it is—for however long it lasts.

It feels like living.

Chapter
TWENTY-FIVE

River

WE SPEND THE NEXT FEW DAYS TOGETHER FROLICKING around Naples, on land and in the sea. Jericho doesn't take any time away from me to work. Not even once. He spends all the time with me.

We hardly even see the staff.

Lauren cooks for us but Corey mostly stays away, doing the work I assume Jericho was supposed to do.

The few times that I see him he barely offers eye contact. I feel a little bad but a wicked part of me still secretly likes that Jericho was so possessive over me.

Today we went sea fishing, then diving. It was amazing and we had such a good time.

We set out early in the morning, almost before sunrise. Now we're on the beach sitting opposite each other. We just cooked the fish Jericho caught earlier over the fire.

It's late and I'm guessing we'll be heading back to the villa soon but I'm enjoying the serenity of us being out here together.

"I like it here," I say, glancing at Jericho.

"Me too." He sighs. "There's a calmness about Europe that I love. I always feel like this no matter where I go in Europe, especially when I'm near the sea."

"There are a few European cities I've yet to explore." I smile. "I've barely been to France."

"Well that's about to change." Jericho smirks. "My mother has invited us to go to Saint Tropez."

"I'd love to go there." I nod and widen my smile, masking the bad memory of me almost going to Saint Tropez before.

That would have been my honeymoon destination if I'd married Sasha. Just before the wedding that was never going to happen he started to show his true colors.

The bastard took his secretary to Saint Tropez instead, while I stayed home, scrubbing the floors of our dinky apartment. Then he had the audacity to come and show me pictures of the two of them on the beach, and the two of them in bed. That's what he used to do to me.

I push the memory out of my mind. It's better I don't think about horrible things from the past.

"I'll take you to Saint Tropez."

"Thank you. It's probably the other place I wanted to go to more than Russia."

Jericho smiles, probably remembering how much I used to talk about Russia when we were younger, then he looks at me with concern. I know he's wanted to ask me more about my life there and about what happened to me. I've been grateful that he's stopped trying to find out. I don't know how much digging he's done, or if he's found out enough to stop asking questions, or if he hasn't dug anymore.

"Would you ever go back to Russia?"

"Just for work. Like if I get into New York City Ballet. If I do,

I'll go anywhere they need me to go and I'd do everything to live the dream again. It would be my second chance."

He moves closer to sit next to me and wraps the blanket around my shoulders.

We stare at each other and I wonder if I'd be more open to talk about my terrible experiences now that so much has happened between us.

I don't know.

"What happened to you, River? I used to love hearing you dream. Back then all you used to do was talk about traveling the world and dancing. I have no doubt New York will take you but I wish you didn't need that second chance. I'm guessing that was because of your ex."

I pull the blanket closer and look away, staring out to what I can see of the dark horizon. I swallow against the knots of my throat. And I realize it's always going to be hard to talk about Sasha. Every time I do, for any length of time, I break down.

"It's difficult to talk about him," I rasp. "Everything about him was bad. I'm embarrassed that I let myself down for allowing certain things to happen to me, to ruin my dream."

"We all have a story like that, Mermaid. We all do." A smirk without humor dips the corners of his mouth.

"There's no way you allowed anyone to humiliate you. *No way.* Not the great Jericho Grayson."

"Try me. His voice is hollow and he stares back at me for a languid moment. The only light we have is the mixture of moonlight and fire but the trouble lurking in his eyes is so vivid, it could be pitch black and I'd still see it.

"My father," he mutters, in that same hollow tone, and this time my insides twist. "My father used to beat the shit out of me every chance he got."

My eyes snap wide. I know Jericho doesn't have any kind of relationship with his father, but he's never spoken about any form of abuse.

"I didn't know."

"It's only my grandfather who knew. He found out years too late. If Knight had known, I'm sure he would have killed our father."

"Oh God, Jericho. I'm so sorry."

"It's okay." He pulls in a breath and reaches for a cigarette in his pocket. He lights up, takes a few puffs, then allows it to dangle between his fingers. "People see me as a strong person. They think I'm ruthless and heartless, cold and merciless. They think nothing bothers me. But they never stop to consider how I got that way."

I'd never have imagined that something like that would have happened to him.

"When did it start?" I ask.

"I was nine. I'd gone to New York to spend the summer with my grandparents, my father came by the house to visit. He brought Bastian along with him. Bastian and I got into a fight that he started by trying to blame me for something he did. I pushed him off me, he fell and cut his arm. Later that night my father caught up with me and punched the life out of me. I'll never forget that night." He shakes his head.

My stomach twists even more.

"My father told me that if I ever let anyone know it was him who did that to me, he'd fly to France and kill my mother. The story I was to tell everyone was that I fell out of a tree and hurt myself. Over the years I had several accidents like that."

He blows out a ring of smoke and looks back at me. "The beating stopped many years later when Knight kicked Bastian's ass. It was the first time that my father saw us retaliate and I guess he must have worried that if Knight found out what he was doing to me, he'd tell my grandfather. We had a few good years, or rather *I* did until I was in my late teens. My father kicked my ass again because I accidentally crashed my car into Bastian's at a party. Months later another fight broke out between Knight and Bastian. That was worse than the first because he almost killed him for calling our mother a slut. That time I didn't bounce back. Instead I turned to drugs."

I'm about to comment, then I note the timeline. He said he was in his late teens. This happened to him when he was with me?

"Jericho, we were together then."

He nods, slowly, confirming, and shocking me further.

"I never knew. How could I have not known? I couldn't even tell."

"I hid it very well." Shame spreads across his face. "Too well. Remember that spring break when I told you I went to France and I'd be away for a few weeks?"

I nod, remembering very well. It was the first time we'd been apart. He was a senior, so I was worried he'd gone to some party beach for spring break.

"I was in rehab," he confesses.

I bring my hand to my mouth.

"That was when I told my grandfather what was happening to me and what had happened with my father. He stepped in and got me the help I needed. I went to him when I realized I was out of control."

"Did he do something about your father?"

"He gave him a taste of his own medicine. I remember seeing him with two black eyes and a broken nose before I went off to rehab. Knowing my grandfather, he would have punished my father in worse ways that could have crippled him. Something more effective than going to the police or exposing him."

"I truly hope so."

"I know he did. I was clean for a few years after rehab but of course my father struck again. This time he tried to send Knight and I back to France. My grandfather stood up to him by getting an injunction on his powers in the company. At that point I'd had enough. I turned to drugs one last time, and it was the most damning. I made some decisions I shouldn't have made. It took finding my dealer dead on his doorstep from an overdose for me to stop. I let myself down because I turned to drugs every time my father struck out. I came back from that person I was. That's how I know you will too."

I gaze back at him, appreciating him sharing his story with me. I can't believe he went through so much.

The relationship with his father is truly ugly to say the least. My story is different, but just as ugly.

Somehow, I feel the strength I needed to share it.

"His name is Sasha," I start. "My ex-fiancé, that's his name. Sasha Konstantin." I clear my throat and take in a slow breath to calm my mind. "He's the reason I needed a second chance. He stopped me from dancing when he changed. He used to beat me. He used to beat me all the time."

The words catch in my throat again, tangling with the fear. That awful fear and terror of wondering if those moments were gonna be my last on earth.

Jericho takes my hand into his and I get that warmth of reassurance again, allowing me to reveal the weakest moments of my life. So I do.

I find myself telling him everything and I round up to the big secret. That I am the reason Sasha is behind bars for the next eight years.

"The police came to me. They'd been watching me for months as they gathered intel on Sasha. They assured me I'd be safe if I helped them. They didn't have enough on him to take him down. I gave them what they needed and they did a good job of making it look like they stumbled on it themselves."

Jericho gives my hand a gentle squeeze but I can see unmistakable worry in his eyes. "Don't worry about him," he says, brushing a wayward strand of hair away from my face.

"I do worry, Jericho. Nothing is ever certain when you deal with men like him. I'm scared he'll find out it was me. People die for less."

"I won't let anything happen to you, Mermaid. You're with me now." He gives me a gentle smile.

"You mean for the next year. After that—"

In standard Jericho fashion, he cuts me off with a kiss. This one is gentle and tender. Softer than the others we've shared. It holds the promise of love and safety. The sort you want to wrap yourself in forever.

He pulls out of the kiss and catches my face. "I won't let anything happen to you. I promise." He lifts my hand with the ring on it and kisses over my knuckles. "You're my wife, River. You're my wife."

Those words open my heart, unlocking something that I can't quite describe, then I do everything I said I wasn't going to do and I fall for him all over again.

Falling into all his promises, his words, and him.

Chapter
TWENTY-SIX

Jericho

WE ACTUALLY HAD A HONEYMOON. A *REAL* ONE.

The kind people talk about for years to come, keep in their hearts as the most memorable of memories, and show off pictures to their friends and family.

The trip was completely different from the one I actually planned that would have seen me consumed with my work the entire time.

Instead I got the guys to focus on the work I had in Italy while I spent all my time with River.

After that first night—*our wedding night*—I realized there was no way on earth that I could have focused on anything business-related with her anywhere near me.

After that night it also felt completely inappropriate to have my wife in a beautiful city like Naples with me working while we were supposed to be on our honeymoon.

Yes, it was planned as a *pretend honeymoon,* but it quickly became all too real while we were still in New York airspace.

We had some good times in Italy.

Now we're back. Back home and back to the real world.

We arrived last night, but that didn't mean we slipped back into the shoes of the fake couple we were supposed to be.

I took her straight to my bed and got the reality hit as soon as the sun came up, when I woke and she wasn't there.

I'd gotten used to waking in Italy with my wife in my arms and the magnolia scent of her swimming beneath my skin.

I wanted that again this morning. Except she'd already left for work and I wasn't sure if she'd left my bed before she needed to think about work.

I left for the day and the time we've spent apart has me reflecting and thinking about the connection we made.

That connection seemed to blossom after our little session on the beach where we shared secrets from our past, the deep ones locked away in our hearts.

Mine was the kind I've only ever spoken about once—to my grandfather.

River told me a lot more than I expected about Sasha and her life in Russia.

Everything she revealed worried me. I'm guessing she was so open with me because of what I told her about my father. What she didn't realize was that was just the tip of the iceberg.

That story led into how I ended up making the worst decision of my life when I got involved with those hackers who stole her father's designs. I couldn't tell her that part. I had to keep that sealed away in my soul.

I also never shared the nitty gritty of why I felt my father treated me the way he did and not Knight.

Sure he was horrible to Knight on several occasions, but he didn't beat him the way he did with me.

I felt I got that treatment because I represented his mistakes with my mother.

It was bad enough that he'd been with her and had Knight when he'd promised to marry Sloane, but then he got my mother pregnant with me.

When he left her it made him look bad in my grandparents' eyes, and they only happened to find out about Knight and me by accident.

My mother was struggling to take care of us and my father didn't care. He still doesn't care. He saw us as pests. That's the type of motherfucker he is.

It's ironic how the one thing I've always had in common with River's father is the hatred for my father. I can just imagine how evil my father must have been in his younger days.

As for River, learning more about Sasha opened my eyes to the real danger she must have been in and again I wondered what the hell her father must have been thinking. She didn't mention him at all even as she spoke about Gina rescuing her. There was no mention of her father and I can't believe that he simply did nothing.

To be on the safe side I took a few further steps to look into Sasha, just to see what we're up against when he's released.

River is right in thinking that the rules change when dealing with men like him. Sasha is in prison for eight years, but as to whether he serves his time is a different story.

I never knew that she had any involvement in putting him behind bars.

So far it looks like he doesn't know either, but people can find things out if they suspect. I don't want her involved in anything like that, especially since she went through hell to escape him.

My morning was consumed with thoughts of my wife. I thought about everything, from her safety to the relationship we have.

I can't go back to how we were before, or rather, the plan I had before, which was to keep my distance. That much was clear from the moment I gave her my name.

I'm just not sure how I can make things work with our temporary business marriage.

It wasn't supposed to feel so real, until it did.

At noon I head over to the cafe across from Grayson Inc. to meet with Luc.

He's already there when I arrive and gives me a cunning smile when he sees me approaching the table, as if he can tell that I've changed.

"Hello friend," he says when I sit.

"Hey."

The waitress comes over straight away and takes our orders, then moments later returns with two steaming cups of espresso and toasted sandwiches.

"You look like you had a good time in Italy." Luc looks me over when the waitress leaves.

"I did."

"I hope you took a bit of my advice." He leans back against his chair.

I sigh, remembering the blissful time I spent with River. "I think I did."

At my confession Luc's expression brightens. "Pray tell."

"There's nothing really to tell." That's a half lie. I just don't want to speak words outside my head yet and give myself hope I shouldn't feel. "I've been thinking. That's all."

Luc smirks and stares back at me with disbelief. "So all you did on your honeymoon with your hot new wife was *think*? You know I was neither born yesterday nor do I believe shit like that coming from your mouth, *Grayson*." He shakes his head at me in an exaggerated manner.

I laugh. "I know, and no, I didn't spend my honeymoon *thinking*."

"Good man." He dips his head proudly. "So I take it you were thinking about how this thing would work between you and River."

"Essentially."

"Just go for it and be with her. That's what I would do. You have the goddess for one whole year. That's having your cake and eating it too. No one has to get hurt. You both enjoy each other for the time you're together, then part ways at the end. No problem."

That type of thinking is exactly where the two of us differ.

Not that I consider my moral standards to be any better than his. We're pretty much the same in that department. It's just that I know he's never been in love before. At least not to my knowledge. I'm certain that if he was at any given point in his life I'd know about it because he wouldn't know what to do with himself.

I on the other hand know there are certain things—*certain secrets*—you can't get away with, or keep hidden, if you claim to love someone.

I never wanted anything close to the darkness associated with the bitter relationship my parents had.

My sins feel exactly like something my father would do.

Keeping secrets like the one he kept from my mother about Sloane feels like what I did. While it might not be the same thing, people's lives were affected.

"I'll see what happens over the next few months." I rest my hands on the table. "We have time."

"Time waits for no one, friend, and I don't want you to let that girl slip away from you again. You two were high school sweethearts, man."

That hasn't escaped me in the least. "Since when did you become the love doctor, Luc?" I try to lighten the conversation. "You're normally the love-them-and-leave-them guy."

He raises his hands. "I'm still that guy, but I'm not an idiot. I just believe that if you have the kind of relationship you and River have, you shouldn't turn your back on it. At least not without making an effort."

I nod, appreciating his words. "I hear you."

"Good."

"So, what's been happening with you?" I decide to change the subject.

He rolls his eyes at me. "A load of shit."

"Like what?"

"The team is getting a new owner. Guess who had a run-in with the new guy in Milwaukee."

God. This is going to be one of those stories of his. Luc is always getting in trouble.

I tilt my head and give him a lopsided grin. "You. Yours truly."

"Me. The one and only."

"What did you do?"

"I called him a dickless baldheaded asshole with a stick shoved up his ass in my last interview with ESPN."

I shake my head at him in dismay. "Why did you do that, Luc?" I don't know why I bother to ask. Luc does these things because he can get away with it.

"That motherfucker deserved it. He and my father were rivals back in the day. He tried to attack my father's integrity to make himself look good. I wasn't going to stand for that when my old man isn't here to defend himself."

"I guess not, what are you going to do though?"

"Not a goddamn thing. As much as he would love to get rid of me, he can't. I made that team what they are. Before me, they never won a single championship so they better pray I don't leave. The prick will just have to put up with me and shut the hell up." He balls one hand into a tight fist then slams it into the palm of the other.

"Hear, hear." I nod and raise my coffee cup like it's a wine glass.

"In the meantime…" His voice trails off and the lightheartedness returns to his face. "I'll be busying myself with dating the list of potentials you never got around to seeing, which is basically all except one."

I laugh. "Trust you."

"You know I don't believe in wasting anything. definitely not a list of the hottest women on this side of the planet. In return, they get me, Luc Le Blanche, the soon-to-be captain of the New York Hawks and hockey god."

It's funny how he can say such sentimental things in one breath then become an actual playboy in the next. It will be interesting to see what he'd be actually like if he met a woman he'd want to keep. I wonder if he'd be like me.

But then… I fucked up.

He hasn't done that yet and he hasn't met the girl who falls outside his rules. I have and I messed it all up. That's why I'm in the mess I'm in and the tug of war is waging in my heart.

"Alright, your highness. Oh great powerful hockey god, come down from your high throne so we can finish our sandwiches and coffee." I laugh while he frowns. "I can't see you from all the way up there." I make a show of gazing heavenward and pretending to look for him in the visible clouds just out the window.

"Very funny, Grayson. You're such a joker." He picks the crust of the bread off the sandwich and throws it at me, just like we used to as children. That was the start of many food fights in the cafeteria at school and summer camp.

We talk and eat for the rest of time, then go our separate ways.

I'm supposed to head back to work for a meeting, but as soon as I start thinking of my beautiful sexy wife my dick has other plans and I don't even make it through the revolving doors of Grayson Inc.

Instead I head to my car and drive out of the parking lot like I'm on my last lap at the Grand Prix.

The closer I get to the theater, the better and better Luc's idea feels to me. Like bitter sweet temptation. Having him suggest this wild idea of being with River and enjoying her for the time we're together almost feels like he's given me the permission I desperately sought and never knew I needed.

It's nearly two. River would normally be teaching at the school today but the dance company needed her to do some extra rehearsals.

She should be at the theater for another few hours, so I head straight there.

She's on stage when I arrive, doing a piece.

I find a seat near the front row of the theater so she can see me. When she does it takes me back to the days when I used to watch her dance.

She used to tame the beast inside me who was always so angry at the world.

It's been years since I watched her dance and the last few times I saw her she didn't know I was there. That was in England.

She was amazing. She was amazing every single time, and my girl is amazing now.

Dressed in a black leotard, River glides across the stage doing a sequence of steps then she goes *en pointe* and into a grand jeté split jump when the music picks up. It's a piece that sounds like it was inspired by Bach's collection of greatest hits.

My thoughts snap when a male dancer joins her on stage and gets real close. At one point they look like they're about to kiss. I figure him to be the love interest and I know they're just acting, but that doesn't do anything for my irritation that he's got his hands on my wife.

An hour later when practice ends I go backstage and find him talking with River. They seem to be going over their steps.

Just before I reach them River lifts her leg into an arabesque and the asshole runs his hand over her thigh. It's too close and too much for my comfort.

"Hey," I call out.

The two of them stop. River smiles at me while the guy, who looks like a clean-cut Disney Prince, narrows his eyes at me.

"Hi there," he says, looking me over.

"Practice is over, I think you've touched my wife enough for today. You can go home now."

He chuckles, thinking I'm joking, but I'm not. River who knows I'm not rushes to my side, laughing offkey.

"You are so funny, Jericho."

I want to tell her there's nothing funny but I decide to bite my tongue and stare the guy down instead.

"Dave, this is Jericho," she introduces me.

I cut her a hard glance when she forgets the most important part of her introduction. "Her *husband*. I'm River's husband." I emphasize the words and she flashes me that death glare she's given me one too many times.

"Yes, my husband."

"I think most of New York knows that fact," Dave replies with a nod. "Congratulations on your marriage. Good to meet you, Jericho."

"Likewise." The answer sounds genuine but I know my face tells a different story.

"Okay." River's voice takes on a high pitched tone, showing her discomfort with my abrasiveness and foreboding presence. "So I'll see you tomorrow, Dave."

She doesn't wait for Dave to answer before she's hustling me away, clearly nervous of whatever is going to come out of my mouth next.

She waits until we're in the hallway and well out of earshot before that glare of hers comes back and she whirls around to face me.

"What in the world are you doing?" She whisper-shouts. "You can't do the whole crazy husband thing with people here."

"I didn't like the way he was touching you."

Her face falls and her lips part. "We were practicing, and Dave is married with children."

"Being married with children never stopped anyone with wanton eyes and cheating hearts."

She continues staring at me with those beautiful lips agape. "Did you just say *wanton eyes*?"

"Yes." I nod.

"Jericho. This is crazy, and what are you doing here?" Her expression relaxes and a look of awe sneaks into her eyes.

"Maybe I missed you, wife." I touch her cheek.

"Missed me? In what ways." The kind of mischief that I like flashes in her eyes.

"All the ways I should, so I came to get you and take you home."

"Take me home?"

I cup her face and she lightly glides her finger over my chest, igniting all the need I have for her.

"I want to take you home and right back to our bed."

"*Our* bed?" River raises her brows. She looks as if she wants to keep up the sexy edge of defiance she has going on, but she's failing and yielding to this thing between us that neither of us can control

"*Our* bed, wife. Come home with me." I move in and kiss her tenderly.

"Okay, let's go home."

We barely make it home. I just manage to park in the garage before I grab her and set her on the hood of my car.

One hungry, filthy kiss leads to me being buried deep inside her, buried to the hilt and losing my damn mind as I fuck my wife on the hood of my car.

Her moans fill me, inside and out. Taking her again feels selfish but I need her.

I fucking need her. The poignant thought makes my thrusts more profound and animalistic. River's body jerks as she comes and her walls clench around my dick, milking me, but still I keep going.

I'm not done yet.

I pick her up and flip her around so she's bending over the hood and I can watch her lush ass jiggle as I pound into her from behind.

We stay like that for a nice pocket of time until we come.

My senses only return for a few heartbeats, then I'm lost again the moment we fall into bed—our bed. There's no fucking way she's going back to that room she was previously in. My room is hers now, my bed hers, my life hers.

And she is mine.

We get in the bed then I can't stop. I keep needing more and more of her and finding excuses to have her one more time.

We're like this for the rest of the week and neither of us goes anywhere. At this point I'm so consumed with her that I can't even remember the way to work.

Monday morning sneaks up on us and I know that if we have a repeat of last week we'll piss off a whole bunch of people. I might not care but she has ballet and that's her world too.

As she lies in my arms, resting her head against my heart we watch the morning brighten before us, and I think of what to do.

I never thought I'd ever be considering Luc's advice on such a deep level, but I am. I've been thinking about it like crazy, my mind doing all sorts of mental acrobatics to work out how it could all *work*.

One year—well, it's not a year now. As of today we have eleven and a half months left to run on the contract.

Do I want to spend the rest of that time in limbo and having these wild sessions then not really putting a label on it? And what about her?

I know her, she's the same as me. She's thinking too.

Not getting too close went right out the window before it even became a thing, so we need to do the alternative.

River shuffles in my arms and I run my finger over the flat of her stomach.

"I need to get dressed, Jericho," she mutters.

"I know, just give me five minutes."

She laughs. "What are we going to do for five minutes?"

I pull back and turn so I can face her. "You can listen to me."

"What will you be talking about?"

I hold her gaze. "I think we should have a fling." That almost sounds juvenile and crazy outside my mind, so when she laughs it's not surprising.

"A fling? Is that what you do over the summer or something like that."

"Yeah, except we do it for a year." I nod.

Damn it to hell, the spark in her eyes shows she thinks it might be a good idea.

"Do married people have flings with each other?"

I take her hand and bring it to my lips. "We can."

"So we're definitely not friends anymore?"

"Not since my dick became obsessed with your pussy."

Her cheeks color. "You are so crazy."

"About you, wife. I'm crazy about you."

She blinks and her eyes become glassy. "I'm a little crazy about you too, *husband*."

"Then let's do it, don't say no to me, Mermaid."

"Yes. I say yes, Jericho."

Chapter Twenty-Seven

River

Six months later

"I HAVE OFFICIALLY DECIDED TO STICK WITH THIS HAIR color," Gina declares, raising her glass of wine and giving her new jet black locks a flick over her shoulder. "For once, I no longer look like a mangy badger."

The table erupts with laughter. Even Dad cracks a smile on his rigid face.

Around the table are Gina, Eden, Dad, Jericho, and me.

We're at Gina's house for a celebratory dinner because I just got a role with the New York City Ballet.

My audition was only a few days ago and I got the call yesterday to confirm the best news ever.

Of course my amazing aunt had to put together an impromptu dinner.

It's worth noting that it would only be an occasion like this that she could manage to get us all together at a table.

God knows what's going to happen for Thanksgiving and Christmas. Dad is usually with me, or I'm with him. Even when I was in Russia one of us would make the journey. This year I can't imagine him sitting at the table with Jericho, but that can be tomorrow's problem or in the next few months.

Tonight I'm happy and my mind is still buzzing with the news of my success.

I can hardly contain myself. I officially start working for the New York City Ballet in two months' time. Until then I still have nightly shows with the dance company and classes at the school, which I've been given the go ahead to continue teaching until the spring term.

My life has changed in so many amazing ways, but so has Gina's.

Now that her treatment and health are stable, Gina looks so different. Right now she looks at least a good ten or so years younger with her new hairstyle which is longer and more beautiful.

"I think you look amazing," I say with a sure nod.

"Thank you my darling niece, and well done again."

Everyone nods and I smile with pride.

"Thanks so much."

"Now let's eat this gorgeous food." She waves her hand over the glorious spread before us as if she's holding a magic wand.

We all tuck in and Gina kicks off the conversation by talking about the new project she and her business partners are working on. Jericho chimes in because he's working on a new project too.

Eden and I exchange awe-filled glances when he takes my hand and holds it on the table for everyone to see.

It's been exactly six months. Yesterday was the six month mark of our marriage, so technically we've been back in each other's lives for almost eight months.

It was close to that time that Jericho and I ran into each other at Club Edge. Or more specifically, I flew past him on my aerial hoop.

So much has happened since. There have been life changing events like Knight and Aurora welcoming their new baby boy into the world. And me getting that second chance to dance for a world-renowned company again.

Jericho gave me my million dollars to spend as I wished so I set out doing all the things I wanted to do.

As Jericho took care of Jones because he didn't want me having any dealings with him, I paid back Gina every cent she spent to save me. I then paid off my father's mortgage on the condo and gave Eden back the money she gave me. As a treat I also sent her on a two week yoga retreat on a cruise to the Caribbean.

I put the rest of money away for myself. For the future. I know I have another million to come but I don't want to be wasteful. The idea occurred to me that maybe I could build a dance school in the very near future. It would be nice to own something like that sooner rather than later.

It's all been so exciting to see the changes taking place, but then there have been the little things too, that have made a massive impact on my heart.

Things like the closeness between Jericho and me.

Since that day when we agreed to this *fling* more has changed between us. All for the better. Six months have gone by quickly and I've found myself thinking about the next six.

I feel like they'll be passing even quicker. That's what happens when you're counting down.

Stop it, River. You promised yourself you wouldn't do this.

Poor me. I have the same thoughts on a daily basis and I have to remind myself of my promise to put things in perspective and protect my heart.

The task might have been easier when I started this journey, but honestly nothing was ever easy when it came to Jericho Grayson.

This is harder because I keep falling for him stronger and faster every single day.

What's that thing people say? That all good things must come to an end.

That's us.

I take a measured breath to push the harrowing thought out of my mind and focus on the slices of roast beef and vegetables on my plate.

Better not to think about it. It hurts less.

We enjoy dinner and have the sort of feel-good conversations that creates a great mood. Once we're all done, Gina calls me into the kitchen to help her with the desserts, but I know she also wants to talk to me away from the group.

"Come here and let me hug you again," she bubbles as soon as the kitchen door closes.

I hug her and I feel like a child again when she taps my head.

"I am so, so proud of you." She nods, bringing her hands to her chest with a relieved sigh.

"Thanks, Gina. That means a lot."

"Please make sure you take a good step back and see how far you've come." She sets her hands on my shoulders.

I nod and think about the advice. "I've come a long way."

"You really have and you have the very best husband anyone could ever wish for you." Her smile brightens.

I smile back, feeling my cheeks heat. "He does take care of me."

"I'd say he does more than that. I'm just so darn happy for the two of you." She hugs me again and we both laugh.

"You next. You have to go on that date with that guy from the hiking club."

She's started hiking again, but not like she used to. She's been doing these organized walks in national parks. The guy who organizes them has been asking her out.

"Maybe," she chuckles.

"Oh good. Maybe sounds very good and positive."

"I thought so. We're probably going to start with a lunch date then see how things go from there."

"That sounds even better."

"Alright Miss Lady, enough of my love life. Let's get the people their dessert. I made the pies using your great grandmother's recipe book and I added extra cinnamon."

Anything in my great grandmother's book is divine.

Gina opens the oven and the scent of heaven hits me. She takes out the apple pie and we prepare individual servings in dessert bowls with ice cream.

My phone buzzes with a text in my jeans pocket.

Earlier Laila the arts director at the New York City Ballet said she was going to send me a link so I could start building my staff profile and do the mandatory online training.

I expect that to be her so I grab my phone.

"One sec, Gina. This should be the director."

"Take your time, I'll be fine." Gina smiles back at me and heads out of the kitchen with two bowls of pie.

I open the message expecting it to begin with some pleasant congratulatory opening because that's how Laila's messages have all begun, but it doesn't.

And it's not from her.

The message says:

Heard you got married, but that's okay.

I'm sure I can fix that problem.

You will always be mine, Baby doll.

I'll see you soon,

Sasha.

My throat closes and my hands shake so hard the phone falls and lands on the floor.

God. Sasha.

He just messaged me.

He said he'd see me soon.

Is he out of prison?

How?

Please God, no. This can't be happening. It can't.

But it is.

Chapter
TWENTY-EIGHT

Jericho

THE MOTHERFUCKER IS STILL BEHIND BARS.

I've just gotten the confirmation that Sasha Konstantin is still an inmate at Fortovoich Prison, yet he got River's number and was able to message her from there.

Although I'm furious he contacted her, I'm more concerned about what he's trying to tell us.

What kind of trouble is on our way?

I couldn't find any details or records discussing Sasha's early release, but I don't think we'll have to wait too long to find out.

He said he'd see River *soon*.

Men like him don't say such things if they don't mean it.

I also believe the asshole will make good on those other promises he made.

I march up the stairs and head up to the bedroom where I left River.

We came straight home after she got the message. We didn't tell Gina what was going on because we didn't want her to worry.

However, River's father knows.

I just had the pleasure of calling Neil to give him an update only to hear him tell me this was expected because he knew how much Sasha loved his daughter. Then he spent ten minutes telling me about how wonderful things were when they got together.

That man tried my patience all night, but everything he said in that conversation pushed my buttons in all the wrong ways. He sounded pro-Sasha and anti-Jericho. I couldn't understand it, when he must have known how Sasha treated River.

Worse, Sasha is in prison, but I suppose that's still better than being Tobias Grayson's son.

Eden stayed with River while I checked things out on Sasha.

I got anyone I knew who could get me intel quickly to work on this as fast as possible. They got back to me within the hour, but I still feel empty.

Empty and fucking helpless.

Those are not good feelings to have when you know your wife is a target for some psycho she was previously engaged to and he wants her back.

I slam a fist into the side of my leg and tamp down the urge to breathe fire.

I calm myself even more when I walk into the bedroom and find River and Eden sitting side by side on the bed.

River looks even paler than she did when she got the message. I guess that's because she's had time to think and allow what's happened to sink in.

Eden stands and meets me halfway. She looks as worried as I feel.

She's just River's friend though. I'm going crazy because it's my job to protect my wife and I feel like I can't. I can't fight what I can't see.

"Is he out?" Eden asks in a hurried voice.

River grabs the edge of the bed, her knuckles turning white.

"No. Sasha is still in prison," I confirm, much to their relief. "I'm still checking things out to see what's happening."

"Okay. That's good right?" Eden looks back at River then at me again. A trace of hope flickers across her face and she tries to smile but it doesn't quite reach her lips.

"It's good for the moment."

Eden's lips part and she stares back at me for a few beats before her chest caves. "Is there anything I can do?"

I shake my head. "No. It's late. You should go home. I'll let you know if there are any updates."

"Alright. Please let me know if you need me to come back or anything like that."

"Of course." I give her a curt nod.

She goes back to River and gives her a hug then she leaves.

I walk over to River and take Eden's place opposite her on the bed.

River stares back at me with an empty look in her eyes. "It's funny, I shouldn't be surprised. I feel like I should have known this would happen. I just didn't know it would be so soon."

"Baby, I don't want you to worry about this."

"Jericho, there is everything to worry about here. *Everything.*" Her voice shakes and quivers. As if it's lost in the wind. "You don't know what this guy is like. He's in prison for a reason. He's dangerous and the worst person I've ever met. There's no point checking things out. It's obvious he's going to be released in the *very* near future, and if he doesn't know now he'll know soon that it was me who sent him to prison. I just know it's going to happen."

She breaks down and the tears come. I pull her in to hold her but it's like she's crying for everything that's ever happened.

Hearing her in so much pain and knowing she must be so terrified breaks me, and I blame myself.

It always comes back to me. One bad choice, one bad move on the chessboard of life and this is what happened.

I allowed myself to become a pawn and I fucked things up for everyone else. Especially River.

If not for me she wouldn't know Sasha, because she would have been with me.

She would have always been with me.

I hold her while she cries herself to sleep. It's only once she's asleep that the answer of what I need to do comes to me.

This Sasha didn't just send her a message, the message was for me too.

He basically said he was going to take my wife away from me.

That is a declaration of war and a challenge that I will accept. Nobody threatens me or what's mine and gets away with it. Nobody.

So I'll do exactly what I do when shit like this happens: face the problem.

On this occasion I need my wingman. The guy I've been purposely leaving out this whole time because I knew he'd be able to see through my web of lies and deceit.

I need Knight.

He's the only one I'd trust at this moment to balance me.

I call him at first light.

"Hey, everything okay?" he asks, sounding unsurprisingly worried. I can't remember the last time I called him this early in the morning.

"I need you to go to Russia with me."

"When?"

This is what I love about Knight. He doesn't waste time asking questions. He'll already know that we'd only be going to Russia for something important.

"Today."

♟

We arrive at Fortovoich Prison at seven in the morning the next day. The time difference between our countries screwed with me.

I wanted to rip through the fabric of time to get here as quickly as possible but we got here as quickly as we *could*. I also had to pull a few strings by calling in favors with off-grid friends who could arrange this visit for us.

No matter who you are, Fortovoich Prison is not the kind of place where you can just make demands, but people all over the world respond to power.

River told me Sasha has his *dangerous* mafia connections.

Well I have mine, too.

Whoever he knows, and no matter how dangerous they are, I'm sure I know just as many people who are the same if not worse. That was essentially how I made this little arrangement today.

River knows I'm here but I didn't make her aware of what I was doing until I was enroute to Russia. I didn't want her to freak out. Honestly I wasn't going to tell her but I felt I should, to give her strength.

Sometimes just knowing you have someone fighting for you helps. It might not solve everything, but it does something.

Knight and I follow the prison guard down a long hallway. I explained the situation to Knight when we met up yesterday to travel. I told him about Sasha, but I never told him about River's part in putting him behind bars. That's not for me to tell.

However, while telling him about Sasha I knew Knight could sense there was more to my story. So much more.

I'm like an incomplete puzzle and people are beginning to see all the spaces where the missing pieces should be.

We round a corner and approach a metal door which the guard opens. It leads into the visitation room for closed visits, so we'll be separated by glass.

I can see it now and I see him—*Sasha*.

The asshole knows I'm coming to see him, but I'd be willing to bet my entire fortune that he never expected me to ride out to the battlefield to meet him face to face.

Sasha is the same age as me but the scars on the side of his face and his full beard make him appear older.

Dressed in a gray jumpsuit with his shaggy black hair an unruly mess, Sasha looks like the sort of hardened criminal you'd expect to see here.

He's got Russian tattoos on his hands and crawling up his arms. They look like knife scars or the sort you get from something sharp, like glass.

Knight hangs back with the guard while I make my way to the chair in front of Sasha.

It's going to be weird talking to him through the glass but I'll make do. It's better than nothing.

"Sasha Konstantin, I got your message." I rest my hands on the counter between us.

"I didn't send you anything, Jericho Grayson," he answers in a deep Russian accent. "I don't know you, rich boy."

I chuckle off-key. "If you send my wife a message on a number you're not supposed to have, that makes that message for me too."

It's his turn to laugh but the sound just infuriates me further.

"I give you credit for coming here, Jericho Grayson, but you are in way over your head."

"Oh I don't think so. It's you who's in over your head. I came here to tell you not to message my wife ever again. Don't fucking do it."

"You got some balls, but do you really think I'm gonna listen to you? Do I look like one of your servants or brown nosers."

"No, you look like a pathetic idiot who won't leave his ex alone when it's clear she doesn't want you, so stay the fuck away. Message her again or go near her…" I make it clear that I'm aware he must be on his way out soon. "Do it and I will fuck you up and destroy you."

He smiles back at me and I don't know what's worse, the smile or no answer.

Sasha just looks at me for a few moments with that psychotic smile on his face and I wait for what seems like forever for some other response.

"What the hell are you smiling at?" I'm losing my cool. That's probably what he wanted.

"You. See you on the other side, Grayson. Enjoy my woman while you can. When I get out of here, I'm taking her back from you. River St. James is not the kind of woman you allow to leave you."

His words… they fill my mind and stay there, still and unmoving as if someone froze them in my head.

This asshole, as bad as he is, knows one of the biggest truths I've had to learn the hard way. That River is not the kind of woman you let go of, yet here I am with a countdown of six months on our relationship.

How do I let her go when the time comes?

How do I let her go and leave her in the world to men like this animal who hurt her.

I'm not going to let that happen.

"Stay away from her, you hear?"

Again he smiles and stares at me with no answer. Frustration gets the better of me and I punch the glass. Of course it's the kind that doesn't break.

If it were, my hands would be around his neck.

"Come on Jericho, we gotta go," Knight says, coming up to me.

"Stay away from her!" I shout at Sasha.

Knight grabs my arm and ushers me away from the glass. I didn't realize it but another guard has joined us. *For me.*

Sometimes I forget the temper I have on me. I wouldn't care if I unleashed it but doing so now wouldn't help anyone. That's the only reason why I go with Knight, but as I leave all I can see is Sasha staring back at me with that I've-already-won smile plastered across his face.

I sit by the floor-to-ceiling glass windows of the hotel room Knight and I are staying in.

I'm smoking a cigar and trying to calm the fuck down, but I still can't.

We've been back from the prison for several hours but I can't shake the bad feeling I have in my gut. There's nothing worse than feeling like your efforts made no difference.

I keep thinking of what I have to do to protect River when I get back.

We're heading home in a few hours. Knight has just gone out to get lunch for us. He should be back soon, then we'll be on our way. I can't wait to leave this place and get home to my girl.

The front door opens and Knight comes in carrying a bag of food. I can smell it from here but I'm not hungry. I can never eat when I'm in fight mode.

Knight walks over to me, sets the bag on the table between us and sits in the chair in front of me.

"I just got some sandwiches from the deli," Knight says. "I wasn't sure what you wanted so I got a range of things."

"Thank you for going."

"No worries." He stares at me and I can practically see all the questions waiting to leap out of his head, but I know Knight won't pounce on me and bombard me with a ton of things he might not get answers for. He'll ask what he thinks will get him answers to the most important questions.

"Go on, ask me." I extend the invitation because I feel like I should.

"Are you sure?"

"Yes."

"Alright, here goes. Do you remember last year when I thought my marriage was over? We sat on the beach by my house and you mentioned a girl. Do you remember that, Jericho?"

"Of course I remember."

It was the first time that I'd mentioned that girl in years but it didn't mean I'd stopped thinking about her.

Aurora had found out all that Knight had done to get her inheritance through their marriage and it nearly broke them up.

That was Bastian's fault but Knight had his own part to play. A part that didn't excuse his actions and decisions to get what he wanted in the empire. I encouraged him not to give up because I felt it could be fixed, but I purposely let it slip that I couldn't fix my relationship because some things can't be fixed.

"That girl was River, wasn't she?" He searches my eyes.

I stare back at him for a beat then nod slowly. "Yes, it was her."

"How did you guess?"

"It's the way you look when you're around her and when you talk about her. I could have believed the story you served us effortlessly, but the way you looked at her tipped me off."

Only a brother would notice something like that.

I put out my cigar and sulk against the cushion.

"You two were a couple in high school," he surmises.

"Yes."

"That's where your story changes, isn't it?" His face hardens and I realize I'm going to have to come clean with everything.

"Yes. That's exactly right."

"And your marriage? Did you make some arrangement with her? Something with a get-out clause that makes sure you both get what you want."

The weight of his stare pulls me under. I don't answer that question.

I don't need to.

All these long weeks and months have gone by, but my brother would have guessed what I was up to from long ago.

"What happened in high school, Jericho? Or whenever you two officially broke up. Why did you keep her a secret?"

"Our fathers were rivals. That's one reason I kept her a secret."

"*Our fathers?*" He narrows his eyes. "I never knew that."

"You wouldn't, besides, our father is so powerful that men like Neil aren't even on his radar anymore." I shake my head with disgust because Father probably wouldn't know who Neil is. "At first I didn't want any trouble for either of us and I didn't want any extra shit with Father. I also didn't want to create more problems for you and him. God knows we had enough to worry about."

"I never want to be the reason you have to make choices like that."

"I know but it was during the time when Father didn't want us to be part of the company."

"Jesus." His shoulders slump and understanding forms in his expression.

"Nevertheless… I decided to fight for her after she graduated high school even when her father warned me away. In the end, what stopped me was me. Something I did."

"What did you do?" His voice is soft and careful, as if he already knows what I'm going to tell him is the type of dark shit you bury away forever.

I take a moment to think about how I'm going to tell him what I did. It's not the easiest of stories to tell and I know he's going to judge me for it. Even if he doesn't intend to, he'll still judge me.

I shuffle in my seat and lean forward, resting my elbows on my knees.

"I took a job that ruined everything," I begin, then the rest of the story flows.

The words fall from my lips like acid, each one burning parts of my character away.

I tell him about the job, the drugs, the mistakes, the consequences I had to pay. I tell him about River's father and the way he lost the use of his legs, then I explain more about why I'm in this arrangement with River and why I can't be with her.

By the time I'm done I feel like a million years have passed by, but I feel light.

I feel like I just broke off a piece of the weight I was carrying and gave it to him to share the load.

"Why didn't you tell me before? How could you keep

something like this from me?" I expected to see more rage in his eyes, not hurt.

"I couldn't. I just couldn't."

"We've always had each other's back but you kept this from me."

"You had your own shit to deal with. It's only in recent months that we've been free of Father's tyranny. Besides, I never expected to see River again. Now I have to be around to protect her. I can't allow Sasha to hurt her."

"Jericho," he says my name in a harsh tone. "If you think that all you're needed for is to protect her, then you're a fool."

"I can't do anything else. I've run away from this for so long because I couldn't bear to see her look at me with such disappointment when she found out what I did."

"I understand that and I see your point, but I'm going to tell you something you told me once that kicked my ass in gear."

"What was that?"

"You're in love with your wife." He nods. "You knew I was in love before I accepted it. I'm telling you now because you need to be told. You didn't stop being in love with River."

I hear those words and I feel like a fool because he couldn't be more right.

I've acted like the guy who could see the sun staring right back at him and still maintain that the day was cloudy.

I *am* in love with my wife.

"Don't tell me I'm wrong, because I know I'm not and you're not going to find it easy to let her go."

"It's not that simple. We've come a long way, and I'm grateful for the time I've had with her, but I still believe she deserves better than me. I can't be with her past our agreement and continue to keep the secret to myself."

"Why don't you allow her to decide that for herself? Have you ever thought about that?"

No. The answer is no, but I think it's a given that I wouldn't have needed to consider that.

Her father can't walk. It's the ultimate price. If he knew, Jesus, if he knew the truth, it would be even worse.

Knight leans forward and stares me down. "If you lose River, you'll regret it for the rest of your life. She's your wife now. There's a difference because you're a different man. She's different too and if nothing else she deserves the truth. She also deserves the option to choose. Don't lie to her, and stop being a coward."

Only he could call me out on being a coward.

It's not a nice thing to be called. Neither is it a label I want to accept.

Denying it would have the added effect of being cowardly.

I can do brave things like walk into a prison and talk big in front of assholes like Sasha, but when it comes to hurting River with the truth, I've been running away for years with my tail between my legs.

I can't argue with Knight. He's right again about everything, but I feel like my back is up against the wall.

I've tried to make up for the past in all the ways I thought would help her and hopefully redeem me, but only telling the truth can give me the complete redemption I seek.

I want to be with River. That is all I want, more than anything in my life, even life itself. Letting her go would kill me.

The pathway to keeping her in my life is telling her the truth. It would be a start, whether she can forgive me or not.

River deserves to know the truth, along with a real explanation of the reason I broke up with her, and I will just have to accept the consequences. For good or for bad.

I have to find the right time to tell her everything, and it has to be soon.

Maybe if she knows how much I've always loved her it might help.

The selfish part of me is desperate for her forgiveness.

I hope she'll allow me to earn it.

I truly hope she can.

Chapter
TWENTY-NINE
River

I'M SITTING ON THE BAY WINDOW SEAT IN THE BEDROOM, going insane with worry.

I've been a mess since I got the message from Sasha.

I haven't been able to do anything besides worry and explore those worries in my all too vivid nightmares.

They're back, but this time I keep seeing Sasha pulling a gun on Jericho and shooting him. That's the image I'm cursed with, so I've barely slept in the three days that he's been gone.

I've barely eaten and hardly left this spot by the window, and I haven't gone anywhere.

Eden has been staying with me, Dad has even come by, and the staff have been even more attentive than they usually are.

Everyone has been great, but this shell of myself where I'm constantly on edge and so terrified I can scarcely breathe is what Sasha Konstantin does to me.

People with my kind of scars find it harder to heal. Our wounds go deeper than the surface. They run deeper past your blood, past your veins, past your soul.

You're never the same again once you get them.

God knows how truly grateful I am to Jericho for going all the way to Russia to face my demon and stare my dragon in the eye to tell him to leave me alone, but I know this won't be over.

That's not how Sasha works.

Jericho is supposed to be coming back later, most likely in the early hours of the morning. I can't wait to see him. Just to see him and know that he's safe.

Then I have to tell him the dreadful decision I've come to.

That I'm leaving…

That I have to leave.

I would never do anything to affect our arrangement, so I'll assure him of that, but I can't stay.

I rest my head against the wall and allow fresh tears to stream down my cheeks as I stare at the shadowy trees in the night, swaying from side to side in the wind.

I close my eyes, disconnecting the vision and all I see is darkness. It swallows my mind, then I hear the faint sound of music. Piano music.

It's my *Clair de Lune*. The boy I love is playing it for me and I see myself dancing.

Warm hands cover mine and caress my skin, then the same warmth touches my cheeks.

"River." Jericho's voice seeps into my mind. He says my name again and the music fades along with the vision of myself dancing.

I open my eyes and I see Jericho crouching before me. He's holding my hand with one hand and touching my face with the other.

It takes me a moment to realize he's real.

"You're home," I gasp, throwing my arms around him.

He rises and holds me tight, lifting me slightly off the ground.

"I just got back." He cups my face and places me back on the bay seat so we're facing each other. "Lauren says you haven't eaten all day."

"I couldn't. I was too worried about you. I'll have a big breakfast later." I try to smile.

Jericho pulls up the stool and sits in front of me so he can hold both my hands.

"I don't want you to worry like this about me."

"Are you serious?" I smirk and blow out a ragged breath. "Jericho, you went to a prison in Russia to confront my asshole ex who has an eight-year sentence. Bad, bad, bad people get that length of sentence. I'm sure that if he wasn't who he is it would have been longer, and now there's the possibility of him getting out sooner. Of course I'm going to worry."

He gives me a soft smile. "I promised I would never allow him to hurt you again, so this is me fulfilling that promise."

"Thank you. Thank you for what you did. You keep saving me in all the ways I can't save myself." Another wave of emotion grips me when I think of everything he's done for me and I blink back tears.

"You don't have to thank me for any of those things."

"I do have to thank you, Jericho. I do. So thank you. For *everything*."

He nods and kisses my knuckles. "Anytime, Mermaid. *Anytime*."

It's time to ask the question that's been on my mind. "What happened when you saw Sasha? How did it go?"

He drags in a steady breath and releases my hands. "It wasn't the best of meetings but he got the message to leave you alone."

My shoulders drop because I know that won't be enough.

"Jericho, what you did is the bravest thing I've ever seen anyone do. It's certainly one of the best things anyone has ever done for me, but Sasha doesn't respond to threats. He thinks he's a god. I um…" My voice chokes when I think of what I have to tell him. "You'll be in danger if you keep pushing back and fighting him."

"I don't care about danger. I won't stop fighting for you."

"That's why I have to leave."

He straightens instantly, his eyes widening, his lips apart, his expression grim.

"No."

"It wouldn't affect our arrangement. I promise I wouldn't allow that to happen."

"Leaving is not an option, and fuck the arrangement. You're staying with me, River."

I press down hard on my back teeth and will myself to keep going. One of us has to do the right thing. It seems like it has to be me.

"Jericho, We're only going to be together for the next six months. Why put yourself and your family in that type of danger for me?" My voice shakes, quivering with every word, and I hate that it's come to this.

"You are my family."

My heart slows on hearing those words. Then it warms when he takes my hands again.

"Jericho—"

"You are my family, River and I can't let you go." He speaks with a meaningful determination I've never heard in him. "I can't do it whether that's now or in six months."

"What?" My voice is so soft I can barely hear it and I give him a narrowed stare, not quite believing what I'm hearing.

"I don't want you to leave in six months. I don't want you to leave me ever."

"You want to stay married to me?" I check to be sure that what I'm hearing is what he's saying.

"Yes. I want to stay married to you. I'll never forget what it feels like to not have you in my life and I can't do that again. I can't watch you from the shadows like I did before, knowing I'll never be able to be with you."

I keep my gaze on his. "You watch me from the shadows?"

He sighs and nods slowly. "I kept an eye on you for years after we broke up. I knew when you left New York and I knew when you went to Russia. When you started touring with the Bolshoi I went to every single country you performed in, just so I could see you live your dream."

I stare back at him in utter shock, my body trembling from deep inside my soul.

I can't believe Jericho did all that for me and it would have been for over a period of years.

And he saw me perform. I remember thinking about him so many times when I got on stage wishing he could see me because he knew more than anyone how badly I'd wanted it.

But he was there…

"You really saw me?"

"Yes and you were amazing." He smiles for the briefest moment. "I couldn't let you go then because I loved you and I still love you now. I love you so much, so yes, I want to stay married to you."

I bite down on my bottom lip so hard I nearly pierce the skin. He would never know just how much it means to me to hear him say those words.

"I love you too, Jericho."

He touches my face. "Do you want to stay married to me, River?" He searches my eyes.

I nod as true joy swells my soul. It's strange to feel like that when I've been stuck in the darkness for days. "More than anything."

Jericho smiles but then the light in his eyes dims. "I wish I'd never let you go. You were always it for me. The one. The one girl I would have wanted to spend the rest of my life with and have everything."

Everything he's saying is so beautiful that my soul leaps but the questions I've always had resurface. All the whys and what-happened questions that have lived in my head all these years.

"You said we grew apart."

He drops his head for a moment, then shakes it. "It wasn't that."

"Then what was it?"

"I got myself in trouble." He speaks in that hollow voice I

remember from when we were in Italy. It holds darkness and pain, but I'm so focused on what he's saying that I pay more attention to that.

"Trouble?" I intensify my stare and process what he's saying.

Trouble. That was why we broke up? All these years I thought he didn't love me it was about trouble?

I think of all the things he's shared with me since we've been together. The drugs and his father. Could the trouble be something to do with that?

"There's.... some stuff I have to tell you."

"What stuff? What trouble was it, Jericho?"

"I need some time... just a little more time before I talk about it. Can you give me that?"

I'm so eager to know that my skin is burning, but the lost look in his eyes compels me to agree.

"Okay. Okay."

"Thank you."

He stands and reaches out his hand to me. I take it and he pulls me in for a hug.

With my mind racing I lean against his chest, listening to the wild beat of his heart.

What did you do, Jericho?

What was so bad that it tore us apart?

It must be really bad if he can't tell me now. I've never known this man to cower away from anything.

He's the rebel, but maybe that was the problem.

Chapter THIRTY

Jericho

It's Monday again.

Three days since I raised the alarm to River that trouble was the reason for the end of our relationship.

I knew by telling her that I'd spoiled the moment and broken another connection between us, but I felt I had to.

Not saying something would have been like giving her false hope, when she needed to have all the information to make the decision to stay with me.

Hearing her tell me she loves me wasn't even something I could savor. Even though I realized I was desperate to hear those words. Starved. Starved for years.

I appreciated that she agreed to give me time. I didn't chicken out by making the request. I just felt I needed the extra time to make sure I say all the right things.

I plan to tell her everything by Wednesday.

No later than that.

Now I'm in the meeting of all meetings. The one I've been waiting for since my grandfather announced his retirement. I've accomplished the goal. This meeting is to award me the CFO position of the Park Avenue branch of Grayson Inc. but I can't even enjoy it.

Knight and I are in the boardroom of Park Avenue, joined by our grandfather and father.

We're at the Park Avenue building because this will be the last time that we meet together as the senior management team of Grayson Inc.

Knight has been working on getting Grandfather to see that we are ready to take over the company. I was so happy weeks ago when he finally agreed.

There will be no more reasons to work with my father, or Bastian whenever he gets back, no need to talk to them or see them.

Everything changes today in the biggest of ways and all I can think about is the past.

"This is a great day for me," Grandfather states, looking at Knight and I proudly.

Father is stiff as usual, full of hate, jealousy, and rage. I know why Grandfather wanted him present, but I wish he wasn't here. I don't like being around him when I'm off my game.

Regardless of how I feel and the worries clawing away at my insides about whether or not I'll have a wife by the end of the week, my father's presence today was a necessity.

Today my father will witness what he feared most.

Today is the day he tried to repress.

I stare at my father as Grandfather starts talking about the early days of the company, and I think that every time those fists pounded into me, breaking bones sometimes, this was what he feared.

The day when his bastards got the chance to have our own legacy.

Today also shows him that although Grandfather is leaving soon, he's still the motherfucking boss and there's not a goddamn thing anyone can do to change how he wants his company run.

Not even me.

The old man wanted me to clean up my act and fall in love. The same way Knight figured me out, I know my grandfather would have done the same thing.

Except he took it a little further because he knows me inside out.

He might not have known about River's existence until the fundraiser, but he knew if I tried to do some contract marriage I wouldn't just pick any old girl. He knew I wouldn't have been satisfied with a so-called business partner.

He knew all of that, so I didn't beat him, he beat me.

"I'm really proud of the legacy I've left behind for Grayson Inc. and to know that the company I spent my life's work on will continue growing from strength to strength." He looks at me when he says that, almost like he can read my mind.

Now that I'm married and he can see how much I love my wife, he knows he doesn't have to worry about me anymore.

I would never spoil this moment for him by letting him know that even though he tried to save me, I still fucked up.

He puts his hand out to me and I stand.

"Jericho, it gives me the greatest pleasure to award you the position of the new CFO. You earned it, son." He nods with the same pride brightening his eyes and shakes my hand.

"Thank you. I appreciate that and all you've done for us." I hope he knows I mean those words.

He nods again, then looks at Knight, who stands.

From the envelope on the table Grandfather pulls out the new certificate of incorporation.

He holds it up so my father can see it, then he shows it to us.

It says Graysons LP. That's our new company name.

Grandfather explained that he wanted the new company name to be pluralized to represent *us*. Knight and me. Two brothers who are as close as brothers who will be starting a new empire that will continue with our own legacy. For our kids and their children and their children until the end of time.

Listen to me not just thinking about kids, but grandkids too and beyond.

I hope I get the chance.

Grandfather hands the certificate to Knight and when he stretches out his hand to shake his, Knight gives him a hug instead.

"We'll take care of it for you," Knight says.

"I know." Grandfather nods, then the warmth leaves his eyes as he looks at our father. "Nothing to say, Tobias?"

I could almost laugh. If there wasn't so much angst in my soul I might.

"Well done," Father says, but he doesn't mean it.

"Alright, that wraps it up, enjoy the rest of the day, boys."

"Thank you." Knight and I answer at the same time.

Grandfather smiles then he leaves with father.

The tension instantly evaporates from the room in my father's absence, but it doesn't leave my heart.

Knight holds up the certificate and smiles at me. "We did it."

"We did."

"But... judging from the look on your face, I assume you haven't spoken with River." He looks me over with concern.

I shake my head. "Wednesday. I'm gonna do it Wednesday. I just needed some time. There's a chance I could lose her so...I just wanted to make sure I thought of everything I need to say."

"I understand. I'm here if you need to talk."

"I know. And thanks."

There's a knock at the door. It opens and Beth, my secretary, comes in.

"Sorry to interrupt you guys. Jericho, your father-in-law is here to see you."

"*Neil?*"

"Yeah. He's waiting by your office."

What the hell is Neil doing here?

Why is he here to see me?

I already touched base with him about Sasha. There's no need for him to come here.

I glance at Knight. He's already looking at me with his jaw clenched and brows knitted. After what I told him about Neil, he knows this visit can't be anything good.

"Alright. I'll go see him." *And see what this is about.*

"Call me later," Knight says and I nod.

"Sure."

I make my way out to my office and find Neil sitting by the window just outside the door. His back is to me so I can't see his face.

Seeing him in that wheelchair pulls on my insides even more today than it has over the last six months.

Probably because I know the moment I tell River what I did, she'll have to tell her father too. Then he'll find some way to make what I did seem like something you could only expect from Tobias Grayson's son.

"Neil," I say his name, getting his attention.

He turns his wheelchair to face me and I notice a brown envelope in his lap. My gaze flicks from it to his eyes.

His face wears the usual unreadable mask but something malicious which makes me feel unhinged lurks in his eyes. It's new and unsettling.

"Jericho, I hope I didn't disturb you."

"Not at all. Do you want to go into my office?" I motion toward the door.

"Sure."

I open the door and hold it for him. He goes right over to the glass wall with the view of the city.

"So this is how the other half lives," he surmises, looking over the view. "I've always wondered if being up so high with a view like this makes you feel like a god."

He's talking more strangely than usual. It's not uncommon

for him to talk in riddles but today seems to carry more of a hidden message.

"Neil."

He turns to face me.

"With all due respect, I'm sure you didn't come to see me to talk about what makes people feel like gods." I wanted to say 'talk about shit' but I decided to choose more respectful words.

Something's not right here and I want to find out what it is. There's no point talking nonsense when we both know there's no universe in which he would visit me to be pleasant.

"No, I didn't, but there was some relevance to what I was saying."

"In what way?"

He fixes his chair so he can face me properly. "I used to have my own office once. It was high up like this. Just that simple thing made me feel like somebody. Did River ever tell you that I got a scholarship to go to Princeton?"

"No, she didn't tell me that."

"Ah... well I did. I always worked hard. I got a scholarship to go to the academy where I first met your father. People like me and mine don't have your kind of money. We rely on scholarships and kindness, but then assholes like your father come along."

"Has he done something more to you recently?" I harden my stare because I want him to get to the point.

"No, but I just found out the apple didn't fall far from the tree. It turns out the son isn't that much different from the father."

The moment he says that I know in my gut that he's found something out that he shouldn't have. Something secret about me.

Shit. This is all I need now, for Neil St. James to have me by the balls, seething under his thumb.

"I'm not like my father," I say, even though I know it's pointless.

"I'll be the judge of that."

He reaches into the envelope and pulls out a document. I

recognize it straight away as the contract of marriage between River and me.

My breath stills in my lungs like a wall has been placed before it, blocking the air from escaping.

I'm the one who's used to digging up dirt on people. Now I'm seeing what it feels like to be on the receiving end of exposure.

"Now tell me if this isn't just the sort of thing Tobias Grayson would do. I knew something was fishy about the whole marriage thing. I argued with my daughter, but I drew a line, you know why?"

I stare at him, not wanting to answer, but feeling forced to. "Why?"

"Because I couldn't do better. I couldn't save her and I couldn't save Gina. Those who can't do better should shut up. But now that I know the truth, I can do something about it."

"How did you find out?" This is too odd for words. How the hell did he uncover the agreement? The contract was scanned into my files and locked away under the security of tight firewalls that should have alerted me if someone hacked my system.

So how did he?

After the shit that went down last year with Bastian and Knight I tightened up security. Bastian hired someone to hack us—someone off the charts good. Someone like me.

Fucking Neil must have done the same damn thing. I can claim to be the tech god, but these things can unfortunately happen beyond anyone's control.

It's like being struck by lightning. No matter what you do to protect yourself it could happen. The chances are as slim as me being hacked, but it can still happen and you can never tell when it will.

"How did you find out?" I ask the question again when the seconds tick by for too long and all Neil does is stare at me.

"Let me worry about that. You have one more important question to ask me."

And I know what it is: "What do you want?"

"Divorce my daughter by the end of the month. Leave her be

once and for all. That is what I want. And here's a little more encouragement." He reaches into the envelope, pulls out a piece of notepaper and tosses it to me. It lands on the floor. "Pick it up."

Asshole. He wants to see me crawl like a dog before him.

With my gaze trained on him, I retrieve the paper.

It has the number and letter combination XY67XQ93 in the center.

It takes me seconds to realize what it is.

The sequence is a hacking code I used back in college.

It's the hacking code with which I created the device those hackers used to steal Neil's designs.

"I know what you did," he declares, confirming my worst fears.

Neil found out the truth.

The truth I've been hiding for the last eight years.

All the blood in my veins turns solid and stops flowing, creating a heaviness throughout my body and deep inside my soul. It pushes against my heart and it clenches so tight I fear it may never beat again.

"I know everything, Jericho Grayson." His voice sounds like an echo on the walls of my mind. "I know it was your fault that I lost everything. You created a device that hackers used to steal my designs and sold them to the competition. You caused me to lose my job, you ripped a hole in the relationship I had with my business partner. Now he's dead and I will never walk again. You did that and you stand there telling me you're not like your father."

"I was tricked."

"Cut the shit, boy. You allowed yourself to be tricked. But you know what? You're right, you aren't like your father. You are so much worse and I don't want you anywhere near my daughter. Sasha had his shortcomings but he was nothing like you."

Speechless, I stare back at him. I don't know what to say.

"Get that divorce or she sees this," he adds. "I tell her the truth."

He's talking about River.

"Cross me and I will expose you. You'll lose whatever you stood to gain from marrying my daughter and you'll lose her too."

He tosses the envelope on the floor and wheels around me, then he leaves.

Feeling numb, I pick up the envelope, knowing there must be more inside to damn me. There is.

Inside is a report showing the tracking pathway to the computer I used back then. It was registered to me. Once again it's odd that Neil would have found information like this when I cloaked myself.

One of the things my grandfather was glad for when this went down was that it couldn't be traced to me. Very few people can track past the cloaking device I used back then, so how did Neil find a fucking way?

Fuck… that's not the problem now.

The problem is that he knows. The secret is out there and he could use everything he knows to destroy me.

I've gone from holding my secrets close to my heart to hanging off the edge of a cliff.

The question now is: what do I value most?

River.

She's the answer. Nothing else matters.

I value her more than anything. Even if Neil exposes my ass to the world and I lose the respect of my grandfather and the empire, I can't lose River.

Not like this.

I have to talk to her today.

I can't wait any longer.

Chapter
THIRTY-ONE

River

"How are you feeling?" Eden asks, sounding hopeful.

She called me just as I was about to leave the house to go for a walk.

I press the phone to my ear and sit on the sofa in the sunroom.

"I think I'm doing better."

"That's good. I was so worried about you."

"I'm okay and tons better than when you last saw me." It's a half truth. I am better than when she saw me but more anxious than I've ever been in my life. I'm still eagerly waiting for Jericho to tell me what happened to him in the past or, I suppose, what happened to *us*.

Part of me wants to be mad at him for not sharing the truth with me sooner—*like years ago*—but I feel I can't be too upset with him.

One; because I have a feeling it's quite serious and two; because he's done so much for me.

That said, the more time that passes, the more angsty I become.

I've told Eden the nicer, more sentimental parts of my conversation with Jericho in regard to us staying together, but I didn't tell her anything else.

The aspect of the trouble felt like one of those things couples should keep between themselves.

It's a good thing she's been away with her students again because I might have changed my mind.

"When are you back at work?" she asks.

"I've decided to have the rest of the week off. I think I'll feel more myself by then." I pray I will be. Last night I had to take sleeping tablets so I could have a decent night's sleep. The nightmares got me again. Last time it took months of therapy to help me feel safe again.

"Make sure you rest."

The sound of Jericho's car pulling up on the drive makes me look through the window. It's not even lunchtime so it's strange he's home at this hour. Also, today's the day he was going to get his CFO position. I assumed he'd probably be at work even longer because it's such a big deal.

What could bring him home so early?

"Eden, I'll call you back later. Jericho's home."

"Alright. Let me know if you need me."

"I will."

"Luv ya."

"Love you too."

We hang up and I make my way into the house to meet him. He's just coming through the door when I reach the hallway.

"Hi," I say first and rush into his arms.

He hugs me, kisses me, then holds me again, this time for a little longer.

"Jericho, what's going on? Are you okay?" I pull back a little so I can see his face.

Something's happened. Looking at him now, and seeing the

concern in his eyes, I can see quite clearly that he's home because something bad happened.

"Was it Sasha?"

My mind goes straight to all the possible, terrible things I know Sasha could do.

Jericho shakes his head. The gesture makes me feel partly relieved but I keep hold of my breath knowing that something is still amiss.

"We need to have that talk now," he explains.

"Oh… Okay. Sure." My heart speeds with adrenaline. I'm glad we're going to have that talk now but I'm more anxious to hear what he's going to say.

"Let's go in here." He points to the living room and we go inside.

My nerves spike when he closes the door. In all the time I've been in this house that door has remained open. The sight of it locked stirs more worry in my soul.

He sits me down on the large sofa and lowers next to me, allowing enough space between us so we can face each other.

He swallows hard and I notice the sheen of sweat beading on the side of his face.

"Did something happen today?" I ask.

"Yes."

"What was it?"

"Your father. He came by the office. He found out about our contract."

I suck in a sharp breath and nearly fall off the seat.

"What? How? I didn't tell him anything. I don't even have a copy of the contract. How the hell did my father find out?"

"I don't know how he found out."

From the ashen look on his face I guess that my father could have only done one thing with that information.

"He threatened to expose you, didn't he?" I stutter, wishing he could prove me wrong.

"He did."

"Oh God. I'll speak to him."

"No."

My brows knit. "Of course I have to. If your grandfather finds out the truth you'll lose the position and—"

"That's not what I'm worried about. There's something more important to me than my job or anything my grandfather could offer me."

I stare back at him, astonished. All he cared about months ago was his empire. "What could be more important than that?"

"You."

"Me?" I point to myself as if needing to check that he's really talking about me. "Why... me?"

"Your father found out about the trouble I got myself in years ago. Years ago when we broke up."

"What was it, Jericho? Tell me. Tell me what happened." Whatever it is, it's clearly something that involves me in some way. Now I want to know more than ever.

"I didn't know what I was getting myself into, but I take full responsibility because I didn't think," he starts then he pauses for a moment.

When he speaks again he takes it back to the problems he was having with his father. As he verges on talking about some hackers who hired him to make a hacking device my stomach twists, but it's not enough of a warning to give me a heads-up that it was the same device that stole my father's designs. I don't know until Jericho says the words, and even as he spells it out my mind is so numb that it can't connect what he's actually telling me.

When the connection forms, it *forms* and sinks deep into my body from head to toe, rooting me to the spot.

Jericho made a hacking device that these people used to steal my father's designs.

Jericho...

My mind races back to that time and everything that happened with my father.

My father, who could walk at that time. Then he couldn't because of this thing that Jericho built. Now my father can't walk and his business partner is dead. Sure, I might be taking it too far by thinking that, but it happened.

It happened and Dad lost everything.

I think back to how Jericho was at that time and I realize he did act strangely.

He hardly wanted to see me.

I was so wrapped up in tending to Dad that I didn't take much notice, but everything makes so much sense now.

Everything, including his willingness to help me in my recent devastation with Gina and even with Sasha.

Jericho felt guilty.

I stand on shaking legs and tremors rush through me.

Jericho stands too, seeing my distress. "River—"

"You!" I cut him off. "It was you. You did all that?"

"I didn't know what they were going to do. You have to believe me. If I'd known I would have never built it, no matter what. I swear to you. I didn't know."

"You think not knowing matters? Jericho, so much happened because of what you did."

"I know."

"My father will never walk again. Not ever. How can you think saying you didn't know makes it okay?"

"I don't think it makes anything better, but I want you to know I didn't intend to cause anyone harm."

All I can do is look at him but I can't see past *this*. The truth.

I understand that he was tricked and I understand that he didn't know, but none of that makes it right. Worst of all, it's taken him all these years to tell me.

All these long arduous years.

"River, I'm so sorry." He steps forward to take my hand but I step back and fold my hand into my chest. "River, I'm truly, truly sorry."

"I… I can't. I can't be with you. I can't."

His hand drops to his side and he stares back at me, looking as if all the life has left him.

I take another step away and then I head for the door. I can't stay here.

I can't.

"I will never stop fighting for you," he shouts just as I yank the door open.

I stop in my tracks and look back at him.

"I'll never stop loving you either," he adds.

I turn away and keep going, hating life so much right now I could tear my skin off.

I head to the garage, jump in my car and drive.

There's no destination in my mind, but somehow I end up at my father's house.

I walk in and find him in the living room watching TV.

When he sees me he smiles but it falters as he takes in my drained expression.

"River, what's going on?" He wheels over to me.

"I know what's happening. Jericho told me you came to see him today."

The color recedes from his face. I'm sure he never expected Jericho to tell me what had happened.

"He did?"

"Yes."

"And what do you think? Do you still believe in your golden boy now? I told you, he's a Grayson. *Selfish as hell.* No matter his excuse, those people think they own the world. They want what they want and when people get hurt they claim they didn't know. His lack of knowledge cost me everything. Everything. I don't want to lose you too."

"You haven't lost me." My lips tremble with my raspy voice.

"Then don't lose yourself in him."

I'm already lost. I'm so damn lost my mind is fractured and I honestly don't know what I'm going to do.

Where do I go from here?

Even if I could forgive Jericho and move on, I'd be torn.

Conflicted and torn between my father and my husband.

Chapter
THIRTY-TWO

Jericho

"A BOTTLE OF VODKA, PLEASE," I SAY TO THE bartender.

"Sure thing," he replies and moves away from the counter to retrieve my drink.

I ended up at the Astoria because I needed to get out of the house. There was also no vodka in my drinks cabinet.

Luc is supposed to be joining me.

He messaged earlier, and I ended up telling him everything had gone to hell. I didn't go into details. Not that keeping things under wrap matters any longer. My life feels like an open book plastered on a wall for everyone to read.

I don't fucking care anymore.

I lost the one thing I cared about when she walked out the door.

The bartender returns with the bottle of vodka and a glass filled with ice.

I take them and head to the booth in the corner to sulk and truly drown my sorrows. Right now, I can't do much else.

A pair of heavy boots comes into view as I pour the first glass. It's Luc.

He sits across from me, rests his hands on the table, and gives me that look of pity that only a concerned friend could show when they know you've hit rock bottom.

"What happened?" he asks.

"River knows everything." I swallow hard and clench my jaw. I never made Luc aware that I'd planned to speak to River after I got back from Russia. I decided against telling him because I didn't want him to discourage the conversation. It feels pointless to clarify those points now that everything has gone to shit. "She knows what I did. Her father found out. He found out about our marriage contract, too."

Luc's brows snap together and he glares back at me as if I just spoke in an alien language.

"What the hell are you saying to me? How the fuck did Neil find out?"

"Your guess is as good as mine." I've been trying to figure it out all day, and I'm nowhere closer than I was when I first began. "He's a software engineer. A real good one, but I suppose he can do a little more than his job requires. Like me."

I guess I finally met my match, even though it still doesn't make one ounce of sense how Neil was able to find out all that information on me going back eight years. If it was just the marriage contract I might give that a pass, but the whole thing is suspicious as fuck.

What's the point, though? I can suspect things all I want, it won't change anything. River will still be gone.

Confessing to her was nothing like when I spoke to Knight. I never expected it to be. In fact, I didn't know what the hell to expect but I guess if I were to imagine her response, she acted exactly the way I thought she would.

I can't blame her. If there was any leeway for understanding,

I'd hold on to the fact that I was tricked. My error is knowing that what I did was wrong. I didn't need to take that job and I should have known that people like the men who hired me would have intended to wreak havoc with a device like the one I created. That was where I went wrong.

"I'm completely baffled." Luc shakes his head. "So now that Neil knows about the past and that you agreed to a fake marriage, what does he want?"

Fake marriage? No Luc. Our marriage was not fake. When I married River, I married her. She became my wife and it felt like I had everything I ever wanted. That day was one of the best in my life. Now she's gone and I wouldn't know where to start in coming up with a grand plan to get her back.

"He got what he wanted. River left me." I gulp down my drink. The harshness burns the back of my throat like fire. That's the only feeling I get from it. Any hopes of numbing my mind are crushed.

Luc sighs. "I'm sorry, man. I… I'm drawing a blank. Maybe there's a way things could still work out."

He doesn't know what to tell me. I wouldn't know what to say either in this fucked-up situation.

"Maybe." I give him a hopeful smile to humor the comment. "If there's a way, I'll find it."

He leans closer and levels me a hard stare. "This might sound pointless to you, but if it were me, I'd want to know how the fuck Neil got all that information. He got into your personal files, Jericho. That's hard enough and bad enough as it is, but it's very suspicious that he would find out this information now and not years ago when it counted. Don't you think?"

I straighten and bite the inside of my lip. The bitterness of everything that's happened today has consumed me so much that I didn't consider that.

"Yes. That's a very valid point." I nod slowly.

Luc sits back. "I don't think this is just him. Software engineer or not, I think he had the right kind of help."

The right kind of help? Now, who would that be?

Who would want to help Neil get my ass in such a way?

The end result, no matter which way I look at it, is losing River.

I have many enemies, but I have a bad feeling and a truly farfetched idea about who this person could be.

Sasha!

What if it was him?

Neil all but worshiped the guy when I spoke to him after that message was sent. He didn't have a bad thing to say about Sasha. Then there was what he said today.

What if I'm right?

I go above board and get the right kind of help from the best people I know who can gather intel on anybody within seconds.

By the time I reach home I already have all the tools I need to hack the universe if I want.

I have no doubt I'll be able to get past any security Neil has in place with no problems and find out what filth he's been up to.

What I'm doing might be pointless, but I'm compelled to do it for several reasons.

First, part of me thinks that if I'm right then Neil, who is pro-Sasha, will do his best to get his daughter back together with that asshole. Despite what's happened, I wouldn't put it past him.

Second, I'm doing this for my sanity. It will literally drive me insane if I don't get answers.

I head to my office, jump on my computer, and hack into Neil's. As expected, he has high-level firewalls, but with my tech I walk through them as if they don't exist.

His emails are what I'm looking for. That is always the best place to start. If I don't get anything from his email, his phone will be my next stop.

I find three email accounts. One for work and two for personal use. Since I doubt he'll use his work email for anything like this, I check the other two. One is so old I'm sure he must have had it since the stone age. The other looks like it was last opened over a year ago.

That's the one I start with because it could have been created for a special purpose. The moment I open the inbox, I sense I'm right.

There is a host of undisclosed recipient emails there. That tends to mean that whoever sent the message didn't want to be tracked.

To narrow my search I decide to filter the emails by their IP addresses. Even though the messages are from undisclosed recipients, the system I have in place is able to find a location.

I'm looking for anything from Russia.

When three hundred of the five hundred emails show themselves as coming from Russia, my stomach hardens.

I open the first message from a year ago and surprise, surprise, it's from Sasha.

He's offering Neil money to keep an eye on River. He also lets him know his sentence will be reduced so he'd be out within a year. In reply, Neil praises him and promises to help.

The next lot of messages are check-ins, until I come on the scene and Neil reports to Sasha, letting him know River is getting married to me. Sasha's reply is an offer of five million to break us up. He then tasks Neil with finding dirt on me that will turn River against me.

Motherfuckers, both of them. Neil, you are one nasty piece of shit.

Five million, though. Wow. I guess the offer was tempting enough to make him disregard his daughter's happiness and safety.

The emails that follow are Neil checking in again, to let Sasha know he can't get past my firewalls. Then an email dated last week shows details of some new hacking tech they secured on the black market. I notice the date of the email is the same day River got that message from Sasha.

God, I remember how awkward the dinner was with Neil. Every time I spoke, he looked like he wanted to burn me alive.

I find the details of the hacking tech and realize it would have definitely been able to hack me because it uses sophisticated AI technology designed to copy the system it's trying to hack. It's like a virus, but it can also duplicate any antivirus software to fight it.

The next message delivers Neil's eureka moment, with all the shit about me from the past and the marriage contract.

That was Sunday night. By Monday morning—*yesterday now*—Neil had received a hundred thousand deposited in his account. No wonder he looked like the god he was trying to call me.

Fucking Neil. He got me good. He really got me.

I sit there for a few moments, staring at the computer screen as I mull over this fresh hell.

Sasha wants River back, so he came up with the perfect plan to take me out of the picture.

I can't allow that fucking monster back in her life. Even if she doesn't end up with me, I won't stand back and allow him to take my wife.

I *won't* do it. That means River needs to know about what her beloved father has been up to.

Fucking Neil. I hate what happened to him as a result of my mistakes, but if he's going to light me on fire his daughter needs to see who he is too.

Gritting my teeth, I decide to do a final check to find out where else Neil might have stuck his nose. I have a number of things going on that I need to protect, including serious clientele money.

I search his hacking code and sure enough, the asshole has been roaming around my private business like he's walking in the park.

Something catches my attention when his code pops a few times during the period before his accident eight years ago.

The majority of listings are to gain access to a link I would recognize in my sleep.

It's the same link those hackers used when I was in college to contact me. I remember it because the middle numbers and letters look like they spell the word 'Rabbit'.

That link was how we communicated.

What I'm looking at is a virtual footprint that exists as a ghost in the system, but my tech allows me to see it as if the link were still active.

That would have been the same way Neil got the details on me from the past.

But why would he be in touch with the same people who wanted to steal his designs? That makes no sense.

I click into the first contact, which shows up like a Discord message, and clarity hits me straight away. The message from the hackers says:

If you sell us those designs, we'll give you two million dollars.

Neil responds by asking for five million.

My mouth drops open, nearly hitting the floor when I realize what I'm seeing. Neil was planning to sell his designs.

Jesus Christ. That's what the asshole was doing.

I get that they were *his* designs, but when you work for a company like Jaeger Tech, who would have put up serious funding, everything you come up with is owned by them.

The next correspondence shows failed negotiations because Neil wanted more money. I can guess what happened next.

I did.

I happened.

The hackers found me. They probably did so because of my connection to Neil through River. People like them check out everybody in your life to discover who will be a threat or who they can use.

I was the latter and, like an idiot, I fell right into their trap.

I'm fairly certain Neil would have known it was the same guys who fucked me over when he found his intel on me, yet he spitefully told me I was worse than my father and allowed myself to be tricked.

What an absolute asshole.

Eager to gather all the shit I can, I click into the last listing of Neil's hacking code. It's dated a few months after his last correspondence with the hackers.

It takes me to a short clip of footage that he wiped from his company's surveillance system.

"Well, well, what didn't you want people to see, Neil?" I speak to the link as the footage loads and begins playing.

It shows Neil walking into his office, where his business partner is sitting behind a desk. The same guy who died that night. I remember his name was Rory.

From the timestamp on the clip, I can tell it's after midnight.

"What are you doing here?" Rory asks.

"How fucking dare you ask me that? They kept you on. You don't even deserve this job," Neil barks at him. "I got you this job, and you decide to screw me over?"

"Calm down, Neil. They suspected you of trying to sell the designs. You should be grateful they didn't do worse to you."

"Grateful? I'll show you what grateful is. Those were my designs. Not yours or anybody else's. They were mine." Neil pulls a gun from his back pocket and points it at Rory, who now freezes in fear.

I stare at the screen wide-eyed and in shock. I'm even wondering if the drink I had earlier is screwing with me, but I know it's not. What I'm witnessing is the night of the accident.

Neil rushes forward to grab Rory, but when he reaches him Rory launches forward to fight back.

Neil shoots him in his chest and Rory cries out, staggering backwards, then he manages to regain his footing and throw himself on Neil.

The two fall to the ground in a flurry of fists, but Neil is still holding the gun.

The gun goes off again. Moments later Neil gets up, not holding the gun anymore. Rory is still on the ground.

This is not the way the world was told this story. Neil reported that it was Rory who went crazy and burst in that night with a gun.

There was also no mention of missing surveillance.

Surveillance which showed the opposite of what Neil stated.

The surveillance the world saw on the news was of him shouting at Rory to put the gun down, then Rory shot Neil just as he turned to run away.

I remember watching Rory kneeling on the floor covered in blood, but Neil told everyone they'd gotten into a fight.

The rest of the blanks fill in as I continue watching the truth unfold. Neil rushes to a computer and types something on the keyboard I can't see, then he looks up in horror as he sees Rory.

"Rory, put the gun down!" Neil shouts. "Put the gun down!"

The clip ends there.

The screen goes blank.

The thoughts in my mind freeze.

I stare at the blank screen, allowing my brain to work through what I just saw but I'm numb from the shock of this discovery.

I click back on the recording and stare at Neil standing by the computer. My guess is that he was hacking the system to wipe the footage. After that, he got shot.

He rushed to wipe the recording instantly so no one else would know what happened.

Fortunately for Neil, he cut the recording at the perfect moment that served to fan the flames of his lies.

What happened that night wasn't even an accident. Neil intended to kill Rory. It seems that it was only Neil the company fired because they knew he was trying to sell the designs.

I'm sure he also doesn't know that this recording still exists, along with everything attached to his name from the hackers. He wouldn't be messy enough to leave such dirty laundry out for people like me to find or use against him.

I intend to do just that.

For the last eight years I've blamed myself for something that wasn't my fault, and because of that I lost the girl I love.

But I was set up.

I got dragged into something that was already going on.

Chapter
THIRTY-THREE

River

JERICHO WALKS THROUGH THE DOOR AND LOOKS AT ME.
He stops by the coat rack and I gaze up at him.
It's strange. It was only yesterday that we last saw each other but it feels like I haven't seen him in years.

His stare is sharp, but within his eyes I still find that spark of love lurking in the background. It makes me want to rush into his arms and stay there forever, but I can't do that.

This is one time I can't listen to my heart, body, mind, or soul, which all still answer to him. I've had to shut down.

Earlier, he called to meet with Dad and me. Jericho suggested meeting at Dad's house to make it easier for him.

Dad agreed easily because he thinks the meeting is to talk about our divorce.

At first I shoved the idea out of my mind because I recalled what Jericho said.

He told me I was more important than his job, but seeing him here now with the large white envelope in his hands makes me think otherwise.

He's had time to think. So have I.

I'm still lost in the wind but maybe he came to the decision that his precious company was worth more to him than I am.

If that's true it would break me, but wouldn't that be for the best?

The conflict between us is so thick I can't even say hello.

"Where do you want me?" he asks, breaking the silence.

"The living room." My voice sounds croaky, as if a frog is hopping around in my throat.

"Alright."

I lead the way and he follows, but each step I take feels like that of a hundred-year-old woman.

We walk into the living room where Dad is stationed opposite the TV.

"Please sit," Dad says, sounding like he's enjoying this.

The sick feeling hits me that he is. Of course, he is. He finally has the upper hand on a Grayson. That *Grayson boy* he forbade me to see.

"Thank you." Jericho sits on the sofa.

I take the armchair and stare back at him wondering how this is going to play out.

I feel like I'm walking around in a nightmare, waiting for my brain to wake me up and tell me this isn't happening.

Over the last twenty-four hours I've experienced every single emotion under the sun. Hurt, pain, disgust, understanding… guilt and conflict.

I'm hurt and disgusted by what Jericho did.

I physically ache when I think that this could be the end of us when I still love him so damn much.

Love compels the understanding that what happened to my father was a repercussion and Jericho didn't intend the damage he caused. That's where I'm conflicted, torn between my love for my husband and my duty to my father.

I feel like a woman torn, but also like the bad guy for them both. I can't support Jericho completely, and when the light of understanding tries to shine on me, I feel like a traitor to my father.

I feel like that again now that Jericho is here.

"I'm glad you came to a decision so quickly," Dad says, jumping into business.

"And what decision do you think I've come to?" Jericho replies with a mirthless grin that seems to throw Dad off-kilter.

"Your divorce."

"No, I have no intention of leaving my wife. She knows that." He cuts me a sharp stare, one that holds determination and strength.

My heart squeezes but I tamp down any joy that swells inside me because that declaration was as good as bringing war to my doorstep.

Dad's face hardens and his eyes become pools of hatred. "If that is your decision, then I'll have no choice but to make good on my threat to expose you."

I snap my gaze toward him. "Dad—"

"No, that's okay, River," Jericho interrupts. "Let him expose me. I'm good with that. People like me rebuild because they can."

I narrow my eyes.

Something has changed, I can tell. Jericho doesn't seem as remorseful as he did yesterday. If anything, he looks like he's ready for the war I just thought of.

But why?

He should be sorry, unless there's a reason for him not to be.

"Your arrogance is very becoming of you. If you're not here to negotiate and you don't care if I expose you, why the hell did you come to my home?"

"I came here to talk about the truth."

"We know the truth," Dad smirks.

"No, we don't. Not all of it. You forgot to mention the five million Sasha promised you if you broke River and I up."

The air drains from my lungs as if someone siphoned it from my body.

I glare at Dad, disbelief making me weak, but I know from the shock on his face that it's true.

"Did you forget to tell her?" Jericho continues. "And let's not forget the hundred grand Sasha gave you yesterday for your good work on finding dirt on me. Something to turn River against me."

"What's he talking about, Dad?" I stand quickly, shaking my head.

"It's lies. He's trying to turn you against me," Dad bites back, but from the bewildered look on his face I know it's he who's lying.

"Dad..."

"It's lies," Dad mumbles.

"Jesus, I would have had more respect for you if you spat in my face," Jericho sneers and pulls out a series of email printouts from his envelope. He gets up and hands them to me.

I scan over the first few and see for myself that everything Jericho is saying is true. Dad has been in touch with Sasha this whole time.

In touch and bargaining with my life as if I'm a piece of meat.

"How could you?" I stare at my father, shock consuming me whole. "After what he put me through, you did this?"

"He loved you," Dad maintains. "He told me he didn't mean to hurt you. He said he was sorry, and he'd changed. You never gave him a chance. Instead, you put him behind bars."

My legs wobble. "Does he know that?"

Dad doesn't answer, which tells me everything.

"You told him."

"He'll forgive you, River."

"I can't believe you did this. I didn't do anything wrong. I just wanted my life back."

"It's you who needs forgiveness," Jericho says to Dad, turning his attention back to him.

"I don't need forgiveness for anything. Get out of my house." The rage on Dad's face is unlike anything I've ever seen.

"I have one more thing to show you and then you can decide why you might *need* forgiveness." Jericho looks away from Dad and turns back to me. "Your father was in contact with the hackers before they approached me."

At first I have to think hard to work out what he's talking about, then I realize what he means.

"Stop it!" Dad yells. "Stop it now!"

"Your father was trying to sell his designs to them, but he wanted more money than what they were offering."

I switch my gaze from Jericho to Dad, who looks like he might implode.

"Stop it now," Dad continues.

"That's when they approached me, a kid who would accept twenty-five grand. What a bargain they must have thought I was." Jericho ignores Dad and continues unearthing his dark secrets. "Your father was fired because his company suspected he was trying to sell the designs, not because they were stolen. But the worst thing he did was this."

Jericho takes out his phone, taps a few buttons, and holds it up for us to see the screen.

I watch a recording of Dad walking into his office at the company. Rory is sitting at the desk. They start arguing, and the truth is revealed seconds later when I watch Dad pull out a gun. My legs give way and I collapse back into the chair.

Dad shoots Rory, then they fight and I hear another gunshot.

Dad gets up and goes to the computer. The clip cuts when he shouts at Rory to put the gun down.

Slowly and carefully, I look at Dad and notice he's gone deadly quiet and ghostly pale.

The same deadly silence that shut him down fills the room. It's not the kind of silence that surrounds you when you're reflecting on your actions, but more the sort that awakens when you know everything is about to change in ways you never wanted.

Dad lied. He lied about everything, killed his friend, and made himself out to be the victim.

Dad killed a man and lied to everyone about *everything*. Even the whole situation with Jericho and the hackers was a setup to undercut Dad because of his greed.

Jesus, Dad set things up to make Rory look like a psycho, and every time he opened his mouth to talk about what happened, he lied.

I can't help but imagine what Mom would think of this. *Of him*. There's no doubt that she'd feel as ashamed of him as I do.

"This is the truth." Jericho puts his phone away and stares at my father. "For as long as I've been in your life I have respected you because of your daughter. You and I had more in common than you thought, but all you ever saw of me is that I'm a Grayson. This is where I draw the line."

Dad is silent. All he does is stare at Jericho.

Jericho walks toward me and I lift my head to gaze up at him.

"I still hurt you. I'm still to blame for my part in this, so take whatever time you need to hate me, but I meant what I said. I have no intention of letting you go." His words of determination send a clamoring shiver through my body. "I won't stop fighting or trying until you love me again, River."

With that promise he steps back, turns, and leaves.

I stare at the empty space he left behind for a few moments too long, as if I can summon him back so I can answer, but I can't speak.

Shock has suffused my entire being and I can't wrap my head around what just happened.

After what feels like an eternity I look at my father and feel like I never knew him.

He meets my gaze with tears in his eyes and a forlorn expression ingrained on his face.

"Why?" My whisper-soft voice is barely audible over the drumming of my heart. "Why did you do this, Dad?"

He swallows hard and sniffles. "I was always a failure in life. Tobias Grayson had everything. He had everything, River."

"Dad. You did this to yourself. *You* did this. Tobias Grayson doesn't even remember who you are."

He hangs his head because he knows I'm right.

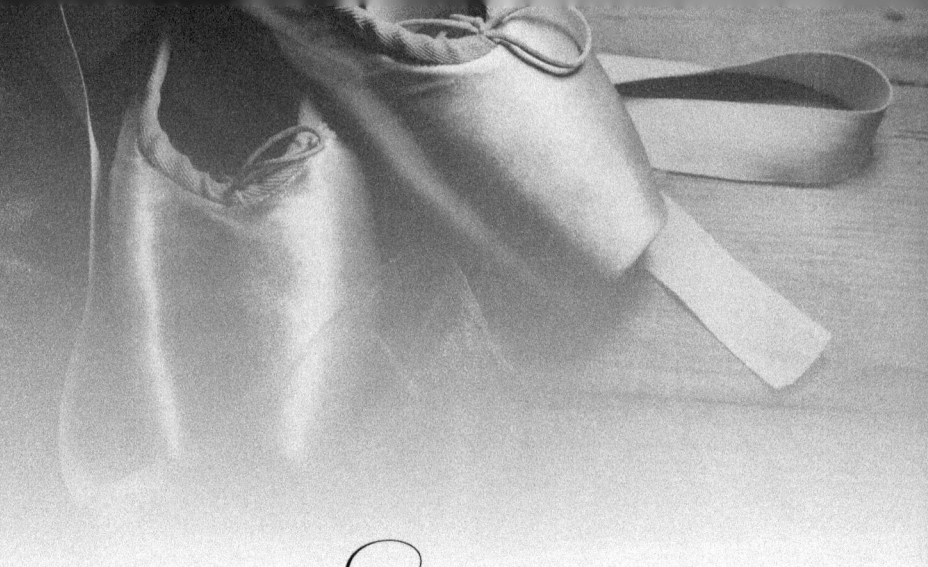

Chapter THIRTY-FOUR

River

DAD TURNED HIMSELF IN AT THE POLICE STATION TWO days ago.

That was probably the most honorable thing he's ever done in his life.

He handed himself in the morning after Jericho came by. Dad called me from the police station and told me.

After the truth was revealed I couldn't stay with him. I could barely look at him, much less speak to him, so I went to Gina's.

She's aware of what's happened—all of it.

As much as I would have loved to shield her from the harsh truths that were exposed, it was one of those things that couldn't be kept from her.

The police have reopened the case and are investigating but there isn't much to investigate with the truth available to see in that missing surveillance.

Rory has also been exonerated. There was something on the

news about it this morning. I didn't watch too much because I couldn't handle it.

I've been staying away from the news but I'm sure once things are out in the open and people realize whose daughter I am and whose wife I *still* am, the press will be hounding me.

I've pushed it all to the back of my mind so I can take one day at a time.

The only thing that hasn't happened is that I haven't heard from Jericho.

I know he's giving me my space and I appreciate that, but there have been moments when I've felt so distressed that I needed him more than anything.

I could have called him but, honestly, I'm embarrassed by what's happened and too upset.

There are so many things to worry about all at once, I don't know what to focus on.

This new revelation about Dad and the past is tearing me up, but the whole Sasha thing is another story.

When it came to Sasha, Dad sounded like the classic deluded person trying to find every excuse in the book to paint a bad person in a good light.

I don't know when I'll be able to speak to my father again and, worse, I don't know when Sasha is going to be released. From those email's Jericho showed me, it seemed like it was soon.

Just like Sasha promised.

Dad knew all along what was going on and kept it quiet. Now I'm left with all the pieces of terror floating in my soul.

Feeling the way I do, I should be tucked away in my bed. Instead I'm at the theater getting ready for tonight's show.

I'm on stage in ten minutes. I was already late arriving and in two minds about showing up, but I felt I had to be here.

I'd already taken way too much time off. I felt like dancing, doing something I love, would provide a much-needed distraction.

At least Gina and Eden are both in the audience tonight. That gives me some comfort. They've already seen the performance a couple of times over the summer, but tonight is about being here to support me.

"Hey, River, you ready to go on?" asks Kate, the stage manager.

My dressing room door was already open, so she's leaning against it.

"Yes, sure. I'll be a minute."

"You sure?" she checks, holding two thumbs up.

"Yes." I nod and smile to reassure her.

I appreciate that everyone here has been so supportive during this time. It's helped me a lot. I can just imagine experiencing the opposite when I go back to the academy.

"Good, see you out there."

She saunters away and I check my hair and face in the mirror once more.

Yesterday when I woke up I had dark circles under my eyes that reminded me of the kind I had in Russia when I was so depressed I used to cry every second of every day.

I look better now but the hollowness is still inside me.

Pulling in a deep breath, I leave. Moments later I'm on stage with the other members of the cast, waiting for the curtain to open.

We've been doing a twist on *Romeo and Juliet* for this production. I have the lead role of Juliet but in this production everything is the reverse.

As I stand here waiting for the performance to begin I realize just how fitting the production is to my life. I've been dancing all summer long not knowing I could easily be Romeo or Juliet. The pain would still be the same.

The music starts and the curtains draw open.

I look into the audience to search for Gina and Eden, but the first person I find sitting in the middle of the front row is Jericho.

He's sitting right where I can see him and he can see me looking right at him.

My heart swells at the sight of him and a wave of emotion

surges through me. It lifts me up and I think of our lives. The past and present.

In the past we were so in love, but I feel like that was just the beginning of what was to come. The present, where we know what love is.

It's us.

I shouldn't be smiling but I am. On seeing that he places his fingers to his lips, then to his heart. It's an old gesture from the past that he made when I was nervous. It means *I love you, and I'm here for you.*

The simple but effective meaning always gave me strength.

It does the same thing now, but there's more power behind it because he's my husband.

I love you, too, Jericho, and I'm here for you.

I spot Gina and Eden in the middle row beaming at me, and I gear up to do what I was born to do.

The performance begins and my newfound strength guides me through the next few hours. I float through every scene effortlessly, separating the real world from the space I have on stage to just be a dancer.

Soon the performance is over and I can't wait to rush into my man's arms.

The audience gives us a standing ovation, but I swear Jericho cheers the loudest for me.

When the curtains close I wrap everything up as quickly as possible. The task that takes the longest is signing my autograph for the fans who have gathered backstage.

Once that's done I practically race toward the dressing room. Jericho will probably be waiting with Gina and Eden for me in the reception area. They've done that after previous performances.

We'd go for a bite to eat after, or a drink but tonight I just want to be with Jericho.

I lock the door and grab my bags to change my clothes, but a shuffle of footsteps in the corner of the room stops me.

This is my dressing room. No one else is supposed to be in

here. Not even the cleaning staff. They usually come in once everyone has gone home.

"Hello," I call out when I hear the sound again. "Who's there?"

"Me, baby doll," a cold, chilling voice answers in a deep Russian accent.

Sasha steps out of the shadows and raw fear bleeds into my heart.

It pierces straight through, as if attached to the tips of a thousand arrows and spreads over my body like darkness swallowing light.

The feeling is fitting. Sasha is dressed in black and the darkness of his heart is suffocating me.

He's here. God, he's actually here.

"Not going to say anything to me? It's been a while." He smiles, causing the scar on his cheek to become more pronounced.

My knees turn to liquid and my brain is hardly any better. My mind scrambles with what to say, and only one thing comes to mind.

"You need to leave me alone."

His jaw clenches and his gaze hardens. "Why? Because you're married? Thanks to your father, I know all about your sham marriage."

"It's not a sham."

"Oh, that's right. Jericho Grayson was the boy who got away. So maybe you want me to leave you alone because it was you who put me behind bars."

The air gets stuck in my throat and I can't breathe past the constriction holding me captive.

"What do you want?"

"You know what I want. Only one thing would get me on a plane here." When he steps forward I step backward, glancing out the corner of my eye toward the door.

It's too far away from me, but if I could get to it, I could run out to the foyer and scream for help.

"What was that?" I decide to keep him talking but the malicious look in his eyes tells me he's already figured me out.

"You. You know I want you. And just for the record you'd have to run at one hell of a speed to get away from me. But it will be fun to watch you try."

He winks at me and launches forward to grab me, but I whirl around and sprint toward the door.

My heart is already tumbling up in my throat and my body is fighting harder than it has strength to move me forward so I can escape.

But just before I reach the door Sasha grabs me and covers my mouth with one large hand.

My screams die on the tip of my tongue.

I never stood a chance.

Chapter THIRTY-FIVE

Jericho

"I'm gonna check where River is?" I tell Gina and Eden.

It's been a while since I saw River's fans leaving the lounge with their autographed copies of the program.

"Okay. We'll wait here. She's probably got her hands full. She was amazing," Gina chuckles.

"She was. I'll just go check, though, in case she needs help with anything." I'm eager to see her. *Desperate.*

When the curtains opened and I first saw her on stage I didn't know how she was going to react.

Seeing her smile at me then and at moments through her performance gave me hope that I was enroute to getting her back.

A lot has happened over the last few days and I know her father turned himself in.

The only other person I've been keeping my eye on is Sasha, but I might not know if he gets out until it's too late.

I make my way down to River's dressing room. She should be inside by now, getting changed.

When I get there the sound of something smashing on the floor followed by a muffled scream has my blood pumping a hundred miles an hour.

Instinct pushes me to kick the door in but I hold back and open it carefully. Once I get a look inside I realize my worst fears have come to life.

Sasha has River hoisted in the air with his hand over her mouth. River looks like a helpless ragdoll in his grasp.

Damn it to hell. The fucker is out of prison. I was too late. Now he's here and he got to her before me.

If I rush in now and alert him to my presence he might hurt her, so I hold back and think of a plan to kick his ass. I need to put him down like the dog he is once and for all.

"You're coming with me, baby doll," he growls in River's face.

No, she's not.

The opportunity to move comes when he walks toward the fire escape.

I grab the fire extinguisher from the wall across from me before I rush in.

I move stealthily, so he doesn't know I'm near until I land the extinguisher right between his shoulder blades.

We're the same height, so when I hit him it's hard and effective.

He stumbles forward, howling in pain and releasing River.

She sees me and dashes to the side of the room, gasping.

When Sasha turns I hit him again with the extinguisher. This time in his face.

No matter how badass he is, that's gonna hurt like a motherfucker. It shows in the blood that spurts from his nose, the bruises that are already forming, and in the sound of his groans, but I'm not done with him yet.

Back in Russia he looked at me as if he would have pulverized me if he had the chance.

This is the beating I wanted to give his ass. I throw myself onto him and we tumble to the ground. He manages to get a few punches in, but they do nothing to me.

He called me rich boy, as if I'd been the pampered prince all my life. I'm sure he knows now that I'm not. I land punch after punch in his face and I can see he's more injured than he wants to accept.

"This is for my girl. How dare you put your hands on her?" I shout in his face and deliver another round of punches.

"Jericho, stop!" River yells when Sasha's arms fall to his side, but I still keep going.

She rushes toward me and when I glance at her and read the panicked look on her face, I stop.

The sight of her in distress tames the beast.

Sasha is out cold. A few more punches might kill him. I won't give him that pleasure. Death is too good for someone like him.

When dealing with assholes like Sasha Konstantin, you don't call the police right away. You go through a different source, who will make sure proper justice is served, then *they'll* call the police.

My good friend Virgo Antonov, a boss in the Russian Mafia came to collect Sasha himself when I made that call.

I met Virgo years ago at MIT. Although he was two years ahead of me, we got on well because of our similar interests. He recently became the leader of his brotherhood, so he was the best person to deal with this situation.

Virgo is the prime example of knowing the right people to get the job done the way you want.

I've been assured that Sasha will go back behind bars to serve the rest of his sentence without the possibility of parole, and he won't bother River ever again.

It will be like he never existed.

So… it's over.

It's all over for the people who were against us, but now we have to deal with the aftermath. *I* have to.

River is traumatized from the whole ordeal of tonight and the events of this week with her father.

We got home, to my house, a few minutes ago.

We went straight up to our bedroom where she sat on the bed and curled into the stack of pillows. I'm crouched next to her and she's holding my hand so tight her knuckles barely have any color.

She looks so frail I feel like I should wrap her in cotton wool. She didn't even get to change out of her costume, and her hair is down and tangled from the struggle with Sasha.

I wish like hell I could have gotten to her sooner than I did. I might have stopped her from experiencing so much terror.

"Do you need me to get you some water or anything?" I ask, kissing her knuckles.

"No. I just need you. Just you."

"You got me, Mermaid."

I kick off my shoes and lie next to her, holding her close so she can feel my protection.

I wake before River the next morning and leave her to sleep while I sort out some business so I can spend the rest of the day with her.

As it's early I head into the garage and work on my Mustang.

When I'm graced with her dainty footsteps an hour later I roll out from under my car.

The moment we see each other, I remember that day in here after she first came to live with me.

I remember the look on her face when she discovered that the piece-of-trash car she was driving was gone. She was ready to hand me my ass.

My, how far we've come, and still there's more.
We're not fixed yet. We're still a work in progress.

"Morning." I stand and look her over. She's changed into one of her little dresses. It's a good sign.

"Hi. I hope I didn't disturb you."

"Never."

She comes closer and stops a breath away.

"How are you feeling?"

"Fragile, but I had to come down to thank you. *Again.* For saving me. *Again.*" She gives me a weak smile. "I wonder if the day will come when I stop needing to be rescued. I'm sure it must be exhausting."

"Not so much. It gives me something to do." I grin back at her.

She gives me a little laugh, but the distress is still swimming in her eyes.

"I'm grateful."

"I know." I touch her cheek, and she leans into my hand.

"Were Gina and Eden okay?"

"They were fine. Just worried about you. I told Gina you'd call her or see her today. I wasn't sure… if you wanted to stay with her. I didn't want to be presumptuous."

She gazes back at me. Despite her distress I find the light I've always loved in her eyes.

"I'm home," she states with reflection.

"Home?" I search her eyes hoping she means that she's coming back to me.

"Home." She nods. "With you. Home is with you. I'm sorry I couldn't be more supportive when you told me what happened." A tear slides down her cheek.

I shake my head and cup her face. "No. I don't want you to be sorry about that. Ever."

"I was so torn."

"It's understandable. I'm sorry we broke up in the first place."

"I'm here now."

"Let's start over." I kiss her quickly and she smiles against my lips.

"From which part? There are good things I don't want to do over."

"But they could be even better if we start at the beginning," I suggest.

She giggles. "I like that."

"Alright, let's do it. Hi, my name is Jericho Grayson and I want you to be my girl. I want to show you off to the world so everyone will know you're mine."

She smiles wider. "Hi, my name is River. I will happily be yours if you promise to be mine."

"Always, Mermaid."

We fall into a kiss and I promise myself that I will never be without her, ever again.

Chapter THIRTY-SIX

River

ROSE PETALS ARE SCATTERED ALL OVER THE FLOOR leading to the bedroom. The floral scent hangs in the air. It's like a scene from the movies.

I've just got home to a message from Jericho letting me know we're about to enjoy another do-over tonight.

This is what we've been doing for the last three weeks, recreating moments and doing everything either the same way we did in the past or differently.

Over the weekend we pretended it was the week before my high school graduation, so we dropped everything to run off to Vegas. We got back yesterday.

The whole recreation thing is exciting, but I also know Jericho is doing this to keep my mind occupied.

Dad was sentenced to life imprisonment for murder two weeks ago. With all the evidence and his confession of guilt, things moved fast.

I still haven't spoken to him, but hearing he was sentenced didn't stop me from feeling bad for him.

I've always taken care of him. The visits during the week to see how he was and making sure he eats came from my heart, but I've had to accept that my father's greed drove him to this.

Only time can heal us, then maybe we'll see what happens. The curse of love is caring and sometimes it will eat you alive if you allow it.

I'm not going to. I promised myself that I would seize my second chance at life and live it.

There is no more Sasha to worry about, no more debts, no more worries.

All I have is the love of a man I've wanted my whole life.

I walk into the bedroom where I find Jericho standing by the window.

He's dressed in a black button-down shirt and black slacks. In my little summer dress, I look underdressed.

On seeing me, he smiles.

"What memory is this? I don't remember rose petals on the floor." I chuckle.

He steps forward. "This isn't a memory. This never happened, but it's about to."

"What is it?"

"This is how I wanted to propose to you."

Warmth spreads over my heart. "Really?"

He moves closer. "Yes. There are a number of things I wanted to say that I never got to tell you."

"Like what?"

He takes my hand with the rings, slides them both off, then gets down on one knee.

"Oh my gosh, you're actually proposing to me again?" I laugh.

"This time, I'm doing it properly." He kisses my hand. "River Marie Grayson, I love you to the moon and back. I would love nothing more than to spend the rest of my life with you. I only want to be married if I'm married to you, I only want kids if they're with you, and I only want to live this life if I get to do it with you. Marry me and be mine forever."

My soul lifts with all the happiness I could possibly feel and I nod. "Yes, of course, I will."

"Thank you. I love you, *wife*." He puts the wedding band on first, then my engagement ring, and stands to kiss me.

"I love you, too, *husband*." I can never get enough of this game of ours. It's like we're on a perpetual honeymoon.

"Now, wife, I'd love nothing more than to feast on your fine body all night."

He plants more kisses on my lips. "That sounds like a good idea. Do I get to feast on you, too?"

"After round two."

His kiss turns hungry and he moves us over to the wall where he strips me naked and licks me from head to toe.

He pauses to shrug out of his clothes, then he returns to my body to give every single part of me the attention it craves.

By the time his cock slides into my aching pussy, my entire body is hungry for him.

Hungry to have him all to myself all night long.

He shoves me up against the wall where he fucks me until I'm screaming his name and my head is spinning.

We don't stop there. We keep going and going, consuming each other as if nothing else exists outside of us.

All there is in my world is him.

Jericho Grayson, my ruthless rebel.

EPILOGUE

River

Three months later

THE CROWD STANDS AND CHEERS, GIVING THE CAST A standing ovation.

Tonight was opening night of the new ballet at Lincoln Center, home of the New York City Ballet.

Tonight's production is an original creation called *Pandora*.

I had the time of my life, and this moment is one I never thought I'd experience again.

I'm not the prima ballerina I was in the Bolshoi, but it doesn't matter.

In this show everyone is a star in their own right.

As usual, my biggest fan is my husband.

Jericho is sitting in the front row looking so proud of me it makes me feel like I'm the only one on this stage.

Next to him are Gina and Eden. They weren't going to miss this performance for the world. Both of them are now in serious relationships. Gina gave Mike, the hiking guy, a chance, and they haven't stopped seeing each other since. Eden met her guy when she was snowed in at a ski lodge in Aspen.

Everyone is happy.

I savor the moment until the curtains close and after, when I meet Jericho in the foyer, I savor the sight of him looking sexy as hell.

In his hands is a bunch of red long-stemmed roses.

"Hello, beautiful, you were phenomenal tonight." He holds the flowers out to me.

"Thank you so much." I take them and stand on the tips of my toes to kiss him.

"Look at this, River." He points to the life-size poster of me in the corner dressed in my beautiful costume. The other members of the cast have posters too around the foyer. It's such an honor to be among them. "That's you, baby. You did it. I'm so proud of you."

I press my hand to his heart. "Thanks. I can't believe it. I'm so happy to have this again."

"I know you are."

I nod and look at the poster. The sad thought hits me that neither of my parents are here to see it, but I know my mother is smiling down at me in heaven, forever proud of me.

As if sensing my thoughts, Jericho kisses the top of my head.

"It's going to be okay."

I nod again. "I think so."

"Good. Now, let's go create some new memories, Mrs. Grayson. I get to spend the rest of the night with the most beautiful woman in the world."

"Thank you, Mr. Grayson, let's go."

Jericho

I hold my nephew against my chest, rocking him to sleep.

Lorenzo is four months old and already has me wrapped around his little fingers.

I'm sitting on the terrace watching my wife and our friends and family gather together for our barbeque.

Although Knight and Grandfather are doing all the cooking, it was my idea to get together now that the weather has turned warmer.

I can't believe that in a few months River and I will be celebrating our one-year anniversary.

It's been quite a year and I love her more and more every day. She's talking heartily with Aurora and the two are laughing.

Knight joins me, sitting in the chair opposite.

He laughs as he looks at me holding his baby, rocking in the chair and humming the tune to *Three Blind Mice*, the only nursery rhyme I can remember.

"My God, this is classic," he says. "I don't know who is more obsessed with my little boy, me or you."

"Me," I tease him. "I'm Uncle Jericho."

"Do you plan to put him down anytime soon, *Uncle Jericho*?"

"Nah, I'm good. While you people eat, I'll happily be on baby duty." I nuzzle my chin against Lorenzo's thick tuft of hair.

"My God, I never thought I'd live to see this day. You know you might be giving your wife ideas of having kids soon."

"That's the idea, bro." I smile wide at him. "Whenever she's ready, I'm ready."

He nods, looking proud of me. "That's good to hear, Jericho. That's really good to hear."

"I'm glad you're happy."

River's eyes find mine and she waves, giving me a bright smile as she takes me in holding the baby. I have no doubt that we'll have our own kids soon. We've already spoken about it. She wants a year with the ballet before we start trying, but if it happens before, it happens before. So, anytime.

I'm good with either option.

"I'd better get back to the cooking." Knight stands and taps my shoulder before he returns to the group.

Just then Luc comes walking up the path looking flustered. He messaged earlier to let me know he was running late.

"You will not believe what just happened to me," he huffs and throws himself down onto the chair.

I straighten. "What happened now? Weren't you on cloud nine only a few hours ago?" He'd gone to Vegas last week and hooked up with a girl he described as unforgettable.

They did the whole no-names thing, but he wanted to find out who she was after she left the next morning.

This morning he located her here in New York.

"It's bad, Jericho. The girl..."

"What about her?"

His jaw tenses. "She's Shawn Jakobe's daughter."

My mouth drops. Shawn Jakobe is the new owner of the Hawks. The same guy Luc has had continuous run-ins with. The guy he called 'a dickless baldheaded something or other' who was his father's rival and as of late wants him off the team.

I bite the inside of my lip. "I see. What are you going to do?"

"That's a very good question. Her father hates me."

I lean back and look at my wife. "That never stopped me. Maybe it shouldn't stop you either."

When I return my gaze to Luc, he raises a mischievous brow. "Maybe..."

ABOUT THE AUTHOR

Faith Summers is the Dark Contemporary Romance pen name of *USA Today* Bestselling Author, Khardine Gray.

Warning !! Expect wild romance stories of the scorching hot variety and deliciously dark romance with the kind of alpha male bad boys best reserved for your fantasies.